Christie Barlow is the number one international bestselling author of nineteen romantic comedies including the iconic Love Heart Lane Series, *A Home at Honeysuckle Farm* and *Kitty's Countryside Dream*. She lives in a ramshackle cottage in a quaint village in the heart of Staffordshire with her four children and two dogs.

Her writing career came as a lovely surprise when Christie decided to write a book to teach her children a valuable life lesson and show them that they are capable of achieving their dreams.

Christie writes about love, life, friendships and the importance of community spirit. She loves to hear from her readers and you can get in touch via Twitter, Facebook and Instagram.

facebook.com/ChristieJBarlow

twitter.com/ChristieJBarlow

bookbub.com/authors/christie-barlow

instagram.com/christie_barlow

Also by Christie Barlow

The Love Heart Lane Series

Love Heart Lane

Foxglove Farm

Clover Cottage

Starcross Manor

The Lake House

Primrose Park

Heartcross Castle

The New Doctor at Peony Practice

New Beginnings at the Old Bakehouse

The Hidden Secrets of Bumblebee Cottage

A Summer Surprise at the Little Blue Boathouse

A Winter Wedding at Starcross Manor

Standalones

Kitty's Countryside Dream

The Cosy Canal Boat Dream

A Home at Honeysuckle Farm

THE LIBRARY ON LOVE
HEART LANE

CHRISTIE BARLOW

One More Chapter
a division of HarperCollins*Publishers* Ltd
1 London Bridge Street
London SE1 9GF
www.harpercollins.co.uk
HarperCollins*Publishers*
Macken House, 39/40 Mayor Street Upper,
Dublin 1, D01 C9W8, Ireland

This paperback edition 2024
1
First published in Great Britain in ebook format
by HarperCollins*Publishers* 2024
Copyright © Christie Barlow 2024
Christie Barlow asserts the moral right to
be identified as the author of this work
A catalogue record of this book is available from the British Library

ISBN: 978-0-00-841323-1

Printed and bound in the UK using 100% Renewable Electricity
by CPI Group (UK) Ltd

For Elaine Houston,
Your words were the loveliest words anyone has ever said to me so far
in my lifetime.
Those words I will never forget.

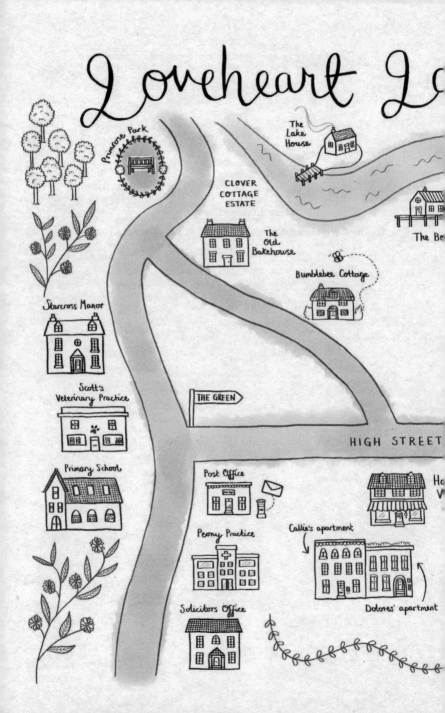

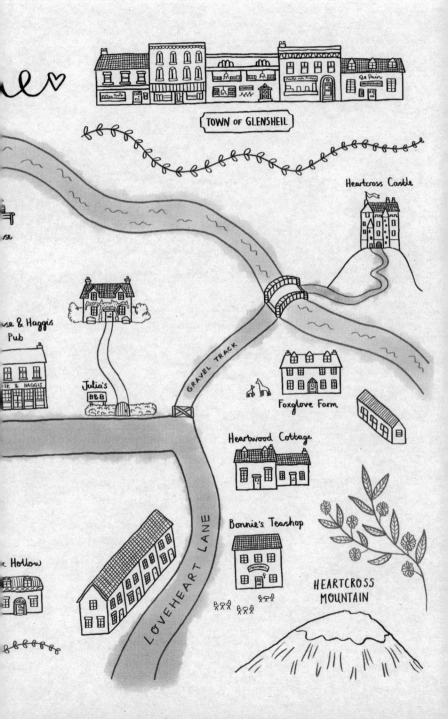

TOWN of GLENSHEIL

Heartcross Castle

se & Haggis
Pub

se & HAGGIS

Julia's
B&B

GRAVEL TRACK

Foxglove Farm

Heartwood Cottage

Bonnie's Teashop

HEARTCROSS
MOUNTAIN

Hollow

LOVEHEART LANE

Chapter One

Elle Cooper hurried towards the bus stop at the entrance of The Heart of the Village, the charming shopping village which was home to the library where she worked, along with a florist and a creperie, among other shops. Consisting of converted nineteenth-century farm buildings and barns, The Heart of the Village was located within the grounds of Foxglove Farm in Heartcross.

The weather app had predicted large dollops of rain would begin to fall by early evening so Elle was grateful to see the bus pulling up. The doors opened and she stepped on board, thankful she'd just managed to miss a drenching as the heavens finally opened.

'Good evening, Miss Elle,' Henry the driver said with a smile as he tipped his cap. 'You made it just in time. How was life at the library today?' he asked, handing her a ticket.

'Full of great expectations,' she replied with a broad smile.

'I see what you did there. Very clever. And how's Irene? I'm missing our daily bus chats.'

'Enjoying retirement! So far, she's been kayaking on the

River Heart, enjoyed spa days at Starcross Manor and has been on a chutney-making course at Bumblebee Cottage!'

Henry chuckled. 'I'm counting the days until my retirement.'

Elle raised an eyebrow. 'Retirement? You're a long way off that, Henry. You don't look a day over forty.' She gave him a heart-warming smile.

'You do flatter me. I'm sixty-five this year and never missed a day's work in my life. Speaking of birthdays, I believe it's nearly yours.'

'It is,' confirmed Elle, her smile a bit forced now. The thought of her birthday had been keeping her awake for a number of weeks. It was her thirtieth this year, and she already knew it was going to be difficult – possibly more difficult than any other birthday before, given what she planned to do to mark it, but it was time.

'That day, you ride for free.' Henry gave her a wink and Elle smiled her thanks before climbing to the top deck of the bus and sitting down in her usual spot.

It was a short ride back to her house on the outskirts of Glensheil. The bus jolted across the track at the bottom of Love Heart Lane and was soon travelling across the bridge towards the town. Elle loved the view from the top deck, with Heartcross Castle towering on one side of the bridge whilst the River Heart tumbled over the rocks on the other. It was the perfect end to her work day.

As she stared out of the window Elle's thoughts turned back to her upcoming birthday. She couldn't believe how far she'd come since she was a teenager and had arrived in Irene's life. Irene had been Elle's foster carer, and they became inseparable. Her manner was always gentle and patient and Elle knew she was going to be a godsend in the coming weeks

– maybe months, possibly years, depending on how long it took – because this birthday was the one when she was finally going to start the search for her biological mother.

Ten minutes later Elle stepped off the bus and took the short walk along the street to reach the red front door of her two-bedroom terraced house, which was a stone's throw away from the River Heart.

As soon as she opened the front door, Elle heard her phone ping. She smiled at the message from an enthusiastic friend who, according to her text, had 'hot gossip' that needed to be shared straight away. Pippa was five years younger than Elle and lived around the corner with her parents. She'd grudgingly moved back home recently after breaking up with her long-term boyfriend, Nick.

After making a coffee, Elle cupped her hands around the hot mug and settled on the comfortable settee, taking a moment to appreciate her surroundings. Growing up, she had always dreamed of owning her own home and here she was surrounded by everything shabby-chic and fluffy pink. Her favourite part of this room was the old Victorian fireplace that complemented the decor perfectly with its original floral embellishments. Even on the darkest days, it still looked so pretty.

Knowing that Pippa would be impatiently waiting for a reply, Elle began typing a message back but before she could finish, the doorbell rang. Elle got up to open the door.

Looking like she was about to spontaneously combust, Pippa erupted into the hallway. 'You haven't replied to my text!' she said, accusingly.

Elle smiled and waggled her phone in the air. 'Give me a chance. It's been exactly three minutes since you sent it.'

The two of them had met at work six months ago. Pippa

had just completed her degree in librarianship and had secured a job alongside Irene and Elle. Elle and Pippa were complete opposites. Pippa lived for fashion, the latest designer shoes and handbags, and spent most of her time watching make-up tutorials on TikTok and purchasing useless items that social media claimed were this week's 'must haves'. Elle, on the other hand, wore her hair in a simple high ponytail, was fresh-faced and bore not even a trace of eyebrow grooming. A social media devotee she was not, instead enjoying the simple things in life – above all, books. Despite their differences, Elle knew the second Pippa walked through the library doors that there was something about the charismatic whirlwind. Her smile was huge, her personality bubbly and, even though they worked together every day, it was at the local book club that they cemented their friendship.

After work one day, Elle had invited Pippa along to the book club that was held at Bonnie's Teashop on Love Heart Lane every Thursday evening. The teashop was owned by Rona and Felicity but the book club was run by Mim, an avid reader.

Bonnie's Teashop embraced all things vintage with its china teacups, delicious home-made cakes and hot chocolate that was to die for. The ambience was just perfect, as far as Elle was concerned, with scented tea-lights that flickered inside glass jam jars and floral bunting hanging from the ceiling.

When they'd arrived at the café, the front of the counter had been open, revealing an array of beautiful cakes on numerous glass-domed cake stands, and their fellow book clubbers were already sitting at a pine table stacked with books, chatting happily amongst themselves.

Mim had welcomed them warmly and they settled down in the plush velvet bucket chairs in front of the window, browsing through some of the books that had been set out for them. A book club was Elle's idea of heaven – a place to share thoughts on books and authors with a group of people who also loved everything bookish.

Once the evening had got underway, and after Mim had introduced Pippa to the group, she had asked the room who their all-time favourite authors were.

'Sam Stone,' Pippa and Elle had declared at exactly the same time, sharing a look that said they both just knew that they were going to be firm friends.

'But three minutes is a long time.' Pippa shivered as she shut the front door behind her and stepped into the warmth.

'Where's your coat?'

'I've only come from round the corner,' she replied, walking into the living room. 'And you have to make opportunities.'

'Make opportunities?' queried Elle, wondering what profound statement Pippa was going to come out with next.

'I might meet the man of my dreams walking down the street and if my outfit is covered up by a coat it's not showing off my full potential.'

Elle couldn't help but look her friend up and down. The dress she wore screamed designer and looked like it had come straight off the catwalk.

'Very daring! And just the thing for nipping round the corner to your friend's house on a very rainy day in February!'

Pippa beamed, posing proudly with one hand on her hip. 'I love this dress – I can't stop wearing it.'

Pippa looked beautiful of course, with her size-eight figure, legs like a giraffe and toned arms. Her blonde bob bounced just above her shoulders and her big blue eyes were enhanced perfectly by her bronzer and nude lipgloss.

'You should try sprucing up your wardrobe, Elle. Stop playing it safe. You have a wonderful figure hiding under your baggy jumpers. Maybe if you started showing it off you'd start attracting some interest from the opposite sex. You do know your biological clock is ticking?' she teased.

Elle gave her a sarcastic smile. She was fully aware of the milestone she would soon be reaching but sprucing up her wardrobe wasn't the top of her priority list right at this moment. No, she was much more interested in discovering the missing pieces of herself and learning about her roots. With constant thoughts of her biological mother filling her mind, she didn't want or need to encourage any kind of romantic interest, except maybe from Noah Jones, who'd disappeared from her life the same afternoon he'd appeared. He was her secret … and one she thought of often.

'And anyway, you said if I wanted to get over Nick, I needed to stop moping around in my trackies and smarten myself up.'

'That's because you didn't get out of bed for days. And I didn't mean for you to wear next to nothing. You'll catch your death in this weather. And what's with the glasses? Since when have you worn glasses?'

Pippa swung a glance towards the mirror on the wall and admired her reflection before glancing down at her watch. 'For approximately twelve hours! I read in a magazine that men find women who wear glasses more attractive. So, working in a library, I think it will make me look more intelligent and very bookish.'

Elle shot her friend her best withering look. But she also couldn't help admiring the fact that Pippa was very much her own person and didn't give a rat's tail what anyone thought of her.

'Anyway, what was it you wanted to tell me? Come on, spit it out! It's hot gossip, you said.'

'So, you haven't heard the latest then?' Pippa looked like she was about to burst as she struggled to pull down the tiny bit of material that was pretending to be a skirt before sitting down on the settee.

'Heard what?'

'Rumour has it that Nick has split up with his new woman. That didn't last long, did it?'

'Hmmm, and you're bothered because?' Elle raised her eyebrows at Pippa.

'He's deleted all evidence of her on Instagram. That's a sure sign.' Pippa pushed her glasses up her nose. 'I know what you're thinking.'

'Which is?'

'I'm completely bonkers and I need to get over my obsession.'

'You read my mind.'

Pippa sighed. 'I need to get over him, don't I?'

'You do! Honestly, I know he's been a massive part of your life, but look at you! You're beautiful, young and intelligent – even without the glasses. That is, you are when you haven't lost the plot,' she said with a smile.

Having watched the relationship break down between Pippa and Nick, Elle was grateful she didn't have that kind of complication in her life at the moment. Pippa had been distraught, her heart smashed to smithereens, and she'd spent ages scrolling mindlessly on social media whilst surrounded by empty pizza boxes. It wasn't Elle's idea of fun.

'But thanks to him, I'm homeless.'

Elle laughed; Pippa did like to exaggerate. 'You're not exactly homeless – you're back living with your parents.'

'Same thing in my book. I mean, who lives with their parents at age twenty-five?' she answered gloomily.

'You do. And at least you're not having to still share space with the two-timing bastard. I know it's difficult, but if you keep stalking him, and trying to find out what he's up to every minute of the day, you're never going to move on. It'll drive you crazy, and you're better than that. I promise, he'll soon pale into insignificance if you stop torturing yourself, and then you'll start to feel better about yourself too.'

'You're right.'

'It's just common sense,' Elle replied diplomatically.

'I know, I know. I wouldn't have him back now anyway.'

'So stop looking at what he's doing! What about the guy from the garage? I thought he'd asked you out? Maybe worth a date?'

'Dave the rave? Have you seen the car he drives?'

Elle laughed. 'It's not all about the car – and at least he *has* a car. And what about what Nick drives? You could hear it coughing and spluttering a mile down the road with that dodgy exhaust. I feared for your life every time you went out in it.'

Pippa laughed. 'Me too.'

'Well, I suppose what the bright blue Corsa lacked in working parts, it made up for with the cream leather seats, dangly dice and what the hell was that air freshener? Very stylish to say the least.'

Pippa raised her eyebrows at her. 'Vintage would be the kindest way to describe that ancient piece of junk.'

They both laughed.

'Are there any other possible contenders?'

Pippa screwed up her face.

'What about Frankie? The guy who comments on all your Insta posts the minute you post them.'

Pippa shook her head frantically. 'Dork city and, anyway, he's ancient. His profile picture must have been through every filter possible. In reality, he's over fifty, looks shifty and sleazes after every young woman out there. He's not even a twenty-tequila type of guy.'

'If you drank twenty tequilas you'd probably end up in a coma.'

Just then they were both startled by the sound of the rain battering against the windowpane.

'Jeez, I don't fancy venturing back out in that tonight,' Pippa said.

Elle stood up and walked over to the window, watching the rain bounce off the pavement. 'Lashing down is an understatement.'

'What about book club?' Pippa asked.

Elle didn't like to let Mim down – she and Rona went to so much trouble to organise everything – but on nights like this, Elle would rather curl up on the settee and watch Netflix. 'It doesn't look like it's going to stop anytime soon,' she said uncertainly.

'Dress code for the evening will be bikini and flippers if we endeavour to go out in that. Heads would turn, especially if we nipped into the pub for a pint on the way,' Pippa joked. 'Is there an author booked for tonight?'

'No, I don't think there is. Mim will understand if we miss one night, especially with the weather being like this. I'm sure we won't be the only ones who want to stay home tonight. Have you eaten?' Elle asked, sitting back down.

Pippa shook her head. 'It's one of those nights when I just

9

want to eat stodge and no doubt it will be steamed veg and chicken at home.'

'How about a takeaway? Oh, and wait until you see what I grabbed from the library today! I'd almost forgotten,' Elle said excitedly, leaning down and digging deep into her bag.

'A takeaway sounds divine,' Pippa replied. 'Come on – show me! What do you have?'

Elle tossed a book in her direction and the grin on Pippa's face as she caught sight of the cover said it all.

'Oh my gosh! The new Sam Stone book! I've been waiting for this to be released,' she marvelled, flicking through the pages.

'It came into the library today. I thought we could read it before it gets borrowed by the masses – perks of the job and all that.'

'Absolutely!' Pippa said. 'Right, I'll text Mum to let her know I'm eating with you, and you text Mim to let her know we'll see her next week.'

As Elle walked into the kitchen to grab the takeaway menus from the pinboard, she tapped out a text to Mim.

'Curry or Chinese?' she asked, passing the menus over to Pippa once she was back in the living room.

'Chicken balti for me,' Pippa piped up, causing Elle to smile. Every time they ordered a curry, Pippa would always have the same old same old, yet every time she swore blind that she would try something different from the menu next time.

'Not going to waste your money then?' teased Elle.

Pippa laughed. 'I thought about it for a teeny second, but what if I didn't like it? I'd be starving and I don't like wasting food or money!'

Chapter Two

The next morning Elle was leaning against the glass panels of the bus shelter waiting for Pippa, who was running late as usual. With the bus due any second Elle glanced up the street and spotted her hurrying towards the bus stop, waving her hand frantically above her head.

Elle tapped her watch. 'Morning. Cutting it fine as usual.'

'Why is it at the weekends I wake up at the crack of dawn, and on weekdays I have to prise my eyes open and force myself to get up?' Pippa was trying to catch her breath and placed her hand on her heart as she winced.

'Because that's life. Don't go keeling over on me before we've even got to work,' Elle said, watching her friend in amusement.

'I'll try my best,' replied Pippa, pointing to the bus that was now travelling up the road towards them.

As soon as the doors of the bus opened, they were greeted by a smiling Henry, who immediately tipped his cap. 'Here they are, my two favourite ladies. Good morning!'

'Good morning,' replied Elle. 'And how are you this blustery morning?'

'Another day closer to retirement,' he chuckled, handing over their tickets. 'Enjoy your day.'

A moment later, they were sitting in their usual seats on the top deck.

'It might be blustery out here but nothing beats the view into Heartcross,' Elle mused as she looked out the window.

'Oh, I agree with you wholeheartedly.' Pippa gently nudged Elle's shoulder. She took a sideward glance at her friend as Pippa flicked her hair over her shoulder and beamed. 'Look at that vision of loveliness,' she whispered, her gaze focused on the stairwell.

Elle turned and locked eyes with the stranger stepping onto the top deck. Immediately she felt herself blush and looked away.

'He's heading this way,' Pippa muttered.

The man sat down on the other side of the aisle from them.

'He even smells gorgeous,' Pippa mouthed.

They both inhaled at the same time, then giggled like a couple of schoolgirls.

'There's something about him. He's mesmerising,' Pippa whispered.

'Do we know him? He seems vaguely familiar. Does he come into the library?' asked Elle, taking another sneaky glance in his direction.

'Does he look like our average customer?' Pippa grinned.

'Don't judge a book by its cover.'

'I think it's love at first sight,' murmured Pippa with a mischievous glint in her eye.

Elle had never believed in love at first sight, until the day she'd met Noah. There had been an intense connection with him the second she'd laid eyes on him and, if pressed, she'd have to admit that it had felt pretty darn close to love.

Noah Jones was a successful author whom Irene had booked at the library to host a one-day writing workshop for disadvantaged children. His warm, charismatic nature was a hit with everyone, but Elle knew the connection she and he had forged was something special. That had been eight months ago now, and Elle hadn't seen him since, but she thought about him often.

'There's no wedding ring. He's possibly still up for grabs,' observed Elle.

'I've not seen him before. He's not local. Where do you think he's going?' Pippa whispered.

'How would I know? I don't have a crystal ball.'

'He's got to have a girlfriend, right?'

'Maybe.'

There were two stops to go before the bus crossed the bridge that linked Glensheil to Heartcross and as they watched, the stranger rang the bell and the bus slowed down, pulling up outside Heartcross Castle.

'He's getting off,' Pippa whispered, linking her arm through Elle's. They must have looked like smitten kittens as their eyes synchronised to watch him disappear down the stairwell.

'Mmm, possibly a newbie in town,' shared Pippa.

'Or a tourist. They do visit in their droves.'

'Fair point.' Pippa leaned over and wiped the condensation off the window with her coat sleeve. 'There he goes, down that alleyway at the side of the bistro.'

He must have sensed they were watching him as he looked back over his shoulder towards the top deck of the bus. Pippa quickly slumped back in her seat leaving Elle to lock eyes with the stranger once again. With a sheepish smile, he paused for a brief moment. Then he dug his hands into the pockets of his green bomber jacket before turning, quickening his step and disappearing from view.

Elle groaned, rolling her eyes. 'How embarrassing.'

She had had a few opportunities to go on dates in the last eight months, but she'd always shied away from a second date. There was no one who'd caught her eye or with whom she had that instant spark – like with Noah.

'Well, that's that, the most excitement we've had on the bus in a long time. We definitely need to find out who that man is!' Pippa insisted.

'Come on, here's our stop,' said Elle, standing up and grasping the metal bar to steady herself.

As the bus came to a halt, Pippa stood up and lost her balance, tumbling into the aisle and then falling onto the seat opposite.

'Steady on.' Elle held out her hand to pull her up.

'It gets me every time!' Pippa exclaimed, finally upright and smoothing down her skirt.

Elle's eyes were fixed on the black rucksack lying on the seat. 'Crikey, look.'

Pippa twirled around. 'The handsome stranger has left his bag! What shall we do with it?' she asked, picking it up and passing it to Elle.

'What are you giving it to me for?'

'Because you're the boss and most responsible one out of the pair of us,' Pippa replied, looking at Elle with amusement.

'I can't argue with that,' agreed Elle, heading down the stairs. 'We could drop it off at the village police station but we won't have time now.' She flitted her eyes towards the electronic sign at the front of the bus which displayed the details of the destination, the next stop and the time. 'We open up in less than fifteen minutes.'

'Have a good day, girls,' Henry chirped as he opened the doors to let them disembark.

'You too, Henry. Oh, Henry, you might be able to help. The man who got off the bus at Heartcross Castle, have you ever seen him before?' asked Elle.

'Afraid not, he's not a regular on my bus.'

'No problem,' she said, slinging the rucksack over her shoulder as they stepped off the bus. 'See you later, Henry, have a good day.'

They began to walk up the driveway of Foxglove Farm, which led to The Heart of the Village, a number of barn conversions turned into shops along with a library.

'Are we going to have a sneaky peep inside the bag?' asked Pippa, with a mischievous twinkle in her eye.

'We can't do that! It's someone else's property.'

'Who's going to know?' Pippa looked at Elle, tilting her head. 'There could be something in there that leads us to the identification of our mystery man.'

Elle had to admit the thought had already crossed her mind. 'No, we're going to do the decent thing and hand it in at the police station.'

'Are you not a little bit intrigued?' probed Pippa, clearly trying to change Elle's mind.

'It doesn't matter whether I am or I'm not, it's snooping,' Elle made clear, taking a sideward glance towards Pippa.

'Spoilsport,' she replied.

Elle had the feeling that Pippa wasn't going to listen to a word she said, and no doubt by lunchtime at the latest the contents of the bag would be known.

Chapter Three

The library was a pretty barn conversion that had been thoughtfully designed and beautifully furnished. From the outside the barn looked much as it always had, with its beautifully weathered stonework, slate roof tiles and duck-egg blue shutters that framed the wooden windows. The addition of big double glass doors adorned with an oak porch flooded the place with natural light.

It was an idyllic place to work and with her passion for books Elle loved coming to work. As she rummaged in her bag for the library keys, she waved at Wilson, the UPS delivery man, who was sitting on the bench underneath the canopy of the creperie.

'Morning,' Wilson said cheerfully, picking up a huge box.

'You're ahead of time today,' Elle replied, smiling as she turned the key in the lock and pushed open the door. There were still ten minutes until the library officially opened and after punching in the alarm code and switching on the lights they all walked into the main room, which without fail took Elle's breath away every time she stepped inside. The fantastic part about the old barn was that its strong sense of history and heritage had been preserved and worked in harmony with its modern interior. The library mixed contemporary furniture with its old features, creating a beautiful juxtaposition. The high vaulted ceiling with its exposed oak beams was another fantastic feature, and the inclusion of a galleried landing full of books was eye-catching and helped to provide defined sections in what was a very open-plan space.

'First things first,' declared Elle. 'Who would like a cup of tea?'

They all headed to the tiny staffroom at the back of the library and Elle placed the mystery rucksack down on the chair in the corner of the room.

'The traffic on the back roads was unusually quiet for once,' Wilson said, balancing the box he was carrying on the edge of the table.

Wilson had been the library's designated UPS driver since Christmas and had gotten to know Elle and Pippa pretty well.

'There's something different about you this morning, Wilson,' Pippa said, eyeing him suspiciously. She stood on tiptoe and reached for a couple of mugs from the cupboard before glancing back in his direction.

Elle gave Wilson a quick look too before scrutinising today's updates, which were pinned to the corkboard. Wilson raked his fingers through his mousy brown hair. He had broad shoulders and, according to Pippa, a six-pack to die for. She didn't actually have first-hand evidence, of course. Wilson just happened to be another man she'd stalked often on social media.

'It's the stubble,' Elle chipped in.

'What do you think?' he asked, stroking his chin and giving a lopsided grin.

'Mmm, I like it.' Pippa scrutinised his face. 'It suits you,' she said, taking out her fake glasses from her bag and putting them on.

'I didn't know you wore glasses.'

'She doesn't. It's the latest fashion accessory, apparently it makes her ooze beauty and radiate intelligence.'

'You definitely don't need them to look beautiful or intelligent,' chipped in Wilson, giving Pippa a heart-warming smile.

Elle noticed that the pair of them had locked eyes longer than necessary. This wasn't the first time she'd witnessed flirtatious banter between them.

'Where do you want this?' asked Wilson, looking at the box he was delivering.

'Can you place it behind the front desk for me?' replied Elle, handing Pippa a mug of tea. 'Have you time for tea?' she asked.

'Not today, but thank you.' Wilson hoisted the box up into his arms. His sleeves were rolled up over his forearms and the muscles bulged as he gripped the box tightly.

Elle watched Pippa with amusement, as her eyes followed Wilson's every move as he disappeared from the room.

Pippa caught her watching. 'What?' she said and grinned, shrugging her shoulders.

'I don't know why you don't just get on with it and ask him out on a date!'

'I don't know what you mean.'

'Of course you don't.' Elle rolled her eyes as they headed to the library floor and switched on the computers. Once everything was up and running Elle set the correct date on the date stamp and they were ready to open.

Wilson had placed the box down behind the desk. 'Do you want me to leave the door open on the way out?'

'Thank you, that'd be great,' Elle replied.

'See you tomorrow,' Pippa shouted after him.

For a moment, Elle stood by the desk and scanned the familiar space. Everywhere looked spick and span. Just then customers began to filter through the door, with Felicity from Bonnie's Teashop running towards the front desk.

'Elle, I need a favour, in return for...' She pushed a white cardboard box over the desk towards her.

'Ooh, what have we here?' asked Elle with a smile, opening the lid of the box to discover freshly baked chocolate flapjacks.

'The use of your photocopier if possible. I need to print off some new menus.' Felicity put her hands together in a prayer-like stance.

This is what Elle loved about this community, everyone helped each other out as much as possible.

'You know that you can use the photocopier any time, but these are most welcome, thank you.'

'You're a superstar. We missed you at book club last night. There were only a few of us ... due to the weather, I'm guessing.'

'I feel guilty for not coming but once I get home...'

'I hear you.'

'What did I miss?'

'We're all waiting for the new Sam Stone book to be released.'

'It's going to be a good read as usual. I'll definitely be there next week, come rain or shine.'

As Felicity made her way over to the photocopier, Elle felt a blast of cool air as the library door swung open. A woman stumbled towards the desk, barely able to see over the pile of books she was juggling.

'Steady! Let me help you.' Elle rushed towards her. She reached out just in time to stop the books toppling from the woman's arms.

'Thank you so much.'

'That's a lot of books you have there.'

'It is, but I always think you can never have too many books. Elle, isn't it? I'm Jenny. I know all about you from your mum, Irene.'

'All good, I hope.'

'Of course!' Jenny smiled. 'I do miss her behind that desk. We used to catch up on all the gossip.'

'I miss her behind this desk too. I'm surprised we've not met before.'

'I usually come in on your day off, as it fits in better around my own work, but I'm off today. And I believe you also know my son.'

'Your son?'

'Wilson. He started working for UPS at Christmas time.'

'Wilson! Yes! You've just missed him. He's already part of the family. Let me get all these books stamped back in for you' said Elle, taking the first book off the pile and opening the cover.

Thud. She stamped the first book back in.

'There's something quite therapeutic about that sound, isn't there? I'm so glad we still do some things the old-fashioned way. Wilson was in a little earlier than usual today.'

'He was up and out with the larks. He has an earlier finish because he and Jack have their first suit fittings this afternoon.'

'For Eleni and Jack's wedding?'

Jenny beamed. 'Yes, it's coming round quickly, isn't it?'

'It certainly is. I love a good wedding and I believe Eleni has the uber-talented Libby Carter designing her dress.' Elle put her hands on her heart. 'Can you imagine? Eleni is going to look gorgeous.'

'Eleni couldn't believe it when Libby agreed. Apparently it was a dream come true.'

Libby Carter was a world-famous fashion designer and sister of Flynn Carter, the business tycoon who owned Starcross Manor and The Lakehouse restaurant.

'Absolutely a dream.'

Elle's invite to Eleni and Jack's wedding was sitting proudly on the mantelpiece at home – it was less than three months away now. Eleni worked at Julia's B&B in the village and Jack was a builder working in the family business. Eleni was also Mim's daughter. They'd been estranged for a few years but everything between them now seemed back on track. Wilson was Jack's best mate – and best man to boot, apparently. Elle smiled, remembering how Pippa hadn't hidden her excitement when she'd discovered Elle's invite to the wedding had those vital words written inside: 'plus one'. Elle hadn't asked her yet, but she knew Pippa was secretly hoping she would soon.

'It should be a good knees-up,' chipped in Pippa, listening in on the conversation.

'Are you coming?' Jenny asked.

Pippa peered up through her fringe and looked in Elle's direction. 'Nah, but I'll be okay sitting at home by myself while you lot cha-cha slide over the dancefloor and drink copious amounts of alcohol. I can always watch reruns of *Take Me Out*.'

Elle grinned at Pippa. 'Shall I get my violin out?'

'No, it's fine!' she replied. 'Weddings are all the same – full of couples that talk about babies and stamp duty. Dull, dull,

dull. And anyway, how many marriages actually last these days? I'll be better off staying in by myself while you all go and have a good time.'

'Pippa is anti-men at the moment,' shared Elle, giving her friend a playful nudge with her elbow.

'But is always up for a party,' Pippa added.

Elle cleared her throat to smother a giggle and looked at Jenny. 'Do you think that's my cue to invite Pippa to the wedding as my plus one?'

'I kind of get the impression Pippa wants to stay home alone,' Jenny replied ruefully.

'No, I'd love to come!' Pippa's eyes widened. 'Are you asking me to be your plus one?'

'Shall I put you out of your misery, Pippa Lawson? Would you do me the honour of accompanying me to Eleni and Jack's wedding?' she asked in her most formal, poshest voice.

Pippa gave her a wide grin then squealed.

'Shhh, it's a library!' Elle whispered.

'Sorry, sorry! Thank you! I thought you were never going to ask.' Pippa threw her arms around Elle. 'I'll need an outfit, and a hat, and you never know, I might even catch the bouquet, but that may be a waste with no actual man on the scene. New shoes as well,' she added. 'And any excuse to buy a new handbag…'

'And breathe,' said Elle, laughing.

'I'm going to leave you ladies to it. I'll see you both soon.' Jenny made her way to the exit and crossed paths with a man whose face looked vaguely familiar to Elle. She narrowed her eyes in concentration, trying to place him.

'Good morning, Elle. Long time no see.'

'Aiden!' welcomed Elle, remembering the familiar face she'd met before on several work courses. 'How lovely to see you. It's Inverness Library you work at, isn't it? What are you doing here?'

Suddenly Aiden looked worried. 'That's right, it *was* Inverness, but as of today I'm working here, at the Library on Love Heart Lane.'

Puzzled, Elle looked towards Pippa, who gave a discreet shrug.

'Human Resources told me they'd sent you an email with all the paperwork. I've been transferred.'

Elle quickly tapped on the keyboard and pulled up her emails on the screen. There it was, the unread email from Human Resources. She quickly read it. 'Oh my gosh, how have I missed that? I'm so sorry, this is probably not the welcome you were expecting but –' she threw her arms open wide '– welcome to the Library on Love Heart Lane!'

'Thank you,' he replied. 'How impressive is this place?' He spun around and took in his surroundings. 'Woah!' He pointed to the window. The rain had eased off and the sun shone through, creating a most spectacular rainbow over Heartcross Mountain. 'It's stunning.'

'I wholeheartedly agree,' came Pippa's reply. The smile on her face widened and Elle noted that she was looking at Aiden rather than the rainbow.

Elle cocked an eyebrow in her direction.

'Before you show me around, could you direct me to the bathroom?' he asked.

'Through there.' Elle pointed.

As Aiden disappeared through the door Elle turned towards Pippa. 'I know that dreamy look.'

'There is a God is all I'm saying!'

'Pippa! This morning there was the man on the bus, then Wilson and now…'

'It's good to keep your options open,' protested Pippa. 'I knew these glasses were going to be the making of my love life.' She waggled the arms of her glasses behind her ears, making Elle laugh as they comically bounced up and down.

'Do not go complicating things.'

'I'm not sure what you mean and shush, he's coming back.'

Elle looked towards Aiden. 'Let me show you the staffroom and get you settled before we set you up on the computer system.'

'Sounds like a plan,' he replied.

Elle picked up the box of flapjacks that was left on the desk. 'Come on, this way.' She dared to look back over her shoulder at Pippa, who winked.

Elle rolled her eyes; she certainly had her work cut out for her sometimes, being Pippa's boss.

Chapter Four

For most of the morning, Pippa had sat amongst the little humans in the children's book corner. Every Monday at eleven a.m. Pippa prised the puppet from the story sack and mesmerised the toddlers with her funny voices and facial expressions while she read from the latest children's books.

'Do you want my opinion?' Aiden asked as he watched Pippa from the front desk.

'What about?' Elle replied, carefully stacking the returned books from that morning into a basket, ready to be filed back on to the shelves after lunch.

'She's a natural.' He smiled in Pippa's direction. 'Just look at her. She comes alive when she's around children.'

Elle looked over. She knew exactly what Aiden meant.

He continued. 'My mum used to sit with me for hours when I was a child, reading the old classics. My favourite was always *Huckleberry Finn*. Maybe that's why I love books so much.'

'The classics are always the best,' agreed Elle.

'Did your mum read to you? Is that why you love books

too?' Aiden gave her a sideward glance.

Elle had been passed from foster home to foster home until she was placed with Irene and couldn't remember anyone ever reading to her when she was small. Once again, her thoughts turned to her birth mother. She had so many gnawing questions that could only be answered by discovering where and whom she had come from. The question that turned over and over in her mind the most was whether her birth mother had ever tried to find her.

Elle had a wonderful life with Irene, a job she loved and a good circle of friends, but there was always a dull ache, a longing to discover exactly who she was, and over the years the curiosity had intensified about the identity of her biological family and the circumstances that led to her being given up as a baby.

'Yes,' replied Elle, telling a little white lie.

'I meant to ask earlier, what happens at lunchtime?' Aiden said as a loud growl escaped from his stomach.

'Pippa and I usually go on separate lunches. We sometimes nip out to Bonnie's Teashop or The Old Bakehouse. There's the pub too, and the creperie. Do you want to come on first lunch with me?'

Pippa was wrapping up the session and caught Elle's eye. She tapped her watch and motioned to say she was off for lunch, and Pippa nodded in acknowledgement.

'That'll be great,' he replied as Pippa appeared beside them with a smile hitched on her face.

'I know it's not the norm to like Mondays, but it's my favourite time of the week,' she said enthusiastically.

'Aiden was just saying what a natural you look with the children.'

'Aww, that's so kind. I do enjoy reading to them.'

'We're going to grab some food. If you get a rush on just let me know and I'll come back to help.'

Walking side by side, Elle and Aiden headed towards the staffroom.

'Would you like a hot drink?' asked Elle, filling the kettle.

'Yes, a coffee would be great, thank you.' He grabbed his rucksack from a chair and sat down at the table.

'Here's where the tea, coffee and sugar are kept. We put a pound in here each week to cover costs but please shout if you notice it running low. Pippa's like a bear with a sore head if she doesn't get her morning coffee fix,' Elle confided, shaking the rusty floral tin.

He smiled. 'I know that feeling. Here.' He flipped a coin across the table. 'My debts are paid for this week.'

Elle popped the money into the tin and made the drinks. They sat down at the table opposite each other and opened their lunchboxes.

'Tell me about Aiden. What brings you to Heartcross? Why the transfer?' asked Elle, but as soon as she asked the question she saw a flash of sadness in his eyes. 'Sorry, I didn't mean to pry,' she added hastily.

'No, it's okay. Honestly, you aren't prying.' He paused. 'It's so I can be nearer to Theo.'

'Theo?'

'Yes, my son.'

'How old is he?'

'He's nearly three. A handful but awesome. Look, I have a photograph.' Proudly, Aiden reached inside his jacket pocket and flipped open his wallet.

Elle smiled down at the picture. 'He's gorgeous. Are you with his mum?'

Aiden exhaled deeply and shook his head.

'No, it's been a difficult few months. It's the usual story – a whirlwind romance followed by a pregnancy. Of course, at the time I believed we were going to be together for ever, but we soon realised we weren't right for each other.'

'It must have been difficult to come to that decision.'

'It was, but on the plus side there's no animosity between Louisa and myself, and our main priority will always be Theo. Even though we aren't together, we both love him with all our hearts.'

'And that's all that matters,' added Elle, taking a sip of coffee. 'Do Louisa and Theo live here in Heartcross then?'

'They've moved in with her parents over in Glensheil and at the moment I'm renting one of the terraced houses on Love Heart Lane. I have to say, opening my curtains and waking up to the stunning scenery is a bonus. I've only been here a couple of days, but there's something about this place.'

'There is,' confirmed Elle. 'And it sounds like you've already been hit by the Heartcross curse.'

Aiden looked puzzled. 'The Heartcross curse?'

'Once you arrive in Heartcross, you never want to leave!' She smiled, thinking of all the residents that had started out here on a holiday and never went home. 'There's Bea who works at Little Blue Boathouse: she came for a two-week holiday to mend a broken heart, got a job at the boathouse and fell in love with Nolan, who was visiting for the summer on his houseboat.'

'There's a book in there somewhere.' Aiden smiled.

'And Libby, Flynn Carter's sister, came and helped him out when his wedding planner resigned…'

'I read about that scandal in the national press. Wasn't there a sabotage plot to steal his wedding business that Libby uncovered?'

'In a nutshell. She was meant to be leaving for a new life in New York after the holidays but fell head over heels for Guy Hart, the filmmaker, who was working alongside her. Now she splits her time between the Big Apple and Heartcross. I tell you, this place has magic powers. I love working here, and the community is friendly and very supportive. What about your family? Are they nearby?'

'I only have my dad. My mum passed away when I was seven – a sudden heart attack.'

'Oh, Aiden, I'm so sorry to hear that. That's so sad. I don't know what to say.'

'Honestly, it's okay. My mum was the reason I ended up going to university to study for a degree in librarianship.'

'Was she a librarian?'

'No, but she always encouraged me to read everything and anything. It was something we always did together. After she died, my dad brought me up. He is amazing and did a superb job of being two parents at once. I was lucky to have the supportive, stable family home that I did, and that my dad never once grumbled about anything. He taxied me from football games to swimming lessons – I even attempted the cricket team but I was a wimp. I used to run in the opposite direction of the ball instead of trying to catch it.' He laughed. 'I was always at my best when I was reading though. Anyway, he was the type of parent that some children could only wish for. I was very lucky.'

His words resonated with Elle in a way she was sure he hadn't intended. Growing up in a stable home was all she'd ever wished for, and that wish came true when she was placed in Irene's care.

'As you can imagine, we're extremely close.'

'I bet he adores Theo too.'

'Without a doubt, but a couple of years ago he moved down to the coast for work. It's a beautiful place he's settled in, and he lives in a little cottage by the sea. I'm taking Theo there for a week in the summer to visit him.'

'That sounds idyllic.'

'What about you? Tell me about Elle. Husband? Boyfriend? Children?'

'Simple answer to that one is no, no and no!' she said, taking a bite of her sandwich.

'Parents? Brothers and sisters?' Now it was Aiden's turn to gently probe before he tucked into his lunch.

'Just my mum, Irene.' Elle always referred to Irene as her mum. Everyone in Heartcross thought that Irene was her biological mum and given that Elle loved her with all her heart, she didn't mind if that's what they believed. As soon as Irene had welcomed Elle to her family, she knew she was going to be settled for life, and when Irene suggested that Elle changed her surname to match hers, Elle had been swamped with emotion, overwhelmed by the feeling of happiness – of belonging.

'Irene. Why does that name sound familiar?'

'You will probably have met her. Mum would have trained you on some of the customer services courses.'

'Tall, lean, with mousy hair?'

'Yes, that's her.'

'I never knew she was your mum. I've met her on a few occasions. She seemed lovely.'

'She is. Mum has just retired.'

'Is that how you ended up working here? Was it always something you wanted to do – follow in your mum's footsteps?' Aiden asked, taking the empty mugs to the sink to rinse them out.

'Yes, when Mum worked over at Glensheil Library, I got a Saturday job there as a teen and loved it that much that I went on to get my degree in librarianship. When this library opened up and they were looking for staff, I knew I wanted to work here. I mean, look at those views!' She glanced towards the window.

'How long has Pippa been here?'

'Just over six months,' Elle replied.

Glancing towards the clock, she was surprised to see that the lunch hour had flown by. Pippa popped her head round the staffroom door.

'We're just coming.' Elle stood up and pushed her chair under the table.

'It's fairly quiet out there. Anyway, what's the verdict?'

Elle and Aiden exchanged a puzzled look.

'Verdict about what? You've lost me,' replied Elle.

'The bag!' Pippa exclaimed, wide-eyed, nodding towards the rucksack on the chair.

'Oh my gosh, I'd forgotten all about it.'

'You mean you seriously haven't had a peek?' Pippa looked amazed.

'I seriously have not!' exclaimed Elle.

'What's going on?' Aiden asked, looking between them both.

'That rucksack over there was left on the bus this morning,' Elle said, tossing her rubbish into the pedal bin then pointing towards the flapjack in the box. 'Help yourself.'

'What Elle means to say is this morning a very handsome man left his bag on the bus, and I think if we take a peek inside, we might discover some sort of identification that'll lead us to our mystery man.'

'But on the flipside, what if it doesn't? The best thing to do is to take it to the village police station after work and let them deal with it. What do you think, Aiden?'

Aiden grinned. 'Don't get me involved,' he said as he held up his hands in surrender.

Pippa tilted her head to one side and sent a pleading glance his way, trying to encourage Aiden to take her side. Her curiosity was obviously in full throttle.

He finally caved in. 'Surely it wouldn't hurt to look?'

'I'm with Aiden,' Pippa agreed immediately, gesturing towards the bag. 'Go on, open it.'

Elle threw the rucksack towards Pippa. 'I'm not touching it. You open it if you want to.'

'Yes, boss!' she replied and grinned. Catching the bag with both hands and pulling rapidly on the zip, Pippa peered cautiously inside before reaching in and pulling out a banana, which she lay down on the table.

'Most probably his lunch?' Elle suggested.

Next, she pulled out a can of squirty cream. Pippa gazed up with a puzzled look on her face and placed it next to the banana. 'Bananas and cream?' She delved in further. 'I've got something else,' she said, gripping a bottle of St Tropez. 'What's this?' she asked, sniffing the lid.

'Fake tan,' said Elle, cocking an eyebrow.

'And tweezers and waxing strips.'

Suddenly they both burst into a fit of giggles, staring at the item of clothing that was currently hooked around Pippa's forefinger.

Aiden took in the sight of the red thong before glancing back over the other items displayed on the table.

'I don't think it takes a genius or a detective to solve this mystery,' he said wryly. 'Your man must be a stripper!'

Chapter Five

After work all three of them walked along the high street towards the police station. which was situated in a building on the Clover Cottage estate.

'Does anyone fancy The Grouse and Haggis for tea tonight?' asked Pippa hopefully, adjusting the rucksack on her shoulder. 'I don't think I can subject myself to much more of sitting around the table with my parents. My father doesn't speak because he's attempting the crossword, in order to avoid any conversation with my mother that might involve him in some job that needs doing around the house.'

Elle laughed and turned to Aiden. 'We could celebrate your first full day at work.'

'I'm in,' agreed Aiden without hesitation.

Five minutes later they walked onto the Clover Cottage estate. Elle pointed towards the cottage. 'This is where Allie and Rory live. Allie is the daughter of Meredith and Fraser, who own the pub, and Rory is the local vet. That's the animal hospital just there, and to the right is the police station.'

The police station was a small stone cottage with daffodils lining the path that led to the stone steps.

'This place looks too idyllic to house any sort of criminals,' observed Aiden.

'It is rather picture perfect, isn't it?' agreed Elle.

'Why is it I always feel like I've done something wrong when I see a police officer?' offered Pippa.

'I know exactly what you mean. My heart suddenly feels like it's racing,' Elle replied, noticing a couple of uniformed officers plodding down the steps of the cottage and heading towards a parked police car.

Aiden grinned. 'Sign of a guilty conscience that, ladies,' he said, bounding up the steps towards the door and looking back over his shoulder at them.

Following swiftly behind him, he pushed open the door and they stepped inside. Elle scanned the room. It was minimalistic, with a pinboard on the stone wall to the right, covered in local leaflets, a counter straight ahead and five plastic chairs lined up against the wall to the left.

Pippa ushered Elle ahead of her and Aiden, so she stepped up and took the bag off her shoulder and placed it on the counter. A police officer who was tapping away on his computer looked up with a welcoming smile. 'Can I help you?' he asked, sliding his chair backwards and standing up to face them.

'Yes, this morning we found this bag on the bus and thought we'd better hand it in,' Elle replied.

The policeman rummaged around amongst some papers on the desk before acknowledging what Elle had said.

'I need to take some details. Did you see who it belonged to?' he asked, poising his pen over the form in front of him.

Pippa nodded and smiled across at Elle before answering. 'Tall, dark and handsome just about covers it.'

The policeman smiled. 'Well, that narrows it down. How about age?'

'I'd say similar to me?'

'Which is?' the policeman asked.

'Mid-twenties,' replied Pippa.

'He was travelling on the 425 bus this morning and jumped off at Heartcross Castle,' added Elle.

'Thank you. That information is a little more helpful,' the policeman replied, smiling kindly in Pippa's direction. 'I suppose I'd better take a look inside.'

Pippa was desperately trying to keep her face under control as she pushed the bag towards him.

'Have you opened the bag at all?' he enquired, looking between all three of them.

Elle and Pippa eyed each other warily, Aiden watching in amusement.

'We may have had a small peep,' Elle offered at last, feeling her face flushing red with embarrassment. The image of the handsome stranger wearing nothing but the red thong flooded her mind, and she bit down hard on her lip trying to suppress her smile.

The policeman unzipped the bag and the three of them fixed their gaze on him while he peered inside.

Pippa stifled a giggle.

The officer looked up, clearly amused, and zipped up the bag before thanking them for bringing it in.

'Is there any chance – if you find out who it belongs to – that you could maybe let us know?' Pippa asked playfully before Aiden grabbed hold of her shoulders and pushed her good-humouredly towards the door.

'Out!' he said, laughing. 'Can you believe this is only my first day working with you lot? Time for the pub. You two have driven me to drink already.'

Meredith and Fraser were in their usual place behind the bar at The Grouse and Haggis, and welcomed Elle the second she stepped inside.

'My usual, please, Meredith, and can I introduce you to Aiden? It's his first day, he's working with us at the library.'

'Welcome to Heartcross. You must be the Aiden that's moved into the house on Love Heart Lane. Rona, who owns the teashop, told us you'd arrived a couple of days ago.'

'That's right, it's a beautiful house in a great location.'

'I hope we'll be seeing you at book club?'

'We'll tell him all about that. I'm sure we can persuade him to come,' Elle said.

'Lovely. Now, as per usual, any newcomer to the village has their first drink on the house,' Meredith announced, reaching for a glass on the shelf above her head.

'Thank you very much,' Aiden said, delighted.

After ordering their food and grabbing Elle's and Pippa's usual table in the corner of the pub they sat down with their drinks.

'Is everyone here this friendly?' asked Aiden. 'If so, I think I'm going like it very much here.'

'They are,' replied Elle.

'Tell me all about this book club.'

'It's the place that cemented our friendship.' Pippa said with a huge smile on her face.

'Tell me more.'

'It's walking distance for you,' said Pippa. 'It takes place at Bonnie's Teashop every Thursday evening and is run by Mim. We read and discuss all genres of books.'

'We also drink lots of tea and eat copious amounts of cake. Rona bakes the most delicious Victoria sponge.'

'It all sounds very civilised,' Aiden mused, sitting up straight and moving his drink out of the way so the waitress could place three plates of pie and chips on the table.

Pippa picked up a chip and blew on it before popping it into her mouth.

'That's hot.' She wafted her hand in front of her mouth and quickly took a swig of beer before taking the pastry off the top of her pie and placing it on the side of her plate.

'Are you eating that?' Elle asked her as she took the brown sauce and vinegar from the waitress, who'd just returned.

'Of course! I'm saving the best bit until last.'

'So do you have any favourite authors then?' Aiden asked. 'I know that's a huge question for librarians. You must have quite a few favourites.'

'Sam Stone,' Elle and Pippa chorused in unison. 'It's a no-brainer,' added Elle. 'But from all the research I've done to find out more about him I've deduced that he's very reclusive. Other than his books, there's no information about him.'

'That's not that odd though. Authors don't necessarily crave the limelight, they just want to tell their stories,' Aiden offered with a shrug.

'Maybe that's true. He shies away from interviews too,' Pippa said.

'His work obviously speaks volumes to many,' replied Aiden.

Elle tucked into her food and watched Aiden and Pippa chatting away. She already knew that Aiden was a great addition to their team, he'd slotted in instantly and was very easy to be around. She knew that Pippa thought so too because she was hanging on his every word.

'And who is your favourite author?' asked Pippa, taking a swig of beer. Aiden didn't think about it for long. 'That's not difficult for me at all,' he stated. 'Noah Jones.'

Elle began to splutter, choking on her food.

Immediately Pippa turned towards her and began to pat her back like she was a child. 'You okay?' she asked.

'Sorry, my food just went down the wrong way,' Elle said, embarrassed, taking a sip of her drink and trying to curb the coughing.

'Are you sure you're okay? Your cheeks look a little flushed.'

'Yes, I'm sure,' replied Elle, knowing that it wasn't the food but the thought of Noah that had her blushing uncontrollably.

'And what makes Noah Jones your absolute favourite?' asked Pippa, looking back towards Aiden.

Elle was half listening to their conversation whilst thoughts of Noah Jones flooded her mind.

She had met him on July the fifteenth last year. On a whim, Irene had contacted the bestselling author through his website and asked if he would host a writing workshop at the library. Irene was amazed when he agreed. The charming – not to mention utterly handsome – Noah Jones had Elle completely flustered from the moment he stepped into the library. She was mesmerised by how utterly gorgeous he was and had to remind herself to breathe. His features were perfect, he was slim and muscular, and his tight white T-shirt had shown off his broad shoulders and strong arms.

He was also warm and funny and completely down to earth. They got on like a house on fire as Elle acted as his assistant for the afternoon. The humour bounced back and forth between them, they caught each other's eye on numerous occasions and Elle felt a spark between them, so much so that she'd found herself praying for time to stand still.

When the workshop had finished, she had been left alone with him. She'd started to collect the handouts left on the desk, and knew he was watching her the whole time. When Elle handed them over, her fingers had brushed against his, leaving her with a fluttering in the pit of her stomach. They were inches apart, his eyes locked on hers, the attraction raw.

'That was a very inspirational workshop,' she'd said, almost whispering.

'Thank you,' Noah answered. 'How long have you worked here?'

'Since it opened.'

'Do you enjoy it?' His eyes were looking into hers with such intensity it made her nervous – in a good way.

'I absolutely love it,' she'd replied.

'Given that you're surrounded by books every day, have you ever thought of writing?'

'After your workshop today, you've inspired me. I might just go home and begin writing straightaway. Don't they say everyone has a book inside them?'

'They sure do,' he'd replied, with a warm smile that melted her heart. 'Here, take this.'

Noah had fished around in the inside pocket of his jacket and handed her his business card.

'My card. Just in case you need any help.'

'With?'

'Your writing,' he'd said, still smiling.

'Oh, yes, my writing. Thank you,' replied Elle.

Without thinking, like it was the most natural thing in the

world, she'd leaned in and kissed his cheek. Taking in his aroma and the scent from his aftershave, her stomach had given a little flip.

'Oh my gosh, I didn't mean to… I was just…'

He'd grinned. 'Don't apologise. And thank you for today. You've been a fantastic assistant.' With their faces still only inches apart, Noah had leaned in and softly kissed her cheek. He'd then pulled back just a little and hovered there. Elle had looked at his lips, every inch of her willing him to lean in for a real kiss. Noah was still looking into her eyes, then his lips had moved slowly towards hers and he'd done exactly what she wanted – he'd kissed her, stealing what was left of her breath. The kiss had been perfect. Every inch of her body had erupted in goosebumps. He'd pulled away slowly. 'I have to run now, but call me.'

'I will,' she replied.

It had only been one kiss – but that one kiss had electrified her heart in a way she'd never felt before.

Looking back now, Elle felt like she had dreamed the whole thing, but that business card was still pinned to the corkboard in her kitchen. She wondered if he ever thought about it too.

Chapter Six

'Earth to Elle,' Pippa said, interrupting Elle's thoughts. 'What are you thinking about?' She narrowed her eyes.

Elle suddenly realised she'd been lost in her owns thoughts and didn't have a clue what Aiden and Pippa had been talking about for the last five minutes or so.

'I'm just telling Aiden it's your birthday on Friday. What are your plans? We could do the pub again, maybe a nightclub? A posh meal? What do you think?'

'It's a tame one for me. Mum's invited me round for tea,' Elle said, smiling.

Immediately, Pippa objected. 'A tame one? It's your thirtieth birthday! There's no such thing as tame. It only happens once. We need to party hard. I've already mentioned it to Isla, Felicity and Allie, not to mention Jinny, Julia and Eleni.'

Elle smiled at Pippa's enthusiasm. 'That is very kind of you but—'

'I don't want to hear any buts—'

'On this occasion I have made plans but let's do a couple of drinks on Saturday?'

Pippa looked disappointed. 'A couple of drinks?'

The question hung in the air.

'Yes, a couple of drinks. I'm not one for a fuss.' Elle knew this coming week her emotions were going to be all over the place.

It was the same every year. It was her birthday yet she knew nothing about her birth or why she was given up. Over the years numerous scenarios had passed through her thoughts. Was her birth mother extremely young? Did her parents force adoption on her? Was she a result of an affair? Did her biological father know she existed? Was there a medical reason? The list was endless and Elle didn't know any of the answers. She always did her best to focus on the positives in her life: Irene, her career, her home and friends. But her reality was that there were so many unanswered questions and she always felt there was a piece of her missing. Her birthday always led her to wonder whether her biological mother had even given her a second thought after giving her up. The older she got, the more desperate she was to know the answer.

Last birthday, she'd spent too long staring at her reflection in the mirror, wondering whether there was another woman somewhere in the world who looked like her. *Would my mother have the same colour eyes? Would she have the same colour hair? Would she have the same mannerisms?*

The only things Elle knew about her mother was that her name was Cora Hansley, her date of birth and an address where she once lived. The only possession she had from her childhood was the shawl she was wrapped up in when her first foster parents took her home. It had managed to survive every foster home alongside her.

Before Pippa could attempt to persuade Elle that they needed to celebrate in style they were interrupted by the sound of jovial chatter. Looking over her shoulder Elle saw that Jack and Wilson were making their way over to the table with beers in hand.

'Hey.' Wilson smiled at them all.

Elle noticed his eyes quickly darting from Pippa to Aiden. She smiled up at them both. 'Hi.'

'How are you, Elle?' asked Jack. 'Is everything good in the land of books at the minute?' He pulled up a stool and sat next to her. Wilson perched opposite Pippa.

'Always good,' she replied. 'I have the best job in the world.'

With his piercing blue eyes, chiselled cheekbones and blond hair, Jack wouldn't look out of place on the cover of *Surfer Weekly*, but he was actually a builder, working in the family business. He was a friendly, genuine guy whom everyone instantly warmed to. Elle had first met him at book club when he'd popped in to pick up Eleni after one of their meetings.

Eleni had been gushing with the news that she'd just got engaged and had spent the whole evening showing off the beautiful diamond ring now gracing her left hand. Jack's proposal was so romantic. He was a friend of Flynn Carter's and the two of them had flown over the village of Heartcross in Flynn's plane, trailing a banner that read: 'Will you marry me, Eleni?' And of course, her answer had been yes!

'How's life with bricks?' Elle asked him.

He laughed. 'Very square and boring to most folk.'

'Yes. In fact, stop there.' She laughed too.

'I'm not sure if you know Aiden?' Pippa chipped in. 'He's

started work with us today after transferring from Inverness. Aiden, Wilson is our UPS guy – I think you might have just missed each other this morning – and this is Jack.'

With quick nods, Wilson and Jack introduced themselves to Aiden.

'I believe you've both been for a suit fitting this afternoon?' Elle said, finishing the last mouthful of her pie and placing her knife and fork down on the empty plate.

'Yes, we have, and as long as I don't put on any more pounds, I think we're all done now.' Jack patted his stomach.

'Jack is getting married in a couple of months' time to Eleni who works at the B&B,' Pippa told Aiden.

'Who is the daughter of Mim,' Elle added.

'Who hosts the book club at Bonnie's Teashop,' Aiden finished.

'That's the one! A man who listens to what you say!' Pippa grinned, obviously impressed.

Aiden leaned over the table and stretched out his arm to shake hands with Jack. 'Congratulations, mate.'

'Are you married, Aiden?' Jack asked.

'No, but I have a son called Theo who's nearly three,' Aiden replied proudly. 'His mum, Louisa, and I aren't together anymore. It's not ideal, but we do our best for the wee man.'

'Did I mention I'm now coming to the wedding as Elle's plus one?' Pippa beamed at Jack and Wilson.

'Excellent,' Wilson replied, smiling back at her with a sparkle in his eye.

'I'd love to get married one day and settle down with a couple of children and a few pets. I can't wait to bake bread and fairy cakes, and sew my own patchwork quilts.' Pippa's eyes were shining.

'Really?' Elle looked at her suspiciously. This was the girl that spent all night watching TikToks and sourcing the latest fashion accessories. 'Well, aren't you the domestic goddess,' she teased.

'Yes, really,' Pippa argued. 'Isn't it every girl's dream to find a prince and have her dream wedding?'

Aiden and Wilson seemed to be listening closely.

'Then you best start the search for your ideal man,' Elle said, swerving the question, but once again Noah Jones was firmly in her thoughts.

Jack's phone beeped and he looked at the text message on his screen.

'Damn. I'd forgotten I should be up at Buttercup Barn with Eleni, to discuss the flowers for the reception. Drink up quickly, Wilson. I'll drop you back home on my way.'

'No problem at all,' he replied.

'Then I've got a bit more work to do after that. The honeymoon won't pay for itself, unfortunately.'

'No rest for the wicked,' Pippa said, grinning at them as they downed their drinks and placed the empty glasses on the table.

'I'll see you in the morning,' Wilson said with a smile as he stood up.

'You sure will,' Elle replied, watching them disappear through the pub door.

'They seem like a couple of decent lads,' Aiden said. 'I actually need to make a move too. I want to nip back and bath Theo and read him a bedtime story. That'll give Louisa a break for an hour or so.'

'Aww, how lovely are you,' Pippa gushed.

Aiden checked his phone before stuffing it back into his pocket and bidding them farewell. As soon as he was out of earshot, Pippa caught Elle watching her closely.

'He's quite nice,' Pippa said dreamily.

'Quite nice?' Elle gave her a knowing look. 'I can tell by the look on your face that you've got your whole future mapped out! I can see you on speed dial to Libby asking her to design your wedding dress. Then the wedding will take place at Heartcross church followed by the wedding breakfast at Starcross Manor, prepared, of course, by world-famous chef Andrew Glossop and filmed by Guy Hart, the best in his field.'

Pippa opened her mouth to protest, then shut it again when Elle silenced her with her hand and laughed. 'Don't you even try to deny it.'

'You know me so well.' Pippa grinned. Anyway –' she steered the conversation into a completely different direction '– about your birthday. I know you said you're spending Friday with Irene but let's definitely do something on Saturday.'

'I'd love to, I really would, but actually, I don't know if I can. Money is a little tight at the minute. I've even been thinking about looking for a part-time job in the evening.'

'Are things actually that bad?'

'They aren't bad as such. I can pay my bills, pay for food, but it just doesn't leave much extra for nights out. Not that I'm complaining, I love being home.'

Pippa was quiet for a moment and then a huge smiled appeared on her face.

'I know that look. What are you thinking about?' Elle asked, intrigued.

'You don't need a part-time job because I know of a better solution.'

'I dread to think,' remarked Elle, hoping that she wasn't going to suggest that her new part-time occupation was the same as the man who owned the rucksack left on the bus. 'Put me out of my misery, and don't you dare suggest I sell feet pictures … or pictures of any part of my body for that matter.'

'As if.' Pippa's grin grew wider. 'How about you get yourself a lodger?'

'I'm one step ahead of you there. I've already thought about that, but it could be a lot more hassle than it's worth. What if they're messy or they drive me insane?'

'Simple. You just need to rent a room to somebody who doesn't get on your nerves and is extremely tidy,' Pippa exclaimed, throwing her arms open then tapping her hands on her chest.

Suddenly the penny dropped. 'You mean you?'

'Yes! Of course I mean me! Well,' she said, grabbing Elle's arm, 'what do you think? It would be so much fun! Late-night girly conversations, film nights … not to mention the extra money will come in handy.'

'It would certainly help me out,' replied Elle, thinking this could be a possible solution.

'Is that a yes then?' Pippa pushed, before standing up with outstretched arms.

'I think it just might be, Pippa Lawson.'

Before Elle could say any more, Pippa pulled her to her feet and hugged her tightly. 'We are going to have *so* much fun! It's going to be like one long girly holiday! When can I move in?'

'How about the day after my birthday?'

'Absolutely perfect!' Pippa squealed before squeezing Elle again.

Chapter Seven

L ying in bed listening to the wind and rain batter the windowpane, Elle knew despite the weather she would have trouble sleeping tonight. It had been the same for as long as she could remember. As soon as it turned midnight on the second of February there would only be one person on her mind for the next twenty-four hours – her biological mother.

Burying herself under the duvet she willed herself to go back to sleep, but it was no use – she couldn't drop off. Through her tired eyes, she watched the clock for what seemed like every second of the night, tossing and turning until around four a.m., when she finally placed one weary leg in front of the other and padded downstairs to make herself a hot drink. Clutching a mug of steaming tea, Elle lingered for a moment at the bottom of the stairs in front of the hall mirror.

'Happy thirtieth birthday,' she whispered to herself.

Staring at her reflection she knew the time had come. As much as she loved Irene, Elle needed to find the missing pieces of herself, even if it meant facing the possibility of rejection. If she was successful in tracking down her mother, would the woman want to acknowledge her existence? Or would the answers she needed so badly prove to be ones she didn't want to hear? Would the whole endeavour leave her with nothing but crushing disappointment? Only time would tell.

With a sigh she climbed back into bed and leaned against her pillows, pulling the duvet up to her chest. As she took a sip of tea, her thoughts tumbled over the past. Moving between various foster homes, she'd experienced a sense of loss on many occasions, and had no experience of positive relationships until she'd met Irene.

Living in Glensheil and working in Heartcross had settled her life into a happy routine. Elle had never imagined she would fit in anywhere, but this place felt like home. She'd made good friends in the village, it was a beautiful part of the world, and she now couldn't imagine living anywhere else.

Elle knew this was the right time – she had a supportive network, gorgeous friends and Irene to help her through the difficult times that might be coming her way. With an anxious feeling swirling in the pit of her stomach, the decision was made.

Elle was ready to find out exactly who she was. She was going to start the search for her mother. Today.

With the torrential rain sounding like bullets, Elle finished her tea and snuggled back under the covers, knowing she would find some kind of closure one way or another.

Whatever the outcome, she was about to embark on the biggest emotional journey of her life, and thankfully she knew Irene would be by her side every step of the way.

She finally managed to doze off for an hour or so, to be woken by the alarm clock. She forced her eyes to open when her phone beeped with an incoming message. The first happy birthday text of the day was from Pippa and there was also an

Instagram story she'd tagged her in. Elle laughed at the collage of photos Pippa had put together, which showcased all the fun they'd had together over the last six months. There was the fancy-dress party for Pippa's birthday at The Grouse and Haggis where she'd insisted everyone had to replicate an outfit worn by Harry Styles in the past five years. Then there was the alpaca racing at Foxglove Farm, where Elle had ended up face-down in the mud after slipping over. In such a short time they had certainly got up to some memorable antics.

After a quick shower, Elle got dressed and ventured downstairs. The rain had finally stopped and according to the weather app the sun would be shining by the afternoon. Deciding on a breakfast of scrambled eggs on buttery granary toast, Elle scrolled through her phone. Already there were messages from Isla, Eleni and Florrie. Suddenly she felt a little teary that everyone was being so kind. Another message pinged. It was Pippa.

Guess what?

No clue! Surprise me! replied Elle.

Two seconds later an image appeared on the screen of Pippa waiting at the bus stop. *I've beaten you to it for the first time ever!*

Elle shook her head, chuckling. *Unbelievable!* she replied, grabbing her bag and coat before heading out of the door and locking it behind her.

As the bus stop came into sight Elle couldn't quite believe her eyes. 'Oh my gosh...' she said as she walked towards a grinning Pippa, who was trying her best to hold on to a bevy of colourful balloons reading 'Happy Birthday!'

'It's a good job the wind has settled down as you would be flying high in the sky!'

'Good morning, birthday girl!'

'Have you gone mad? Everyone's looking at you.'

'Let them look. It's my best friend's birthday and I'm going to make sure you're spoilt rotten, all day.'

Much to Elle's embarrassment, Pippa began to sing 'Happy Birthday' at the top of her voice. A number of amused onlookers standing in the bus queue joined in with the three hip-hip-hoorays at the end of the song.

'Thank you,' Elle whispered, shooting Pippa a look that meant *behave*, but judging by the look on her face there was going to be no chance of that.

'These are for you.'

'What am I meant to do with all these?' Elle looked at the colourful balloons bobbing up and down in the air.

'At least hold half because you might be right, I could be taking to the sky at any minute.'

'How many are there?'

'Thirty, of course, a colourful dancing balloon for every year of your life. Thirty years old ... how do you feel? I feel no different from when I was younger except for the wrinkles.'

'You have no wrinkles.'

Pippa leaned towards Elle and attempted to flex the skin on her forehead. 'Botox in three places but that is not to be repeated.'

Elle laughed. 'My lips are sealed.'

'What were you like when you were younger? I can imagine you being top of your class, the most popular girl in the school, no doubt head girl.'

Pippa was so far off the mark. During her childhood, Elle was passed from pillar to post, family to family. She'd moved around the country more times than a travelling circus and lost count of the number of schools she'd attended, never staying in one place long enough to have any stability or make any real friends until she'd moved in with Irene and become part of the communities in Glensheil and Heartcross.

Wrestling with the fifteen balloons in her hand Elle saw the bus trundling up the road towards them. She stared, not quite believing her eyes, and her pulse began to race as she recognised the face staring back at her from the new poster on the side of the bus. There he was advertising his brand-new book – Noah Jones, a face she never expected to see on her birthday. Elle knew she was catching flies but his eyes melted her heart and he was still as utterly gorgeous as she remembered. There was only one word to describe the face on the poster – hot. Immediately, her thoughts went back to the kiss they had shared and her whole body erupted in goosebumps. He was perfect.

'What's up with you? You've suddenly gone quiet,' Pippa observed, trying to control the balloons she was holding.

'Nothing, absolutely nothing,' replied Elle, knowing that wasn't strictly true.

'Well, just look at that.' Pippa had spotted the poster. 'Noah Jones's new book is out very soon. He's a little easy on the eye, isn't he?'

'Isn't he just,' murmured Elle, her thoughts distracted as the bus doors opened and they were met by Henry's huge smile.

'Here she is! Happy birthday, Miss Elle.'

'Thank you so much, Henry! I hope you're not going to charge us for the balloons today?'

Pippa was fighting her way up to the top deck as the helium balloons were attempting to fly off in every direction.

Henry laughed. 'No. And as promised, you ride free today.'

'Thanks, Henry, you're so kind!'

Fifteen minutes later, they arrived at the library and were greeted by Florrie, the local florist, holding a bouquet of the most beautiful lilac roses that Elle had ever seen. 'It's a good job I went for flowers and not balloons!' Florrie grinned, reaching up and grabbing the string of a balloon that was trying to escape. 'You nearly lost one there. Happy birthday, these are for you.'

'Florrie, these are gorgeous, thank you so much.'

'You're very welcome.'

'Please could you reach inside my bag and grab the keys? I think I'm going to struggle to get through the door.'

Florrie reached in her bag and then opened the door. 'Here you go,' she said, placing the bouquet in Elle's arms. 'Enjoy the rest of your birthday.'

'I'll get them in water as soon as I can.'

Once inside the door, Elle weighted the balloons and let them dance each side of her desk.

'How lovely is that?' she exclaimed, taking in the aroma of the roses. 'And such a beautiful colour.'

'I bet you're feeling loved today!' said Pippa. 'I love birthdays, it's one of the best days of the year.'

Elle immediately felt a surge of emotion. For her it was completely different – birthdays had never been a source of celebration. She'd always felt that something – some*one* – was missing from her life. Trying to stay composed, she swallowed a lump in her throat. 'Yes, I'm feeling loved. It's great to have such wonderful friends,' she replied.

In the staffroom, Pippa threw her bag on to the table and rummaged around inside. 'Here!' She pulled out a small gift wrapped in pink-spotted tissue paper with a bow on top.

'For me?' Elle asked, smiling.

'Of course it's for you! I didn't just get you balloons; this is your proper present.'

'You're spoiling me. Thank you very much.' Elle took the gift and pulled on the ribbon before carefully unwrapping the blush-coloured paper to reveal a small box. Lifting the lid she gave a tiny gasp. Inside was a gorgeous pair of silver earrings in the shape of books.

'Oh, they're perfect, thank you!' she exclaimed, immediately wrapping her arms around Pippa and hugging her.

'What's going on in here?' Aiden asked, walking through the staffroom door and placing a large white cardboard box on the table.

'It's Elle's birthday today!' Pippa said, smiling, scooping up the torn wrapping paper and rolling it into a small ball before tossing it into the bin.

'A birthday, you say? It's a good job I brought you this then.' Aiden gestured towards the box. 'Go on, take a look.'

Elle raised the lid to reveal a mighty fine-looking birthday cake. 'Oh my gosh!' The cake design showed the library with 'Happy 30th birthday Elle' iced on top.

'This is amazing. It has to be one of Rona's creations.'

'It is,' replied Aiden. 'If you look closely at the little pile of books you'll see they're by one of your favourite authors – Sam Stone.'

'It's just brilliant and very thoughtful – and it looks scrumptious.'

'It's chocolate cake on the inside,' added Aiden, displaying a dimple as he grinned at both of them.

'My favourite!'

'Oh, and I nearly forgot,' he went on, pulling a slightly creased card from the inside of his jacket pocket. He handed it to Elle and pressed a swift kiss to her cheek.

'Happy birthday, Elle.'

'I think there's only one thing for it. Who fancies a slice of birthday cake for breakfast?' she asked.

'Absolutely a must!' confirmed Pippa. 'There's fifteen minutes until opening time,' she added. 'Let the sugar rush begin.'

Pippa switched on the kettle whilst Elle took plates out of the cupboard and put them on the table before cutting the cake into pieces. 'It seems an absolute shame to eat it. It's the best cake I've ever seen.'

Pippa had already taken an enormous bite and Elle laughed as cream oozed down her chin.

All three of them sat in silence aside from the odd murmur of appreciation at how delicious the cake was, and soon every morsel had been hoovered from their plates.

'That was the best breakfast I've had in ages. Thank you, Aiden.'

'Is there time for another slice?' Pippa looked longingly at the cake.

'No! And you'll feel queasy if you eat any more! Save some for lunchtime.'

Pippa blew a sad kiss at the leftover cake as Aiden shut the box and Elle placed the plates in the sink.

'Wilson hasn't arrived with any deliveries,' Elle said.

Looking up at the clock, she added, 'He's usually here by now.'

'Maybe all your birthday presents are too heavy for him to carry from the van,' Pippa joked, grinning as she held the door open so Aiden could walk past her on to the library floor.

'Or maybe it's simply because we don't have any deliveries today. I'll fire up the computers. Here, take these.' Elle threw a bunch of keys towards Pippa. 'Can you open the front door?'

'Yes, of course,' she answered, catching the keys.

Pippa disappeared towards the front door while Aiden and Elle headed towards the main desk.

As soon as the doors were open a stream of people filed into the library. Wilson, juggling a box, followed swiftly behind.

'Here he is. Morning, mate.' Aiden reached out and took the box from him.

'Sorry I'm late!' His face was flushed. 'It's been one of those mornings.'

Jenny walked in behind Wilson. 'What he means is that it's my fault.'

'For once, Mum, I'm not going to argue.' Wilson smiled, quickly kissing her cheek. 'I'll catch you at teatime,' he said, waving as he dashed back outside into the courtyard.

'He'll forgive me,' Jenny said. 'The internet isn't working at home, and I was wondering whether I could use that computer over there?' She nodded towards the desk on the other side of the room.

'Of course, that's what it's there for,' Elle replied. Then, noticing how tired she looked, she added, 'Do you need any help with anything?'

'No, thanks, I'll be fine,' she replied, walking over to the computer, scrabbling inside her bag as she went.

Grunting noises from the other side of the room made Elle look in Aiden's direction. He'd opened the box and was grappling with a poster that was too large to manage by himself. 'Urghh,' she heard him mutter before he thumped the poster in the middle to try to straighten it out.

Elle hurried towards him. 'Here, let me help,' she said, pulling up a chair and reaching towards the top as Aiden smoothed down the bottom half.

'Thank you,' he said, finally securing it to the wall with some drawing pins. They both took a step back and gazed at the poster.

Pippa joined them. 'Sam Stone's latest novel,' she said admiringly. 'What a marvellous cover. In fact, I finished reading the book last night.'

'What did you think of it?' asked Aiden.

'Absolutely awesome as usual. It was one of those books I couldn't put down. Hence why I have huge bags under my eyes this morning,' she said, pointing to her face. 'The only downside is, now I'll have to wait months for his next book.'

They stared at the poster for a moment longer before Pippa moseyed over towards the children's corner and Aiden began to put returned books back on the shelves.

Drifting back towards the front desk, Elle noticed Jenny was still sitting at the computer. Even though she was staring at the screen, she looked distracted. Twisting her wedding ring round and round on her finger, she exhaled before scribbling something in her notepad then closed it quickly.

Elle walked up behind her and Jenny started.

'Sorry, I didn't mean to make you jump. Is everything okay?' Elle noticed a tear roll down her cheek. She quickly pulled out a tissue from her pocket. 'Here, take this,' she said softly. 'It's clean.'

Jenny dabbed the corner of her eyes. 'Thank you. Yes, ignore me. I'm just having a moment – nothing to worry about.'

Elle could see Jenny was far from okay. There was sadness written all over her face, but Elle didn't want to pry or draw attention to it.

'Let me make you a cup of tea.'

Jenny nodded her appreciation. 'Thank you, that would be lovely,' she replied, her voice faltering.

Elle gestured towards Pippa that she was going to the staffroom for a moment and five minutes later returned carrying a tray of mugs and biscuits for everyone. The library was quiet aside from an elderly couple standing amongst the children's books with a toddler in tow, chatting with Aiden.

With a smile, she placed a mug of tea and a plate of chocolate biscuits in front of Jenny.

'Thank you.'

'A chocolate biscuit always works wonders for me,' said Elle, dunking one into her tea. 'If you need anything, please give me a shout.'

Jenny nodded.

Elle walked over to Aiden, who was kneeling down next to a little boy, showing him a book on steam engines. The boy was making train noises and giggling infectiously.

'I'll pop your drink up here, Aiden,' Elle told him, placing the mug on a high shelf away from the toddler.

'Thanks, Elle. While you're here, can I introduce you to Louisa's mum and dad?' he said, gesturing towards them both.

'Pleased to meet you,' she said, smiling. Glancing over at the small boy on the beanbag, she said, 'And this has to be Theo, right?'

'It sure is,' Aiden replied with a huge grin across his face.

'Well, there's no mistaking he belongs to you. Two peas in a pod,' she exclaimed, passing him the tray before she knelt down next to the little boy, who looked up at her with huge hazel eyes.

'You're a handsome little fellow, aren't you?' She held out her hand towards him. 'I'm Elle, and I'm very pleased to meet you.'

Theo looked up towards his dad before his wide eyes met hers again.

'Shake Elle's hand,' Aiden encouraged.

Theo shyly grabbed her hand before letting go and hiding his hand behind his back. He had such an adorable face.

'It was lovely to meet you both – oh and you too, Theo.' Theo gave her a cheeky smile over his shoulder. He was now holding on to the edge of the shelf, happily pulling off every children's book he could lay his hands on and stacking them in a pile on the floor.

Pippa was hovering at the back of the room, helping a student. As Elle headed back towards the reception desk, she noticed that Jenny had disappeared. She looked around the library then spotted her through the window walking across the courtyard. Elle didn't like to see anyone upset and hoped that whatever was troubling Jenny would sort itself out soon.

'Gosh, what's that?' she murmured. Sitting in the middle of the front desk was a parcel wrapped in pink birthday paper and bound with ribbon.

She fixed her gaze on the handwritten label.

It read: *For Elle Cooper*

Elle looked over her shoulder and swung her gaze around the library but there wasn't anyone nearby and she couldn't work out where the parcel had come from. Aiden was by the door, saying goodbye to Theo and Louisa's parents and Pippa was up in the galleried landing. The library had been extremely quiet this morning, and in the past ten minutes she hadn't noticed anyone else pass through.

She slid the parcel towards her, picked it up and turned it over. There was no postage mark so Elle knew it must have been hand delivered.

'Pippa!' she whispered loudly and held up the parcel.

'What have you there?' Pippa asked, heading down the stairs and walking towards her. 'Who is it from?'

Elle shrugged. 'I found it on the desk.'

Pippa peered over her shoulder. 'It's addressed to you. Another birthday present! Come on, open it,' she encouraged.

Grasping hold of the ribbon Elle pulled, then ripped open the wrapping paper.

Staring back at her was a copy of Sam Stone's new book. She picked it up and flipped it over.

'I don't understand,' she murmured, mystified. 'It doesn't say who has sent it. There's no note or card.'

'I don't understand either,' replied Pippa. 'We already have one in the library.' Taking the book from Elle's hand she fanned through the pages, then gasped loudly. She grabbed hold of Elle's arm then wafted her hand frantically.

'Are you having a heart attack?' Elle asked, not sure if she should be amused or concerned by her friend's antics.

Pippa thrust the book back towards her. Her eyes were wide and she could barely speak. Waggling her finger towards the book, she stuttered, 'L-Look at the front page!'

Elle did as instructed and opened the book to the first page. Wide-eyed she looked back at Pippa.

'Holy moly!'

It read:

Dear Elle,
> *Happy birthday!*
> *Best wishes,*
> *Sam Stone*

The writing was stylish, written in in real ink.

'What's going on?' Aiden asked, appearing at the side of the desk. 'What have you got there?'

Pippa couldn't hold back. 'Elle Cooper here has landed the best birthday present ever. A signed copy of the new Sam Stone novel. Look!' she enthused.

'How cool is that?' Aiden said, as his eyes darted towards the page.

'I don't get it. This is off-the-scale amazing and just the best present…'

Pippa pretended to look hurt.

'You know I love the earrings but how would Sam Stone even know I existed or where I worked?' asked Elle, puzzled. 'And how did it get here?'

'I've no idea. It's a mystery but a very lovely one,' chipped in Pippa.

Elle's mind was racing with all the possibilities.

'Maybe it was Mum?' She looked at Pippa and Aiden. 'Maybe she had a contact after working in the library all those years.'

'That doesn't make sense, because she would have just given it to you tonight. She would have wanted to see your reaction,' Pippa said, taking the book from her hands again and flicking through the pages. 'And if Irene had a contact that knew Sam Stone you would have heard about it before now.'

'Very true,' agreed Elle, still thinking. 'What do you think, Aiden?'

He shrugged. 'I think Pippa's right. If Irene had a contact, you would have known about it by now.'

Elle couldn't believe she'd received such a wonderful gift. Someone knew something about how it got here, and she was going to try her damnedest to find out who and how.

Chapter Eight

The rest of the day passed quickly and Elle felt loved for every single minute. Isla had popped in and gave her a meat hamper from the farm shop. Flynn and Julia had given her a voucher for a spa day up at Starcross Manor, and Bea from The Little Blue Boathouse had given her a voucher for a luxury champagne day cruise. After telling Pippa a little white lie about why she wasn't travelling back with her on the bus this evening, Elle locked the library door behind her and Aiden. The next bus out of the village was due in a little over an hour, which would still give her plenty of time to be out of the library before the cleaners arrived and to arrive at Irene's in time for tea.

Switching off the lights in the main foyer, Elle felt her heart racing. She sat down at her desk, her hands slightly shaking as she brought up the Salvation Army web page. She was already familiar with the form she had to complete as she'd researched it many times but her emotions were all over the place now that it was time to actually fill it out. She felt hopeful yet fearful of what – if anything – she was about to discover, but she knew she had to take the chance if she had any hope of ever knowing exactly who she was.

Taking a sip of water, she tried to calm her nerves as she began to read section one of the guidance notes. Elle had the information that the Salvation Army needed to begin the trace. She'd googled the name Cora Hansley on many occasions but with no results. Elle hoped that the Salvation Army would be more successful.

After completing all the relevant details, she took a moment to check back over the form and printed it off. After scanning the form and attaching a photo of her birth certificate, she paid the fee online and swallowed a lump in her throat, she briefly closed her eyes as she hovered the mouse over the 'send' button before she pressed it down. Hearing the whoosh of the email leaving her sent box, she knew it had gone. As she stared at the screen her head and heart were in battle. She began to wonder if she was doing the right thing? Or were some things better left in the past?

There was no going back. Her search for her biological mother was now in the hands of the Salvation Army. She exhaled and tried to calm her rapidly beating heart.

There was no guarantee they would even be able to trace her mother, or, if they did, that she would want to be found, but this was a start. And even if they weren't able to uncover any information, Elle knew she wouldn't be any worse off than she was now. Or at least that's what she kept telling herself.

Fifteen minutes later, she was still looking at the screen, trying to digest the scale of the journey she was just about to embark on. But whatever the search threw up she knew she could face anything with Irene by her side. Finally shutting down the computer she grabbed her signed Sam Stone novel and her bag and jumped as she heard a voice.

'Are you still here, Elle? You're working late. Look at those balloons. Do we have a birthday in the house?'

The cleaners, Gwen and Julie, were strolling towards her, Gwen pushing a hoover and Julie with her arms full of cleaning products.

'Yes, it's mine! Thirty today.'

'Happy birthday,' they chorused.

'Any plans for tonight?' asked Julie.

'I'm having tea with Irene,' she answered. 'If you would both like a slice of cake there's some left in the staffroom.'

A moment later, armed with her gorgeous blooms and a handful of balloons, Elle paused briefly outside the library.

There was a hive of activity in The Heart of the Village. Isla was closing the family farm shop and Florrie was taking inside the buckets of beautiful flowers that lined the pavement outside her florist shop. Feeling emotional, Elle waved to them both before setting off down the driveway towards the bus stop on Love Heart Lane.

Arriving at Irene's house in an emotional state, she knocked on the door and waited. As soon as the door opened, she was met with a broad smile.

'Gosh, I've missed seeing you! Come here! Happy birthday!' Irene threw her arms wide and hugged Elle like she'd just returned from a year's travelling round the world.

'I've missed you too,' she replied, smiling at the overzealous welcome as she placed the bouquet of roses on the hall table and let the balloons dance at the foot of the stairs.

'How are you?' Irene asked. 'It takes some getting used to, not seeing you every day.'

'I'm good,' Elle replied weakly, causing Irene to study her closely.

'That doesn't sound convincing.' Irene looked sceptical.

'Okay, you can read me like a book,' Elle acknowledged, unbuttoning her coat as the fresh aroma of home-baked bread hit her.

'Mmm, that smells divine,' she murmured, slipping her arm through Irene's as they walked towards the kitchen.

'Your favourite, but I do appreciate you're now thirty, so do you really want home-made bread with fish fingers and tartare sauce? We could order—'

'Of course I do,' Elle interrupted.

'Okay, and guess what it's followed by?'

'Eton mess?' Elle added hopefully.

'Of course.'

'Thank you! Even though I have to admit, I've had cake for breakfast.'

Irene pulled down the oven door and took out a baking tray. 'If you can't have cake for breakfast on your birthday, when can you?' She smiled, turning the temperature up on the oven before placing the freshly baked loaf in front of Elle on a breadboard.

With a mischievous grin on her face, Elle leaned forward, but before she managed to pinch a little from the corner of the loaf, Irene playfully swiped her hand.

'Damn,' she muttered, rolling her eyes.

She smiled. 'You, young lady, can wait another twenty minutes for your tea.'

'Okay, okay, but it just looks so delicious – especially this bit here that seems to be looking straight at me.' Elle managed to break a little bit off and pop it into her mouth before Irene playfully struck her again, this time with the tea towel.

Elle shot her a mock regretful look, then carried on eating with a huge grin on her face.

'Cup of tea or a glass of wine?' asked Irene, hovering at the fridge door.

'It's my birthday and Friday night – let's go for the wine!'

'Agreed!'

After pouring the wine Irene popped the fish fingers in the oven, set the timer and they went into the living room. Irene sat down opposite Elle on the settee and sipped her wine.

'I've been thinking about you all day today. How've you been?' she asked. 'I'm assuming you've been all over the place emotionally?'

Elle looked up and met Irene's heart-warming smile.

'I've been spoilt rotten by my friends. Pippa greeted me at the bus stop with thirty balloons! Honestly, I thought she was going to fly high in the sky if the wind caught her at the wrong moment.'

Irene laughed.

'Those beautiful roses are from Florrie and Aiden brought in a cake decorated like the library. Which reminds me. I've not told you yet but we have a new member of staff. Aiden from Inverness has transferred to our library. You'll have met him on training courses.'

'I remember. He's a lovely lad.'

'Everyone has just been fantastic, but...' Elle blew out a breath.

'You've always had something or someone in the back of

your mind on your birthdays,' Irene said, leaning across and touching Elle's knee.

Elle nodded. 'I've been thinking a lot recently about who I am. It's not just about the woman who gave birth to me – even though that's a huge part – it's also about knowing who I truly am. Does that sound daft?'

Irene shook her head. 'Of course it doesn't sound daft. It's very understandable.'

'This past year, I've been happier than I've ever been before,' Elle shared. 'I have a fantastic job, my own home and of course you.'

'I know.' Irene nodded. 'But...'

'But...'

'There are questions you need answered – about your mother.'

'Yes,' Elle replied softly, nodding. 'It's the right time.' She lightly thumped her chest. 'In here, there's a dull ache that never goes away. On some days the ache is a little less but on my birthday it intensifies. It's hard to explain but as time is passing, it's beginning to get worse. Over the last few years, I've become more emotionally balanced. My life has settled down. I have stability and I know that's down to you and my friends in Heartcross.'

Irene cupped her hands over Elle's.

'And then there's Eleni and Jack.'

'What do they have to do with anything?' Irene asked.

'They're getting married, embarking on the next stage of their life, and I want the fairy tale, the happy-ever-after, too, but I feel I need some sort of closure about my past before I can look forward to my future.'

'I can understand that.'

'Irene, I've set the wheels in motion. Today, after work, I

sent the form to the Salvation Army and started the search for my mother.'

'Oh Elle, that's good news, hopefully.' Irene's eyes welled up with tears.

'Yes, but I'm a little worried about us too.'

'Us? As in you and me? Why?'

Elle paused for a second. 'Because everyone who's come into our lives in the last few years thinks you're my mum. How are you going to feel when people begin to discover the truth?'

'This is about what's best for you, and whatever happens, I'll be with you every step of the way. You know I will.'

Elle's voice faltered a little as she blinked through tears. 'Thank you.'

'It'll all be okay, you know.'

'I hope so. It's the first thing on my mind in the morning and the last thing I think about before I go to sleep.'

'It's definitely time then,' Irene said reassuringly.

A tear rolled down Elle's cheek. 'I know it sounds daft, but I feel like I'm a jigsaw puzzle that's waiting to be completed, and there are two more pieces to fit in.'

'Two?' Irene prompted.

Elle hesitated. 'Maybe finding my mother will lead me to discover who my father is too.'

'It might or it might not. Who knows? You need to prepare yourself for every possible outcome. All we can do is wait. These types of searches can take weeks or even years, and your mother might not want to be found.'

'Or she could have passed away.'

'That is also a possibility,' Irene admitted. 'But you need to keep an open mind and be hopeful, think positive. The only way we're going to discover the truth is if we find your mother, and even then she might not want to talk about it.'

Elle knew Irene was talking sense, and she might just have to accept not knowing where or who she came from, despite the feeling of abandonment that still ached deep inside her.

'I know.'

'Have you spoken to anyone else about this?' Irene asked.

Elle leaned forward and took a sip of wine. 'I've thought about talking to Pippa about it all.'

'But you haven't yet?'

Elle was silent for a moment.

'Once I've crossed that line, there's no going back. She'll know you aren't my biological mum.'

'Pippa isn't a gossip. She'll support you. I know she will. Have a think about it.'

'I will,' Elle agreed. 'She's going to be moving in with me next week, which will help me out financially too.'

'I think that'll be good for you – not just for the money but for the company too.'

Just then they were interrupted by the oven timer beeping.

'You go and wash your face. I've set the table in the dining room.'

'Thanks, Irene.'

'What for?'

'Just for everything.'

'You don't need to thank me.' She smiled lovingly. 'I'll dish up and then you can tell me all the gossip from work.'

'And you can tell me what you're doing with your days now you aren't up at the crack of dawn.'

After Elle had finished touching up her make-up in the downstairs bathroom, she opened the door to the dining room and smiled. Irene had done a superb job of setting the table, and she'd even tied the balloons to the back of Elle's chair like she'd done from the very first birthday that Elle had spent in her care. On top of her happy birthday napkin lay a small gift wrapped in shiny silver paper.

A few seconds later, Irene appeared in the doorway clutching two plates brimming with food.

'Wow, there's enough to feed a small army!' Elle exclaimed, sitting down at the table and staring at the plate in front of her. 'Back to healthy eating next week.'

The home-made bread was cut into large doorsteps, the sandwich piled with fish fingers and crisp iceberg lettuce. She lifted the top of the sandwich and smeared it generously with tomato ketchup, then put the bread back on top and pushed it down using a little force, which for some reason always seemed to make it taste better. By the side of the sandwich were a handful of thick-cut chips and a freshly prepared salad.

'This looks absolutely delicious. Thank you,' she enthused, picking up her fork and stabbing a chip with it before popping it into her mouth.

'There's a pot of tartare sauce there too. Would you like a top-up?' Irene said, hovering the wine bottle over Elle's glass.

'Oh go on then. It is my birthday after all.' Elle held up the small gift on the table. 'Is this for me?'

'It is indeed.' Irene pulled out a chair and sat down opposite her. 'Open it.'

Without hesitation, Elle ripped open the wrapping paper to reveal a burgundy box. Slowly opening the lid she saw sparkling back at her the most stunning diamond ring she'd ever seen.

Elle's voice cracked with emotion. 'Irene, it's beautiful! Absolutely exquisite. But I can't accept this, it must have cost a fortune.'

Irene dabbed at her eyes with a tissue. 'You can and you must because I want to give you this. As you know, when my husband died unexpectedly of coronary heart disease, I thought my own life was over, but then you arrived at just at the right time. I needed you as much as you needed me. I think of you as my own daughter and I wouldn't want to give it to anyone else. This was my mum's and I'd like you to have it.'

Irene held Elle's gaze and a tsunami of tears cascaded down Elle's cheeks. 'Irene, I don't know what to say, except I'm truly honoured. It's absolutely beautiful.' Elle took the ring out of the box and slipped it on to the fourth finger of her right hand before holding her hand out to show it off. 'I can't believe it, it fits perfectly.'

'Will you treasure it?' Irene asked.

'With all my heart,' Elle answered, overcome with emotion.

'You mean the world to me, Elle. I know you might not have had the best start in life, but I can feel it in here –' she said, pointing to her heart '– that it's your time now. I was one of the lucky ones. My relationship with my mum was one of love and respect; we were best friends. She always had my back and I always had hers. It was us two against the world, the same way it's you and me against the world. I know I'm not your blood, but as far as I'm concerned, you're my daughter. I thank the universe every day for bringing you into my life.'

Overcome with emotion, Elle was unable to speak.

'This ring is very special to me, and I'm glad that I can pass it on to you.'

Irene's kind words had hit Elle hard. She bit her lip, but she still couldn't stop the tears from falling. Standing up, she walked around the table and threw her arms around Irene, who gently kissed her hair.

'Now let's eat,' she said, smiling up at Elle. 'Before it gets cold.'

Elle sat back down at the table and sank her teeth into the enormous sandwich. 'Mmm, delicious,' was all she could manage as the tartare sauce oozed from the bread.

They sat and ate in silence for a while before Elle finally spoke. 'So how are you finding retirement?'

Irene gave a little chuckle. 'At first, it felt like I'd just taken an extended holiday, but now it's beginning to hit me, and I have to say I'm missing the library.'

'We're missing you too. It's not the same without you there.'

'I'm keeping myself busy though,' she said. 'I've joined a walking group.'

Elle raised her eyebrows. 'A what?'

'A walking group.' Irene laughed. 'Don't look too surprised. I decided I needed to do a little more exercise, and though anything too strenuous is beyond me, I do like a stroll. Every Monday and Wednesday morning we meet by the church and go for a ramble – well, that's what they call it.'

'How did you hear about it?' Elle asked as she devoured the rest of her sandwich. 'Sorry, I shouldn't talk with my mouth full,' she said, grinning. 'You always used to tell me off for that.'

'There was a poster in the window of The Old Bakehouse so I thought, what the heck, why not. There was a lovely group of men and women that turned up. They'd all been before on numerous occasions, and I was definitely the new girl. But they made me feel very welcome and the company was great. Most of the walkers live around here, and it was nice to get out in the fresh air and just chat about everything and anything.'

'Are you going again?'

'Yes, I think I will. It gets me out of the house for a couple of hours.'

'You'll be climbing mountains next!'

'Ha, I wouldn't go that far.'

'I don't believe you for a minute! Walking this week, climbing mountains next week, then you'll progress to skydiving!'

'My feet are staying firmly on the ground!' insisted Irene. 'But tell me about your day. How was work? Were you spoilt rotten?'

'I was. Look at these.' Elle tucked her hair behind her ears to reveal the earrings that Pippa had bought her.

'They're gorgeous, very pretty indeed,' Irene exclaimed. 'And very apt given you work in a library.'

'And I told you about the cake that Aiden bought me.'

'You did.'

'Changing the subject, do you remember Jenny?'

'Jenny is lovely. She often popped in and I've missed our chats. She's such a down-to-earth, easy-going person.'

'Her son, Wilson, is the new UPS guy and he also happens to be Jack's best friend.'

'Eleni's Jack?'

'Yes. He's best man at their wedding.'

'Isn't it just a very small world.'

After catching up on the gossip they finished their meals and Elle clasped her hands over her stomach. 'I don't think I could manage another mouthful. Can we wait half an hour until dessert?'

'Of course.' Irene smiled. 'Let's sit back in the living room. We can tidy these plates away in a little while.'

Elle stretched out her fingers again and stared at the ring.

'I'm glad you like it.' Irene touched her arm affectionately before she followed her into the living room.

'It's my favourite present.' Suddenly she remembered the mysterious Sam Stone book delivery. 'I can't believe I've forgotten to tell you this! Look what I have.' Elle fished inside her bag, pulled out the book and passed it across to Irene.

'Sam Stone's latest! I was going to ask you about this one. Can you reserve me one at the library?' she asked. 'Or is this the library's copy?'

Elle couldn't hide her excitement. 'Look at the first page. Go on. It's not the library's copy, it's my copy.'

Elle watched Irene's expression change to one of shock as she opened the book and focused on the birthday message written inside.

'I have no idea where it came from. I was going to ask you, did you know? But judging by the shock on your face, you must have no clue either.'

'You have a signed copy from Sam Stone? *The Sam Stone?*' Irene repeated, just in case Elle hadn't heard her the first time.

'It's an absolute mystery. One minute I'm cleaning the empty mugs off the desks and next there's a parcel sitting slap bang in the middle of reception addressed to me.'

'And you didn't see who put it there?'

'No, not at all.' Elle shook her head. 'And it wasn't posted either.'

'Hand delivered then? Now that is a mystery,' Irene mused.

'At first, I just thought it was a normal copy of the book, but then Pippa spotted the inscription.'

'Written with what looks like a fountain pen too,' Irene

commented. 'Proper ink. Do you think it's fake?'

'Why would anyone send me a book with a fake signature? What would be the point of that?'

They stared at each other for a moment, mystified.

'But how does Sam Stone know who you are?' Irene quizzed.

'That's what I said. I've no idea.'

'Wait until you show them at book club next week!'

'I know. Poor Mim will be hyperventilating – she's a number one fan too.'

They both took a sip of wine and Irene kept flicking through the pages of the book.

'What a day it's been for you,' she said.

'It's been a rollercoaster of emotions, to say the least.'

'What exactly happens next with the search for your mother?' asked Irene.

'From what I read on their website, the Salvation Army will contact me if they manage to trace her, so it's just a waiting game now.'

'It's scary, but exciting at the same time.'

'And it might be that the search never uncovers anything.'

'Whatever the outcome, I'll be here waiting with you every step of the way,' Irene said, leaning over and clinking her glass with Elle's. 'Happy birthday, Elle.'

'Thank you. I've got a feeling this one will be a birthday to remember.'

They smiled affectionately at each other. Elle didn't know what she would do if she didn't have Irene in her life. She was her rock, and she loved her dearly.

'And the day I took my first step on the path to possibly discovering who I am,' Elle said hopefully as she chinked her glass against Irene's for a second time.

Chapter Nine

'Steady,' Elle shouted as she saw the ladder wobble.

'Whoa, this looks easier than it actually is!' Pippa was clinging desperately to the top of the ladder.

'Why do you think I'm not up there?' Elle added, laughing, trying to steady Pippa's balance.

'What we need is a man,' Pippa grumbled, fighting with a piece of wallpaper that seemed to have a mind of its own.

'Ha, we don't need a man. Just think: girl power!'

'I am, but it's not doing it for me right now,' declared Pippa, ripping the air-bubbled piece of paper from the wall and dropping it to the ground before climbing down the ladder in a huff.

They'd spent the whole of Saturday morning dragging every piece of furniture out of the spare bedroom and the rest of the day stripping off the old wallpaper. Not only had they found what looked like a mouse's tail behind the old chest of drawers, but they'd also discovered layer after layer of woodchip wallpaper. The idea had been to decorate the room before Pippa moved in, but now the pair of them wished they hadn't started it. It would have been easier just to apply a fresh lick of paint, and gloss over the skirting boards.

'Urghh, I'm losing the will to live,' Pippa declared, slumping to the floor and putting her head in her hands.

'You and me both,' Elle replied, sliding down next to her.

'It looks so easy! How can it be so difficult to hang a piece of wallpaper straight?'

'Maybe that's why we work in a library and we aren't decorators.'

'I wouldn't mind, but papering the walls is meant to be the easy part! Imagine us trying to cut and measure around the windows.'

'Oh God. I don't even want to think about it.'

'Well, we have two options. The first is that we could give up … and the second is that we could give up *and* drown our sorrows in alcohol.'

Elle looked at Pippa. 'The second option sounds the best one. Shall I nip to the corner shop?'

'Come on, let's both go. We can get cleaned up and grab a bag of chips from the chippy too.'

'Sounds like a plan.'

Pippa stood up and kicked the screwed-up wallpaper just as the doorbell sounded. She smiled at Elle. 'Maybe that's our knights in shining armour coming to help us out.'

'Knights? We should be so lucky! It's more likely to be next door, asking if I'll feed their cat while they're away this weekend.'

Pippa looked disappointed.

The doorbell rang again.

'Coming,' Elle shouted, bounding down the stairs and opening the door to discover Wilson, Jack and Aiden grinning back at her.

'The cavalry has arrived!' they all chorused.

Elle was dumbfounded. 'What are you all doing here?'

Wilson thrust his phone in the air. 'We are your knights in shining armour!'

Elle was a little suspicious that Wilson had used exactly the same phrase as Pippa. She glanced over her shoulder to see Pippa hovering on the bottom stair, looking rather sheepish.

'I'm assuming this is your doing?' She pointed at Pippa, smiling.

'Absolutely! Thanks, lads. We were beginning to lose the will to live.'

'We have wallpaper paste, brushes, scissors, gloss, masking tape – oh, and not to mention a bag of chips each for the lovely ladies.'

'Thank God!' Elle exclaimed, ushering them inside. 'But shouldn't you lot be doing something more exciting on a Saturday night?'

'We *were* in the pub but we couldn't leave you to struggle. And then we bumped into Aiden, so we roped him in too,' said Wilson, stepping inside.

'Wrong place, wrong time for you then, Aiden.'

'Luckily for you two, I've just finished decorating my own house, so I've had a lot of practice.'

Elle smiled gratefully at them. 'I could kiss you all.'

'Here you go – chips! Why don't you two go and devour this lot while they're still warm and point us in the direction of the room,' Jack said, handing Elle a white plastic carrier bag. The smell of chips drenched in salt and vinegar was absolutely divine.

'Thank you! You lot really are our knights in shining armour,' she replied.

Without any hesitation, Pippa pointed them up the stairs

and directed them to the bedroom on the left. They watched as the three of them disappeared before she whisked Elle towards the kitchen, smiling.

'You're terrible, Pippa!' Elle said, laughing as she placed the bag on the table and grabbed a couple of plates.

'I know,' she agreed. 'But they didn't have to come, did they? They could have pretended they were busy.' Pippa plonked herself at the kitchen table and began to unwrap the chips.

'True,' Elle replied, rattling around in the drawer for knives and forks before sliding a tray across the table towards Pippa. 'Here you are. Let's eat in the living room.'

'I didn't actually think they would come,' she admitted, popping a chip into her mouth.

'Who are you trying to kid?'

Pippa looked up with a wicked glint in her eye.

'From what I've seen – or call it woman's intuition – I think *both* Wilson and Aiden have a teeny crush on you. I think you knew they would turn up.'

'Maybe!'

'What are you up to, Pippa Lawson?'

She arranged her face into an innocent expression. 'Nothing. I just realised I wasn't cut out for decorating.'

'I think that goes double for me. I wouldn't even climb the ladder!'

Although Pippa hadn't moved in yet, Elle was already enjoying her company. The house had certainly come alive.

They could hear the sound of activity above and music filtering down the stairs.

'I love this song,' said Pippa, as she began to lip-sync to Adele's 'Hello'.

'There's never a dull moment with you around, is there?' replied Elle, laughing as Pippa mimed to the song flawlessly.

Just at that moment a bus rattled past and as Elle glanced out of the window she met the eyes of Noah Jones once again – which was an odd coincidence because every time Elle heard the first line of this song, it reminded her of him. Playing scenarios over in her head, she often wondered what would happen if she picked up the phone and rang him.

'Hello, it's me,' she'd say, hoping he would know who was calling. She wondered what he was doing right now.

Even though his number was still on the corkboard in the kitchen she'd never called him, firstly because she was too nervous, secondly, because she had no intention of writing a book and thirdly, because too much time had passed. But she still got flutters in her stomach every time she thought of him.

'Earth to Elle.'

She met Pippa's inquisitive stare.

'What are you thinking about?' Pippa probed.

'Nothing,' she replied, quickly.

'I completely forgot to ask – did you have a lovely time with Irene last night?' asked Pippa, placing her tray on the coffee table then cradling her stomach in her hands.

'Yes, the food was delicious and she gave me the most beautiful gift! A ring – it was her mother's.' Elle held out her hand towards Pippa to show her. 'What do you think?'

'Wow! It's beautiful,' she said, holding Elle's hand up to the light to get a better view.

'I told her you were moving in and she thought it would do me the world of good. Are your parents all right about it?'

Pippa nodded. 'Yes, Mum was a little tearful – again. But it's not as though we've not been here before.'

'How are you feeling about Nick now?'

'Nick who?' She smiled. 'Exes are exes for a reason, and it's time to move on.'

'Well, at least that's something,' Elle said. 'All we need to do now is finish decorating your room and it's full steam ahead. I wonder how they're getting on up there.'

'Hey, slackers, any chance you're going to switch the kettle on? We are *dying* of thirst,' Wilson requested as he popped his head around the living room door.

'I'm on it!' replied Pippa, standing up.

'You have a lovely house here, Elle.' Wilson cast his eyes around the room.

'Thank you. I love it,' she replied, offering him a leftover chip from her plate.

Pippa smiled. 'How many teas and how many coffees?' she asked, standing in the doorway unscrewing the lid of the tea canister.

'Look at this one – she's already making herself at home,' Wilson teased.

'Let's hope she's as enthusiastic about washing the pots and cleaning the bathroom,' said Elle with a smile, standing up and taking her empty plate into the kitchen.

'We're all tea and one with sugar,' he said to Pippa. 'Thanks. I best get back to it. We're already papering the second wall.' He gave them a thumbs-up before turning round and disappearing.

Elle caught Pippa's eye and posed the question she'd been wondering about for a few days now. 'Do you prefer Wilson or Aiden?'

'How can I choose? Anyway, what about you? Isn't it about time you found someone now you've hit the big three-o?'

'Me? I'm quite happy by myself.'

'Mmm, really? Come on, you must have your eye on someone. When was the last time you went out on a date?'

Elle paused then took the plunge. 'I've gone on a few dates in recent months and I had a very brief encounter eight months ago – and we are talking brief – but all the dates I've been on, I just didn't seem to click with any of them.'

Pippa raised her eyebrows. 'Brief encounter?'

'Yes, but there's nothing to tell. He was in my life for one afternoon and that's about it.'

'Are you sure there's nothing to tell? Because if it was that brief why would you even mention it?' Pippa tried to probe further, spooning sugar into one of the mugs of tea.

'Look at you, Detective Pippa.' She laughed.

'Mmm, I'll delve into this more,' Pippa said, eyeing her suspiciously. 'But not before we get these drinks up to the lads.' She grabbed a tray and Elle followed her up the stairs.

They could hear the boys laughing and joking as they reached the landing.

'Teas are here,' Pippa chirped as she rattled the door handle.

'Out!' they all chorused. 'You can't come in until we've finished.'

Aiden appeared in the doorway and pulled the door shut behind him. His sleeves were rolled up and his shirt was covered in splodges of wallpaper paste. 'Thank you,' he said, taking the tray from Pippa's hand. 'Now, you two get yourselves downstairs and relax,' he ordered, standing firm in front of the door so they couldn't see the progress of the work.

'Can we just have a little peep?' begged Elle.

'No! Now go!' he said, shooing them away.

'You're never going to finish all this tonight,' Pippa said, giving him a twinkly smile.

'You'll be amazed at what we can do when we put our minds to it.'

'Are they still here?' they heard Jack shout from the other side of the door.

They raised their hands in defeat. 'Okay, we're out of here!' Elle playfully pushed Pippa lightly towards the stairs. Soon they were settled on the couch with a glass of wine.

'*Bridget Jones's Diary* or *Notting Hill*?' Elle asked, pressing the remote control and scrolling between the two films.

'Definitely Bridget Jones,' Pippa replied, taking a sip of wine.

'Excellent choice!' Elle held up her glass. 'I think we should have a toast. It was one of your better ideas suggesting you move in and I'd like to formally welcome you to your new home!'

Pippa chinked her glass against Elle's.

'I don't mean to go all slushy on you but thank you. Since we met, you have brightened up my days and it's great to have a best friend that has enriched my life as much as you. I'm really glad our paths crossed. This is going to be so much fun!'

Elle smiled warmly at Pippa. She wholeheartedly agreed. She was really glad their paths had crossed. For the first time in her life she felt like she had a friend she could open up to. Perhaps Irene was right – maybe it was about time she let someone else in and shared what was going on in her life.

'Wake up, sleepy head.'

Elle felt herself being lightly shaken. Opening her eyes, she looked up, startled, to find Wilson standing over her.

'Sorry, I didn't mean to make you jump,' he whispered.

'Where's Pippa?' asked Elle, sitting up and stretching her arms out in front of her.

'She's over there.' Aiden's voice was still low as he nodded towards the chair.

The light from the television was flickering across Pippa's face. Her legs were draped over the arm of the chair and she was curled up under the blanket that Elle kept by the side of the settee.

'What time is it?'

'Just gone three a.m.,' Jack said, checking his watch.

'You're kidding me. It must have been hours since the film finished,' Elle exclaimed, suddenly feeling wide awake. 'I'm so sorry! I didn't mean for you all to be here this late.'

'This is the first time I'll ever be rolling in at three a.m. sober,' Wilson said, smiling as he zipped up his coat.

'It's all finished, Elle. We hope you like it,' Jack added, touching her arm.

'You're kidding me?' she said again.

Aiden smiled. 'I'm sure you've just said that!'

Elle was dumbfounded. 'You lot really are our knights in shining armour. I can't thank you enough. *We* can't thank you enough,' she added.

'Just remember – the paint is still wet on the skirting boards and the windowsill, so be careful. Don't put anything on there until it's completely dry. Oh, and we've put the curtain rail back up for you too, and we've taken up the carpet. We've left all the old wallpaper and carpet outside the back door. I hope that's okay?' Aiden asked.

'You hope that's okay? You guys are total sweethearts – my heroes in fact,' she said, standing up and beaming from ear to ear.

'We aim to please, but now, if you'll forgive me, I really

need my bed. I have to be up in five hours as I'm taking Theo swimming in the morning.'

'Yes, go, and thank you all again!' Elle pressed a kiss swiftly to each of their cheeks before they disappeared quietly by the front door. Locking it behind them, she glanced back round the living room door to check on Pippa, but she was still fast asleep. She was itching to see the room and couldn't wait any longer. Hurrying up the stairs, she opened the bedroom door and gave a tiny gasp – she couldn't believe her eyes.

The room that had once worn an overcoat of dust and woodchip wallpaper and oozed neglect had now been transformed into an exquisite space that could have featured in the latest edition of *Country Living* magazine. Well, maybe that was a little bit of an exaggeration, but the lads had done a magnificent job. The rosebud wallpaper was hung to perfection, trimmed neatly around the sockets and windows, they'd stripped back the multi-coloured carpet to reveal beautiful oak floorboards that had been hidden, and they'd positioned the bed in the middle of the room with the bedside table next to it. They'd worked so hard, and Elle couldn't thank them enough. It would have taken her and Pippa weeks to get it looking as good as this.

Suddenly hearing the stairs creak behind her, Elle swung round to see Pippa.

'I must have fallen asleep. Are they still here?' she murmured, still looking drowsy.

'No,' Elle replied, smiling. 'They left about five minutes ago.'

Standing on tiptoe Pippa peered over Elle's shoulder. She ran an approving eye over the room and Elle watched as a huge smile spread across her face.

'What do you think? Do you like it?'

'Do I like it? I absolutely love it! Look at it, what a transformation! I'm so happy!'

'It is amazing. I can't thank them enough,' Elle added.

'And the room looks bigger now they've taken up the carpet and that mucky pink wallpaper has been stripped away,' observed Pippa. 'It has a lovely airy feeling to it. All I need now is a rug at the side of the bed and a pair of curtains.'

'Are you okay to sleep on the settee tonight and then tomorrow we can go and collect your stuff and move you in officially?'

'I can't wait!' Pippa replied. Opening her arms wide, she pulled Elle in for a hug.

Chapter Ten

Waking up with the sun streaming through the small gap in the curtains made a change. For weeks now, it seemed, Elle had woken to the sound of rain, but this morning everything seemed calm outside. Sitting up in bed, she stretched her arms above her head and yawned before reaching for her phone.

Last night, in her dream, she'd kissed a man. It had seemed so real, and as she sat there remembering it, there was only one man on her mind. Opening her internet browser, Elle googled 'Noah Jones'.

Her heart gave a tiny leap as Noah's handsome face smiled back at her from the screen.

'Does Noah Jones have a girlfriend?' Elle blurted to Siri and instantly regretted the question as Pippa rapped gently on her bedroom door. 'Who are you talking to?' she asked, opening the door. 'I've brought you a brew.'

Siri suddenly piped up as Pippa placed the mug of tea down on the bedside table. 'I have found this on the web for "Does Noah Jones have a girlfriend?"'

Pippa looked at Elle with pure puzzlement on her face while Elle frantically silenced her phone.

'Right, budge up, Elle Cooper. Noah Jones? The author? Why do you need to know if he has a girlfriend?'

Elle patted the space next to her before cupping her hands around the mug and taking a sip.

Pippa plumped up the spare pillow and lay next to her. 'Get talking, Cooper.'

'Damn that Siri is all I can say!'

Elle tilted her phone towards Pippa so she could see the image of Noah on her screen.

'Oh, I know how gorgeous Noah Jones is and I'm delighted to see his face every morning when we climb on the bus. But why—'

'We kissed,' interrupted Elle.

Pippa laughed. 'In your dreams, maybe.'

'No, we really did.'

Pippa looked sidewards and studied her face 'You're being serious, aren't you? Tell me everything.'

'Before you started work at the library, somehow, miraculously, Irene persuaded Noah to come in and inspire a group of students from the local college. I was his assistant for the afternoon and we hit it off straightaway. Just before he went home we kissed.'

'And?'

'And nothing.'

'Let me get this straight, you kissed *the* Noah Jones and it was mutual, not a fangirl moment?'

'Yes and yes.'

'And now?'

Elle smiled. 'He pops into my head quite often.'

'Have you had any further contact with him?'

Elle shook her head. 'Not since that afternoon but I do have his number.'

Pippa bolted upright. 'You have his number? Have you ever rung it?'

'No, he only gave me it in case I ever needed any help writing a book.'

'Since when have you ever thought about writing a book?'

'Exactly – that's why I haven't rung him.'

'Do you know how lame that sounds?'

'What do you mean?' Elle asked, perplexed. '"Call me if you need help", he said. I've not called him because I don't need help and I'm not writing a book!'

'Elle! No man would give out his business card just to help you with your writing.'

'He's a genuine guy.'

'I'm not disputing that, but giving you his card meant he wanted you to ring in general, not just for that one specific reason. Where does he live?'

'London, I think … according to Google.'

'What does it say on social media? He must have author pages knocking about?' she said, taking control of the phone and bringing up Elle's Instagram app.

'Ah,' Pippa confirmed. 'According to his bio, he does live in London.'

Elle sighed. 'Miles away.'

'Let's see what he has on Twitter.' Pippa waited for the app to load. 'And why aren't you following him on Twitter?'

'For the same reason he's not following me.'

'Well, let's put a stop to that nonsense.'

'What do you mean?'

'You are now!'

'Pippa!'

'To be fair, he has that many followers, he might not even notice, but look – his brand-new book is out very soon and he's doing a tour. There are no dates or venues confirmed yet, but maybe we should make the effort and pop along to one of them.' Pippa gave an encouraging smile.

'No! He might not even remember me.'

'You shared a kiss. Of course he's going to remember you.'

'It was months ago. Can you remember everyone you've kissed?'

'I try to deliberately forget most of them but I think if Noah Jones has forgotten like you say –' Pippa rolled her eyes, making it clear she did *not* think that was the case '– then it's about time he remembered you.'

'You're starting to worry me, Pippa. What are you thinking?'

'Look at your profile picture. It screams librarian,' she said, turning the phone in Elle's direction.

'I *am* a librarian.'

'But it's dowdy. There's no colour to your clothes or your cheeks. In fact, it doesn't even look like you've brushed your hair.'

'But that's what I look like,' Elle protested.

'We need a punchy bio, an up-to-date picture… There are so many filters and apps these days – who actually looks like their profile photo anyway?' Pippa continued.

'Me – I do!'

'Then that's where we're going wrong.'

'We?'

'Yes, we! It's a good job I've moved in, Cooper. We need to get your life back on track.'

'Oh God,' was all Elle could manage.

'Leave it in my capable hands. I follow all the latest fashion and accessory accounts on Insta and TikTok. What we need is for you to watch a few videos, decide what kind of image you would like to portray and then we can transform you into a sexy goddess.'

'I don't like the sound of that. I'm quite comfortable how I am.'

'Really? Look at your PJs – they have pigs all over them.'

'They're comfortable and I've had them for years.'

'You can tell. I think I've moved in just at the right time. We need Noah Jones to wonder how the hell he let you slip through his fingers. Trust me.'

Elle was beginning to wonder what she had let herself in for.

Chapter Eleven

I t was Sunday night and The Grouse and Haggis was packed.

'Where do all these people come from? Shouldn't they be at home watching TV or something?' Pippa said as they weaved through the sea of people towards the bar.

'It's carvery night,' replied Elle. 'The only time you can pile your plate high with as many roast potatoes and slices of roast beef as possible, like food is going out of fashion, and no one bats an eyelid.'

Suddenly Elle noticed Eleni at the bar, chatting to Mim.

'Keep your eye on the prize, I'm just nipping to the bathroom,' she said, handing Pippa a ten-pound note.

'Eye on the prize?' Pippa queried.

'Yes, the queue. Don't let anyone push in, otherwise there will be arguments.'

Pippa grinned at me. 'The usual?'

Elle nodded before waving across to Eleni and Mim, who'd spotted them.

By the time Elle returned, Pippa had been served and was

sitting down at a table alongside Eleni and Mim. She pulled up a stool and reached across to pinch one of Pippa's crisps.

'Perks of being your landlady,' she declared, before popping it into her mouth before Pippa could object.

That afternoon they'd lugged all of Pippa's belongings from her family home to her new room. Elle had never seen so many clothes or shoes in her lifetime, and what's more, Pippa seemed to have a different coloured handbag for every day of the week. Her mum had joked that Pippa could set up her very own boutique. She had tried her best to hide her tears as she stood on the doorstep and waved them off.

'Shall we fight our way through to the bar again and pay for a ticket for the carvery?' Elle suggested, suddenly feeling ravenous.

'No need!' Pippa smiled as she handed one over. 'It's on Fraser – a moving-in present.'

Elle smiled towards Fraser, the landlord, and he caught her eye. She waved at him, mouthing, 'Thank you', and he nodded in acknowledgement.

'Are you two eating?' Elle looked between Eleni and Mim.

'Yes, I'm just waiting for them to bring out a fresh tray of roasties.' Mim smiled. 'And I may even be tempted to try a sticky toffee pudding for dessert.'

'I believe you kept my fiancé up until the early hours last night,' said Eleni.

Pippa grinned. 'Yes, sorry about that. It was my fault.'

'They did a marvellous job,' Elle chipped in. 'You wouldn't recognise the room. This time last week it was a junk room and now it's been totally transformed.'

'It'll do Jack good. He needs to get the practice in so he can decorate the nursery.'

As Elle and Pippa watched, Eleni slowly looked down

towards her stomach and patted it before looking back up at them. She grinned.

'No way! Really? You're expecting? Aww!' Pippa jumped up and moved round the table to give Eleni a hug.

'This is amazing news! Congratulations! How far gone are you?' Elle asked.

'It's still very early days, only eight weeks. It's not what we would have planned just before the wedding, but we're very happy and I can't wait to be a mother. My destiny is calling…'

The next words were a blur for Elle. Eleni's words tumbled over in her mind as her brain contemplated her own situation. She wondered what her biological mother had thought when she first discovered she was pregnant. Was she happy, like Eleni, or was it the worst thing in the world to have happened to her? Elle tried to push the unanswered questions out of her mind. All she could do was wait to see if her search would uncover something concrete.

'Although I've started to feel hideously sick all the time,' Eleni added. 'We wanted to keep it quiet a little longer, but I have the slight problem of the hen party fast approaching, and if the bride-to-be is only drinking soft drinks, I'm sure questions will be asked.'

'Oh, of course,' Elle replied, glancing quickly towards the food queue as her stomach let out a huge gurgle.

'Hen party? Did someone say hen party?' Pippa grinned.

'Ha! First of all, she blags an invite to your wedding—' Elle began.

'As your plus one, and anyway who else are you going to take?' Pippa pretended to look hurt.

'And now she wants to gate-crash your hen party!' Elle joked.

'You're more than welcome to come, Pippa,' Eleni piped up.

'We're thinking of having the hen do sooner rather than later,' Mim added.

'Thankfully it's not long to the wedding now,' said Eleni, 'though there's still loads left to organise. Fingers crossed I won't bloom too much in the next couple of months, otherwise my dress may need to be altered.'

'What are the plans for the hens then?' asked Elle, keeping a close eye on the food queue, which thankfully was now dwindling.

'We thought maybe a meal up at the Starcross Manor or over at The Lakehouse.'

Elle noticed Pippa's face fall and gave her a gentle nudge with her leg under the table to encourage her to look a little more enthusiastic.

'I'm sure that'll be absolutely lovely, and you can count us both in,' Elle declared, standing up and clutching her ticket for the carvery. 'Who's coming for food?'

Five minutes later, their plates piled high, they began to tuck in.

'What's been going on in the land of books this week?' Eleni asked. 'Anything interesting?'

'It's been fairly quiet, hasn't it?' replied Elle, glancing at Pippa and wondering why Noah was the first thing to pop into her head again. He was beginning to make a habit of that.

'Quiet?' exclaimed Pippa. 'We've had a new employee – not to mention your unexpected birthday present.'

The weekend had been so busy Elle had totally forgotten

about that. 'Oh my gosh, both had slipped my mind. I'm sure Jack's mentioned Aiden, he's transferred from Inverness—'

'*Very* easy on the eye,' Pippa chipped in.

'And I've received a mysterious birthday present, which no one seems to be owning up to.'

'Oooh, was it a good present?' Mim asked, intrigued.

Pippa smiled. 'You could say that.'

Both Eleni and Mim were staring at Elle with anticipation.

'Here's the thing … on Friday, my birthday—'

'Get on with it! Eleni will have had the baby by the time you finish this story,' Pippa demanded, laughing.

'There slap bang in the middle of the reception desk in the library was a parcel addressed to me.'

Pippa rolled her eyes. 'You'd think she was an author the way she's stringing out the story. What Elle is trying to say is that inside that parcel was a copy of the new Sam Stone novel.'

Eleni and Mim looked a little disappointed by the reveal.

'Is that it?' Mim asked, looking between the two of them.

'Not quite,' Pippa continued, hitting Elle's arm. 'Go on!'

'I was trying until you rudely interrupted.'

'There's more?' Eleni queried.

'It was a signed copy from *the* Sam Stone, wishing me a happy birthday.'

Both Eleni and Mim gasped.

'Get away! You're pulling our leg.' Eleni's eyes narrowed. 'It's a well-known fact that Sam Stone barely autographs any books.'

'Honestly, I'm not pulling your leg. It's all very bizarre. One minute I'm making a cup of tea and chatting to Aiden and his gorgeous son—'

'Cut to the chase,' Eleni said, grinning.

'And the next I'm opening a present from Sam Stone.'

Eleni and Mim looked at each other with puzzled expressions.

'Surely it's a practical joke? Someone's faked the signature,' suggested Mim.

'That thought did cross our minds, but if it was a joke, no one has owned up to it,' Elle answered.

'Yet,' Mim chipped in.

'And we've no idea how it appeared on the desk. The library was nearly empty, and neither of us saw anyone put it there,' Pippa added.

'Was it posted?' Mim asked.

Elle shook her head.

'There was a handwritten label,' Pippa piped up.

'It's someone who knows you work in the library?' Mim raised her eyebrows.

'That's what I said,' confirmed Elle.

'I'd die for a signed copy of any Sam Stone book. How lucky are you?' Eleni added.

'Very,' Elle replied, still mystified by the whole thing.

'How can we discover how it got there?' Mim asked.

'I've no idea,' Elle replied.

'Well, that's easy,' Eleni shared, and they all looked over in her direction and waited patiently. 'Contact him on social media. Tweet him.'

Elle laughed.

Pippa's eyes widened as she turned towards Elle. 'Why didn't we think of that? That's a brilliant idea.'

Before Elle could answer, Pippa had grabbed her phone off the table.

'Passcode,' she demanded.

The laugh faded from Elle's voice as soon as she realised Pippa was serious. 'We can't tweet him. What would I say?'

'Too late, I'm in,' she said, grinning from ear to ear.

Damn.

'Fancy not having a passcode.'

'I've never needed one before!'

Before Elle had a chance to object, Pippa had tweeted and the phone had been placed back on the table.

Almost immediately, it pinged.

They all stared at it.

'Gosh, that was a quick reply. What does it say?' Mim looked towards Pippa.

Pippa glanced at the notification, then looked at Elle. She was silent.

'What's the matter?'

Pippa passed Elle the phone.

Elle hesitated before scanning the notification on the phone.

Noah Jones is now following you.

Elle felt her heart miss a beat.

Chapter Twelve

S everal drinks later Elle and Pippa left The Grouse and Haggis with their arms linked and ambled across the bridge into Glensheil.

'Why don't you send him a message?' Pippa suggested.

'Who?'

She rolled her eyes at Elle. 'You know exactly who I'm talking about. Noah.'

'And what am I going to put? "Remember me? We spent the afternoon together."!'

'That would set the cat amongst the pigeons. Which afternoon was it anyway?'

'It was the fifteenth of July,' Elle replied without hesitation.

Pippa raised her eyebrows. 'You actually know the exact date?' She stared at Elle. 'I can't remember what I did last week, never mind eight months ago! But I suppose if I was lucky enough to share a kiss with Noah, the date would be firmly planted in my mind too.'

'I'm sure he won't even remember,' Elle said, deliberately avoiding her question.

'Yes, he will. He's followed you back.' Pippa squeezed her arm, then did a tipsy celebratory dance on the pavement.

Elle laughed. That's what she loved about Pippa, she was good fun and didn't take herself too seriously. 'He probably follows everyone back.'

'We could soon put that theory to the test.' Pippa had that mischievous glint in her eye again.

'Let's not, eh?'

'Okay, boss. But your love life is going to be non-existent unless you take risks. Anyway, what's the plan for the morning?' Pippa asked. 'We don't want to be tripping over each other in the bathroom. What time do you normally get up?'

'Around six.'

They strolled in silence for a minute, until Elle noticed a familiar figure walking towards them.

'Look,' she murmured under her breath.

Pippa looked up. 'Oh no.'

Strolling in their direction was Nick, Pippa's ex. They hurriedly crossed the road, hoping he wouldn't notice them.

'He texted me this morning.'

'Are you kidding me? You've kept that quiet. Did you reply?'

'No, and I've not replied to any of his texts, though I've been tempted. He's sent me a few now, but I've made myself remember all the pain he caused me. He just keeps saying he's made a huge mistake.'

'We already know that.'

'Oh, and that he's sorry.'

'And let me guess: if he could turn back the clock...'

Pippa nodded. 'Oh lord, he's spotted us – he's coming over.'

Elle looked up to see Nick heading straight for them.

'Hi,' he said, hovering sheepishly in front of them on the pavement, his hands stuffed firmly inside his coat pockets.

Silence.

'Hi,' Elle said. Awkwardness was hanging in the air.

'Have you been anywhere nice?' he asked, doing his best to make small talk.

Still Pippa didn't speak.

'Just the pub,' Elle offered, dodging the sudden glare Pippa shot her for providing such information.

More silence.

'I'll leave you to it then. It was lovely to see you both,' he said, pausing for a moment before he reluctantly moved past them and kept walking. They turned slightly to watch him go and saw him glance over his shoulder as he turned the corner.

'Are you okay?' Elle asked tentatively.

'What does he expect me to do? Stand there and make small talk or even ask him how he's doing?'

'I'd say by the worn-out, washed-up look on his face that he's not doing too brilliantly.'

'He's regretting what he did,' Pippa agreed. 'I know I shouldn't be happy with other people's misfortunes, but I kind of think he's got what he deserved. He's girlfriendless and back home living with his parents – unlike me, who's put all that sorry mess behind me and moved in with you!' She managed a smile.

'Exactly. So, no more stalking him on Facebook to see if he's single.'

'Nope. I couldn't care less. I'm well and truly over him. It's about time I moved on.'

Just then a car slowed down next to them. The window rolled down and Aiden beamed at them.

'Do you ladies need a lift?' Aiden asked, his hand poised on the gear stick. 'I'm heading into Glensheil.'

'Yes, thank you, Aiden.' Elle opened the front door on the passenger side and climbed in whilst Pippa clambered onto the back seat.

'Well, hello, little man,' Elle heard Pippa say as she fastened her seat belt. She looked over her shoulder and was met with two big brown eyes staring back at her.

'Hello, Theo, how are you?'

Theo hid his head in his hands, then peeped cheekily through the crack between his fingers.

'We've not met before,' Pippa said, holding her hand out, but Theo kept his face hidden.

'Didn't you meet him when he came into the library?' Elle asked.

Pippa shook her head. 'No, I was helping that student with her coursework, remember? I didn't have a chance. You're a handsome chappie, aren't you?' she said in a rather cooey voice as she tried to tickle his tummy. Theo let out the cutest giggle Elle had ever heard.

'What have you pair been up to today then?' Aiden asked.

'We've been moving all of Pippa's stuff across to her new room.'

'Thank you by the way.' Pippa leaned forward and placed her hand on Aiden's shoulder. 'It's very much appreciated.'

He turned his head towards her and Elle noticed a look between them.

'Anytime,' Aiden replied warmly. He looked away as he pulled away from the kerb, but Elle observed him catch Pippa's eye again in the mirror once they were on the move.

'What have you two been up to today?' Elle asked.

'We've been to the zoo,' Aiden replied as Theo let out a

huge roar from behind them and everyone laughed. 'And we've just had tea and I'm dropping him back at his mum's.'

'I think he quite liked the lions!' Pippa said, smiling at Theo.

'Yes, and hopefully I've tired him out and given Louisa a chance to recharge her batteries. Even though he's beginning to sleep in his own bed, he keeps waking up early now he realises he can get out of it.'

Pippa's voiced jumped an octave. 'How grown up are you, sleeping in a big bed?'

Theo looked up and gave her a huge smile.

'You're wasted working in a library,' Elle said to Pippa, admiring the warm interaction between the two of them. 'You should've become a teacher.'

'You'd make a brilliant teacher,' Aiden agreed. 'Usually when Theo meets anyone new, he cries – and look at him smiling away. He can't take his eyes off you!'

A moment later Aiden was turning into their street and pulled up just outside the house.

'Thanks for the lift,' Elle said as she unclipped her seat belt.

Pippa pinched Theo's cuddly toy and ruffled it against his cheek. For a second Aiden and Elle just watched as she made a fuss of him.

'See you tomorrow, Aiden – and hopefully see you soon, little fellow,' Pippa said, smiling, as she climbed out of the car and waved at Theo through the window.

They stood on the pavement watching the car drive up the road.

'Mmm, never mind Theo – Aiden couldn't take his eyes off you either.'

Pippa smiled. 'I don't know what you mean.'

'It's obvious to anyone that you find each other attractive.'

'Do you think it's too soon after Nick?'

'If you like him, ask him out for a drink. It can't hurt. Just enjoy his company and see where it goes.'

'I'll think about it but in the meantime let's get the kettle on and we can discuss your next move.'

'My next move?' asked Elle, watching Pippa bound up the steps towards the front door.

'Yes! I only have two words for you.'

'And they are?'

'Noah Jones.'

Feeling her heart race faster at the very mention of his name, Elle put the key in the front door. Since the notification had popped up on her phone, it was all she could think about. Smiling at Pippa, she said. 'We'd best get that kettle on then.'

Chapter Thirteen

On Monday morning, the library was unusually quiet. Elle was sitting at the computer behind the reception desk. Since sending the form to the Salvation Army she'd fallen into the same routine, when she arrived at the library, of checking her emails right away. Scrolling through her inbox she could see that there was nothing out of the ordinary and no email with any news about her biological mother. She couldn't help feeling a little disappointed, but it was still very much early days.

'Anything interesting?' she asked Aiden, who was perched on a desk in front of her, browsing through the latest newsletter, which was distributed to the library every week.

'There are lots of new publications this week.'

'Anyone we might know?' asked Elle, knowing that the release of Noah's new book was imminent. Before she'd got in the shower this morning, Elle had lain in bed with a brew scrolling through Noah's Twitter feed. There'd been a couple of new posts from bloggers eagerly awaiting the new release, which of course he'd retweeted. Elle had hovered over the private message button a couple of times but she felt unsure about sending a message. What exactly would she say? It would be embarrassing if he didn't remember who she was, and the follow back was just a goodwill gesture.

After stalking Noah for a while, she switched over to own profile and scrutinised it. She wasn't into social media like Pippa and found it awkward taking a selfie but she realised Pippa was right, her profile picture lacked any sort of life.

Aiden interrupted her thoughts. 'Did you recognise any of those names?' he asked, looking over in Elle's direction.

'I don't think so,' replied Elle, who hadn't heard a word he'd said, her mind having taken a wander.

'Who are you trying to kid?' Pippa whispered to her as she reached over the desk and changed the date on the stamp.

'Huh?' she replied.

Just then they heard a squeal of delight and looked over at the main entrance.

'Theo!' Aiden exclaimed. 'I'd recognise that noise anywhere.' He held out his arms while Theo stumbled towards him. Aiden promptly threw him up in the air and caught him.

'Pippa, let me introduce you to Louisa's parents.'

Pippa shook both their hands and smiled politely.

'I hope you don't mind, but we thought we'd bring Theo along to your children's session this morning. Aiden has been singing your praises.'

'Mind? Of course I don't mind.' Pippa beamed, holding out her hand to Theo as Aiden placed both his feet back on the floor.

'Would you like to help me set up?' she asked Theo, who nodded and grasped Pippa's hand tightly.

Aiden and Elle watched them as they walked slowly behind the desk to grab the story sack before making their way over towards the colourful beanbags in the children's area.

Louisa's parents wandered after them, pulling out a couple of chairs and perching beside the beanbags.

'Singing her praises?' Elle repeated, smiling at Aiden.

'What?' he asked, suppressing a smile as he returned to the desk and began tapping away on the keyboard.

'Here they all come now,' Elle said as the library door swung open and a small army of children ran wildly towards the beanbags shouting Pippa's name, only to be shushed by parents reminding them they were in a library.

'She's definitely got a way with the little people,' she added.

Pippa's animated voice filtered across the room to them. 'Not only do I have a fantastic story for you today, but we have a special guest.'

Theo was sitting proudly on her knee.

'This is Theo. Can we all give him a wave?'

Both Aiden and Elle smiled across the room as the session got underway.

'You like her, don't you?' Elle probed.

'I think so,' he answered truthfully. 'But it's not that simple, is it?'

'Why not?'

Aiden gazed back over towards the pair of them. Theo's face was shining with joy as Pippa began to read this morning's story, the puppet in her hand moving animatedly.

'Theo will always come first – and then there's Louisa.'

'Where *is* Louisa?' Elle asked, wondering why her parents had brought Theo along to the session instead of her.

Aiden exhaled. 'That's part of the problem. I think she's struggling a little at the minute.'

'In what way?' Elle asked cautiously.

'I think it's down to moving back in with her parents. Don't get me wrong, David and Barbara are worth their weight in gold, especially with Theo – we couldn't manage without them – but I don't have to live with them, and I suppose once you've had your own space, it's difficult to live by someone else's rules again and…'

'And what?'

'And she's been hinting that maybe we should give it another go for Theo's sake.'

'How do you feel about that?'

'It wasn't working, otherwise we wouldn't have made the decision to separate in the first place. At the moment, I think she's experiencing a whole range of emotions. Theo is happy and settled, and I help out as best I can. Sometimes it's lonely for me at night having no one else around, but although I'm very fond of Louisa, it's better this way, and in time it will get easier for both of us.'

'You have to do what's right for you and Theo.'

He nodded. 'I know, but I worry that if I started dating so soon, Louisa wouldn't cope.' For a moment, his eyes flitted back to Pippa.

Elle touched his arm affectionately. 'What will be will be.'

He smiled at her warmly. 'Thanks for listening, Elle.'

'Anytime,' she replied, grabbing the small ladder and walking towards a group of students who she'd spotted were having difficulty reaching a book.

How lovely was Aiden? It must be difficult for him too, Elle realised. He'd also experienced massive changes in his life, and to go from seeing your son all the time to just snatching every moment possible with him … it had to be heart-wrenching. In the short term, he was sacrificing his own happiness to ensure Louisa had a chance of becoming happy once more.

———————

The morning flew by and at lunchtime Elle was perched on a stool in the staffroom, tucking into a cheese and pickle sandwich as she watched the drizzle run down the windowpane. At the moment, all it seemed to do was rain, and she couldn't wait for the summer months to be upon them once more. Just like her morning routine, Elle's lunchtime routine prioritised checking her emails. Every time she saw a new message arrive her heart began to race but none of them were from the Salvation Army.

'That's a huge sigh,' Pippa said, smiling as she entered the staffroom. Reaching for the radio on the worktop, she cranked up the volume. 'I love this band!' she declared, dancing around the table towards the fridge. After grabbing her lunch, she jigged her way back towards the radio and turned the volume down.

Elle looked at her with amusement.

'Chocolate?' Pippa asked, sliding a bar towards her.

'You know I'm trying to lose a little weight for the summer.'

Pippa peered out the window. 'I shouldn't worry. With British summertime being what it is, it'll probably just continue to chuck it down.'

'Oh sod it, you're right.' Elle changed her mind, pulling open the wrapper.

'So come on, what's up with you? Don't think I've not noticed.'

'Noticed what?' asked Elle, breaking off another slab of

chocolate.

'That since your birthday you seem distracted. I often catch you lost in your own world, and as soon at that machine pings out there with a new email you're the first to check what it is.'

'I always check the emails.'

'Mmm, but it's never been first priority. I'm just saying, if there is something bothering you, you can talk to me, you know.'

'I know,' Elle pondered whether to share with Pippa why she was checking the emails at every opportunity but was there a point talking about an email that might never arrive? 'How cute was Theo this morning?' she asked, deliberately changing the subject.

'He's a gorgeous little boy, isn't he?'

'You seem to have taken to him.'

'You know, he clung on to my leg all the way through that session and Aiden had to pry him off me when it was time for him to go home.'

'Aww, bless him.'

'Louisa's parents were lovely too, and I helped Theo choose some more books to take home.'

'It must be difficult for them all at the moment with all the changes that are going on. David and Barbara must have had a shock when Louisa turned up back home with Theo.'

'Ha, yes, Barbara mentioned that she's permanently on the go, with interrupted sleep, but you do what's best for your kids, don't you?'

Immediately Elle thought of Irene and her biological mother. 'Yes, you do.'

'How did you feel when Aiden read out the list of authors this morning?' Pippa was watching Elle closely.

'What do you mean?'

Pippa's eyes widened. 'I knew you weren't listening because you didn't flinch at all. You should think about playing poker.'

'Busted! I was—'

'Distracted,' interrupted Pippa. 'I'm watching you.'

Elle rolled her eyes. 'Who was on it?'

'Who was on it? Who are you trying to kid? At home, you've taken to sitting in the front window so you can watch the hourly bus drive past just so you can glimpse his picture on the side. Come on, tell me I'm wrong.'

Elle smiled. Pippa didn't miss a trick. She reached across to the bulletin that Aiden had left on the table. Pippa pointed to the relevant piece of information.

'Right there. Noah Jones will be signing books in *this* town during his tour.'

Pippa's words washed over Elle in slow motion as her eyes fixed on the information. She knew her mouth had fallen wide open and hundreds of nervous butterflies erupted in her stomach.

'He's coming here?' Elle said, her voice shaky.

Pippa grinned at her. 'You might be seeing your Mr Jones sooner than you think.'

Pippa had been right, she'd been distracted this morning and missed this vital piece of information. Suddenly, she felt very nervous – but also a little excited.

'He's not my Mr Jones and just because he's going to be in the same town as us doesn't mean we're going to bump into him, does it?' she said.

'It's a pretty small town and we definitely will if we go to his book signing. After all, why wouldn't we? We *are* all about the books … we work in a library.'

'We'll both be working.'

'No, we won't.'

'Why not?' Elle asked.

'It's on a Saturday.' Pippa stared at her, waiting for her to process the information.

'Where at?'

'Venue to be arranged.'

Elle couldn't think straight. She felt flustered.

'So? Shall we go?'

'Let's see a little nearer the time,' Elle answered, trying to play the whole situation down. 'I've got a lot going on at the minute.' The words left her mouth before she could stop them.

'Such as?' Pippa stared her down.

'Oh you know.'

Pippa shook her head. 'No, I don't know.'

'It's just a figure of speech,' replied Elle quickly, telling a little white lie and feeling a twinge of guilt.

'Back to Noah. I think you'll find this an opportunity not to be missed.'

It had been eight months since Elle had set eyes on him; *of course* she wanted to see him again. She'd played that very scenario over in her mind most days since Noah walked out of the library. But something was troubling her – what if he didn't remember it the same way, and she'd over-fantasised the whole thing? She gave herself a little shake. Of course she hadn't. They'd kissed and it had made her feel like she'd never felt before.

Maybe this was the month to be taking chances and stepping out of her comfort zone. If she didn't go to his book signing, Elle knew she would always wonder, 'What if'.

'I have to say, I think I agree with you,' confirmed Elle, smiling. 'After all, we *are* all about the books.'

'And you, my friend, are all about Noah Jones.'

Chapter Fourteen

Stepping under the canopy of Rona's colourful hanging baskets, Elle opened the door of the teashop and welcomed the rich aromas of coffee and cake. As the little bell tinkled above their heads Rona turned from where she was standing behind the counter chatting to Mim, and looked over towards the door.

'We have a new member,' enthused Elle as she gestured towards Aiden.

'Welcome to book club! All new members are welcome but only on one condition – that you must love books.' Mim gave him a welcoming smile.

'I think I can safely say I fit into that category.'

'And I believe you're here with some exciting news.' Mim touched his arm. 'I'm fit to burst but please excuse me for just a moment.' Mim walked off towards Eleni and Julia, who had arrived, leaving Elle and Pippa looking at each other in wonderment.

'Erm, what aren't you telling us?' Elle asked Aiden. 'You know I don't like secrets.'

Aiden couldn't take the smile off his face. 'You'll just have to wait and see. I've promised Mim that I won't tell a soul until it's announced.'

'Until what's announced? You're acting all very cloak and dagger. You have to tell us!' insisted Elle but Aiden wasn't up for sharing whatever information he had.

'Urggh, you're being frustrating,' added Pippa.

Aiden held up his hands. 'Sorry! But a promise is a promise.'

'Whatever it is, it better be worth the wait,' added Elle.

'I don't think you'll be disappointed,' he replied, looking a little smug.

'Don't you just hate it when someone knows something you don't?' Pippa huffed lightheartedly, waving to Isla and Felicity, who were sitting on the other side of the room.

Irene had grabbed their usual table and once they'd made themselves comfy Elle cast her gaze over the delicious-looking Lemon Drizzle cake on display under the glass dome on the counter.

'I'm never going to lose weight. Everywhere I go there's scrumptious-looking cake. A slice of that has my name written all over it.'

Rona walked up to the table. 'Here he is, my new neighbour. How are you settling in, Aiden?'

'This may sound daft and I know it's only been a matter of days but it feels like I've lived here for a long time. I feel so settled already.'

'That's good to hear. Now can I get anyone any refreshments before Mim starts?' Rona's pen was poised over the paper.

Irene looked around them all. 'I think, by the way everyone

is drooling, that I can say a slice of cake for everyone and a couple of pots of tea.'

Rona nodded. 'That's a good choice. And how are you, Irene? Are you enjoying retirement?'

Irene smiled. 'I can't grumble, even though this retirement lark takes some getting used to. My body clock still thinks I should be up at six-thirty a.m.,' she said, grimacing. 'I long for a lie-in.'

'Oh no! Hopefully that'll sort itself out soon.'

'Fingers crossed, because by the time I get to nine a.m. all my chores are done and sometimes it feels like a very long day.'

'You can always nip across and tidy up our place,' Pippa suggested with a huge grin on her face.

'There's nothing like a bit of cheek,' Irene replied, smiling across at Pippa before delving into her purse. 'I'll get these – my treat.'

Taking the signed Sam Stone novel out of her bag, Elle placed it on the table, knowing everyone would be excited to see it.

When Rona brought the slices of cake and drinks to the table, she noticed the book. 'Is this the signed one? I've heard all about this. You were the talk of the teashop yesterday. Rumour has it the whole thing is a complete mystery.'

'It is, but surely it can't stay a mystery for ever,' added Elle, looking around the table.

'May I?' Rona asked.

'Of course!' Elle handed her the book.

Rona handled it carefully and opened it to read the inscription. 'Elle, this is simply amazing,' she said.

'I know,' I replied.

Rona gestured to Felicity to come across. She was soon by her mum's side. 'Tell Elle what we found out on the internet about Sam Stone.' The page was still held open on the inscription.

'If this is real then it's very valuable. He barely autographs books. In fact, from what we read it sounds like he's signed less than twenty books … ever.'

Elle's eyes widened. 'If that's true, then how and why have I got an autographed copy? I really wish I knew.'

'You're extremely lucky as whoever has organised this must have friends in high places. I wouldn't let that copy out of your sight.' Felicity returned to her table and Rona handed the book back, leaving Elle wondering how exactly this fantastic birthday present came to be in her possession.

'Whoever organised this won't be able to keep it a secret for ever,' Irene said confidently, smiling up at Mim, who had come over to take a look at the book.

'Wow! This is amazing,' Mim said, taking the book from Eleni. 'I just heard what Felicity was saying and she's right. Sam Stone barely autographs any copies. This is just incredible. And talking of Sam Stone… With Aiden's bit of news added into the mix, this is going to be a book club to remember.'

'What do you mean, "talking of Sam Stone"?' asked Pippa.

'You'll have to wait and see…' Mim had a huge smile on her face. She clapped her hands together to get everyone's attention before standing in her usual spot at the front of the teashop. Pippa whispered, 'She is such a tease! There must be something in the water tonight. First Aiden with his secrets and now Mim.'

Aiden grinned. 'But soon you'll know everything.'

A moment later, Mim was explaining why this week's choice of book had her hooked from the very first page. Then everyone listened intently to each other's points of view and discussed various aspects of the plot before it was time to choose the next read. Mim and the room fell silent as they watched Rona pass a cardboard box over the counter. Elle knew by the look on Mim's face that whatever was in that box was something special. 'You're not going to be disappointed,' confirmed Mim, looking around the room. She flipped open the lid and pulled out a paperback, which she hugged to her chest before turning the cover around for everyone to see.

'Ta-dah!' she chirped. 'Here's the book club's next read. This is the new thriller by—'

'Noah Jones,' Pippa finished, giving Elle a tiny nudge.

'How has Mim managed to get all those copies of his brand-new book when we've not even got our library copy yet?' Elle whispered to Pippa, who shrugged.

Mim continued. 'But I don't recommend you take this one to bed with you.'

'I bet you want to take it to bed with you,' Pippa whispered discreetly with a wicked glint in her eye.

'Otherwise you'll be sleeping with the light on,' added Mim. 'And we're lucky to have a free copy each.' Min grabbed a handful and began to hand them out.

'Has anyone read anything by Noah before?' Mim asked the group. A number of readers nodded and began reeling off some of Noah's previous book titles.

'He's very swoonworthy, isn't he, Elle?' said Irene. 'He came into the library, was it around June time?'

'July the fifteenth,' replied Elle.

'You have a good memory,' replied Irene.

Elle's heart was racing just at the mention of his name as well as her memories of the first and only time she'd seen Noah.

'I want to know how Mim has got so many copies.' Pippa shouted the question over to Mim.

'That's the next bit of news … it's thanks to Aiden.'

Both Elle and Pippa stared at Aiden, who grinned. 'And Aiden has some amazing news to tell you all.'

'She's going to say he'll be visiting our book club,' Pippa jokingly whispered again to Elle.

Irene raised her eyebrows. 'What is going on with you two? Why all the whispering?'

'Nothing,' Elle replied, shooting Pippa a warning glance.

'You share the news, Mim. I know you're dying to tell everyone.'

Mim clasped her hands together and looked around the room. 'Aiden –' she gestured towards him '– has transferred from Inverness Library, where part of his job was to work directly with authors and organise events at the library. Noah Jones is going on tour, signing copies of his brand-new book…'

'She's going to say he's coming here,' Pippa repeated.

'Don't be daft,' Elle uttered under her breath.

'…And Aiden had arranged for Noah to sign copies of his new book at Inverness Library, but now he's transferred here, he's persuaded Noah to come and sign books at the Library on Love Heart Lane, which was confirmed about thirty minutes ago! How utterly fantastic is that?'

Elle's mouth had dropped wide open.

'You're catching flies.' Pippa nudged her.

Elle's thoughts were whirling all over the place. Her heart was racing and she couldn't believe the words she'd just heard.

Everyone began to chatter excitedly.

'I can't believe you didn't tell us,' exclaimed Pippa as she looked at Aiden accusingly. 'When? Do we have a date?'

'I've just forwarded you the email with all the details on it.'

Elle took out her phone and checked her inbox. There it was, an unread email from Aiden confirming the attendance of Noah Jones at the Library on Love Heart Lane.

'How lovely! That's one not to miss,' Irene enthused, smiling as she read the blurb on the back of the book. 'This looks a really good read too.'

'If you bring your copy along on the evening, Noah will take great pleasure in signing the book for you,' Mim shouted over the happy conversation that had erupted throughout the teashop.

Pippa tipped her face towards Elle.

'You're staring at me,' Elle observed, knowing the exact reason why.

'How are you feeling? This is fate. I'm telling you it is. You're going to get to see your man again.'

Nervous was how Elle was feeling … yet also excited. She'd often wondered if their paths would ever cross again.

'It's meant to be,' Pippa whispered.

'You two are whispering again.' Irene looked at them both before turning towards Aiden. 'You've done very well. This will be brilliant for the library and the community. All the publicity will enhance the profile of the library and hopefully you'll get a few more members signing up.'

'Let's hope so. It should be a good night. He was very kind to courier across the copies of his book.'

'Very kind indeed,' added Pippa. 'Was it just email contact with Noah, or have you managed to have phone conversations with him?'

Pippa had asked the very question that was on Elle's mind.

'I managed a quick call with him today and he said he looked forward to the visit, and that he's fond of this part of the world and Heartcross.'

'Oh I bet he is,' Pippa mouthed to Elle.

Elle didn't trust herself to speak. She wanted to ask Aiden whether he had mentioned her at all in the conversation – but surely Aiden would have said something if he had, which led her to suspect that Noah had forgotten meeting her and their kiss.

Mim tapped the side of her mug with a spoon to bring the chatter under control. 'It's all happening in our little community of Heartcross – because that's not the end of my news. But first we have a celebration.'

'I'm not sure I can take any more surprises,' Elle murmured, still trying to process that sooner rather than later her path would cross with Noah's.

'Do we have a date for the book signing?' asked Isla. 'I need to put it in my diary.'

'We do, March the seventeenth.'

'That gives us enough time to spruce up your appearance and groom those eyebrows of yours,' teased Pippa.

'What's wrong with my eyebrows?' Elle asked, alarmed.

'Everything, but don't worry, I'm going to be in charge of your destiny.'

'Oh God,' were the only words Elle could muster up.

'Shhh, listen. Mim has more news.'

'Before I share with you all some other exciting news I'd like to wish one of our longstanding members of the book club a very happy birthday for last Friday. Not only is she our chief librarian and always wearing a smile, but she is also a kind, heart-warming member of our community who goes out of her way to help others.'

Irene had sneaked to the back of the teashop and appeared holding a birthday cake. Eleni lit the candles and when Mim started singing 'Happy Birthday' to Elle, everyone joined in.

'Thank you,' exclaimed Elle, with her hands on her heart. 'I wasn't expecting this. What a fantastic cake.' With a big puff Elle blew out all the candles at once.

'And *now* we have some news about Sam Stone, the man himself,' Mim continued.

'Exciting,' said Isla from the other side of the room.

Mim held up a leaflet and wafted it in the air. 'To all you aspiring authors out there, this is for you.' She quickly circulated copies to everyone in the room.

'It's a writing competition,' observed Irene, quickly scanning the leaflet.

The leaflet encouraged any aspiring writers to compose a short story about their life for a national magazine. Sam Stone was judging the competition and would present the winner with an award and a copy of the published story at a ceremony at Starcross Manor.

'*The* Sam Stone is coming to Heartcross?' Elle couldn't quite believe what she was reading.

'Gosh, it's all happening tonight! Noah Jones *and* Sam Stone in the village.' Pippa looked over the leaflet then placed it on the table. 'You couldn't make it up,' she said. 'It's times like this I wish I could write.'

'This, again, will be brilliant publicity for the library,' added Aiden. He stood up and with the leaflet in hand began to chat to Mim.

'I'm just nipping to the bathroom,' Pippa said before weaving her way through the tables and chairs.

As soon as Pippa was out of earshot, Irene tapped the leaflet and glanced at Elle. 'What do you think about this?'

'It's an amazing opportunity for all those wannabe writers out there. I can't believe the presentation is going to be at

Starcross Manor. I can guarantee now that we all will be hanging around the entrance, hoping for a glimpse of him.'

'I think you should give it a go,' encouraged Irene.

Elle wasn't sure whether she had just heard her correctly. 'Me? Why would you even think of me? What have I got to write about?' she asked, taking a sip of tea.

'Your story is a fantastic one.'

'My story?' quizzed Elle.

'Against all odds, the girl did well. You could have easily ended up on the streets or bitter about life. But look at you! You're kind, beautiful … the list is endless. And when your story is written and you win the competition, you can add being a published writer to your many achievements,' Irene said proudly, patting her knee.

'But no one knows my story, not even Pippa. People only know what I choose to tell them.'

'When you came to my door, you'd hardly been to school, you had moved homes that many times. You could barely read and write – and now look at you, you're chief librarian! You could have easily given up on life but you didn't, you fought every step of the way.'

For most of her childhood, Elle had been illiterate. Over the years it had become easier and easier for her to hide it as she'd never stayed in one school long enough to be assessed or for anyone to care. Over time she adapted and learned to cope but Irene had quickly discovered Elle's secret and secured her a Saturday job working alongside her at Glensheil Library when she was sixteen, so that she could take Elle under her wing and invest the time that was needed in teaching Elle to read and write.

Elle owed Irene a debt of gratitude. She'd guided Elle to become the independent woman she was today and Elle loved her for that with all her heart.

'Think about it. You're an inspiration to me and you could be to others,' encouraged Irene. 'Your story gives other people in your situation hope. They might struggle with not knowing who they are, or where they've come from. Like you, they may feel there is a piece missing from the jigsaw. But as you've proved, you don't have to let your past define you.'

'But we don't know the ending yet, do we?' Elle said, her voice suddenly emotional as she thought about the search for her biological mother.

'No, we don't, but you don't need to mention that if you don't want to,' Irene said thoughtfully. 'Personally, I think it would make a very emotive read and could help inspire other young people in the same situation.'

Elle glanced back at the leaflet, mulling over what Irene had just said. She liked the idea of helping anyone to be the best that they could be, and especially helping those who were or had been in the same situation as her. Despite her uncertainty about who she was, Elle knew that since meeting Irene her life had turned around – and that could give people hope.

'When's the closing date?' Irene asked.

'Mid-March,' Elle replied, before slipping the leaflet into her bag.

'That gives you plenty of time if you want to enter, and I'm here to help. You can do this, Elle – give it a go. What's the worst that can happen?'

Elle looked up to see Pippa and Aiden wandering back towards them. 'Shush, here's the others.'

Irene nodded.

'I can't believe this one has kept his contact with Noah Jones a secret,' Pippa said as she looked at Aiden.

'I haven't kept it a secret. I've just rearranged things at short notice so that my favourite author visits our library on his tour rather than the one I used to work at. I mean, who doesn't want to come to Heartcross when it has everything? He'll probably thank me for the change of venue!' Aiden smiled at Pippa and Elle noticed her blush.

'Looks like we have yet another cake to eat,' said Elle. 'It does look amazing though.'

'Oh, the hardship,' replied Pippa.

Irene stood up. 'I'm just going to catch up with Mim and Rona before we head off.'

'And I need to get home too,' added Aiden, picking up his copy of Noah's new book.

He shouted goodbye to Mim and thanked her for a wonderful evening before he headed out the door and crossed the lane to his whitewashed terraced house on the other side.

'*I mean, who doesn't want to come to Heartcross when it has everything?*' teased Elle, repeating Aiden's words.

'Mmm, this isn't about me,' mused Pippa, handing Noah's book to Elle. 'Now hold it up.'

'Why?'

'Just hold it up and smile.'

Pippa picked up Elle's phone off the table and with a click she took a photo.

Elle stole a puzzled glance at Pippa, who was still grinning but now tapping frantically on her phone.

'What are you doing?'

'Just adding a post to your Instagram… #WelcometotheLibraryonLoveHeartLane #NoahJonesNewBook'

'What have you done?'

'I've added a post announcing Noah's appearance at the library along with a photo of you and his book, captioned:

We can't wait to welcome you back to the Library on Love Heart Lane.'

Elle's heart began to race as she stared at the post. 'You've tagged him.'

'Of course I have. Let's see if he remembers you now. That's not a bad photo, to be honest, but I still stand by your brows needing tidying up.'

Still staring at the screen, Elle watched as her notifications began to ping. The post was already clocking up likes.

'Anyway, like we've said before, it's unlikely he'll reply – especially with that many Instagram followers. He probably misses half his notifications.'

'Mmm,' Elle agreed, even though there was a tiny part of her that was hoping he *would* see the post. But as his following was huge and increasing by the day, it was doubtful he would notice it.

'What a night,' Pippa continued. 'Who'd have thought Heartcross was going to welcome two of our favourite authors in such a short time?' She pressed a hand to her heart and mimed a swoon. 'Noah Jones and Sam Stone.'

Elle rolled her eyes.

'Are you ready for home?' asked Pippa, standing up and sliding her arms into her coat.

'Yes, I think so. I'll just check with Rona to see if she has something for us to take this cake home in. It was such a lovely gesture, but the amount of cake I've been eating recently is no good for the diet.'

Irene was wrapping things up on the other side of the room, giving Eleni a hug. As though Rona had read Elle's mind, she suddenly bustled towards them carrying a large white cardboard box. 'Here, take this for the cake,' she said, placing it on the table.

'Thank you, Rona, and thank you, Mim, this was such a lovely gesture.'

'You're more than welcome! You didn't think we'd let your birthday slip away without any notice, did you?' Mim touched her arm affectionately before saying goodbye to all the other book clubbers. 'Same place, same time next week,' she called over the chatter.

'Are we ready?' Irene asked, grabbing her bag from underneath the table.

'Yes, we're ready,' replied Elle, hearing her phone beep as she slipped her books back into her bag.

Glancing at the screen of her phone, Elle did a double take. Her mouth fell open. She passed the phone to Pippa.

Noah Jones liked your post.

Pippa's eyes widened.

Sheer pleasure mixed with apprehension ran through Elle's body – and then she saw that he'd also replied with a comment.

I can't wait to see you all back at the Library on Love Heart Lane and I hope you all enjoy my latest book. Please let me know!

Instantly, nervous butterflies began to flutter busily around her stomach. When she came out tonight, she'd had no idea that Noah would be visiting the library or that their paths were going to cross again so soon. The only thing that was on Elle's mind now was: would he acknowledge the kiss that had happened between them the last time they saw each other?

Chapter Fifteen

Pippa had spent ages straightening Elle's hair before backcombing it to give it some height. She then pulled it into a tight high ponytail that actually made Elle's eyes water. The living room now felt like the bedroom of a messy teenager, with clothes thrown over the back of the settee, make-up scattered all over the coffee table and the latest Lewis Capaldi album playing on Pippa's iPhone.

'I'm nearly done,' Pippa declared, swiping more blusher across Elle's cheekbones. 'Ta-dah!' she said, turning the mirror towards Elle. Elle did a double take and a small noise escaped from her throat.

'What do you think?' Pippa asked, standing back and studying Elle's face like she was a professional make-up artist.

'I think I look like one of those ridiculous porcelain dolls that you find abandoned on a dusty shelf in a charity shop.'

'Eww, those things are ugly.'

'My point exactly – and that's where I'm going to end up.'

'Where?' Pippa asked, smudging in Elle's eyeshadow with her finger.

'On the bloody shelf!'

'Trust me, no man is going to be able to resist this smoky eye make-up,' she said, cranking up the music. 'You look the business.'

'That's what I'm worried about.'

Elle was still staring open-mouthed at her reflection, tilting her head from side to side.

'You need to pout like this.' Pippa demonstrated.

'You look ridiculous.'

'Go on – give it a try!'

'You'll be advising me to inject collagen next – and Botox,' Elle replied, laughing as she pouted back at her.

'Now it's you who looks ridiculous.'

Elle swiped her hand playfully. 'All this for a brand-new profile picture.'

Pippa laughed. 'You'll thank me for this when your new look lands you a hot date with Noah.'

Elle swallowed, feeling a little flutter of nervousness at the mention of his name. 'Let's hope he goes for the half-dead porcelain doll look then, hey?' Elle grinned. 'Pass me some wine. I think I need it.'

'What do you think of these?' Pippa was now holding up a couple of dresses.

'Very bright,' Elle replied, wondering why she'd agreed to let Pippa give her a makeover. She was quite happy with her oversized hoodie, tattered jeans and Converse.

'And that's what we want … bright. Not the dowdy librarian look. Here, go and try them on – and grab a couple more, too.'

Reluctantly, Elle browsed through the collection of outfits that Pippa had laid out on the settee.

'What's this?' she asked, picking up something that resembled a onesie.

Pippa laughed. 'It's a jumpsuit. Get with it!'

'It looks like my PJs.'

'They're the latest fashion! They're in every magazine right now.'

'This is exactly why I don't do fashion, and I don't read magazines.'

Hopefully in another hour this torture would be over.

'Go on, take these,' Pippa insisted, thrusting a pile of clothes into Elle's hand and pushing her up the stairs. 'And do not mess up your hair,' she shouted after her.

Five minutes later, Elle shouted from the top of the stairs like a sulky teenager, 'I feel so uncomfortable.'

Pippa popped her head round the corner of the living room and stared up the stairs. 'Wow, you look different – pretty good in fact. I reckon jumpsuits are your thing,' she said with enthusiasm.

'Do you now? I feel like I'm wearing a Babygro.'

'Get yourself down here! Let's have a proper look at you.'

Strolling down the stairs was uncomfortable to say the least. Elle's knickers kept rising up her backside and for the umpteenth time she attempted to pull them down.

'Stop fidgeting,' Pippa ordered. 'And give me a twirl.'

Unwillingly, Elle gave her a twirl with a forced smile along with jazz hands.

Pippa bent down underneath the coffee table. 'That outfit will look great with these,' she said, hooking a pair of strappy peach stilettos around her fingers and holding them in the air.

'I'm not sure,' replied Elle, thinking immediately of her comfy – flat – Converse.

'These are the height of fashion. Pop them on! Luckily for you, we're the same size,' Pippa replied.

'More like unluckily for me,' Elle muttered, slipping on the shoes. As soon as she stood up she wobbled from side to side.

'Now walk around the coffee table so I can have a proper look at you.'

Thrusting her hips forward, Elle began to strut around the table in time to the music, pretending she was on the catwalk. She moved unsteadily as the heel of the left shoe got entangled in the rug, and reached out towards Pippa, knocking her glass of wine out of her hand.

'Whoa, okay, maybe let's ditch the heels,' Pippa agreed, quickly using a make-up wipe to mop up the spilled wine.

Thank God for that, Elle thought, kicking them from her feet.

'But what about this look in general?'

'I feel like a drag queen, and I look like a drag queen – and not a good one at that,' Elle shared, slumping on to the settee. 'If I have to go to all this trouble to impress Noah, is it really worth it?'

'Trust me, you look amazing. You do trust me, don't you?'

'Hmmm.' Elle replied. 'I'm not entirely sure – the jury's still out on that one.'

'Let's take some photos and see how you look.' Pippa wasn't taking no for an answer. 'Come on – get posing,' she said, picking up her phone.

'I can't, I feel stupid.'

'I'll tell you what – I'll disappear into the kitchen. Now stand in front of the fireplace,' she demanded.

Elle had never felt as uncomfortable in her own skin as she did at that moment. Taking selfies wasn't something that came easily to her, unlike Pippa, who'd spend ample time photographing herself.

'Tilt your chin up – and the other one,' Pippa joked, as Elle grappled with her phone, trying to get it to focus.

'It's no use, I can't even see all of myself,' Elle exclaimed.

Pippa slowly lifted up Elle's arm until the top half of her body came into view on the screen. 'How do you not know how to take selfies at your age?'

'Because I don't need to spend my time posing, pouting and posting pictures just so any Tom, Dick and Harry can give them a like to make me feel wanted. I'm quite happy with people liking me in the real world, for who I am.'

'The lady doth protest too much,' Pippa replied, dismissing her answer. 'Now start clicking.'

Elle took a deep breath and pressed the button.

'OMG, that looks awful.'

Pippa peered over her shoulder. 'Mmm, yes, that one doesn't do you justice. Do it like this.' Taking the phone from Elle's hand, Pippa smiled and then took numerous photos of herself before stopping and staring at them.

'Ooh no, definitely no, don't like that or that one,' she said, deleting them straightaway. 'That one's okay-ish, that one is a no… That's the one,' she exclaimed, grinning, holding out the phone towards Elle.

'Actually, not bad,' Elle agreed.

'Then we do this, this and this and look!' Pippa twisted the phone back towards Elle.

'Jeez, Pippa, you look like you've just shed ten pounds and have been sunning yourself on a Caribbean island! Where did you get that tan from?' Elle spluttered, amazed at the image staring back at her.

'Filters. Easy peasy and … posted,' she said. 'Your turn.'

Elle held the phone up again, feeling self-conscious.

'I can't do this – it feels so unnatural.'

'I'll go in there and top up the wine while you snap to your heart's content,' encouraged Pippa, picking up their empty glasses and disappearing into the kitchen, closing the door behind her.

Five minutes later, after the initial awkwardness had passed, Elle was getting into the swing of things and beginning to enjoy herself.

'Can I come back in yet?' Pippa shouted from the other side of the door.

'Of course!' Elle replied.

'Let's have a look at what've you got.'

Elle looked over Pippa's shoulder as she flicked through the photos.

'What about that one?'

'No, I look like a rabbit caught in the headlights.'

'Maybe,' she said, biting her lip. 'This is the one!'

Elle tilted her head to take a proper look. 'Yes, it's not too bad.'

'Not too bad? It's perfect. Let's do this, this and this. Now what do you think?'

Elle stared at the photo in disbelief. In the blink of an eye, Pippa had made her look fresh and fashionable.

'Where's that wrinkle gone from the bridge of my nose?'

'We don't need that – I've airbrushed it out,' Pippa replied like it was the most natural thing in the world. 'That is what you would look like with a little bit of Botox.'

'I am not having Botox.'

'Ah, why not?' Pippa pointed to her own forehead. 'Everyone does it.'

'I'm really glad I'm not everyone.'

'This is the one. Now upload it and let's get the show on the road.'

Still unsure, Elle hedged. 'I don't think I need to do this. I did manage to get a kiss by being just me, you know, and these photos don't really look like me. Just remind me why we're doing this again.'

'To attract male attention.'

'But it's the wrong attention if they think this is a true representation of me. I'm just being honest. As much as I've had a little fun today, I think the best thing is to be true to who I really am. I can't pretend to be something that I'm not. Please don't be disappointed in me.'

'I get it. You know exactly who you are and you're comfortable in your own skin. I wish I had self-esteem like you.'

This was the ideal time to share with Pippa that she had no clue who she was and had struggled with her self-esteem for the whole of her life until she became part of Irene's family. But she didn't. They'd had a lovely couple of hours and as much as Elle had protested, she'd actually quite enjoyed dressing up and spending time with Pippa. What she didn't want to happen was for the mood to be brought down. With a glass of wine in one hand, Elle picked up her phone and sank into the settee.

'Please tell me you aren't checking those emails again?' Pippa was sitting next to her. 'It's been every two minutes recently. You're becoming obsessed.'

Once again this would be the ideal time to share with Pippa the reason why her heart began to pound every time her phone pinged with a new mail to her inbox, but again, right now there wasn't anything to tell – and she didn't want to get a few glasses of wine inside her, become all maudlin and spend the evening talking about her childhood.

'And there it is again…' Pippa rolled her eyes as Elle's phoned beeped again.

'That's not an email, that's an Instagram notification.' Elle opened the app. 'There's a private message.'

'Who's it from?' Pippa asked, leaning in towards Elle's phone.

Elle's eyes widened. 'Noah Jones.'

'Stop teasing me! Now who is it really from?'

'Noah Jones,' she repeated, turning the phone towards Pippa so she could read the message.

Hi Elle, Do let me know if you enjoyed my latest book and I hope to catch up with you at the library on my tour :-) x

'Look at Noah sliding into your DMs. Don't try and tell me he doesn't remember that kiss.'

Elle felt a smile hitch on her face and her heart leapt.

'And there's a kiss.'

The first thing Elle had spotted was the kiss.

'If you want my input, Elle Cooper, he's not coming to our library for Aiden's sake. I think there is someone else he would prefer to see … he's sent you a *DM*,' Pippa emphasised.

Still staring at the DM, Elle turned Pippa's words over in her mind, hoping that her theory was correct.

Chapter Sixteen

I t was four o'clock on Sunday morning, and Elle was wide
  awake.

No matter how hard she tried, she couldn't sleep. During
the night she'd constantly been refreshing her emails in the
hope that answers about her past would land. Pippa was right
– she was becoming obsessive.

After tossing and turning for hours, Elle quietly pulled her
body out of bed and silently padded down the stairs, heading
towards the kitchen to make a cup of tea.

Waiting for the kettle to boil she noticed the writing
competition leaflet sticking out of her bag. Looking over the
leaflet and reading the criteria for entry, Elle realised she met
every single one. She hadn't written anything before or been
published but she knew she had a lot to get off her chest.
Maybe if she did write her life story down it would help her to
feel a little more comfortable in her own skin, whilst inspiring
others to realise that no matter how hard your background is,
it's down to you to make your life as happy and successful as

possible. Even though Elle could put on a front to everyone around her – except Irene, who understood her perfectly – she knew she would never be truly happy until she had all the answers she needed about her biological parents.

After making a cup of tea, she took the leaflet into the living room and fired up her laptop. Reaching for a notepad, she wondered where to start. The thought of helping other children growing up in foster homes spurred her on.

With Irene's words whirling around in her mind – *Your story is a fantastic one. Against all odds, the girl did well* – Elle found herself rereading the leaflet.

Irene was right – she'd overcome so many obstacles in her life and there were countless times she could have hit the self-destruct button and veered off the right path.

Thinking back to her early years, Elle remembered how she'd battled with crushing disappointment due to her lack of stability within a family unit. They say school days are the best time of your life – but not for Elle. She'd dreaded school plays, sports day and parents' evenings. There was no one to watch her and no one interested enough to read her report cards. Also, she never had time to make friends before she was shipped off to somewhere new.

But during the last fifteen years, her confidence had slowly grown through hard work and determination. Her self-esteem flourished when Irene believed in her and encouraged her to read. Irene helped her understand that you could accomplish anything as long as you believed in yourself and whatever you put into life was what you were going to get back.

Looking at the notepad, Elle thought back to various author interviews she'd read in the past, where they'd talk about the inspiration behind their stories and how they wrote. They seemed to be divided into two camps – those who plotted, made wall charts and knew every twist and turn in their book before they put pen to paper, and those who flew by the seat of their pants. She was definitely a fly-by-the-seat-of-your-pants type of girl, and the words from one author interview in particular – Noah Jones's – had always stuck with her: *Write from your gut.*

Pushing the notepad to one side, Elle fired up her laptop, opened Word and stared at the blank screen in front of her before typing: *My story: February 2nd, 1993 – where it all began.*

Already feeling emotional, she blinked back tears. She swallowed as she struggled to think of an opening sentence. Eventually she abandoned the laptop.

She crept quietly back upstairs hoping not to wake Pippa. Pulling out the stool from underneath the dressing table in her room she stepped on it and grabbed a box from the top shelf of the wardrobe before sitting on the edge of the bed. With the box resting on her knees, she removed the lid. Lying inside was the shawl that had accompanied her through every foster home along with a rent card with Cora Hansley's birth date and address, which was dated around the time Elle had been born. Elle had no idea where the card had even come from but along with the shawl it had survived every foster home. When she was eighteen, she'd travelled to the address but the trail ran cold. No-one knew of Cora Hansley.

Elle picked up the shawl and hugged it tight.

Burying her face in it, she inhaled the distinctive smell that lingered amongst the stitching. A smell she couldn't describe or recognise. She thought back to how frightened she was as a child, when there was always a fear of the unknown future, never knowing where she would end up next. All she'd ever wanted was to be loved and feel a part of something. Taking the shawl back downstairs, Elle draped it over her knees and rested the laptop on top of it. Taking a deep breath, she murmured, *'Write from your gut.* Start at the beginning.'

She started to tap the keys frantically as words began to spill out onto the screen at a pace she couldn't stop. Overcome with emotion, she felt tears flowing down her cheeks as her words turned into sentences and then paragraphs.

Before she knew it, she'd written over three thousand words. Glancing up at the clock, Elle was amazed to see it was fast approaching 7.30 a.m.

She began to read over what she'd written and couldn't believe that staring back at her was a short story about her life.

She heard the creaking of the stairs just before Pippa breezed into the living room with a smile.

'You're up early,' she observed.

Elle opened her mouth to reply, but no words came out past the lump in her throat.

Pippa paused by the coffee table. 'Hey,' she said softly. 'You look awful. Are you sick?'

Elle shook her head.

'Have you been crying?' Pippa's eyes were on her as she walked around the table and sat next to her. 'What's the matter?'

Elle couldn't hold back the tears and again they began to cascade down her face. Pippa opened her arms and Elle fell into them.

'Come on, it can't be that bad. How long have you been down here?'

'Since the early hours.'

'Whatever it is, it's going to be okay. We can sort it together,' Pippa soothed in a calming voice.

'It's been a long night.'

'And you're cold,' she said. 'I'll pop the kettle on, get you something warm to drink, then, if you want to, you can tell me all about it.'

A couple of minutes later, Pippa handed Elle a steaming hot mug of tea. 'There's two sugars in there,' she said. 'I think you need them.'

Elle nodded and cupped her hands around the mug. Pippa gave her a reassuring smile. 'What can I do to help?'

Elle smiled at her with bleary eyes. 'You're a really good friend and you came into my life at just the right time, like Irene.'

Puzzled, Pippa didn't take her eyes off Elle. 'I don't understand. What do you mean? Do you want to tell me what is going on here?'

'I think I probably do.'

Elle sipped her tea. Pippa remained silent.

'I don't know where to start.'

'Try the beginning,' Pippa urged gently.

'There's something I need to tell you about my mum.'

'What about her?'

Elle hesitated before saying, 'Irene is not my biological mum.' She watched the look on Pippa's face change as her words registered.

Elle picked up the writing competition leaflet. 'Remember you said that you'd bet I was always top of my class, was the popular kid at school and had bundles of self-esteem? Far from it. Irene suggested I wrote my story and enter it into Sam Stone's competition. She said it could inspire other young children that are going through the same situation I went through.'

Elle turned the laptop towards Pippa. 'Here, read this.'

Pippa took the laptop off Elle and balanced it on her knees. Within seconds, she was in an emotional state, a tear sliding down her cheek as she continued to read. When she finished, she looked up, her eyes blurry. 'Oh, Elle, I had no idea about any of this. You've kept it all well hidden.'

'Until now.'

'Your story is so sad but also so inspirational. This is emotional stuff and it's written so well. It's clear it's come straight from the heart.'

'Thank you. That's what I was intending even though I've never written a thing in my life. I cried writing it and I feel exhausted, but I'm relieved to have got everything off my chest. Once I started to write, I couldn't stop. It may be inspirational but it isn't a childhood I'd have wished on anyone.'

'Was it really difficult growing up?' Pippa asked tentatively.

Elle nodded. 'I'd see all the other children being dropped off in the playground by their parents. They'd be smothered in kisses and have their friends around for tea. I envied the bond they had. I was never mistreated or anything like that – I was always fed and watered – but I never felt like I belonged. It was more that I felt like I was an inconvenience, I suppose.' Her voice faltered a little. 'There was always a piece of me missing.'

'Oh, Elle, but look at you now.' Pippa squeezed her knee. 'And Irene is the best surrogate mum anyone could ask for.'

Elle smiled. 'I know she is. I'm very lucky that we found each other.'

'I didn't have a clue that Irene wasn't your biological mum. You even look similar,' she said, sipping her tea.

'I think it's the hair,' she replied, twirling a strand around her finger.

'And you have the same surname.' Pippa looked puzzled.

Elle nodded. 'Yes, I changed mine by deed poll.'

'Honestly, I'd have never guessed in a million years.'

'It was Irene's idea, just like she suggested I write my story for the competition.'

'After reading it, I think you've got a very good chance of winning.' Pippa smiled. 'Have you any clues about your biological parents?'

Elle shook her head. 'No – except for my mother's name. Remember, on my birthday, I didn't come home with you on the bus?'

'Yes.'

'That's when I filled in the form and started the search for her. I'd wondered for years and always thought she might come looking for me ... but I also wondered if some things were best left in the past.'

'There could be numerous reasons she hasn't come looking.'

'Such as?'

'She might be worried about rejection, or that you could be settled and happy, and her sudden reappearance might catapult your life into disarray.'

'I suppose.'

'Do you know why she didn't keep you? Did she leave any kind of letter of explanation?' Pippa asked tentatively.

Elle shook her head. 'No, all that I have is an old rent card with a name, address and date of birth but I don't know where that came from. I don't know anything else, except my surname before I changed it was Hansley.'

'Did you say you only started the search last week?'

'Yes, on my birthday, using the Salvation Army service. I've tried googling her for years but I've never found anything.'

'What happens now?'

'I sit and wait.'

'*We* sit and wait,' Pippa corrected her. 'Is this the reason you're constantly checking your emails?'

'You don't miss a trick.'

Pippa leaned over and touched her arm affectionately. 'I'll be here for you every step of the way.'

'I've at least had an acknowledgement email to say the Salvation Army have received my form. Who knows how long it will take, but you know how it is when you're checking your emails every two minutes, hoping the news you want has landed in your inbox.'

'I definitely know that feeling. I keep checking mine hoping that Harry Styles has finally noticed me on Twitter and thinks I'm sex on legs,' Pippa said, with a tiny laugh.

'I think there's more chance of my email landing than yours.'

'Yep, you're probably right. And are you really going to enter this in the competition?' Pippa asked, nodding towards the laptop.

'Do you honestly think it's good enough?'

'Of course, I do – it's the best thing I've read in ages. It's full of raw emotion and it's going to be inspirational to other children who are experiencing – or have experienced – what you went through.'

'Pippa, for now, please keep all this to yourself.'

'Of course – it goes without saying.'

'Thank you.'

'Why don't you get yourself back to bed and try to get some sleep? You need to rest. I'll clean up down here.'

Elle nodded. 'Thank you. I feel exhausted.' Clutching her shawl, she walked towards the door then hovered.

'I'm so glad you're here,' she said.

'Me too,' Pippa replied warmly.

Chapter Seventeen

'Shall I or shan't I?' Elle asked nervously as both she and Pippa stared at the computer screen, upon which was Elle's entry for the writing competition.

She'd spent the last two weeks polishing the entry, checking the grammar and proofreading it. 'I think it's ready to go.'

'That would be a shall,' Pippa encouraged. 'And hurry up or we'll miss the bus.'

'It's now or never.' Taking a huge breath, Elle hit 'enter'. The email was gone. 'There's no turning back now.' Her eyes were wide with the panic that had suddenly hit her.

Pippa hugged her tight before pulling away slowly. 'I know that was a big moment for you … but now you need to get your coat, otherwise we'll be late.'

Twenty minutes later, they were standing outside the library doors.

'You will remember to keep quiet about my competition entry, won't you?' Elle repeated, pausing in the oak porch that framed the entrance to the library.

'Of course, I've promised,' replied Pippa. She noticed Aiden hurrying across the courtyard from the creperie. As soon as he spotted them he waved. Pippa tapped her watch, grinning at him.

'I don't want anyone knowing, I suppose to save face a little in case I don't win.'

'It's our little secret – just as long as when you win, I can go with you to meet Sam Stone.'

'That's a deal. But now I've sent it, I'm starting to panic a little.'

'Why?'

'Because it was all so personal – writing about the shawl and revealing Irene isn't my mum.'

'Irene knows and she's good with that. There's no need to panic. Now shush – here's Aiden.'

'Good morning, ladies,' he said cheerfully, bounding up the steps towards them.

Pippa narrowed her eyes at him. 'You're full of the joys of spring.'

'Just high on life,' he replied, grinning and fishing around in his pocket before pulling out a letter.

'I'm under strict instructions to hand you this.' He passed the envelope to Elle.

'From whom?' Elle asked, opening the library door.

'Yes, from whom?' Pippa's mouth and eyebrows were twitching with curiosity.

'It's from Eleni – an invitation to the hen do,' Aiden replied as Elle punched in the alarm code. 'It's to both of you.'

'Exciting! We need a good night out.' Pippa took the envelope from Elle, who immediately took it back.

'It's addressed to me.'

Pippa huffed and headed inside.

After hanging up their coats and storing their lunches in the staffroom, they put on their lanyards and declared themselves ready for work.

'Monday mornings do come around a little too quickly for my liking,' Aiden added, tossing his pound coin into the tea-fund caddy. 'Did you two get up to anything interesting this weekend?'

Elle and Pippa exchanged glances and hesitated. They'd spent the majority of the weekend putting the finishing touches on Elle's competition entry.

'That silence speaks volumes,' he said, looking between the pair of them.

'Nothing whatsoever,' Pippa piped up. 'Just a quiet one for us.'

Aiden looked sceptical but shrugged and happily changed the subject. 'Jack's invited me on the stag do. I know I'm a newbie but they're doing everything they can to welcome me to the village,' he said cheerfully, walking out on to the library floor.

'Where are you going?' Pippa asked.

'Unfortunately, I've signed the Official Secrets Act. If I tell you, I'll have to kill you.' He winked as he switched on the computer.

'That sounds more fun than our meal out.'

'You don't *have* to come,' Elle said playfully. 'No one is twisting your arm.'

Pippa shrugged. 'I suppose it beats staying in by myself –

unless I gate-crash the stag do. You wouldn't mind if I tagged along, would you, Aiden?'

'Don't answer that, Aiden. She's only teasing, and remember Eleni is in the early stages of pregnancy – she isn't going to want to go clubbing until the small hours.'

'I know,' replied Pippa.

'I'm sure you'll have your chance one day and we can party hard then. I'm just wondering who'll be lucky enough to marry you.' Elle flicked her eyes towards Aiden, who promptly blushed and pretended he hadn't heard.

Pippa discreetly poked Elle in the ribs and cocked an eyebrow.

'Did you do anything nice over the weekend, Aiden?' Elle asked, quickly changing the subject.

'I met up with the lads Saturday night. Nothing heavy – just a few beers because I looked after Theo yesterday.'

'Aww, what did you get up to?'

'We went to the park, fed the ducks and had a picnic, though he spent half the time giggling and trying to throw my sandwiches to the ducks instead of the stale bread. He's developing a little personality of his own.'

'Bless him,' Pippa and Elle chorused.

'How's Louisa?' Elle asked

'Yes, she's okay. She's starting a part-time job today, and now we're both settled, Theo's going to stay over with me a couple of nights a week so we can have some real boy time together.'

'Aww, that's nice.'

'I'll start filing these back in the gallery area,' he said, wheeling a trolley of books towards the staircase.

Elle glanced up at the clock. 'Has anyone seen Wilson this morning? He's a little late.'

They looked towards the door, and just then Jenny came through it. 'Wilson's running late – there's a flat tyre on the van but he will be with you as soon as possible,' she said, answering Elle's question. 'The computer at home is playing up again. Would it be possible to use yours to check my email?' she added.

'Of course,' replied Elle. 'It just needs switching on at the wall and will take a moment or two to load.'

Watching Jenny walk towards the computer, Pippa leaned in towards Elle. 'Have you checked yours yet?'

With Pippa watching over her shoulder, Elle logged on to the system.

'One hundred and twenty-eight new messages.' Elle quickly began to scroll through them and turned towards Pippa. 'Nothing from the Salvation Army.' She sighed.

'I know it's disappointing but keep the faith.'

'I just want answers and I'm not good at this waiting lark.'

'I can't imagine how difficult it is – but there's something to take your mind off of it.' Pippa pointed to an email on the screen.

The email was titled 'Noah Jones's upcoming visit to the Library on Love Heart Lane.'

Elle clicked on the email. 'It's his schedule, his arrival time, how many books will arrive ahead of the signing, and a note to say we should receive posters in the next few days to distribute around the town and village to advertise the event.'

'And no keeping one of those posters for yourself. The last thing I need is coming home to discover you've pinned them around the house.'

'As if… Okay, maybe just one,' agreed Elle with a smile.

'We do need to pull out all the stops for this event,' Pippa continued. 'We need fresh flowers in the corners of the room, maybe even a buffet, along with teas and coffees.'

'Good idea,' replied Elle. 'Are you all done?' she asked Jenny, noticing she'd finished on the computer and looked disappointed.

'Yes, thank you. I'll catch you later.' She waved and stood aside as Florrie walked through the doors holding a beautiful bouquet of flowers.

'Great timing! You're just the florist I wanted to see,' enthused Elle. 'We have a very special book signing coming up at the library and we thought we could do with a number of floral displays to brighten up this area.'

'I've heard! I'm a huge fan of Noah's, read every book, and it will be my absolute pleasure. Drop me an email with budget and colours.'

'Perfect and what beautiful blooms those are. I can smell them from here.'

'They're gorgeous. Someone has got exquisite taste! I have to shoot now; the van engine is running. It's my busiest day of the year.'

Elle looked at Florrie. 'Oh my gosh, it's Valentine's Day isn't it? It totally slipped my mind, what with not having a significant other.'

With a huge grin on her face Pippa extended her arm. 'I'll take those.'

'Have a lovely day!' Florrie waved as she disappeared back through the door.

'Aiden or Wilson?' Elle whispered, glancing at the flourish of pastel-coloured roses and freesias.

Pippa inhaled. 'What a gorgeous scent.'

'Come on, who are they from?' probed Elle.

Pippa pulled out the small white envelope and paused.

'They aren't for me.'

'Oh no, have they been delivered to the wrong place?'

She shook her head. 'No, they're for you.' She held the flowers out to Elle.

'For me?' Elle repeated, puzzled, taking the bouquet from her. Sure enough, the envelope was addressed 'Elle Cooper'.

'Come on then, open the card.'

'It's probably Irene,' Elle said heartily, slipping the card out of the envelope. 'This is the kind of thing she'd do.'

She read the card and looked a little puzzled. 'Very interesting,' she said.

Pippa stared at her for a few seconds, waiting for her to elaborate, before she took the card from Elle's hand and read the message aloud.

Dear Elle,
>*Happy Valentine's Day!*
>*Love from*
>*Guess who xx*

'Guess who? That's a let-down,' Pippa said, clearly disappointed.

'I suppose that's what Valentine's Day is all about – sending anonymous gifts.'

'Blooming annoying though! First the Sam Stone book appears and now these flowers.'

'Do you think they're connected?'

'I never thought of that. I really don't know who these could be from.'

'Ooh, what have you got there?' Aiden asked as he came up behind them and swept the duster over the front desk.

'Flowers,' Pippa answered, stating the obvious. 'It's Valentine's Day.'

'Who from?'

'That's the question,' Elle replied, still mystified. 'We've no idea.'

'You'd best go and put them in some water,' Aiden suggested.

'Have you discovered any admirers today, Aiden?' Pippa asked, fishing for gossip. 'Any special plans for this evening?'

'Plans for this evening include a microwave meal for one, unless anyone fancies keeping me company?'

'That sounds like either one of us would do!' Pippa said, hitting him playfully.

'Just keeping my options open,' he joked before heading towards the photocopier to help a customer load the empty paper tray.

'And why didn't you jump at the chance?' Elle whispered to Pippa once he was out of earshot.

Chapter Eighteen

'Come on, what are your plans for tonight?' Elle insisted. 'Why not take Aiden up on his offer?'

'There are a couple of options I'm mulling over.'

'Which are?'

'I could go out to dinner with Harry Styles or, as a backup, I could attend a film première with Cillian Murphy.'

'And failing that?'

'I think you mentioned yesterday that you're going to Irene's for tea? I could come with you. I quite fancy fish and chips.'

'You're more than welcome.'

'Thank you. Now, given that it's the most romantic day of the year, tell me – have you replied to Noah's message on Instagram yet?'

Elle shook her head.

'Have you stalked him today on his socials?'

'I've barely had time to do anything yet.'

'There's no time like the present. Let's have a look at what he's up to today. After all, it's Valentine's Day!' Pippa insisted, whipping her phone out of her pocket.

'Noah Jones,' she murmured to herself as she waited for the app to open. 'Honestly, I think I spend half my life waiting for apps to load.'

Elle smiled at her impatience. 'I don't think holding your phone up to the window actually makes it load any faster.'

'Little do you know, Cooper,' she said, stretching her hand further in the air. 'Right, let's have a look,' she said, tucking her hand under Elle's arm and holding the screen in front of them. 'Here he is – Mr Noah Jones.'

Elle dropped her gaze to the screen.

'It appears that Noah Jones is spending this Valentine's...' Pippa scrolled her finger up and down the screen.

'Probably with his girlfriend,' Elle claimed.

'Doing nothing,' Pippa said. 'There's nothing on his socials.'

'That's probably because he's all loved up and hasn't got time to tweet today.' Elle felt a tiny slump in her mood. Why hadn't she messaged him back? She could kick herself.

'Such a pessimist.' Pippa put the phone back into her pocket. 'I suppose we best do some work and hope your mystery man doesn't stay a mystery for too long, because I'm dying to know who he is.'

'You and me both,' replied Elle, pointing towards the door, through which a flustered-looking Wilson had finally arrived.

'I'm sorry I'm late. A flat tyre is not what you need first thing in the morning.' He looked towards Pippa. 'I was hoping we'd have time for a chat this morning but I'm already late. I'll put your deliveries against the back wall so they aren't in the way of the reception, then I need to get going.' Wilson stacked up the numerous boxes then turned back towards Pippa. 'I'll text you at lunchtime,' he said, touching her arm as he walked past.

Once Wilson was out of sight, Elle turned towards Pippa. 'Why would Wilson be texting you at lunch and what was that look between you?'

Pippa shrugged her shoulders dismissively.

'Why do I get the feeling there's something you're not telling me?'

'Shhh,' she said as Aiden wandered out of the staffroom clutching a mug of tea.

'There's a cuppa on the table for you both,' he said, before grabbing the duster and heading towards the shelves.

Luckily for Pippa, Elle's interrogation was interrupted by a steady flow of customers exchanging books, and for the next ten minutes the only noise in the library was the thump of the date stamp and the turning of pages.

'Gosh, that was a bit of a rush.' Pippa sat back in the reception desk chair when she finally got a breather.

'Wasn't it just. Don't think I've forgotten the conversation before the rush.'

'Don't! I'm feeling bad enough as it is.'

'Feeling bad about what? What do you mean?' Elle cast her eyes around the library. There was no one in sight. 'You've clearly got something on your mind. I can tell. Come on. Staffroom. Let's grab a quick five minutes.'

Pippa took a breath once they were seated with the door firmly closed. 'There's no easy way to say this except to say it how it is. The other night I met up with Wilson and we slept together.'

Pippa certainly had Elle's full attention now!

'You slept with Wilson,' she repeated.

Pippa nodded.

'I wasn't expecting that, I have to admit.'

'I can't say I was either.'

'How did that happen?'

Pippa raised her eyebrows.

'I obviously know how it *happens*. You know what I mean – when, where and how did it come about?'

'You were out, visiting Irene I think, and Wilson had followed me on Instagram. We flirted a little and I invited him around. We chatted, had a glass of wine and before I knew it we were kissing and one thing led to another.'

'I can't leave you alone for a minute. And it happened just like that?'

'Yes.'

'And was it just a one-off?'

'He wants to see me again, but I'm feeling really embarrassed about the whole thing,' Pippa admitted.

'Why? You're single.'

She lifted her head for a fraction of a second and looked towards the door before she spoke. 'Because I think I actually like Aiden, and now I've gone and slept with his new mate. I've messed it all up.'

'That is a bit tricky.'

'I do like Wilson – well, actually, who wouldn't? He's kind, considerate – not to mention easy on the eye – but I don't get that nervous flutter in my stomach—'

'Like you do with Aiden,' Elle interrupted, instantly thinking of Noah, as that's the way he made her feel.

'Like I do with Aiden,' Pippa repeated.

'What are you going to do?'

'I've no idea. I've made the situation really awkward, and then there are even more complications with Aiden.'

'Which are?'

'He's only recently separated from Louisa, and there's Theo to consider.'

'How do you feel about dating a man with a small child?'

'I hadn't really thought about that. It's a whole new ball game to me, but Theo is adorable and I see him as a bonus.'

Elle smiled. 'Who wouldn't?'

Suddenly Aiden popped his head around the door. 'Hey, I'm on my own out here and I think these ones are for you, Pippa,' he said, holding out a bouquet of twelve red roses towards her.

'Thank you,' she replied, taking the flowers and then watching the door shut behind Aiden as he returned to the library floor.

'Awkward,' Pippa said as she breathed in the scent of the roses.

'Beautiful flowers though. Are they from Wilson?'

Pippa nodded as she read the card. 'Yes. What am I going to do?'

'Firstly, put those in water, and secondly, if you receive such beautiful flowers after only one night, he's a keeper!' Elle joked.

Pippa rolled her eyes. 'Don't. I'm feeling bad about the whole situation.'

'Come on. We best get back out there.'

When they returned to the library floor, they found Aiden sitting behind the front desk. He looked preoccupied.

Checking her phone, Pippa whispered to Elle that she'd already received a text from Wilson. 'He's asked me out tonight.'

'And are you going to go?' asked Elle, keeping her voice low.

'It's difficult, he's sent me the most beautiful flowers and…' Pippa glanced across at Aiden. 'I feel terrible.'

'It is a dilemma. How about we stick to my plan?' Elle suggested.

'Fish and chips with Irene?'

Elle nodded.

'Yes, I think that's the best plan.'

Chapter Nineteen

'You girls have been very popular today,' Irene said as she was greeted by an armful of blooms when she opened her front door.

'And we've brought fish and chips,' said Elle, holding up the white carrier bag in her hand.

'I'm not sure which smells the best – the flowers or the chips.' Irene opened the door wide. 'The only deliveries I've had today are the newspaper, a charity bag and a coupon for a free cup of tea from the local garden centre,' she continued, chuckling. 'Pop your flowers in the front room and then you can tell me all about who sent them.'

Elle placed the bouquets in the front room and followed Irene and Pippa into the kitchen.

'I can't believe neither of you has a date tonight,' said Irene, dishing up the food. 'You two take a seat.'

'Pippa has had two offers of dates—'

'Lucky girl,' Irene interrupted.

'Whereas I've had none.'

'You could have had one of mine,' Pippa said, grinning,

squeezing brown sauce all over the plate of fish and chips that Irene had just placed in front of her.

'Let me guess your two.' Irene smiled at Pippa. 'Wilson and…'

Pippa raised her eyebrows, waiting for the second guess.

'Wilson and … please don't tell me it's the ex, Nick,' Irene added, wide-eyed.

'No, of course not,' Pippa replied. 'Actually, he's not even crossed my mind today.'

'Have you had any texts from him?' Elle asked curiously.

'I wouldn't know because I took your advice and blocked his number. If he has been texting, he's been talking to himself.'

'I know Wilson sent you some flowers because I bumped into Jenny in the teashop and she might have mentioned it.'

'What did she say?' Elle asked before Pippa could get a word in edgeways.

'That Wilson's like an excited puppy every time he leaves for work, knowing the library is his first stop.'

'Oh God,' Pippa said, looking towards Elle.

'He's a lovely lad,' Irene said, puzzled.

'He is,' admitted Pippa.

'But?'

'She likes Aiden too,' added Elle.

'Now that *is* a dilemma. Hearts are going to be broken.'

'Irene!'

'And don't think it's escaped my noticed that you were armed with flowers too.' Irene tilted her head, waiting for Elle to share who they were from.

'I'd tell you if I knew but your guess is as good as mine. I have no clue – it's yet another mystery gift.'

Irene looked surprised. 'Another one? You mean like the Sam Stone book?'

'Yes.'

'You must have an inkling?'

'I haven't, honestly, but they're from someone who knows I work at the library.'

'So there's no man in your life at all?' Irene prompted, not failing to notice the look between Elle and Pippa. 'Don't leave me in suspense. There's something going on here.'

'It's Noah Jones,' Elle finally admitted. 'But there's absolutely nothing going on.'

'*The* Noah Jones? The *author* Noah Jones? Noah Jones who will be visiting the library very shortly?'

Pippa grinned. 'The one and only.'

'And how long has this been going on?'

'I've just said there is nothing going on,' Elle protested.

'I don't understand. Have you seen him recently?'

'The last time I saw him was at the library. We had a moment but nothing has happened since.'

'He seemed a very nice lad.'

'And we're on a mission to get Elle noticed when he returns,' Pippa said proudly.

'This bright spark here,' Elle nodded towards Pippa, 'decided my profile picture looked very librarianish and that we needed to jazz it up to gain some male attention.'

Irene shook her head, laughing. 'Librarianish? I'm not sure that's even a word.'

'Here, take a look. We took some photos.' Pippa thrust her phone at Irene.

'Is that even you? You look like you've been holidaying in the Caribbean for a couple of weeks.'

'That's exactly what I said. It's done with an app. It's meant to make you look fresh and hip.' Elle rolled her eyes. 'Thankfully, I came to my senses and didn't allow this one to post them.'

'Such a spoilsport,' Pippa chipped in.

'And we have no idea who your flowers are from, Elle?'

Elle shook her head. 'My detective work failed at the first hurdle. Just before we left work I did text Florrie and asked if she could share with me who'd sent them but as I suspected, she wasn't at liberty to say!'

'I love a bit of intrigue,' replied Irene. 'If someone has gone to the expense of sending such beautiful flowers, I hope they'll reveal themselves very soon.'

All they could do for now was sit and wait.

Chapter Twenty

They arrived home from Irene's around nine p.m. and after removing their make-up and changing into their PJs they settled on the sofa with a mug of hot chocolate each. They were fifteen minutes into watching *Pretty Woman* when they heard a knock at the front door. Neither of them wanted to answer it and they dithered for a few seconds before the knock came again.

Whoever it was evidently wasn't going away.

'It's your house,' Pippa said, grinning. 'You go.'

'Why doesn't anyone knock on the door when we're dressed up?' Elle exclaimed.

'Cos that's life,' replied Pippa, watching Elle reluctantly get up to open the door.

Wilson was standing on the step. 'Hi.' He cleared his throat. 'Is Pippa in?'

'Yes. Pippa, it's for you,' Elle shouted over her shoulder, then smiled at Wilson, who appeared a little subdued.

Pippa appeared in the hallway and met Wilson's gaze. 'Hi.'

For a second there was an awkward silence before Elle took control.

'Would you like to come in?'

'If that's okay?'

'Of course,' Elle answered, holding open the front door. 'Come on in.'

As soon as Wilson stepped into the living room, he said, 'I've interrupted you, haven't I?'

'It's fine.' Elle smiled warmly. 'The film hasn't started properly yet. Would you like a drink?'

'Yes, that would be great.' He perched on the edge of the settee next to Pippa.

Heading out of the living room, Elle could sense the atmosphere was a little tense. From the kitchen, she heard Wilson speak first. 'Did you get the flowers?' he asked.

Pippa gave a tiny gasp. 'Oh, Wilson, I'm so sorry. I got distracted and forgot to text you back. The flowers were lovely. They're over there.'

Elle peeked out and saw Wilson glance at the flowers displayed in the vase sitting in the window.

'You didn't answer my text about dinner tonight and I've been sat waiting, not knowing what to do.'

'I'm sorry,' replied Pippa. 'It was a genuine mistake on my part. I only remembered when I was round at Irene's with Elle, eating fish and chips, and then we got talking again … and it slipped my mind again. I know that sounds like a lame excuse.'

Wilson looked relieved. 'You've been at Irene's?' His expression was earnest, his mood obviously lifted.

'Yes, I went with Elle.'

'Can I ask, are we okay?' Wilson asked softly. 'I just want to tell you I wasn't looking for a quick fling, Pippa… I'm still not looking for a quick fling.'

Elle decided this wasn't the moment to walk back into the living room so she waited on the other side of the door.

'Wilson, you are so lovely—' Pippa began.

'But…' Wilson interrupted.

'Funny and handsome too,' she added. 'And just a genuinely decent bloke, but I have to be honest with you. I'm not interested in taking things further between us. I'm so sorry if I've hurt you.'

Wilson looked down at the floor. Elle knew it had definitely sounded like the end of the road for them, when it hadn't even properly begun.

'Sorry, I feel like a right idiot,' he managed to say. 'I shouldn't have come round.'

'Don't be daft – and don't ever apologise for being such a lovely person.'

He let out a defeated sigh before standing up and putting on a brave smile. 'If you ever change your mind, please come and find me. I really like you, Pippa.'

'I will – I promise,' she said, standing up and hugging him. 'Friends?' she whispered.

He nodded.

After hearing Wilson leave, Elle stepped back into the living room. 'You did the right thing if you didn't want it to go any further,' she reassured.

'It doesn't make it any easier though. I feel dreadful about the whole situation.'

'I can imagine. Is the reason you've turned him down because you've decided you like Aiden?' probed Elle.

'I think it is – which is daft because there isn't anything going on between me and Aiden.'

'Well, not just yet.'

Pippa smiled. 'Every time I hear Aiden's voice, it sparks off a swarm of fireflies in my stomach.'

'That's a good sign.'

'It is … except I've probably messed that up now. I shouldn't have gone out with Wilson. What if Aiden finds out?'

'Don't beat yourself up over that now. It was just bad timing. These things happen. You're only human.'

'Aiden's probably got enough going on in his life right now – and anyway, he might not even be looking for another relationship so soon after Louisa.'

'That's very true,' replied Elle, remembering the conversation she and Aiden had had. 'It must be difficult when you have a child with someone and you go your separate ways. But I do know Louisa is struggling a little bit with the changes in her life – the break-up, moving back in with her parents and generally being on her own.'

'Do you think there's a possibility they'll get back together?'

'Apparently she's mentioned the idea, but Aiden was adamant that wasn't going to happen. There's no connection there now except for Theo, as far as he's concerned.'

She nodded, unpausing the film. 'Julia Roberts gets her happy ending … why isn't life that simple in the real world?'

'If only,' replied Elle, the thought of Noah suddenly creeping back into her head.

It was the following morning in the library. The door opened, letting in a blast of cool air, and Wilson walked silently up to the front counter, managing only a slight smile before placing the deliveries on the desk and heading out again.

'Wilson?' Elle shouted after him, but he just waved and continued without saying a word. Wilson normally had time for a chat in the morning, and the only reason Elle could think of for his hurry was that he might be avoiding Pippa. She vowed she would catch up with him after work tonight to make sure he was okay.

'What's up with Wilson this morning?' Aiden asked, appearing behind Elle. 'He wasn't his usual cheery self.'

'Probably just a busy morning,' Elle replied. It was a little white lie but it wasn't her business to discuss what she knew. She just hoped that things between Wilson and Pippa would get back to normal in time.

'And what's up with you?' asked Elle. 'You look a little miserable.'

'I am, a little,' he replied, shuffling some papers on the desk.

'Do you want to talk about it?' she asked, glancing around the library. Pippa was on the other side of the room, returning books to the shelves.

'There's nothing I can do about it anyway,' he replied.

'About what?' asked Elle.

Aiden glanced in her direction.

'I saw them.'

'Who?'

'Wilson and Pippa.'

'Saw them when?'

'Last night – Valentine's Day. I was driving past and saw him leave your house. It was him who sent her the flowers, wasn't it?'

Elle nodded. 'But it's not quite what you think.'

'Why's that then?'

Elle was in a difficult situation. On the one hand, she was loyal to Pippa, but on the other, Aiden was standing in front of her hoping she was going to tell him what he wanted to hear.

Elle hesitated. 'They aren't going out together...' she confided.

'I've put you on the spot, haven't I?'

'A little,' she admitted. 'Pippa isn't going out with Wilson. They're just friends – good friends. How's Louisa?' she asked, changing the subject as she noticed Pippa walking towards them.

'She's started her new job now, which seems to have perked her up a little. She's socialising a little more and hopefully getting her life back on track.'

'That's good to hear then.'

'What are you two talking about?' Pippa asked as she approached the desk.

Aiden and Elle exchanged a glance before he replied. 'My microwave meal for one last night,' he said, smiling as he leaned across the desk to answer the phone.

'Hello, you've reached the Library on Love Heart Lane; this is Aiden speaking, how may I help you?'

There was silence for a moment while the person on the other end spoke.

'Who's calling please?' Aiden asked, looking towards Elle. He put his hand across the receiver and whispered. 'It's the Salvation Army for you.'

Feeling her pulse race, Elle looked at Pippa, who stared back at her in shock. Neither of them spoke, but they held one another's gaze as Pippa perched close by on the edge of the desk and Elle took the phone from Aiden.

'Hello,' Elle said, her voice shaking. All she could think was – had they traced her mother?

'Hello, is that Elle Cooper?'

'Yes, speaking.'

'This is Ann Blears. I'm ringing from the Salvation Army. Are you okay to talk right now?'

'I am.'

'I've phoned your mobile and left you a message, but I thought I'd try this number too.'

Elle quickly took her phone from her pocket. It was switched to silent and there was a missed call and a voicemail from a number she didn't recognise.

'Can I just confirm some personal details with you?'

Ann took Elle through a serious of security checks and as the seconds ticked by Elle's thoughts ran wild. She started shaking.

'Elle, we have some news for you.'

'Please just tell me.' Elle's heart was beating so fast she thought it was going to burst through her chest.

'We are pleased to tell you that your search has been successful. We have found your biological mother.'

Elle gasped, clasping her hand to her mouth. She lowered herself on to the reception chair and briefly closed her eyes while she digested the information. She'd waited to hear those words for a long time. 'So soon. Is this real?'

'Yes,' replied Ann. 'Are you okay? Have you got someone with you?'

'Yes, I have my friend with me,' replied Elle, reaching across and taking hold of Pippa's hand for moral support. 'Does she want to see me?'

Elle closed her eyes again, waiting for the answer.

'Yes. Your mother has written you a letter, and we'll post it to you First Class today. You'll be allocated a caseworker – Emily Kirk – and she'll liaise with you both about the next steps. All the details will be in the letter. Do you have any more questions at this stage?'

'Can I ask how long she has been searching for me?'

'The second of February just gone.'

Elle gave a tiny gasp.

'Is there anything I can help you with today?'

'No, I don't think so. Thank you.'

In shock, Elle put down the receiver and met Pippa's gaze.

Placing her hands on her chest, 'They've found her. I can't believe it; they've actually found her.' Elle tried to compose herself but it was no use. The emotional impact had hit her like a high-speed train, and her cheeks were wet with tears. 'She's sent me a letter. She wants to see me.'

'Oh Elle, that's such wonderful news. I'm so happy for you.' Pippa stood up and wrapped her arms around Elle, hugging her tight.

Aiden, who had been stood silently at the side of the desk for the duration of the call, gently cleared his throat. 'I'm not exactly sure what's going on here, but is everything okay?' he asked tentatively.

Through her tears, Elle managed a nod. 'It's more than okay, I think.'

'Come on,' Pippa said, gently placing her hand beneath Elle's elbow and leading her towards the staffroom, away from prying eyes. 'Can you man the fort?' she asked Aiden.

'Of course,' Aiden confirmed.

Sitting down in the staffroom, with the adrenaline pumping through her body, Elle looked up at Pippa through blurry eyes. 'I can't believe they've found my mother, and so soon. I was trying to prepare myself for never knowing and now I don't have to. I feel so shaky, numb even.'

Pippa hugged her tight again. 'This is amazing. What happens now?'

'She's written me a letter, and she wants contact.' Elle breathed unsteadily. 'I can't believe it. Am I dreaming?'

Pippa pinched her on her arm.

'Ow! What are you doing?'

'You felt that, so you're not dreaming. Elle, this is real.' Pippa gave a tiny squeal.

'This is really happening?'

'Yes!'

Once again, they hugged each other tightly.

'Elle! This is fantastic news!'

Elle was sitting on Irene's settee, her feet tucked underneath her.

'I have so many questions. Do you know how long she's been looking for you?'

Elle's tears were threatening to fall at any moment but she squeezed her eyes together and took a deep breath. 'Ann, the lady from the Salvation Army, told me that her request was logged on the same day as mine – my birthday.'

'That just shows she's never forgotten you.' Irene wrapped her hands around Elle's.

'Why now though? Why after all these years has she only just decided to come looking for me?'

'That's a question you'll have to ask her. Maybe it's the right time in her life too. Everything happens for a reason.'

Elle nodded. 'Ann said that once I've read the letter – if we both are agreed – they can arrange a meeting for us.'

'How are you feeling about that?'

'Terrified. Excited. Hopefully the letter will arrive tomorrow if they've posted it First Class. I'm not sure I'll sleep tonight.'

'That may be a little difficult with all this on your mind.'

'I just keep thinking, do I look like her? Do we have the same mannerisms?'

'Even though the wait is hard, you'll soon know all the answers – and I'm here for you every step of the way.'

'Thank you.'

'What are you going to do about work tomorrow?'

'I'd like to stay home but I already feel like I've let Pippa and Aiden down by leaving early today.'

'Don't be daft – they'll understand,' she said. 'Does Aiden know the reason you left today?'

'He will now. I've told Pippa it was okay to tell him.'

Irene nodded. 'Good call.' She put her arms around Elle. 'Everything will be okay,' she promised.

'What're your plans for the rest of the day?' Elle asked, slowly pulling away.

'No plans whatsoever. I've a few errands to run but they can wait. Why, what are you thinking?'

'I'm thinking a walk along the river, catch the boat to Primrose Park and maybe treat ourselves to lunch at Starcross Manor?'

'Perfect. I'll go and wash my face and clean myself up.' Irene smiled warmly. 'Tomorrow will soon be here.'

'I know I shouldn't wish my life away,' said Elle, 'but this is one of those times when tomorrow can't come soon enough.'

Chapter Twenty-One

After they left Irene's house, they walked along the River Heart and caught the water taxi towards The Little Blue Boathouse. Roman, the skipper of the boat, tipped his cap as they stepped on board and took seats near the back. It was a short ride across the water and soon they were walking through the gates of Primrose Park. The weather had begun to change in the last couple of days, and even though there was still a slight chill in the air, the first signs of spring were beginning to burst through.

The entrance to the park was impressive, with two stone statues framing the wrought-iron gates, and the bandstand an iconic feature. They took the path leading through the oak trees, the daffodils adding pops of yellow and orange all around. 'This is one of my favourite times of year,' said Irene, standing still for a moment to watch two squirrels chase each other along the path.

They walked a little further. 'Even the pond looks like it's come alive this morning with the sun reflecting on the water,'

Irene said, leaning against the railing and watching a young family throw bread to the ducks.

'Do you think you'd like children one day?' she asked tentatively.

This was a question that Elle had often thought about and the simple answer was yes. Knowing that she had so much love to give and that her child would have a completely different upbringing from hers, she couldn't wait to enjoy the life journey of her own little human one day.

'Without a doubt,' she replied, smiling.

'I think you'd make a wonderful mother.'

'But I need to meet a lovely man to settle down with first.'

'It'll happen when you're least expecting it. It did for me,' Irene replied with a chuckle.

Elle smiled at Irene. 'Mint choc chip ice-cream has a lot to answer for.'

She grinned. 'It certainly does! I put on half a stone that summer visiting the ice-cream van that Neville worked in.'

Elle linked her arm through Irene's as they began to walk again.

'But it was worth it. Neville was helping his dad that summer. I can still picture his cheeky smile from the van window when he asked what ice-cream I wanted. Every time I saw him, I had swarms of butterflies, but tried to play it cool. I didn't think he'd even look in my direction.'

Elle smiled. 'Playing it cool is overrated.'

'The van was always parked over there.' Irene pointed to a clearing behind a well-tended garden. 'That garden hasn't always been there. It was once a purpose-built paddling pool, and that's where my friends and I spent most of our summers. We used to set up camp under that tree so we could watch Nev in the van.'

'Do you miss him?'

'Every day. It feels like there's a massive void in my life. People say it gets easier in time – and time's a great healer – but it still seems very raw to me.'

'I can't imagine.'

'Sometimes my dreams about him are so vivid that when I wake up, it takes me a minute to realise it was only a dream.'

Elle squeezed her arm.

'We had a wonderful life together, and I treasure that time. My heart will never soar for anyone else like it did for Neville.'

For a moment, they ambled along in silence, lost in their own thoughts, and then Elle spotted a familiar figure up ahead. Theo was giggling as a woman pushed him back and forth on the swing, his small hands gripping the rope for dear life.

'Do you know them?' asked Irene, following Elle's gaze.

The woman gave Theo one more huge push on the swing before perching on a bench next to a man Elle didn't recognise.

'That's Theo, Aiden's son, and I'm assuming that must be Theo's mum, Louisa.'

'Who's the man?'

'I have no idea but they seem close.' Elle watched as he placed his arm around Louisa's shoulder then nuzzled her neck. He whispered something in her ear, causing Louisa to throw her head back and laugh. They seemed very at ease in each other's company and only a few seconds later, he pulled Louisa towards him, cupped his hands around her face and kissed her deeply.

'Oh my,' Elle muttered, thinking about Aiden, who'd been so convinced she'd react badly if he started dating again. From where she was standing, it looked like Louisa had well and truly moved on.

'They don't look like just friends,' Irene commented wryly.

'I have to agree with you there,' Elle replied, just as Theo suddenly caught her eye. A huge grin spread across his face and he pointed at her.

Louisa stood up and glanced in their direction.

'I think we'd better introduce ourselves,' Irene said. 'Otherwise, she'll be wondering how Theo recognises you.'

Elle waved towards Theo.

'Hi,' she said, making eye contact with Louisa. 'I'm Elle – I work with Aiden at the library and had the chance to meet Theo and your parents when they visited. This is my mum, Irene.'

'Lovely to meet you both,' replied Louisa. The man sitting next to her didn't utter a word, giving just a half-hearted and somewhat awkward smile.

'Hello, little man,' Elle said, moving over to Theo and giving the swing a little push.

Immediately, he let out an infectious laugh. 'More!' he shouted as Elle gave him a couple more pushes.

'Not in work today?' Louisa asked.

'Day off,' replied Elle.

'It's a lovely day for it,' Louisa said, glancing up at the sky.

'Yes, it is. The weather certainly makes a difference. Anyway, we'll leave you to it. Enjoy the park, Lovely to meet you, Louisa.'

'You too,' she said and sat back down on the bench.

They could hear Theo's giggles fade away as they carried on walking along the path.

'Was it just me or was there a slightly uncomfortable atmosphere there?' Irene asked when they were finally out of earshot.

'You felt it too? I didn't know whether it was just my imagination acting up.'

Irene shook her head. 'She didn't introduce us to her friend.'

'Who clearly wasn't just a friend – which is very strange because Aiden told me that Louisa had suggested they give things another go.'

'Really?'

'Yes. He wanted to ask Pippa out, but he hasn't because Louisa has been very down about all the changes in her life, and he didn't want to cause her any more upset.'

'How lovely of him to put his life on hold and sacrifice his own feelings. But judging by what we've just witnessed, there's no need,' Irene observed, discreetly looking back over her shoulder. Elle followed her gaze to see the group now strolling towards the entrance of the park.

'Do you think I should say something to Aiden?'

'I think you're going to have enough to deal with over the next twenty-four hours. Concentrate on what's important in *your* life.'

'Hmmm, yes, I think you're probably right,' replied Elle, knowing she would be sitting by the letterbox until the letter from her biological mother arrived. Just at the very thought her heart began to race again.

Chapter Twenty-Two

E lle had been awake and staring at the clock for most of the night. She was willing the time to pass quickly, but of course it felt like the longest night ever. All she could think about was Cora Hansley. She wondered what sort of night she was having, knowing her letter was on its way to the daughter she gave up.

There were other thoughts also turning over in Elle's mind. What sort of life did Cora have and where did she live? Did she have a family of her own? Hopefully the answers to her questions would soon be answered.

Just past eight a.m. Pippa gave Elle a huge hug before she left for work, and told Elle to ring her the second she had any sort of news.

'You'll be okay?'

'Yes,' replied Elle, forcing a brightness into her voice that she didn't feel, knowing that no matter how hard she tried to hold it together she was soon going to be an emotional wreck.

As soon as Pippa left the house, Elle forced herself to eat a bowl of cereal even though she wasn't hungry, then took a quick shower. After that, all she could do was wait. Ten minutes later there was a knock at the door and she nearly jumped out of her skin. 'Recorded delivery,' she murmured, putting her hands on her chest. 'Of course, it will be recorded.' With her pulse racing she hurried to the front door to find Irene standing on the step smiling back at her.

'What are you doing here?' Elle asked, opening the door wide. 'You gave me the fright of my life. I thought you were the postman.'

'Oh my, I'm sorry. I didn't want you waiting on your own.' She kissed Elle's cheek then hung up her coat before settling on the chair in the living room.

'Thank you,' said Elle, relieved she didn't have to do this alone.

'You look absolutely exhausted,' Irene added. 'Did you get any sleep?'

'Not a wink.'

'Have you eaten?'

'I've managed a few mouthfuls of cereal but I don't have much of an appetite.'

Elle couldn't settle so she hovered at the window, hoping to glimpse the postman and willing him to hurry.

'It's like waiting for a kettle to boil.'

'Try and relax. The postman isn't going to get here any quicker. What time does he normally come?' asked Irene, her voice calm and soothing.

'I'm not sure as I'm usually at work during the week, but at weekends it can be any time before lunch.'

She smiled. 'Let's hope he'll soon be here and in the meantime let's try and keep your mind off the wait.'

Elle nodded, though that *was* all she was thinking about. 'Are you going to Eleni's hen-party next week?' she asked.

'I've got my invite.' She pointed to the invitation propped up next to the clock on the mantelpiece.

'Yes, I've already checked out the menu and the feathered beef has caught my eye; it sounds delicious.'

'I've not had a chance to look yet, but Pippa and I are going so you're more than welcome to come with us,' said Elle, switching on the TV and hoping that would distract her until she heard the clang of the letterbox. The news played out.

'It's always doom and gloom, isn't it? I think they should make it the law that one day a week, they only report good news – to give the country a bit of a lift,' Irene suggested.

'I think that sounds like an excellent plan.'

After making a cup of tea, they sat in silence watching the TV. Elle was lost in her own thoughts, not knowing what the letter was going to uncover. Sitting near to the window, she saw the familiar red post van park in its usual spot at the end of the road.

'He's here.'

Irene sat up and glanced out of the window. It felt like forever watching the postman deliver to the five houses before her on the street. They watched him walk up the steps then heard the letter box clang and the sound of the post falling onto the mat.

Neither of them moved. They stared at each other.

'I daren't look,' admitted Elle, feeling her heartbeat quicken. 'I actually feel sick.'

'Take some deep breaths,' encouraged Irene. 'Whenever you're ready. There's no rush.'

Elle didn't know what she was expecting to happen but once she began to read the letter, everything would become very real, very quickly. Standing up, she took a big breath and walked towards the hallway. Picking up the post she saw that there were two letters – the first a bank statement and the second an envelope with the Salvation Army logo printed on it. With a fast-beating heart, Elle returned to the living room. 'It's here.'

'Would you like me to stay or go?' asked Irene tentatively.

'Please stay.' Whatever Elle was about to discover, she wanted Irene by her side.

Sitting on the settee Elle opened the envelope. Inside, she found a smaller envelope and a document from the Salvation Army outlining the details of when Cora Hansley's request was logged and when they'd received the letter. The caseworker that Elle had been allocated had added a note saying that she would take care of any further correspondence or liaisons between the two of them.

Despite Elle's anxiety about its contents, actually holding a letter from her birth mother in her hand felt good. The writing on the envelope was small and neat. Her hand shaking, Elle opened it carefully, pulled out a sheet of cream-coloured paper and stared down at the words written on it. Overcome with emotion, her eyes blurred with tears and she found it difficult to focus.

Irene touched her arm and handed her a tissue. 'Here, take this. Do you want me to read it to you? Would that make it easier?'

Elle nodded and passed the letter to Irene without saying another word. She read it aloud.

Dear Eleanor,

I'm struggling as to how to begin this letter, and even as I write, the pain is twisting in my heart. Since the day we parted, you have always been in my life, my head, my heart, and not a day has passed without me thinking of you. I never thought I'd have the chance to write this letter to you, and I pray you find it in your heart to forgive me one day for the choice to give you up.

During the early nineties, I was in a stable relationship with a lovely man called Matt Harrison when my life took an unexpected twist. My parents – Jane and Mike Thomas – were tragically killed in a boating accident in the south of France, and from that moment on my life seemed to spiral out of control.

At the time, I worked three jobs trying to make ends meet while Matt worked on his novel, his dream being to become an author. He spent every hour he could tapping on his keyboard, waiting for that publishing deal to land. He was going to take the world by storm, but he never got a break and money was tight. Dreams weren't paying the rent.

We lived in a dingy flat in one of the less salubrious areas of Morley. Music would pound above our heads and we could hear arguments through the wafer-thin walls at all hours of the night. It really wasn't a nice place to live.

Some months, we had to skip the rent – and even meals at times. After a while, I began to resent the fact that I was working myself into the ground, out at all hours, whilst Matt stayed home, following his dream and not bringing in any money. I became more and more depressed.

At first, I was taking antidepressants I'd been prescribed by the doctor, but they weren't enough. My relationship with Matt was falling apart, and I began to siphon off the rent money to buy stronger drugs from a dealer who lived in the flat above us. Soon it was too late. I was an addict – I couldn't live without the pills.

Matt had no idea. He was too caught up in making a career for himself. He didn't notice my mood swings, or the fact I'd lost a couple of stone in weight, and I began to steal to keep the dealer off my back, but eventually I racked up a debt I couldn't pay back.

Things went from bad to worse and the dealer started to threaten *me. I knew that I could never pay the money back and being scared for my life I ran. I left Matt without telling him anything because I was so deeply ashamed. I never saw him again.*

When I left I didn't know I was pregnant and I lived on the streets, visiting soup kitchens and begging for food wherever possible, but stealing anything and everything to feed my addiction.

The evening of 2ⁿᵈ February was bitterly cold. I was slumped against the doorway of a café. It was after hours and the shutters were down. There wasn't a soul in sight when I started to experience pain like nothing I'd ever felt before. It was only when I got the urge to push that I realised I was about to give birth. There was a light on in the flat above the café and I screamed and banged on the door so loudly that the owner appeared. She had a baby on her hip, which she promptly took back upstairs, but when she came back a few minutes later, she was armed with blankets and a pillow and made me up a makeshift bed on the floor of the café. If it wasn't for her, I dread to think what would have happened. She rang for an ambulance but you were almost here.

Irene took a breather and looked across at Elle. 'How are you doing there?'

Elle took a moment. To hear about the tragic death of Cora's parents – her grandparents – was one thing, but discovering her mother had been terrified and all alone in the world and the fact that her father possibly didn't know she existed even now…

'It's strange to hear her address me by my proper name. No one has called me Eleanor for as long as I can remember.'

Irene gave Elle a smile. 'It's a beautiful name. Do you want me to carry on?'

Elle nodded.

You were born in the early hours of 2nd February. From what I could see, you were perfect – chubby even, which was a good sign considering I'd barely eaten for months.

You cried the moment you made an appearance and I was relieved. The lady gave me clean clothes – we were of a similar build – and she cleaned you up and wrapped you tightly in a shawl. I held you in my arms and hugged you tight while she made me some food.

The lady disappeared upstairs to check on her own child and it was then that I decided I couldn't take you back on the streets. You deserved a better life.

I scribbled a note on the order pad to look after my beautiful baby, whom I wished to name Eleanor. I told her you might need medical attention due to the drugs I'd taken and that I loved you. I laid you down on the floor and kissed you goodbye.

As I paused at the door, I could hear the sirens in the distance. I knew you were going to be safe. My heart was breaking, but I knew I was making the right decision. I couldn't take you with me. I needed to get myself clean. I came back to you one more time and whispered. 'I love you,' before disappearing into the night. But I never forgot you, and I celebrate your birthday every year.

It took me a while to get my life back on track. One cold evening, I'd ventured into a shelter and was recognised by one of the volunteers – an old friend of my mum's. She kindly took me in and looked after me. She transformed my life, got me clean and helped me to find a job. Then I met a wonderful man named George. We have a son together, and now, after all these years, I've finally shared my past with them both. Hopefully one day we'll all meet and we can make a fresh start.

When you've had time to digest all this, I hope you can find it in your heart to forgive me.

I have no idea how to finish this letter, but I hope it's not the end – only the beginning for the both of us.

All my love,
Cora x

Elle and Irene sat in silence, Elle's head whirling as she tried to digest all the information.

'I always thought the hardest part was not knowing, but I can't even imagine how hard it must have been, feeling that scared and addicted to drugs. Not knowing where you would be sleeping each night. I know what it's like to feel that you're in the big wide world on your own and it's a very lonely place to be without any real support.'

'I think Cora's been very brave to share all this with you,' responded Irene, 'especially about her addiction. She could have kept it to herself but instead she's been completely honest. And it just shows you're two remarkable individuals. You've both had an incredibly rough time in life, but you've persevered.'

Elle nodded.

'And now she has made a good life for herself and it sounds like she has a beautiful family. She wants to start again with you, which is wonderful.'

Elle took the letter from Irene and reread it herself. 'Matt Harrison. He has to be my father, right?'

'It sounds like that's possible. Where do you go from here?' Irene asked tentatively.

'I want to meet her if she's in agreement and I'd like to discover a little more about my father. Even if she never saw him again, she would know his date of birth, the area he could possibly be living in…' Elle glanced over the information from the Salvation Army. 'It says if I want to meet her then I can give the caseworker a call and she'll organise a time and place.'

'Whatever happens, I'm always here for you, Elle.'

'Thank you,' she said, picking up the phone and dialling the number on the letter.

'Good morning, Emily Kirk here. How may I help you?'

Elle took a deep breath. 'Hi, this is Elle Cooper, I've received and read the letter you forwarded to me and I'd like to arrange a time to meet my biological mother.'

Chapter Twenty-Three

At 6.45 p.m. Elle heard the front door open.

'Hi, honey, I'm home,' Pippa shouted, traipsing up the hallway towards the living room. She gave Elle a smile. 'I could murder a cuppa. Do you want one?'

'How was work?' Elle asked. She was curled up in the corner of the sofa, Cora Hansley's letter resting on her lap.

'Busy! All the posters and books arrived for Noah's book signing. I took it upon myself to order the flowers from Florrie and I bumped into Rona, who said she would be delighted to help with refreshments, cake and sandwiches. And the reason I'm late is because I've put up some of the posters around Heartcross.'

'You've certainly been earning your salary today. I should take a day off work more often.'

'Never mind work. I know you sent me a text to say the letter arrived but I want to hear everything.'

After making the tea Pippa sat down next to Elle. 'How are you feeling?'

'Battered, bruised, anxious, sad, happy… I think I've experienced every emotion possible this afternoon. I do now know how I started out in life, which has answered numerous questions, and I know that my mother loved me and thought she chose the best possible start for me.' Elle swallowed. 'I think she thought I would be adopted into a loving family and would want for nothing. I don't think she anticipated that I'd be passed from pillar to post through my childhood years. I'm not sure how she'll feel when she learns that bit of information, but she thought she was doing the right thing. Everything could have worked out so differently. It seems we both didn't have the best start.'

Elle handed Pippa the letter. 'Here, have a read.'

By the time Pippa finished she had tears in her eyes. 'I don't know what to think. It's a very emotional story and she clearly did love you.'

'It was just the wrong circumstances for her to be able to raise me herself.'

'Cora's life seemed to spiral out of control so quickly – it must have been hard losing her parents so suddenly and then having the constant worry about money. I wonder what happened to Matt Harrison. At what point did he realise she was never coming home?' added Pippa.

Elle had already asked those questions herself. This afternoon she'd googled Matt Harrison but, there were hundreds of men with the same name.

'It's too awful to even think about,' Pippa continued. 'Goodness knows what must have been running through his mind. Did he think she'd run off with someone else?'

'Maybe. I wonder if he tried to look for her,' added Elle. 'He might even have filed a missing-persons report.'

'Who knows? It wouldn't have been that hard to disappear

in those days, before everything was online and so easy to trace. And her state of mind must have been so unstable, dealing with drug addiction… And to run like that, she would have been constantly looking over her shoulder, petrified in case the dealer hunted her down.'

'I can't even imagine,' replied Elle, a lump forming in her throat. 'She must have been so scared.'

Pippa nodded. 'There's no address on this letter,' she suddenly exclaimed, flipping it over.

'I know. Her address is deliberately kept off it in case I make the decision not to make any further contact.'

'So at this stage we don't have any idea where she lives? I'm assuming it must be this country?'

'I'm assuming that too.'

'At least Cora has finally found happiness. She has George and a son. And you've finally found happiness with Irene. What happens now?' she asked curiously.

'I've already rung the caseworker and asked her to set up a meeting for us.'

'All systems go then?'

'All systems go,' Elle repeated.

As they finished their tea, Pippa's phone pinged from the table.

'Aww,' she said, glancing at her message. 'That reminds me – I have news! Aiden asked me on a date.' Pippa beamed from ear to ear. 'That's him texting now.'

'No way! I'm so happy for you. I do think you make a lovely couple. And I hope you let me return the favour you did me.'

'What favour?' asked Pippa, looking puzzled.

'I'm going to give you a makeover and make you look like a porcelain doll, and back-comb your hair so much it makes your eyes water.'

'Not a chance, I'm not that stupid.' Pippa grinned. 'However, you can share a glass of wine with me whilst I get ready. It's the day after Eleni's hen party.'

'Deal,' replied Elle.

Chapter Twenty-Four

'How do I look?' asked Pippa, swishing her hair over her shoulder before placing one hand on her hip and twirling to the side.

'I'd say you're dressed to impress,' Elle said with admiration.

'You don't think this lipstick is a little too much? It's not my usual colour.'

'It's a little on the bright side but, as usual, you manage to carry it off.'

Pippa pouted at Elle, then blew her a kiss.

Tonight was Eleni's hen party, and Elle looked forward to seeing everyone.

'The taxi is picking us up in half an hour – don't you need to get ready?'

'Hey, cheeky!' Elle threw a cushion at her. 'I *am* ready.' She was dressed in a ditsy floral dress that fell to her ankles, a cute cardigan and her ever-so-faithful white Converse.

Pippa looked her up and down. 'You need to show a bit of flesh and pop some heels on.'

'I am absolutely fine the way I am. Did you ever find out where the boys were off to on the stag?'

'No,' Pippa replied. 'I couldn't get Aiden to spill the beans.'

'Talking of Aiden, it's your date tomorrow, isn't it?'

'Yes, at his suggestion, we're going to the cinema, but he was a little strange when he asked me…' Pippa paused.

'Strange in what way?'

'He told me not to tell anyone.' She raised her eyebrows.

'Whyever not?' Elle asked.

'The only explanation he offered was that Louisa is struggling with life and he doesn't want to upset her, which it may if it gets out. I know it's commendable that he's thinking about someone else's feelings, but I want to shout it from the rooftops. Either he's moved on or he hasn't. I really don't want to get caught up in a love triangle. All I want is a drama-free life.'

'How things have changed,' Elle remarked with a grin, wondering if this was her cue to share that she'd seen Louisa with a man in the park.

'He kind of said that she keeps suggesting they give it another go and that she still has feelings for him.'

'Really?'

'Don't sound too surprised – he is quite a catch, you know.'

'It's not that.'

Pippa had been fiddling with a loose thread on the hem of her skirt, but looking up she caught Elle's gaze. 'What is it then?'

'I may be speaking out of turn but…'

'Go on.'

'Irene and I saw Louisa at the park. I didn't know who she was, but Theo recognised me and we wandered over to them.'

'What's so unusual about that? Little kids like going to the park.'

'It was the fact she wasn't on her own.'

'What do you mean?'

'She was sitting on the bench kissing another man, and when we went across to introduce ourselves, she didn't introduce him.'

Pippa raised her eyebrows.

'It's possible that Louisa isn't struggling as much as she's making out.'

'Mmm, it sounds like a case of she doesn't want him but doesn't want anyone else to have him either. Do you think she's trying to make Aiden feel guilty for whatever reason?'

'It's possible, but who knows?'

Elle glanced at her watch then looked out of the window. They still had a few minutes before the taxi was due.

'Changing the subject,' Pippa announced, swigging the rest of her drink back as Elle did the same. 'Here's to a good night!'

After collecting Irene, they travelled to a popular French bistro on the edge of town. It was the perfect place for Eleni's hen do, sophisticated yet inexpensive, with hearty traditional food and a stunning art deco interior.

'Oh look, there's Jack, Aiden and Wilson standing outside the bistro,' Irene said, leaning forward and paying the taxi driver.

'I wonder what they're doing here,' murmured Pippa, trying to step out of the taxi in a sophisticated manner, which was a little tricky given she was wearing the shortest skirt possible. She tried to pull it down.

'There's no point trying to cover yourself up now,' whispered Elle.

'I just feel a little self-conscious. I wasn't expecting to see my ex standing with my future date on the street.'

'Ex is pushing it a bit – you only had a one-nighter with him.'

'Shush! You know what I mean.'

'Hi, Irene, ladies,' Wilson greeted them, avoiding eye contact with Pippa.

Was it Elle's imagination or was Aiden also avoiding eye contact with Pippa? There seemed to be a strange atmosphere lingering in the air. Elle looked at Pippa, who raised an eyebrow.

'We've just been for a quick drink with Eleni, Mim and Mum. There's a whole group of them inside,' added Wilson, still not looking in Pippa's direction.

'Am I invisible?' whispered Pippa.

'I think it's about time you men disappear,' Elle ordered, shooing them away. 'This is a girls only night.'

'Ha, we know when we're not wanted.' Jack grinned as he patted Aiden and Wilson on the back. 'Don't you worry, we're on our way.'

As soon as they were out of earshot Pippa asked, 'Was that just my imagination or have I been mugged off?'

'Mugged?' Irene asked with a puzzled look on her face. 'I didn't see anyone pinch your handbag.'

'Mugged off – it means ignored, left hanging,' Elle explained, watching Irene enter the restaurant as she and Pippa hung back.

'I was, wasn't I?' Pippa looked worried. 'Did you see Aiden's body language?'

It wasn't like Aiden to be so aloof – in fact it was very out of character. He'd stood on one side, facing away from her with his feet planted firmly on the ground and his hands stuffed in his pockets, and had mostly looked in the opposite direction.

'I'm confused. The other day he was asking me out on a date and now he's completely ignoring me in public. What's going on?'

'I've no idea. Do you want me to text and ask him?' Elle offered, not knowing what else to say.

'Oh God, it's Wilson, isn't it? They've been talking. Do you think he's told Aiden we spent the night together? Aiden will never come near me now.' Her eyes were wide, worry written all over her face. 'I knew this would cause a situation.'

It was a thought that had already crossed Elle's mind but she hadn't wanted to say anything. 'Let's not jump to any conclusions. Try not to worry about it now – there's nothing we can do about it tonight,' she soothed, looking through the window to see Irene holding up a wine glass and madly waving at them to come inside.

'We best get ourselves in there – otherwise they'll be talking about us. So, forget Aiden, forget Wilson and don't let it spoil the evening. Tonight is all about Eleni.'

'Agreed,' replied Pippa, but the look on her face was telling a different story. She reluctantly followed Elle into the restaurant with one last glance over her shoulder but the boys were now nowhere in sight.

———

An hour later, after a delicious banquet, Elle was fit to burst and couldn't manage another morsel.

'Dessert, anyone?' Eleni chirped, patting her stomach. 'I'm

taking advantage of this eating-for-two lark! I don't know or care what is fat or what is baby!'

'Not sure what my excuse is,' Elle replied, laughing before patting her own stomach. She glanced over at Pippa, who'd been particularly quiet throughout the whole meal. She'd played with her food on her plate, drunk copious amounts of wine and hadn't stopped messing around with her phone.

'Hey, are you okay?' Elle whispered.

'Not really – I feel sick to my stomach.'

'Why, what's going on?'

'Aiden is reading my texts but isn't answering them.'

'There could be a number of reasons: lack of signal, caught up with the boys as they're on a night out...'

'And so are we but if someone wants to text you, they will.'

'I know it's easier said than done but you've got to try and put it out of your mind until you can have a proper conversation with him. Aiden has to be in touch at some point – he's invited you to the cinema tomorrow.'

'That's true.'

'Sit tight, turn your phone off and come and join the party.'

'It's not exactly rocking though, is it?'

Elle shot Pippa a stop-blooming-moaning look and put a smile on her face.

'I think you'll find Isla has some news but you've been too preoccupied to listen.'

Pippa looked up. 'Anything interesting?'

Isla and Felicity were sitting at the opposite end of the table, grinning like Cheshire cats. Isla was clutching a leaflet and held it up for Pippa to see. 'Ta-dah!' she shouted down the table.

'What does it say?' Pippa queried.

'Ladies night!' confirmed Florrie.

Isla had a mischievous look on her face.

'Who's up for seeing Dangler Dan in all his glory?'

'Dangler Dan? Such a classy name for a stripper,' joked Elle.

'Did someone mention a stripper?' Suddenly Pippa came alive and grabbed hold of Elle's arm like an excited child. 'Did I hear you correctly?'

Elle shook her head in jest. 'Trust you to start paying attention now.'

'You didn't think this was it, did you?' Eleni said, laughing and pointing towards Pippa. 'A sophisticated meal followed by cups of coffee and mints?'

'Well, I did wonder!'

'I may be pregnant but I've not developed baby brain yet!'

'I knew you wouldn't let us down, girl. The Full Monty, now that's more like it!' Pippa exclaimed, clapping her hands together.

'I'm not sure if it's The Full Monty,' Mim added quickly. 'More like a local lad trying to earn a few extra quid by taking his kit off.'

'And if you look outside now, you'll see our carriage awaits!' Mim announced.

Everyone sitting at the table turned towards the window and gasped.

'Only the best for my daughter,' she said, smiling, and handed her credit card to the waiter. 'And tonight's meal is on me!'

One by one, they thanked Mim before quickly finishing off the rest of the wine.

'Now let's get this show on the road!' exclaimed Felicity.

They all grabbed their bags and walked excitedly out of the bistro.

'This night might not turn out so badly after all,' Pippa

said, smiling as she once again wrestled with her skirt before climbing into the back of the limo.

'Grab yourself a glass of champers, girls,' ordered Eleni. 'And would someone be kind enough to pour me an orange juice?'

Chapter Twenty-Five

The limo pulled up outside the club, where there was already a queue of shrieking, scantily dressed girls with their arms linked, tottering on their heels.

'They'll catch their death dressed like that,' observed Irene.

'It makes me cold just looking at them,' added Jenny.

Both women gripped the lapels of their coats tighter.

'You know you've definitely reached the next stage of your life when leaving home without your coat is not an option,' Elle said, giving a twirl in her coat. There was no way she had any intention of being cold on the way home.

The hen group joined the back of the line and chatted amongst themselves as the queue began to move slowly forward.

'I can't believe it's only going to cost me ten pounds to watch some dishy man get his kit off on a Friday night,' Pippa marvelled as she rummaged through the loose change in her purse.

'I've happily got to my time of life without ever seeing a

strip show,' admitted Mim, with a twinkle in her eye, 'but I have to admit I'm a little intrigued.'

Eleni chuckled. 'I can't believe I'm actually queuing up with my mother to watch this kind of show!'

Once inside the foyer, they could hear the music blaring from a room at the far end of the club. An unsmiling woman sat behind a dated oak ticket booth, her hair harshly scraped into a bun and secured by a black velvet scrunchie. Electric blue eyeshadow covered her lids and thick red blusher striped her cheeks.

'Are you sure we aren't coming to watch *Rocky Horror*?' Pippa whispered in Elle's ear.

'That's next month,' replied Elle, nodding to the tatty poster pinned up behind the woman.

'You must be over eighteen to enter. Prepare for nudity. No touching the act and no photography allowed,' she intoned as she blew a bubble with her gum and slapped a pink ticket down on the counter. 'Ten pounds please.' She held out her bony hand.

Once everyone had paid, they entered the club.

'Are we all ready?' Pippa asked, clapping her hands together. 'Let's go find out what Dangler Dan has to offer!'

Following Mim, they filed into a packed, sweaty room that was a sea of pink feather boas and flashing deely boppers, which were bouncing along to the song 'I Predict a Riot'.

'If it wasn't for our pregnant hen, I could cause a riot,' Pippa giggled.

'Behave! Actually, have you seen Eleni? She looks rather pale,' observed Elle.

'Possibly tired,' suggested Pippa.

'I can hear you! Honestly, I'm fine, really. I'm just grateful that you haven't made me dress up in a stupid outfit or pinned learner plates all over me,' chipped in Eleni, pointing towards another hen that hadn't escaped the embarrassing torture.

'There's time yet – let's see what I have in here…' Felicity pretended to rummage in her bag. 'Only joking!'

Everyone's spirits were high and after they'd managed to fight their way to the bar they found a vacant space to stand.

'I think I need to sit down,' Eleni said, fanning herself with a beer mat while Mim grabbed a chair from a nearby table. 'It's so hot in here. I'm going to overheat.'

'Here, have this,' Mim offered.

'It's going to get even hotter when Dangler Dan makes an appearance,' added Pippa, taking a sip from her wine glass.

The music suddenly stopped and the lights dimmed. There was a loud cheer and as the waiting crowd began to chant, an unruly group of women surged towards the stage.

Pippa raised an eyebrow, laughing as she grabbed Elle's hand and pulled her towards the crowd.

'What are you doing?'

'We're getting the best view.'

Elle snagged a glance over her shoulder. Isla, Jenny, Irene, Eleni and Mim were still standing at the back of the room, while Florrie and Felicity had totally disappeared.

'Where have those two gone?' Elle murmured, standing on her tiptoes and trying to spot them over a sea of deely boppers.

'Forget them. Come on!' They carried on snaking their way through the crowd until they managed to land a prime spot right at the front of the stage.

'Why are we waiting, why-y are we waiting?' the crowd chanted, the whole room vibrating as everyone stamped their feet.

'So will Dangler Dan be a fireman, a construction worker or a—'

As the music struck up and the curtains lifted, Pippa screamed. 'Policeman!'

Elle laughed at the helmet tipped over his eyes and the huge truncheon he carried in his hand. He'd packed his muscly upper half into a very tight shirt and his thighs were bulging through his trousers.

'Now that's what you call orgasmic,' stated Pippa.

'I have to admit he's rocking that look.' Elle nodded approvingly.

'He is undeniably a damn fine-looking man.' Pippa observed, not taking her eyes off him.

He began to slowly unbutton his shirt and when it finally hit the floor, the girls went wild.

'The hormones in here are on fire. If he's not careful, they'll be carrying his charred body from that stage before this song finishes,' Elle exclaimed.

He turned to face the crowd. 'Off, off, off,' they screamed as he launched his hat into the crowd.

As the hat sailed over them, their eyes followed it and they watched a group of women push and shove each other to claim the prize.

'Jeez, it's carnage – they were nearly fighting for real!' Elle exclaimed.

'Look!' Pippa pointed and the pair of them burst out laughing as Felicity gave them the thumbs-up from the side of the stage where she was proudly standing, wearing the helmet.

'I might have known!'

Looking back towards the stage, Elle said, 'He reminds me of someone.'

'I know, I thought the same,' mused Pippa. 'I don't usually forget a face.'

Elle's breath caught in her throat as she grabbed Pippa's arm.

'It's him!'

Pippa gasped as the same realisation hit her. 'It is!'

The incredibly attractive man from the 425 bus was now standing in front of them wearing nothing but a red thong.

'It looks like he's been reunited with his rucksack!' Elle laughed.

Dan – aka the man from the bus – moved to the front of the stage, and the women started shoving each other, their hands thrust forward trying to grab hold of his leg. His eyes twinkled at every girl in the room.

'Look at them – they're falling at his feet,' observed Elle.

'It's like he's seducing them with his eyes.'

'And the rest!'

Dan hooked his finger under the red thong and pulled it down slowly, gently teasing the crowd. 'They're like a pack of wild animals!'

He turned his back towards the crowd and glanced over his shoulder. Elle's eyes caught his and one side of his mouth lifted in a sheepish smile before he shot her and Pippa a cheeky grin. They both squealed with laughter.

'I think he's recognised us!' Pippa shrieked.

'I think you might be right!'

The crowd was still yelling 'OFF, OFF, OFF.'

Dan faced the screaming girls and whipped off his thong. Elle had never heard noise like it. The lights went down and the room fell into darkness. It was at that moment that Elle felt something being thrust into her hand as boisterous applause filled the room and the lights snapped back on. The stage was empty and Dan was gone. The crowd began to disperse in every direction.

'That was the best half-hour I've had in a while. What have you there?' Pippa asked, looking down at Elle's hand.

'A card,' Elle said, flipping it over and reading it. 'A business card – for Daniel Jones, Entertainer.'

'He was definitely that. Where did you get it from?'

'Someone put it in my hand when the lights went out.'

Pippa cocked an eyebrow. 'There's some writing on it,' she said, squinting at the handwriting.

'What does it say?'

'Meet me at the stage door in twenty minutes.'

Pippa grabbed hold of Elle's arm and squealed, 'Elle Cooper! Grab your coat – you've pulled!'

Chapter Twenty-Six

Once the performance had finished, another set of doors at the back of the room was flung open, leading to a disco that was now open to the general public.

'Shall we go for a dance?' Pippa asked, grabbing her drink.

'It would be rude not to, but where is everyone?' Elle asked, spinning her head around and looking at the crowd of people.

'What do you mean? This place is packed.'

'I mean, where's the gang gone?'

Pippa pointed. 'There's Florrie and Felicity, they're already in the disco.'

'I actually think I need some air,' said Elle, suddenly feeling hot and bothered.

'Ha! You just want to see if Mr Dan appears at the stage door in erm … ten minutes' time now. The clock is ticking.' Pippa tapped her watch.

'Don't be ridiculous,' Elle protested, delving into her bag and searching for her phone.

'I bet he doesn't give his card out to just anyone.'

'I bet he blooming does!'

'Yes, you may be right,' Pippa replied, laughing.

'Six missed calls from Irene!' Elle exclaimed, quickly swiping the screen so she could read the text message she'd sent.

'What does it say?' Pippa asked, looking over her shoulder at the screen.

'Irene, Mim and Rona have taken an early dart.'

'Aww, that's a shame. So, that leaves Eleni, Isla and Jenny unaccounted for.'

They both scanned the room but they couldn't spot any of them in the mass of writhing bodies.

'Maybe they're in the toilet.'

'Possibly.'

Feeling a tap on her shoulder, Elle spun round to see a panic-stricken, pale-faced Jenny standing behind her.

'You need to come.'

Elle and Pippa both looked at each other. 'Whatever's the matter?' asked Elle.

'It's Eleni. She's feeling unwell. Stomach pains.'

Hurrying towards the foyer, Elle spotted Eleni leaning against the wall, clutching her stomach. She cried out. 'The pain is getting worse.'

'Do you think it's the baby?' Elle asked.

All Eleni could manage was a nod.

'Okay, deep breaths and don't panic. Has someone phoned an ambulance?'

'I just want Jack.'

'I've tried to ring Jack,' added Isla. 'But it just goes to voicemail.'

'Pippa, phone an ambulance,' Elle instructed then looked back towards Eleni. 'Don't worry, we'll find him.'

Pippa strode over to the hatch and asked the cashier the full address of the club, relaying the information down the phone. Once the ambulance was on its way, she hung up.

'Jenny, can you try and ring Wilson and leave him a message? And Pippa, try Aiden too.'

They both nodded.

'I think I'm going to be sick,' Eleni blurted.

'Okay, do you think it would help if we moved you outside or are you more comfortable here?'

'I need some fresh air.'

'We can manage that,' Elle said softly. 'Jenny, can you grab a chair from over there so Eleni will be able to sit down outside?'

Eleni was doubled over in pain, her head bent low, her hands cradling her stomach. Elle carefully wrapped her arm around her and they slowly walked towards the exit. Once they were outside, they waited for Jenny to appear with a chair.

'Here's Jenny and Pippa now.'

Jenny placed the chair in a doorway further down the street from the entrance to the club and Pippa wrapped a coat around Eleni's shoulders.

'The ambulance won't be long now.'

Eleni perched on the edge of the chair and they all stood on the pavement in silence, praying everything was going to be okay.

Eleni whimpered. 'The pain is getting worse.'

Elle glanced up the road for any sign of the ambulance but she couldn't see anything.

'I wish it would hurry up,' Jenny whispered in Elle's ear.

'Any news from Jack or Wilson?' Elle asked.

Pippa checked the phone and shook her head. 'No, nothing as yet.'

'Does anyone know which club they've gone to?'

'No,' Pippa answered.

'Please don't let me lose the baby, please don't let me lose the baby,' Eleni muttered over and over. Elle watched in horror as Eleni's face crumpled and all the colour drained from her skin. She gripped the side of the chair and began to sob. 'I think I'm bleeding,' she whispered.

Just then they heard voices filtering through a door behind them.

'What's this place?' Jenny asked, looking up at the sign above their heads.

'Stage door,' Elle said as the phone in Pippa's hand started ringing.

'It's Jack,' Pippa exclaimed, pushing the phone into Elle's hands. 'You speak to him.'

Elle put the phone to her ear and her mouth went dry. 'Jack, it's Elle.' Her eyes filled with tears. 'We're waiting for an ambulance. It's Eleni...'

'Jack is going to meet us at the hospital. He's on his way now,' she reassured Eleni after hanging up the call.

'At last!' Jenny exclaimed. 'I can hear the sirens.'

At first, they seemed miles away but they soon became louder and louder.

'They're nearly here – not long now. Hang on in there,' Elle said.

Eleni couldn't speak; she just clutched her stomach.

'Mim! We haven't phoned Mim!' Pippa cried, taking the phone back and quickly scrolling through Elle's address book. 'I'll ring her now.'

'It's here,' Elle relayed, relieved to see the ambulance

speeding down the road towards the club. Jenny stood on the edge of the pavement, waving her arms frantically in the air, hoping the paramedics would see her. A crowd had started to gather on the pavement, and there were hushed whispers as the ambulance drew to a halt. The sirens were switched off but the blue lights still whirled.

The doors swung open and a paramedic made his way over to Eleni.

'She's pregnant,' Jenny announced immediately.

'And I think I'm bleeding,' Eleni sobbed.

His manner was calm as he asked Eleni a series of questions before taking her blood pressure and strapping her to a chair.

'You're in the best possible hands,' Elle tried to reassure her.

'Please can you come with me in the ambulance?' Eleni asked.

'Of course.'

The paramedic lifted her into the back of the ambulance and started hooking her up to a machine.

Elle turned back to Jenny and Pippa. 'If I go in the ambulance, are you all okay to follow in a taxi?'

'Yes, of course,' they said in unison.

'Can you pass me my bag?' Elle asked, nodding towards the chair in front of the stage door. Right at that moment, the door opened and a group of girls who were hovering nearby started squealing as they recognised Dan stepping onto the street. His eye caught Elle's then his expression quickly turned to one of concern as he clocked the ambulance.

'Are you ready?' the ambulance driver asked Elle, ushering her inside. Grabbing her bag, she glanced back at Dan and noticed someone else standing next to him. She did a double take as her eyes locked with Noah Jones's. He was standing only a few steps away from her.

'Elle,' he mouthed, but she didn't have time to respond. The ambulance door was slammed shut and they sped off towards the hospital, sirens blaring.

Chapter Twenty-Seven

As soon as they arrived at the hospital, they whisked Eleni off up the corridor and into a room out of sight. She'd spent the journey with her eyes shut tight and hadn't spoken. Elle kept hold of her hand the whole time. Even though Elle hoped she was wrong, there were signs that Eleni might have already miscarried.

Pippa and Jenny arrived five minutes after the ambulance and found Elle in the waiting room, holding a cup of coffee. Mim and Jack were both on their way.

'I don't know what to say,' Pippa said softly.

Jenny shook her head. 'Me neither.'

'Jack should be here soon. Has anyone heard from him since he jumped in the taxi?' asked Elle.

Pippa pointed. 'He's here now.'

Jack rushed through the doors, quickly followed by Aiden and Wilson.

'Where is she?' he demanded. His cheeks were flushed and he was close to tears.

Aiden and Wilson lingered behind him.

'They've taken her through to a room. I'll let the nurse know you're here,' Jenny said, patting his arm and hurrying over to the reception desk at the far end of the room.

'How is she?' Tears brimmed in his eyes.

'She's in a lot of pain. One minute she was okay and the next...'

'I feel so helpless,' he murmured.

Jenny hurried back over to them. 'The nurse is coming now and she'll take you to Eleni. In fact, here she is.'

They all watched Jack disappear up the corridor.

'This is not a good end to the night.' Wilson kissed his mum on the cheek and sat down on the chair next to her.

None of them knew what to say. All they could do was wait.

They sat in silence for twenty minutes before Jenny made a suggestion. 'Why don't you boys get yourselves home? You aren't going to be able to do anything here, and if there's any news, we'll be in touch.'

Aiden began flicking through his wallet. 'I've got enough cash to get us all home. What do you think?'

Wilson gazed up from his chair. 'I'm not sure. I feel like we should stay.'

'Honestly, that's very kind but there's no need. Go home and get some rest. Mim will be here shortly and she doesn't need all of us hanging around.'

Pippa rubbed a weary hand over her face. 'I'm feeling tired too. Would anyone mind if I travelled back with the boys?'

'No, not at all. You three go.'

'Aiden, Wilson, is that okay with you?' Pippa asked.

'Of course,' Wilson replied.

'There's a taxi rank just outside.' Aiden turned towards Elle. 'Please let us know if there's any news.'

'I will – I promise.'

'This is awful, isn't it?' Jenny said once they were alone. Her eyes glistened with tears. 'I feel so helpless. This was meant to be a night to remember and now it's one for all the wrong reasons.'

'Do you want another coffee?' asked Elle.

Jenny shook her head. 'No, thank you, I'm fine.'

Elle noticed a tear run down Jenny's cheek and passed her a tissue.

'Thank you.'

Jenny seemed lost in her own thoughts and Elle wondered if she'd possibly been through the same situation in the past.

Twenty minutes later they were still waiting in silence. Then finally the door at the end of the corridor swung open and the sound of footsteps could be heard. Elle's eyes met Jack's and immediately she knew it wasn't good news.

He stood in front of them. His voice was quiet. 'She's lost the baby.'

Elle squeezed her eyes shut as Jenny stood up and wrapped her arms around Jack. Jack sobbed.

Once Jenny pulled away, Elle hugged Jack too. 'I'm so sorry. I don't even know what to say, as nothing will make it feel better.'

'Just having my friends with me is a help. Thank you for travelling with Eleni in the ambulance. You're a good friend, Elle.'

'You don't need to thank me. Anyone would have done the same.'

'She's finally drifted off to sleep.'

'How are you feeling?'

'Numb' was all he could say as he perched on the edge of the chair.

'Shall I get you a coffee?' Jenny asked.

He nodded and she walked off down the corridor towards the coffee machine.

'They said they don't know why it happens – it just does,' Jack said, sounding completely defeated. 'We didn't plan to have a baby so early on, but that doesn't mean I hadn't got my head around being a dad.'

'I know,' Elle replied sympathetically.

Jenny returned from the coffee machine and handed him a cup. 'Thank you,' he said. 'And please, get yourselves home. There's nothing anyone can do here.'

'Do you want us to fetch you anything?' asked Jenny.

'No, I'm fine. Mim should be here any second, and she's picked us up a few bits and pieces – in fact here she is now.'

They all looked up to see Mim hurrying through the doors of the hospital. The second she locked eyes with Jack he shook his head. 'We've lost the baby,' he murmured, the tears still falling. Taking him in her arms, she whispered, 'I'm so sorry, Jack.'

Elle looked at Jenny, who nodded towards the door. They slipped away quietly, leaving Jack and Mim in a tight embrace of grief.

Chapter Twenty-Eight

E lle and Jenny travelled back home in a taxi together. They sat in silence for the whole journey – there was nothing more they could do or say. When the taxi pulled up outside Elle's house, they hugged each other and said goodnight.

As Elle stepped into the house, she saw that Pippa had been kind enough to leave the living room light on for her, which Elle switched off before wearily climbing the stairs to bed. She peered around Pippa's bedroom door to see she was fast asleep. After getting changed for bed, Elle opened her phone. She had only two per cent battery left. Her thoughts turned back to the second before the ambulance doors were shut, when her gaze had locked with Noah's. She didn't have a clue why he was there, but he'd recognised her, he'd said her name. She loaded up his socials, wondering if he'd sent her a message or if there might be any posts explaining why he was there, but as soon as his profile loaded, the phone died.

Exhausted, she put her phone on charge and slipped under

the duvet. The moment her head hit the pillow, Elle was asleep.

When she woke the next morning, her mood was sombre and her thoughts immediately turned to Eleni and Jack. It had been such an awful end to what should have been a lovely fun evening. Hearing a gentle rap on the door, she looked up as Pippa popped her head around the door with two mugs of tea. 'I took a punt you were back. I thought you might like one of these.'

'Thank you.' Elle sat up in bed and clasped one of the mugs. Pippa slid into the bed next to her.

'What do you say in situations like this?' murmured Pippa.

Elle shook her head. 'I'll text Jack in a little while to see if there's anything we can do, but in situations like this, you always feel helpless. It'll be something they need to deal with together.'

'Why do bad things happen to nice people?'

Elle shrugged. 'Sometimes life is very cruel.'

They sipped their tea for a moment. 'How was your journey home with the lads?'

Pippa sighed. 'Strained. Aiden ignored me for most of the journey and just fiddled about on his phone. I tried to make small talk but that's exactly what it was – I'd ask a question and he'd answer in a few words or less. Other than that, we travelled home in silence.'

'What was Wilson doing at this point?'

'He was resting his head against the window with his eyes closed, but I'm pretty sure he was just pretending to be asleep to avoid having to make conversation. The taxi dropped him off first…'

'Which just left you and Aiden in the taxi alone.'

'Yes, so I took the opportunity to ask him if something was wrong and it was just like we'd feared.'

'He knows you slept with Wilson.'

Pippa nodded. 'Yes. Apparently, Wilson confided in Jack that we'd spent the night together and that he wanted to see me again. Then, last night in the pub, Jack asked Wilson how we were getting on.'

'In front of Aiden?'

'Yes, which was a little unfortunate, and as you can imagine, Aiden wasn't very impressed with me. I tried to explain it was just one of those things, a spur-of-the-moment decision, but he just stared resolutely in the other direction until the taxi pulled up outside our house. It was awful. If I could turn back time…'

'But remember, you haven't done anything wrong. If you wanted to be with Wilson, you could be. You're not, because you prefer Aiden.'

'I do feel crappy about it all though.'

'It's just really bad timing.'

'And anyway, Elle Cooper,' Pippa said, leaning forward and picking up the business card from the bedside table, 'I think we need to have a chat about this card and the sudden appearance of Mr Noah Jones last night.'

'At first, I thought I was hallucinating; I even did a double take! He was definitely there, wasn't he? I didn't just imagine it?'

Pippa passed Elle the business card. 'He was definitely there. You're really no detective, are you?'

'What do you mean?'

'Look at his business card! Noah and Dan have one thing in common,' Pippa shared.

'Hopefully not a red thong.'

Pippa rolled her eyes. 'Their surname!'

Elle looked at the card. 'Brothers? Maybe?' she said, amazed. 'That would explain why he was there last night.'

'Let's have a look at his posts from last night,' Pippa suggested, unplugging Elle's phone from the charger.

'I really do need to set up a passcode.' Elle nudged Pippa's arm.

Pippa searched through Noah's socials. 'Here you go. Instagram. There's a photo of him and Dan captioned: *The boys are back in town.*'

Pippa studied the screen. 'That's the club we were at last night. Look – that's the same bar.'

'He mouthed my name just as the ambulance doors shut. What happened after it pulled away?' Elle asked.

'A group of girls surrounded him and Dan. They were all chanting Dan's name as Jenny and I jumped into a taxi and followed the ambulance to the hospital. I think you should message him. You've got nothing to lose.'

'And say what?'

'Actually, I think you need to check your notifications first. You have an unread message.' Pippa passed the phone to Elle.

Elle clicked on the arrow in the corner. 'It's from Noah.'

Elle stared at the screen. It read:

Are you okay? What was with the ambulance? Noah x

'Answer him.'

Elle thought for a moment and then typed:

Yes, all OK. The ambulance was for a friend.

'You can't leave it there,' Pippa insisted, reading the message. 'You need to ask him a question to keep the conversation going.'

'I'll just add … I was surprised to see you there?'

'Good plan – we might discover if our suspicions are true and he is, in fact, related to Dan.'

Elle's phone pinged.

'That's quick by anyone's standards. Well?' Pippa asked impatiently. 'Is it from him?'

'Yes.' Elle read his message. 'He says that he hopes my friend is okay, and yes, he's in town visiting his parents. He was at the club last night to see his brother and apparently he noticed me from backstage during the performance.'

'This is sounding very good,' Pippa interrupted.

'He gave Dan the business card to put in my hand when the lights went out as he assumed I'd lost his last one.' Elle's eyes widened and she bit her lip to try and tame her smile.

Pippa raised her eyebrows. 'There you go. He wants you to get in touch. He's clearly been thinking about you as much as you've been thinking about him.'

'You can't assume that from that message.'

'Yes, you can. He's given you his business card … again. He wants you to ring him.'

Elle lifted her hair off her neck and twisted it into a bun, then let it cascade back over her shoulders while she pondered. 'Maybe.'

'There's no maybe about it. Why don't you just add, "It was good to see you last night, if only for a split second"?' Pippa encouraged.

Elle typed the message and hit send. She had nothing to lose.

They both stared at the phone like it was about to explode – and then there was nothing.

Elle sighed. 'Maybe that was a little too keen and we've frightened him away now.'

'It's only been a couple of seconds. He might have nipped to make a drink or is having a shower. He might even be working.'

'On a Sunday?' Elle replied, swallowing her disappointment.

'He's a writer, isn't he? He might be up to his eyes in edits or something.'

'More like back to bed with a girlfriend for lazy Sunday sex.'

Pippa tutted and rolled her eyes dramatically. 'Such a pessimist!'

They both jumped as the phone beeped.

'Ha! This time it's my phone,' Pippa said, taking it from the pocket of her PJs.

'Who is it?'

'Aiden,' she said, slowly swiping the screen.

'And it says?'

'"Are you still up for the cinema?1.30 p.m.?"' Pippa read.

'See!'

'There isn't even an apology for his behaviour last night.' She turned the phone towards Elle.

'Okay, maybe he thinks it's six of one, half a dozen of the other. Here's the thing – he still wants to go. I think this is a man apology.'

'And how do you make that out?' She looked at Elle as if she'd just said something absolutely ridiculous.

'Because he's texted first – and not only that, he's brushed over the subject because maybe he's a little embarrassed about last night. This is his way of saying, "I was hurt and overreacted, but only because I really like you."'

'A simple sorry would do.'

'As the saying goes: men are from Mars and women are from Venus. Just go with it and if needs must, talk to him about it when you see him.'

'What will you do this afternoon?'

'Me? I'm going to nip over to Irene's before I cook up a magnificent roast for when you get home. Then you can tell me all about your date.'

'You're *so* good to me!'

'I know – and don't you ever forget it.'

'I won't, and to prove it I'm going to knock us up a couple of bacon butties to keep us going, and then you can help me choose my outfit.'

'You need an outfit for the cinema?' Elle asked bemused. 'But it's dark!'

Pippa raised her hand to her chest. 'One must look good always,' she projected in a dodgy Shakespearean voice.

'Come on then – let's get breakfast.' Elle threw back the covers as her stomach gave a loud rumble.

'Your phone just beeped again,' Pippa said.

It was a response from Noah:

It was good to see you too x

Elle's eyes widened.

Pippa squealed. 'Oh my lord!'

Chapter Twenty-Nine

S lumped on the settee in her faithful old trackies and sloppy sweater, Elle was half watching *Virgin River* while continually staring at Noah's last message. It all seemed very surreal. Over their bacon butties, Pippa had declared this was fate and Elle's life was all coming together. It wasn't going to be long until Noah was signing books at the library and even the very thought of it was putting Elle in a spin.

She could hear Pippa bounding down the stairs just before her friend shouted, 'Close your eyes! I'm dressed to impress.'

Elle squeezed her eyes shut obediently and waited.

'Ta-dah! How do I look?'

When Elle opened her eyes, she saw Pippa had plumped for a hoodie, jeans and Converse, which was not her usual attire.

'You've taken me a little by surprise, I have to admit. It's not your usual sexy knock-'em-dead kind of look.'

'Ha, that's where you're mistaken!' Pippa had a glint in her eye. Unzipping her hoodie she disclosed absolutely nothing underneath but a black satin push-up bra that showed off her ample cleavage.

Pippa gave her shoulders a little shimmy.

Elle rolled her eyes. 'Only you.'

'But,' Pippa added, zipping her hoody back up, 'he isn't going to know what assets I'm hiding under here unless things get steamy – and then I'll knock his socks off. In the meantime, I'll sport a toned-down look and leave it to Aiden to make a move.'

'Very good plan. Put the ball in his court.'

'Exactly,' she said, grabbing her bag off the chair. 'What time are you leaving for Irene's?' Hearing a car horn beep, she looked out of the window. 'That's Aiden now.'

'I may as well head out as well.' Elle got to her feet and switched off the TV. 'Have a fantastic time, and I hope everything isn't as fraught as last night.'

'Thank you.' Pippa hugged Elle. 'Say hello to Irene for me, please. And I can't wait for my roast. You're a keeper!'

After grabbing her coat and waving at Aiden, Elle watched them drive off up the road. Heavy rain and thunder had been predicted for later, but at the moment, Elle was enjoying the calm before the storm.

When Elle arrived at Irene's house, she had a massive smile etched on her face. It was no wonder, given that she'd been thinking about Noah from the time she left home until the time she reached Irene's front door.

Hearing Irene chit-chatting away to someone inside, Elle rang the bell.

'You wait there,' Irene commanded, leaving Elle wondering who she was talking to.

The door opened. 'Good afternoon,' Irene chirped brightly, then immediately crouched on the floor.

'What are you doing?' Elle asked, perplexed. 'Have you lost something?'

Irene smiled up at her. 'Not quite,' she said, then all became clear. Behind her, Elle heard a tiny yelp and then she saw, sliding towards her on the wooden floor, the cutest ball of chocolate-coloured fluff she'd ever set eyes on.

'Oh my life!' she shrieked, bending down and scooping the tiny pot-bellied puppy up into her arms. 'He's absolutely gorgeous,' she exclaimed, stepping into the hallway.

Irene stood up and grinned. 'Let me introduce you to my new companion – Buddy.'

'Hello there, Buddy! Aren't you cute? How long have you had him?' Elle asked, juggling the puppy in her arms as she unfastened her coat. 'You never said anything yesterday.'

'Approximately three hours – and my life has never been so chaotic!' Irene smiled affectionately at Buddy.

Elle followed her into the living room then settled on the rug with the energetic whirlwind tugging at the cuff of her hoodie.

'Where did you get him from? He's so adorable.'

'One of the ramblers' daughters breeds Labradors, and I couldn't resist. I need a bit of company in the day, and he's the perfect excuse to venture out in the fresh air.'

'It's those paws – they're huge! He'll grow into them one day though … and those eyes – look at those, Irene. I'm already in love.'

'Yes, he does have the knack of making you fall in love with him instantly.'

'Ouch,' Elle yelled, her voice jumping an octave. 'And not forgetting those razor-sharp teeth.'

Irene laughed.

Elle scooped the puppy up again and held him in front of her face. 'We do not bite Auntie Elle – otherwise you'll have nowhere to stay when Irene goes on holiday.'

Laughing, Elle realised her voice had gone all gooey, and she buried her face in his fur as he let out a tiny bark, as though he'd understood her request.

When she put him back down on the floor, he scampered towards his teddy bear and grabbed it in his teeth. Elle giggled as she began to pull the bear and he tugged back with surprising force. His bum waggled in the air and he growled softly as Elle dragged him around the floor.

'Would you like a drink?'

Elle shook her head. 'I'm okay but thank you. It's just a quick visit as I need to nip to the shops before the heavens open.'

Irene nodded. 'Where's Pippa this afternoon?'

'At the cinema with Aiden, thankfully.'

'Thankfully?' Irene asked.

'It was a little touch and go for them last night. Jack let slip that Pippa and Wilson had shared a moment together, and Aiden wasn't too impressed.'

'Oh dear. And what about you?'

'Me?' Elle asked.

'Noah is coming to the library soon. How are you feeling about that?'

'It will be nice to see him,' replied Elle, suddenly realising her hand wasn't being pulled anymore. She looked down to see Buddy had climbed on to her lap and was now curled up, fast asleep.

She stroked his head softly. 'I saw him last night,' she remarked.

'You saw Noah last night?'

Elle nodded. 'I honestly thought I was seeing things. When I climbed into the ambulance, he was standing on the pavement. I actually did a double take.'

'Did you speak, did he recognise you?'

Elle nodded and passed Dan's business card over to her.

'Why do you have a business card belonging to the stripper? I don't understand.'

'Look at the writing on it.'

Irene's eyebrows rose. 'You didn't meet the stripper, did you?'

Elle laughed. 'Not in the way you're thinking. When the act finished and the lights went out this card was thrust into my hand. I didn't know what to think. But look at the name.'

'Dan Jones,' Irene read out loud.

'He's Noah's brother. Noah was backstage and he noticed me in the crowd. Goodness knows what he must have thought of me being on the front row enjoying every second of the show.' Elle shook her head in embarrassment. 'He asked Dan to put the card in my hand and I didn't know until this morning.'

'This morning?'

'We exchanged a couple of messages online. Out of all the strip joints in all the world… Can you believe that Dan Jones is not only the man that left his bag on the bus, but also Noah's brother?'

'It's Fate!' declared Irene.

'That's exactly what Pippa said.'

'Your life is all coming together, mark my words … and

exchanging messages sounds very promising.' Irene gave Elle one of those looks that meant she knew best.

'We'll see,' Elle said, trying to play the whole thing down.

'Any news on a meeting time with Cora?' asked Irene.

'No, but I'm hoping it's sooner rather than later. I'm dying to know what she looks like and how she turned her life around.'

'How are you feeling about it all now you've had time to digest the contents of the letter?'

'A little more settled. Growing up, I felt angry at the situation, especially not having a stable upbringing, but I think with age you realise life is never that simple.'

'That is very true.'

'I truly believe that Cora gave me up thinking I would have a better life and a stable family. It wasn't her fault it didn't turn out the way she hoped – until I met you. I think she'll be devastated when she learns the truth.'

'If I could change the past for you, you know I would, but hopefully now you'll be able to build a relationship with Cora and look forward, not backwards. It will be an emotional time.'

'I know. I'm nervous about meeting her.'

'When you see each other I'm sure there will be lots of tears but you both want this and I think it will be the making of you.'

'You're wonderful, Irene. You do know how much I love you, don't you?'

'I do, and I love you too.'

They both turned their heads to Buddy, who'd begun to snore lightly. 'Just look at him. What's the timescale with this little one? How soon can you take him out for a walk?' asked Elle, smiling at him.

'He's had his first batch of injections and his second lot are tomorrow. Then normally another two weeks after that, though he can roam around in the back garden in the meantime.'

'I bet you can't wait.'

'I can't, but apparently they don't need that much exercise when they're puppies. I've thought about taking him to obedience classes, though – look...' Irene held up a chewed shoe.

Elle laughed then checked her watch. 'I'm up for coming with you if you need a training partner but in the meantime, I promised I'd cook Pippa a roast dinner for when she gets back from the cinema, and I need to grab some potatoes.'

'You certainly can't have a roast without roasties,' Irene replied. 'Fingers crossed the date has gone without a hitch.'

Elle glanced down at Buddy. 'Aww, look at him,' she said, smiling.

'I know. He's just so cute.'

Reluctantly, Elle handed the bundle of cuteness back to Irene who laid him down gently inside his puppy pen and closed the gate.

'I'll come over after work on Tuesday, with Pippa if she's free. I'm sure she'd love to meet Buddy.'

'That'd be great.'

After kissing Elle on both cheeks, Irene stood in the doorway and waved her off.

'It's going to rain,' she shouted after her. 'Hurry.'

The sky had indeed darkened.

'I will,' Elle bellowed, picking up speed and burying her hands in her pockets. The heavens opened soon after, but thankfully she'd reached the corner shop in record time.

By the time Elle had paid for the potatoes, the rain had worsened. Sheltering under the roof that jutted over the shop doorway, Elle watched the rain bounce off the pavement. People were racing along the street with their coats over their heads, trying to keep themselves from being drenched.

She was just about to make a run for it when she sensed someone standing next to her.

'Hey,' came a male voice.

Elle glanced over her shoulder to find the gorgeous eyes of Noah Jones staring back at her. It took everything in her power not to gasp out loud.

'Hey back,' she replied, thankful her voice sounded relatively normal even though her heart was beating nineteen to the dozen. His eyes did not leave hers.

'It looks like you're deciding whether to make a run for it or not.'

'You read my mind,' she replied, though she was thankful he couldn't *actually* read her mind, given that all she could think about was how utterly gorgeous he was.

They watched the rain bounce off the parked cars in the road. 'I'm not really dressed for this.'

Elle noticed he wasn't even wearing a coat, which was extremely brave in this weather. Instead, he was dressed casually in a tight white T-shirt, faded jeans and Converse. Elle was doing her very best not to stare at his toned abs or breathe too deeply – the aroma of his aftershave was already causing her stomach to flip.

'Where are you going?' he asked.

'Home,' Elle managed to say.

'Is it far from here?'

'About five minutes.'

'Come on then. I'll walk you,' he said. 'This rain doesn't look like it's giving up anytime soon and I've got an umbrella.'

'Are you sure?'

'Absolutely. Here.' He extended his arm and draped it around her shoulders. His hazel eyes bored into hers and Elle felt her entire body trembling. He was definitely striking, and she hoped it wasn't too obvious she was blushing.

'It's that way.' She pointed up the street and stepped out of the doorway.

Just then they saw a flash of lightning and their eyes flicked upwards. Thunder rolled across the dense black sky, and in an instant the rain became heavier. Another jagged bolt of white split the sky.

Noah took the bag of potatoes from Elle's hand. 'Are you ready to make a run for it?'

'As ready as I'll ever be. We're going to get drenched!'

'That's half the fun,' he said, looking at her from under his dark eyelashes and giving her a playful smile. There it was again, that explosion of flutters in her stomach.

They took off up the street, the rain bouncing off the pavement. Despite Noah's umbrella, Elle's shoes were sodden in seconds.

A second burst of thunder, even louder than the first, rumbled across the sky and Elle flinched. Noah passed her the umbrella then grabbed her other hand. They both glanced at the angry storm clouds above, then Noah began to run faster, pulling Elle along behind him.

Neither of them spoke as they ran. They reached the steps of Elle's house in six minutes flat.

There was a huge crack as lightning flashed above them again. 'This is me,' she said, bounding up the steps and handing the umbrella back to Noah before rummaging in her bag for the key. 'Would you like to come inside?'

Noah was soaked to the bone. Little droplets of rain fell from his hair and a smidgen of chest hair curled over the top of his T-shirt. She fought the urge to wipe the raindrops from his forehead. Their height difference meant she'd been holding the brolly too low for him, so he'd had to run most of the way without its protection.

He hesitated for the slightest of moments. 'That would be great, but only if you have time?' he said, flashing her a smile that showed off his perfect white teeth.

There was something about the way he smiled at her that made her heart skip yet another beat.

'Yes, I have time.'

'Then I'd love to,' he replied. 'Now open that door! In case you haven't noticed, I'm drenched.'

'I hadn't noticed,' she said as she stared towards the wet T-shirt clinging to his torso.

He followed her gaze and *she* knew *he* knew she was staring.

Once they were in the hallway, she pushed her own wet hair from her eyes and risked a tentative look in the mirror. Damn, that really wasn't a good look. Her mascara had blackened her eyes, her nose was red and her hair was limp. This was definitely not the look she wanted when meeting Noah again.

'That was a downpour and a half,' he said, smiling, raking his hand through his hair and sweeping his wet fringe from his eyes. 'Am I okay to kick off these wet shoes?'

'Of course! And let me get you a towel – then I'll pop the fire on. It's the least I can do. Go in there and make yourself comfortable.' Elle nodded towards the living room. Noah disappeared through the door and Elle hurried up the stairs, reminding herself to stay calm. She couldn't believe it – Noah was really in her living room.

———————

Elle quickly dried her hair and pulled a brush through it before using a facial wipe to remove the mascara from round her eyes. Then she touched up her make-up before grabbing a towel from the airing cupboard.

When she walked back into the living room, Noah was kneeling in front of the fire, which he'd already managed to light.

'Here, take this,' she said, handing him the towel. 'Would you like a warm drink?'

'You read my mind! A cup of tea would be perfect.' He smiled, rubbing the towel over his arms. 'One sugar please,' he called after Elle as she headed to the kitchen to switch on the kettle.

While she waited for the water to boil, she looked back through the gap in the kitchen door. It was so surreal – the man she'd had on her mind since their kiss all those months ago was now sitting in her living room. She watched as he peeled his T-shirt from his body and dried himself with the towel.

Elle couldn't take her eyes off him. His body was wonderful, his muscles toned to perfection. With a stomach full of butterflies, she wandered back into the living room clutching two steaming mugs of tea. Noah had started slipping the T-shirt back over his head. As he did so, she averted her eyes towards the fire.

'I hope you don't mind – I was a little sodden.' He smiled and the corners of his eyes crinkled.

'No, not at all,' she replied, placing his mug on the table and deliberating over where she was going to sit. Feeling a good type of nervous, she perched on a chair next to the fire. Noah looked sideways at her.

'How's your friend?' he asked, sitting down on the rug and stretching his legs out in front of the fire.

'Friend?' she asked.

'Last night – the ambulance.'

'Oh, yes, sorry. Unfortunately, she suffered a miscarriage.'

'I'm so sorry to hear that,' he said sadly.

'It was her hen party too – she's getting married very soon. It had been such a fun evening up until that point.'

'I noticed you were all very entertained by my brother.' He raised an eyebrow at her and Elle blushed. 'I'm just teasing! Anyway, tell me all about you. What's happened since I saw you last? How's work at the library?'

'I love it there, but Irene has retired now. I miss seeing her every day, but she's only up the road. And look how well you're doing – another book out soon,' she added, changing the subject.

'Yes, that's why I'm here – visiting Dan, catching up on the family and attending a few book signings. Is this your place then?' he said, switching the conversation back to her again.

'Yes, all mine.'

'Boyfriend? Husband?' His eyes caught hers and the question hung in the air for a split second.

'No boyfriend, no husband – just Pippa, my housemate. She recently moved in with me after splitting from her boyfriend. She moved back with her parents for a while, but I think once you've made that step to move out, it's difficult to live by their rules again. What about you?'

'No boyfriend or husband.' He grinned, making Elle laugh.

'Are you originally from around these parts?' she asked, and gave a little shiver.

'You're cold,' he said. 'Here – sit by the fire.' He made room for her on the rug and Elle sat beside him, stretching her legs out in front of her. The heat from the fire was inviting, and she rubbed at the goosebumps on her arms.

'Yes, I'm originally from around here,' he said, answering her question. 'My parents still live here, and so does Dan, obviously.'

'Where do you live now?'

'I moved to London a while back.'

Elle knew that, of course, from his social media but she didn't want him to think she'd been stalking him. 'And how long have you been there?'

'I moved just after I saw you last.' His eye contact was strong and she wondered if he thought about the kiss they'd shared as much as she did. 'I thought it would be cool to say I'm a writer living in London. The aim was to spend most of my days wandering through the city and parks, finding inspiration wherever I walked. Or maybe writing in coffee shops next to the Thames while sipping cappuccinos.'

'And is that not what you do?'

'I mainly sit in my apartment with only myself for company.'

Elle laughed. 'It sounds lonely.'

'It can be,' he replied. 'And how is Irene? Your mother, right? Is she enjoying retirement?'

'Irene's my foster mum, which I know may sound a little weird at the age of thirty, but she's good, and she is very much enjoying retirement. She's just got herself a small bundle of fluff to keep her company.'

'A puppy?'

'Yes, a chocolate Labrador called Buddy.'

'A handful, I'm sure.'

'But a cute handful.'

'You said Irene's your foster mum?'

Elle hesitated for a moment. That was the first time Elle had admitted to anyone new in her life that Irene wasn't her biological mum.

'I don't mean to pry,' he said.

'You're not. I mentioned it,' Elle replied, pulling her knees up to her chest and wrapping her arms around them. 'I'm just going through a very emotional time at the minute. Irene is my rock – my whole world in fact – but recently I started the search for my biological mother.'

Noah's eyes widened. 'That's big. And?' he asked. 'Any news?'

Elle nodded, not trusting herself to speak for a moment. Noah sat in silence and sipped his tea, waiting until she was ready.

'I was given up at birth and passed between foster families. For years I battled with my own demons – feeling like I was never wanted – and I never stayed in one place long enough to make any real friends. It was Irene's love and care that saved me. That sounds dramatic, I know, but it's true.'

'It must have been tough.'

'It was. I learned to go under the radar at school, and I struggled. It was Irene who discovered I couldn't read.'

'You couldn't read?' Noah looked astounded. 'You work in a library.'

Elle smiled. 'It wasn't that difficult to hide. I'd changed schools so many times that no one ever noticed, and I learned to get by.'

'Gosh, Elle, I can't imagine what you've been going

through all these years,' he said, leaning towards her and touching her knee, like it was the most natural thing in the world.

'Irene is a very special person. If it wasn't for her...' Elle felt the emotion welling up inside her, just as it always did whenever she thought about Irene's kindness and love for her. 'She taught me to read, and she's helped me to overcome so many barriers in life – she built up my self-esteem and taught me I was enough even though I always felt there was a piece of me missing. I will be eternally grateful for that.'

'It sounds like everyone needs an Irene in their life.' Noah smiled.

'They sure do. I started the search for my biological mother on my birthday and shortly after, the Salvation Army confirmed they'd found her. It came as quite a shock – I'd convinced myself it would take years to track her down. She wrote me a letter explaining why she had no choice but to give me away. I always wondered what type of person could give up their newborn baby, but when I read the letter, I realised I shouldn't ever have judged what I didn't understand.'

'I think that's something we're all guilty of from time to time, but life is never simple.'

Elle nodded. 'Cora Hansley – that's my biological mum's name – started looking for me on the same day I started my search for her.'

'What a coincidence,' Noah said softly.

'It was the second of February – my birthday.'

'It sounds like she never forgot you.'

'In her letter she said that not a day goes by without her thinking about me.'

'So, what happens now?' Noah asked.

'We've both agreed that we want to meet up.'

'How are you feeling about that?'

'Scared, excited, nervous, physically sick. What if she doesn't like me?'

With a smile, Noah rolled his eyes. 'Elle, who on earth wouldn't like you? You're beautiful, warm, funny … the list is endless.'

She could feel herself blush at his kind words. 'Thank you. It's all just a waiting game now,' she replied.

'Come here.' Noah stretched his arms out and Elle hugged him.

'I think you needed that,' he whispered and softly kissed the top of her head.

'I think you might be right.' She pulled away and felt his hand drop to the small of her back. They stared into the dancing flames of the fire and sat in silence for a moment.

'What about you? What's next for you?' asked Elle.

'It's mainly work, work, work. When I'm not writing, I'm editing, and when I'm not editing, I'm promoting.'

'That sounds very busy.'

'It is.'

'So it's all work and no play?' she added, lifting one shoulder and playfully bumping it against his.

His eyes sparkled. 'No play at all lately.'

His hand brushed against hers on the rug and her whole body tingled. 'I do remember, you know,' he said. 'I've often thought about our moment.'

Elle smiled. His gaze was intense, causing every hair on her body to stand on end.

'Me too,' she replied. The attraction between them was strong and clearly mutual, given that he was looking at her with such adoration. She wanted to embrace the tingling feeling flooding her body. She wanted him to kiss her just like he had done back then.

Noah moved a little closer, until they were mere inches apart. His lips lingered next to hers. Elle felt dizzy, her eyes locking with his before she dropped her gaze to his lips…

The moment was interrupted as his phone beeped and Noah slowly pulled away.

He read the text. 'Damn it. I should currently be sitting down for a Sunday roast with the family.'

'Double damn it.' Elle wanted him to stay for longer.

'I don't want to go but I have to go. This conversation isn't over though, Cooper.'

She pressed her lips tightly together to hide her smile and watched as he stood up and disappeared into the kitchen with his empty mug, which she heard him place next to the sink.

'I was just thinking the same thing,' she murmured when he was out of earshot.

Through the open door, Elle saw him hover by the kitchen table for a moment, and wondered what he was doing.

'Cooper! You've still got it.' He was now leaning against the kitchen door. In his hand was his business card, which had been pinned to the corkboard in the kitchen.

'Why the hell did you never ring the number?'

His gaze met hers, and neither of them faltered. She stood up and he walked slowly towards her. She felt her heart racing. Elle had never felt desire like this before. No one had ever come close.

'You have my number, so ring me. No excuses, and failing that…' He tapped the card lightly on the end of her nose, then flipped it on to the table next to her phone.

'Failing that, what?' she asked, standing close to him.

'Then I'll see you at the library for my book signing. Do not let me down.'

'I think I can make that; after all, I do work there,' she replied, smiling.

'It's a date then,' he replied.

'A date,' she repeated.

Tilting her face towards his, Noah pressed a soft kiss to her lips. 'Until next time.' He pulled away slowly and Elle watched the vision of loveliness disappear into the hallway. She followed him. As he opened the front door, he looked back over his shoulder and they grinned foolishly at each other. A moment later he was gone.

Once again, Noah Jones had knocked her off her feet.

Chapter Thirty

E lle heard muffled shouting from the hallway as she
bolted upright.

'Elle, are you home?' Pippa bounded into the living room
and plonked herself down on the settee. 'I've shouted for you
twice! Who's been having a sneaky kip in front of the fire?' She
grinned. 'That's a sign of old age, that is.'

'What time is it?' asked Elle. Once Noah had left, Elle had
poured herself a glass of wine and snuggled down on the
settee but must have dozed off soon after.

'Five o'clock, and I'm ready for my roast. I've worked up a
right appetite.' Pippa grinned.

'Your date went well then?'

'Very well.'

'I have bad news about the roast,' Elle confessed guiltily.

'Which is?'

'I fell asleep before I could make anything.'

'You're kidding me?'

'Afraid not – and I've had an unexpected visitor.' Elle tried
to control the smile on her face but failed miserably.

'Sounds intriguing! I'll pour myself a glass of wine and we can swap Sunday afternoon stories.'

'And you might as well grab the takeaway menu from the drawer while you're in there.'

'Pah! You had one job this afternoon, Cooper,' Pippa shouted from the kitchen. A few seconds later she was perched on the other end of the settee.

'How was the film?' Elle asked.

'It started well, but got a little hazy towards the end.'

'You're terrible.'

'I can neither confirm nor deny.'

'The question is, are you going to see him again?'

'Of course I am. Tomorrow morning, nine a.m., at work!'

'Apart from work!' Elle rolled her eyes.

'Nothing was arranged as such, but I hope so.'

Elle could hear the excitement in Pippa's voice, and she was truly happy for her friend. She deserved a little bit of happiness after her disastrous relationship with Nick.

'And your afternoon? Tell me all about it.'

'I popped in to see Irene as arranged and I was introduced to the newest member of the family. He's this big,' Elle demonstrated, gesturing with her hands, 'with gigantic eyes and the largest paws you've ever set eyes on.'

'No way, Irene's got a puppy?'

'Yes, the most gorgeous chocolate brown Labrador called Buddy.'

'I can't wait to meet him. He sounds adorable.'

'I've said we'll nip over after work on Tuesday, if that's okay with you?'

'Would love to! I can see why you were too preoccupied to make dinner.'

'There's a little more to the story.' Elle's smile grew. 'I did go to the shop to buy the potatoes, and I had every intention of starting the dinner when I got back, but the heavens opened and I was caught in a massive thunderstorm. I was standing in the shop doorway deciding whether to make a run for it when…'

'When…' Pippa was winding her hand around in circles, willing Elle to continue.

'There was Noah, standing right next to me.'

Pippa's eyes widened. 'Noah Jones?'

'Noah Jones,' repeated Elle. 'He offered me his umbrella, and I offered him a cup of tea and a towel.'

'Tell me everything,' Pippa insisted. 'This has made my day.'

'We got soaked in the thunderstorm so I let him spend a short time drying out in front of the fire.'

'You've had Noah Jones sitting on the rug, drenched to the skin, on a Sunday afternoon?' She narrowed her eyes at Elle. 'And?'

'And just before he went, we may have shared another kiss.'

Pippa's eyes widened. 'I'm loving this. I wasn't expecting that.'

'I wasn't either – it just happened. And as he was about to leave he noticed his business card on the pin board and told me to ring him.'

'This is promising.'

'I think you might be right,' replied Elle, feeling a nervous flutter in her stomach at the thought of seeing him again, chatting with him on the phone.

Pippa held up her glass. 'Let's have a toast.'

'What are we celebrating?'

'Thunderstorms, love, life and libraries … because if it

wasn't for the Library on Love Heart Lane, we would both be dateless.'

'I've not got a date yet.'

'*Yet* being the key word!' retorted Pippa. 'You've just kissed him again. Some girls can only dream of kissing him and here you are on a Sunday afternoon…'

'I'll drink to that.'

'Cheers!'

They clinked their glasses together.

'To the Library on Love Heart Lane,' Elle repeated, wearing the biggest smile.

'Was it a good kiss?' asked Pippa.

Elle laid her hands on her heart. 'Just the best.'

Pippa squealed with delight. 'You're forgiven for not cooking the roast. Pizza?'

'Sounds good to me.'

Chapter Thirty-One

'Come on, Elle, hurry up. We're going to miss the bus at this rate,' Pippa shouted from the bottom of the stairs.

Elle stared into the bathroom mirror. Yesterday, after they caught up with each other's news and after she'd climbed into bed, her mood had dipped a little. Noah had made her feel completely at ease and she'd easily shared information with him, but after she checked out his social media, she realised that once his book tour was over he'd be heading back to London. In the grand scheme of things it was silly to be worrying about it, knowing she was getting ahead of herself. They weren't even dating and had only shared a couple of kisses. But Elle had lived with the feeling of rejection and abandonment for years and it was a feeling she didn't want to have again any time soon.

Last night she'd lain in bed looking at the business card. She wanted to text him, but was it too soon, if she'd only just seen him that afternoon? There was nothing from him in her messages and, feeling a little disappointed, she eventually put her phone down on the bedside table and drifted off to sleep with Noah still very much on her mind.

Elle shouted back, 'I'm coming.'

'You took your time.' Pippa was waiting impatiently, holding open the front door while Elle grabbed her bag and coat.

'There's still plenty of time, and anyway I've never known you this keen to get into work before,' Elle teased, even though she knew that this time they were really cutting it fine.

On the bus, Elle wasn't in a talkative mood. She sat in her usual seat, gazing out of the window and watching the town whiz by.

'Right, come on – what's up with you?' Pippa probed. 'Last night you were on a high, and this morning you're not your usual self.'

'Nothing, honestly. I just didn't get much sleep.'

'Would that have anything to do with Noah?'

Elle sighed. 'It's silly really.'

'Come on, tell me.'

'I really like him – I always have.'

'And the problem with that is?'

'The distance. If we did start seeing each other, would it just be limited to weekends?'

Pippa raised her eyebrows. 'Are you seriously worried about that?'

Elle nodded.

'It's very early days. Take one day at a time, and don't forget he's a writer.'

'What do you mean by that?'

'Surely he can write anywhere. It's not as though he works in an office and has set hours. He could even write in the library and you could swoon over him from the reception desk. You really are overthinking this.'

'I hadn't thought of that,' Elle replied, mulling over Pippa's words.

'That's because you're too busy thinking of all the reasons why it might not work.'

'Sometimes I wish I was more like you. You're so confident around men.'

'Focus on each day and what will be will be.'

'One day at a time.'

'One day at a time,' Pippa repeated, with a slight smile.

'When did you become the wise one?' Elle nudged her with her elbow.

'Since wearing these glasses.'

They both laughed.

Fifteen minutes later, they stepped off the bus at the bottom of Love Heart Lane. Elle tilted her face up towards the sunshine. 'Thunderstorms yesterday, bright sunshine today.'

'It certainly makes everything seem a lot brighter.'

'Good morning, ladies.' Aiden had sneaked up on them as they walked up the drive of Foxglove Farm towards the library.

They both jumped and turned around. Aiden was rustling two white paper bags.

He grinned. 'One for you and one for you.'

'Oooh, what's in there?' Pippa exclaimed, taking her bag from him and peeping inside.

'A warm pain au chocolat, fresh from Bonnie's Teashop.'

'Thank you,' said Elle, taking the bag. She noticed Wilson parking his van at the side of the library.

'You two go on in,' she insisted, handing the keys to Pippa. 'I just need a quick word with Wilson.'

Pippa raised her eyebrows.

'Go on,' Elle shooed. 'And stick the kettle on. I'll be there in two minutes.'

Aiden and Pippa disappeared inside while Elle waited for Wilson. He soon appeared, juggling numerous packages in his arms.

'Hey,' she said. 'I just want to make sure you're okay.'

Wilson looked glum, disheartened and even exhausted. There was no smile forthcoming.

'Not really,' he replied.

'Here, let me take those from you,' Elle said, reaching forward and taking the packages. 'Is there anything I can do? If you want to talk about it, I'm here.'

For a second, Wilson looked like he was about to say something, but then he changed his mind.

'I'm a great listener, you know.'

Wilson managed a half-smile as a group of students filed into the library. 'I know and thank you.'

'Is it Pippa?'

Wilson shook his head. 'A little … probably a lot. Rejection is never a nice feeling and we've just got a lot of family stuff going on at the moment.'

'You know where I am if you need anything.'

He nodded. 'Thanks, Elle.'

She watched him walk back to his van. Just as she was about to go into the library she heard her name being called.

She spun around to see Irene hurrying across the courtyard, waving something frantically in the air.

'What are you doing here so early?' Elle asked, wondering what all the urgency was about.

Irene thrust a white envelope into her hand.

'Where did you get this?' asked Elle, looking down at the envelope, which she saw was addressed to her.

Irene tapped it with her finger. 'I'm no Sherlock Holmes, but it has the Salvation Army logo on the envelope. Do you think this is it?'

Elle couldn't take her eyes off the envelope.

'I've been up for hours. Buddy is absolutely adorable, but he's just like a baby. He's howled all night and I've hardly slept a wink.'

Elle smiled – Irene did look exhausted. 'I've not known many babies that howl.'

'You know what I mean! In the end, I kept him company in the kitchen and spent most of the night cooking. I nipped over to yours first thing, but you'd already left for work so I let myself in and popped you a casserole in the fridge for later. When I was leaving, I saw this was lying on the mat, so I drove here as fast as I could.'

'Thank you,' she said, turning the letter over in her hand.

'Do you think this is the letter about your meeting?'

'There's only one way to find out.'

With a racing pulse, Elle headed towards the staffroom with Irene following close behind. Was this the moment she discovered more information about her mother and the date they would finally meet? As soon as they were in the staffroom, Elle sat down at the table. 'I feel so nervous.'

She opened the envelope and pulled out the letter inside.

'It's from Emily, the caseworker. She's identified a meeting place.'

'And?'

Elle gave a tiny gasp. *No, surely not*. She reread it.

'What is it?' Irene urged. 'What does it say?'

'I wasn't expecting that.' Elle felt herself trembling. 'My mother is here.'

Irene glanced towards the door in amazement. 'Here?'

'No, not here as in the library.'

'Where then? What do you mean, Elle?'

Her mind was in overdrive as the words left her mouth. 'My mother lives in Glensheil.'

'You're kidding me!' Irene picked up the letter and began to read. 'What are the chances of that? Saturday – she wants to meet you on Saturday in Primrose Park.'

'I feel sick with nerves. It's all moving so quickly.'

'I can't believe she lives so close.'

'I could have been walking past her in the street. This is surreal.'

'That is a possibility.'

Elle wiped a lone tear away from her cheek with the back of hand. 'I'm actually going to meet my real mother. Do you know what feels so calming about this?'

'What's that?'

'That it's here, in Heartcross, a place I feel so settled and safe in.'

Irene kissed the top of her head. 'It's all coming together.'

Chapter Thirty-Two

E lle spent the rest of the week in an emotional state. Both Pippa and Aiden were patient with her, and she tried her best to keep busy, but her mind wasn't on the job. The meeting with her mother was scheduled for the same day as Noah's book signing at the library, which sadly couldn't be helped. Pippa and Aiden had offered to organise it all, to take the pressure off Elle, and she was thankful that all she needed to do was turn up on the evening of the event.

Cora Hansley was constantly on Elle's mind and she wondered if her biological mother was as nervous as she was. Elle had rehearsed many conversations in her head over and over again, trying to figure out what she would say when they came face to face, but knowing it would all probably go out of the window when they actually did.

Today was Thursday, which meant it was book club, and it would be the first time they'd seen Eleni since her miscarriage. Elle had bumped into Jack at the shops earlier in the week and he'd said she was coping well and throwing her energies into wedding plans, which sounded like a good thing.

Elle glanced at her watch: six p.m. Pippa was meeting her at book club as she'd gone out for tea with Aiden and Theo, and they would be dropping her off at Bonnie's Teashop afterwards. She was meeting Irene at the bottom of the street in about ten minutes' time and they were going to make a quick stop at the cemetery on their way. It was the anniversary of Neville's death, and even though Elle had never met Irene's husband, she felt he'd always been a part of her life since Irene had taken her under her wing.

Heading up the street, she saw Irene ahead talking to a man. After they finished their conversation, the man kissed her cheek and walked off in the opposite direction. Irene turned and waved at Elle.

'You look nice.' Elle gave her a smile.

'New jacket. Not my usual colour but I thought I'd give it a go.'

'It really suits you.' Elle admired the jacket before changing the subject. 'Who was that?' she asked.

'Just someone.'

'What do you mean, "just someone"?' Elle linked her arm through Irene's.

'Let's talk,' said Irene and they began to walk.

As they strolled past The Old Bakehouse and Bumblebee Cottage towards the church, a smile appeared on Irene's face, followed by a tiny look of anguish.

'Is everything okay?'

Irene took a deep breath. 'I need advice,' she said, taking a sideward glance at Elle.

'*You* need advice? That makes a change.'

'That was Arthur,' she said.

'Arthur?'

'He's a friend of mine.'

'A friend as in a *friend*?'

'That's what friend usually means.'

'Would you like to tell me about Arthur?'

'I think I would. Arthur is one of the ramblers, and we seem to have hit it off quite well.'

'Aww, Irene, that's lovely. But judging by the look on your face, you seem a little worried about it.'

'It's Neville,' she answered, pushing open the wrought-iron gates leading to the churchyard. The last time they'd visited Neville's grave was on Christmas Eve. The day had been misty and the sudden drop in temperature had given the whole place an eerie feel. Today, however, the cemetery was an array of yellow, daffodils dancing along the path leading to the gravestones.

'Can we sit on that bench over there for a minute while we talk?'

'Of course,' Elle answered.

'Let me tell you about Arthur. He's a lovely man, a widower, so we have that in common. He has a grown-up daughter, Jessica, who's one of those theatrical types.'

'Theatrical types?'

'Yes, she's currently touring the country with *Mamma Mia!*'

'I love that film – it's one of my favourites. Is that the production that's on at Glensheil Theatre at the minute?'

'Yes, that's the one. But I feel it's too difficult.'

'What's too difficult?'

Irene glanced towards Neville's grave. 'Neville was the love of my life, and I've started to get close to Arthur but…' She tried to put on a brave face but her eyes teemed with tears.

'But?'

'I have these pangs in here, like I'm betraying Neville.' Irene clutched her chest.

Elle placed her hand on her mother's knee.

'No one will ever replace Neville,' she said softly, 'but I'm also sure he wouldn't want you to grow old alone – or be lonely for that matter.'

'I still feel like I'm being disloyal.'

'Aww, Irene, that's just not the case. It's okay to move on. It doesn't mean you've forgotten him – you still have all those wonderful memories.'

'It's just very hard.'

Elle's heart ached for her. 'Tell me about Arthur. What's he like?'

Irene glanced at Elle, her eyes twinkling at the mention of his name, and a smile grew on her face. 'He knew today would be difficult for me, and he popped by this morning with a bunch of flowers.'

'That's lovely.'

'Like I said, we met in the walking group. After his wife died, he joined the group to make new friends and take a little exercise. He's funny, kind and thoughtful. We have loads of things in common. We both like to eat out and go to the cinema, and we've even talked about joining the bowling club. It's just so easy – there are no awkward silences when we're together.'

'Good-looking?'

Irene blushed. 'I think so.'

'I think I best look up this Arthur for myself!' Elle teased.

Irene chuckled.

'I think you should grab this little bit of happiness while you have the chance.'

Irene smiled at her. 'I suppose you're right.'

'How does Arthur feel?'

'He says one day we will be rocking together in the old

people's home,' she said, giggling as she rummaged in her bag for a packet of sweets. 'Here, have a pastille. I always find the black ones are the nicest.'

Elle popped the sweet into her mouth. 'Arthur sounds like he wants to be part of your life then.'

'I think he does.'

They sat for a moment, staring across the cemetery. 'Shall we go and see Neville?'

Irene nodded and pointed to the flower vendor. 'Let's get a bunch first.'

After they'd purchased the flowers, they made their way towards Neville's grave.

Elle hoped that one day she would find a love as true as Irene and Neville's – they really had been soulmates. She instantly thought of Noah. With everything that had been going on in her life this week, she'd been preoccupied with thoughts of her meeting with Cora, but she looked forward to catching up with him at his book signing.

Watching Irene lay the flowers on the grave, Elle passed her a tissue to dab her teary eyes. 'The emotion gets me every time. Our love was the most wonderful thing in the world. I really hope that someday you find someone just like my Neville.'

Elle hugged Irene, her thoughts still firmly fixed on Noah.

'Welcome to Thursday night book club!' Mim announced, standing by the counter in the teashop. She clapped her hands together and all eyes turned towards her. 'Two minutes until we start, so get yourselves settled.'

Elle and Irene were sitting in their usual seats by the window, sipping tea from beautiful vintage teacups. Elle glanced out of the window on to Love Heart Lane and noticed Aiden's car pulling up outside. He leaned over and kissed Pippa on the cheek before she clambered out of the passenger side and waved at Theo.

'She's all loved up.' Irene pointed towards her.

The bell above the teashop door tinkled and Pippa walked towards them with a huge smile on her face.

'Dare we ask what you're smiling at?' Elle enquired.

'Just life! That's all!' she trilled, still smiling.

Elle could hear the happiness in her voice. 'I'm made up for you. You deserve to smile again after everything Nick put you through. It'll just be me that's left on the shelf.' Her eyes flicked towards Irene who also smiled.

'What's that look for? What have I missed?' Pippa asked.

'Irene has met a wonderful gentleman from her walking group.'

Pippa's eyes widened and she grinned. 'Tell me more, Irene, tell me more!'

'His name is Arthur.'

'Apparently, he's very thoughtful, kind, generous and easy on the eye,' Elle added.

'When are we going to meet this lovely man? We definitely need to give him the once-over, don't we, Elle?'

'Absolutely!'

'Well, actually … I've not mentioned it yet, but Arthur has invited us both out for a meal with his daughter Jessica,' she said to Elle.

'Jessica is currently starring in *Mamma Mia!* at the theatre in Glensheil. They're on tour,' added Elle, for Pippa's benefit.

'Oooh, I love *Mamma Mia!*,' Pippa exclaimed. 'Maybe we should try to get tickets. I love a night at the theatre.'

'The last show is tomorrow,' replied Irene.

'That's a shame, maybe next time.'

'Arthur's booked a table on Sunday, Elle, if you'd like to join us?'

'I would! It will be lovely to meet them.' Elle gave her a heart-warming look. 'I knew this retirement would be good for you.'

'I'm hoping it stays that way.'

'And just like you have always been here for me, I'll always be here for you.'

Irene gave Elle an affectionate hug. 'That's what families are for.'

Elle's heart melted at Irene's words. She knew, whatever happened with her biological mother, that she would always love Irene unconditionally.

Chapter Thirty-Three

The following day, Elle was perched behind the desk in the library with lunchtime fast approaching. She flicked through the pages of a book she'd been trying to read for ages, but the words just weren't sinking in. After rereading the same passage several times she finally gave in and closed the book. Maybe it was just the mood she was in. The only thing she could think about was that this time tomorrow she'd be face to face with her mother. Nerves were starting to get the better of her.

'Penny for them.' Pippa nudged Elle's arm. 'You're very preoccupied.'

Elle looked up. 'I'm just thinking about tomorrow.'

'I can come with you, if you like.'

'Thank you, but Irene is going to be there.'

Pippa nodded. 'I'll be there when you get home.'

'And thank you for doing all this.' Elle gestured to the library floor.

'It's looking good, isn't it? I did wonder how you'd cope with seeing multiple posters of your heart-throb pinned around your workplace. I have to see if these posters do him justice. If they're true to life than he's extremely hot.'

'I have to agree.' Elle grinned.

Pippa and Aiden had organised everything for Noah's book signing. Florrie had delivered umpteen floral displays, which decorated the signing area beautifully, and the shelf behind Noah's signing table was stacked end-to-end with display copies of his books. Rona was dropping off a couple of long trestle tables after the teashop closed this evening, along with cups and saucers and a couple of aluminium urns. The buffet was being delivered tomorrow afternoon.

'I've organised the publicity. We have Aidy Redfern coming along from the local newspaper. He said there's a good chance this will make the local TV news.'

'That's good,' replied Elle, distracted.

'You don't sound like you mean that.'

'I do, I just feel terrible. I've not even messaged Noah to wish him good luck or tell him I'm looking forward to seeing him. All I can think about is this meeting tomorrow.' Elle held out her hand 'Look, it's shaking. My heart feels like it's continually racing, I can't eat and I can't sleep. I don't think I have ever been as nervous about anything in my life.'

'I can't imagine how you're feeling.'

'My main fear is that after everything we've been through to track each other down, what if…' Elle took a breath. 'What if she doesn't like me, or I don't like her? Should it all just be left in the past?'

Pippa slid into the chair next to her. 'But if that happens – and I'm sure it won't be the case because who could not like you? – but if that does happen you have answers. You'll never be wondering "what if". You know who you are, where you've come from.'

Elle nodded. 'I just want it all to be perfect.'

As she took one last look in the mirror, Elle's stomach performed a double somersault.

'You look beautiful,' complimented Irene.

'What do you wear when you meet your mother for the first time?' Elle glanced down at her clothes. In the end, she'd opted for jeans with a smart but casual blouse.

'I don't think she'll be looking at your clothes,' Irene said softly.

Elle stared at her reflection one last time.

'Right, I think I'm ready…' Her voice faltered.

Pippa was standing in the doorway. 'Come here.' She stretched out her arms and hugged Elle tight. 'I'll be back here for five p.m., waiting to hear all about it.'

Elle managed a nod.

'And I know the timing isn't the best but don't worry about the library. Everything is ready for Noah's book signing tonight.'

'Thank you.'

'Here,' Irene said, handing Pippa her front door key. 'I hope Buddy doesn't drive you too insane.'

'I can't wait to look after the little ball of energy. I've even worn long sleeves so those sharp little fangs don't leave any war wounds.'

They all laughed, lightening the mood a little.

Pippa pressed one last kiss to Elle's cheek before she grabbed her coat and disappeared through the door.

Elle looked towards Irene. 'I think I'm ready.'

She hoped her head and heart *were* ready for whatever was going to be thrown at her in the next couple of hours.

With Irene by her side she ambled down towards the River Heart and took the water taxi to The Little Blue Boathouse, where they disembarked and took the path leading towards Primrose Park.

Trying to calm her beating heart, Elle glanced at Irene. 'I feel sick with nerves.'

'That's understandable – it's a big day and emotions will be stirred up for both of you. It's natural. Just don't make any assumptions. First impressions aren't everything but they are important.'

Elle nodded.

'Just be yourself.'

They walked through the gates of Primrose Park. 'You tell me where you want me to sit and I'll wait for you,' Irene said warmly. 'Take as long as you need – there's no rush. I'm not going anywhere.'

Primrose Park was busier than usual because the local Scout group was holding a fundraiser. Two large gazebos housed refreshments while smaller tables covered in floral tablecloths had tombolas, a bottle stall and a hook-the-duck game.

Up ahead, Elle spotted a familiar figure.

'Oh no,' she murmured. 'I never thought that there would be people here I know. Look…'

She nodded towards a picnic blanket laid out on the grass, where Wilson was sprawled out with a flask and a book.

'I hope he doesn't spot us. How long have we got?' Elle asked anxiously.

'Twenty minutes or so,' replied Irene. 'How are you holding up?'

'I feel like I'm about to crumble.'

'Shall we have a short walk around the gardens?' suggested Irene. 'I've got something to show you.'

They took the path around the bandstand and headed towards the lake at the back of the woods. 'Neville used to love fishing here. I'm going to transport you back to my youth.' Irene pointed to a path that Elle wasn't familiar with.

'What's down here?'

'This leads to an old cottage, right on the outskirts of the village. Back in the day it used to belong to the park ranger – Mr Preston, if I remember rightly. He was employed to maintain the gardens in the park. It's been empty for a fair few years, but I believe it's about to be auctioned off.'

As they followed the path Elle gazed at the old stone cottage. 'Look at that, it's still full of character – and how beautiful are those duck-egg blue shutters and the gorgeous oak porch?'

'It is indeed,' Irene replied, standing still for a moment.

The garden behind the cottage was vast and overgrown.

'The forgotten cottage. Look at this place – it's like something out of a novel,' exclaimed Elle, taking a look all around her.

Irene gave her a warm smile. 'It's a very special place.'

She began to walk across the grass and Elle followed. Up ahead there was a gate. Irene twisted the wrought-iron knob and led Elle into an overgrown vegetable patch with a small potting shed just beyond it. Irene headed towards the old oak tree. 'Come and look at this.' She pointed at the trunk of the tree, her eyes glistening with tears. 'Good times,' she murmured.

There, carved in the tree, was a heart with the words 'Neville loves Irene' etched inside it.

'I lived and breathed the bones of that man. He's still in here.' She placed her hands on her heart. 'He was taken too soon, but I still feel him. Every day.'

They stood in silence and Irene traced the heart with her fingertip before gently brushing away a tear.

'I truly wish you could have met him.'

'Me too.'

'We tried for children, you know. It was agonisingly painful when all our friends were falling pregnant and we didn't. We were constantly being asked when we were going to start a family. Some marriages wouldn't have survived the heartache, month in, month out, but the love we shared was one in a million. *Neville* was one in a million.'

Irene turned towards her and held her gaze. 'You were the daughter we never had. He would have been so proud of you, Elle.'

Elle swallowed a lump in her throat.

'And whatever happens today, just remember it will never change my love for you. I want you to have the best life and a happy one.'

Elle's heart soared for Irene. She was the best thing that could have happened to her.

After a few seconds, Irene kissed her fingertips and pressed them to the heart on the tree, then turned towards Elle.

'Are you ready?'

Elle nodded.

It was time for Elle to meet her mother.

Chapter Thirty-Four

They walked slowly towards a bench close to the spot where Elle was meeting Cora Hansley.

'Shall I wait here?'

'Yes, this will be perfect. Thank you, Irene.' It wasn't too near the tiny café, which was an extension of Bonnie's Teashop and situated at the back of the park, but it wasn't too far away either.

Irene placed her bag down on the bench then held Elle's elbows with her hands. 'You're shaking. It's a big moment, isn't it?'

Elle nodded.

'Try and relax. Just remember she wants this as much as you, otherwise she wouldn't be here.'

Not trusting herself to speak, Elle kissed Irene on the cheek.

'I'll see you soon. Good luck.'

Elle took a deep breath, and, with mixed feelings of excitement and trepidation, slowly walked towards the designated meeting place. After a few steps, she glanced nervously over her shoulder. Irene gave her a reassuring smile.

Oblivious to everything around her except her own thundering heartbeat, Elle carried on walking.

The café was up ahead. The first thing Elle noticed was a woman sitting on one of the tables outside. She didn't know whether Cora would be waiting inside or out – but before she could figure out what to do, the woman at the table looked up at her.

'Hi, Elle.'

Elle's breath caught in her throat. She'd hoped that she wouldn't bump into anyone she knew, but it was too late.

'Hi, Jenny. It's a lovely day for it.' Elle tried to keep her voice bright despite the nervousness that was swamping her whole body. She didn't feel like making small talk, but she knew she couldn't ignore Jenny. Quickly she scanned the inside of the café but everyone was sitting in groups and there didn't seem to be anyone on their own.

'Have you been to the fair?' asked Jenny.

'No, not yet.'

'I'm just grabbing a pot of tea. Would you like one?'

'I'm actually just going to grab some water. Is there anything you want whilst I go inside?'

'No, but thank you.'

Trying to keep her nerves under control Elle stepped inside the café. As much as she liked Jenny, she didn't want anyone witnessing the moment she met her mother. After paying for the water Elle wandered back outside and looked up the path but there was no one in sight. Now she felt a twinge of panic. What if Cora had changed her mind?

'I've just seen Wilson near the entrance to the park. He's sitting on a picnic blanket reading.'

Jenny nodded. 'He's waiting for me.'

Elle looked at her, puzzled.

'I'm waiting for someone,' Jenny added, her voice faltering. 'What are you doing here?'

'I'm waiting for someone too,' Elle said, taking a seat on the bench next to her. 'And you look as nervous as me.'

Elle's pulse began to race as she studied Jenny's face. She forced herself to breathe calmly, even as she realised that the face staring back at her resembled her own. Surely, she couldn't be…

Elle looked away, her thoughts running wild. She was letting her imagination run away with her. This wasn't Cora Hansley, this was Jenny.

She glanced one last time up the path, but there was still no one else in sight.

Elle hesitated before finally asking, 'Are you Cora Hansley?'

Jenny looked at her in shock, her eyes searching Elle's as she registered the question she'd just been asked.

'Are you Cora Hansley?' Elle asked again.

'Yes.'

Elle tried her best to hold on to her tears, but it was no use. They began to roll slowly down her face.

'I think that someone you're waiting for might be me. Are you … my mother?'

'Yes,' replied Jenny. 'Eleanor Hansley, my beautiful baby.' She released her own tears as they fell into each other's arms. 'I can't believe I've found you,' she whispered. 'It's been too long.'

Chapter Thirty-Five

Holding hands, they looked at each other through blurry eyes. Elle took a deep breath. 'But I don't understand. Your name isn't Cora Hansley. It's Jenny – Jenny Hughes.'

Jenny's eyes slid briefly from Elle's. 'My real name is Cora Hansley, but when I needed a fresh start, I changed it.'

'Fresh start?'

'Oh, Eleanor, I don't know where to begin.'

It was strange hearing someone call her by her full name. It was one she never used; she'd always been known as Elle. She saw a shadow of disappointment pass across Jenny's face, and blinked away fresh tears.

'I let you down,' said Jenny. 'I let everyone down.'

'Don't say that. The past is the past – we can't change it,' Elle said warmly, knowing this must be as hard for Jenny as it was for her.

Jenny took a deep breath. 'My name was Cora Jennifer Hansley. Jennifer is my middle name; Hansley is my maiden name.'

She took a deep breath.

'Matt Harrison was my childhood sweetheart, the one I wrote about in my letter. He's your father. He didn't deserve the way I treated him. Our life was difficult – money was sparse and I was tired of working so many jobs, out until all hours of the evening. He was a lovely man – handsome too – but my life spiralled out of control after my parents died.'

'The grief must have been overwhelming,' Elle said softly.

Jenny nodded and dabbed at her tears.

'Do you know what happened to Matt … my father?'

She shook her head regretfully.

'No. I haven't even gone looking for him. I've thought about him often over the years, but what would it achieve? We were besotted with each other once, but I'm married to George now and we have Wilson. No doubt Matt will be married with a beautiful family of his own. He deserves that. Some things are just better left in the past, but I'd like to apologise to him for the hurt I caused. That was unforgivable.'

As Jenny took a few steadying breaths, they watched a young mother walk by. She was pushing a pram and making cooing noises at a newborn baby. They both smiled at the excited toddler running alongside the pram, pointing towards the swings in the play area of the park.

'I missed out on all that,' Jenny said sadly. 'We missed out on all that,' she corrected. 'You smiled at me, you know. I know people would say you were too young to smile, but you did.' Jenny broke down completely then, no longer able to maintain eye contact with Elle. 'I'm so sorry,' she said, over and over again, as she wept. She looked exhausted. 'You have to know how difficult it all was.'

'For years I didn't know what to think. There were moments I hated you, then there were moments I hoped you would come looking for me.'

Jenny's face crumpled in pain. 'Oh, Eleanor,' she said, touching her knee.

'But now I understand and it's okay, honestly it is. I know it was impossible for you at the time. Taking a baby onto the streets... I dread to think where I would have ended up – where both of us would have ended up.'

It was Jenny's turn to listen, and she held Elle's hands as she asked tentatively, 'Did you have a happy childhood?'

Elle shook her head. 'This is probably not what you expected to hear but I just existed from day to day. My earliest memory is at primary school.' She swallowed a lump in her throat. The memory was so clear it felt like yesterday. 'The class had baked biscuits for Mother's Day – small heart biscuits that we'd decorated. The school invited our mums in for the afternoon, and I had to watch as everyone's mothers started to file into the classroom. Everyone's except mine. They all looked so happy, praising their children for making such wonderful biscuits. No one came for me. The memories of that foster family are so vague,' she said. She scrunched her eyes in an effort to remember, but there was nothing.

'I'm so sorry. I really am. My heart ached for you every birthday, every Christmas, every Mother's Day. Don't ever think it didn't,' Jenny murmured.

'I always felt like I never fitted in. I felt alone. I was moved from family to family and it wasn't until I met Irene that my life began to have some meaning.'

'I thought Irene was your biological mum. I just had no idea. Why would I?' Jenny's gaze met Elle's. 'No one in the village ever mentioned it.'

'No one would realise. When the library opened on Love Heart Lane, we came as a pair and that's when we were introduced to the community. I've only recently told Pippa – when I started the search for you.'

'Irene is one in a million.'

'She is,' replied Elle, holding back more tears.

'I'll be eternally grateful to her. You were my little angel and she brought you up. For years, the only thing that kept me going was the hope that we'd be reunited one day, and not a day's gone by that I haven't thought about you. You've always been in my heart,' Jenny confessed. 'Can I ask, how did you know my details to start the search?'

There was a rent card that somehow got moved with my belongings every time I was allocated another foster home. It was only when I got older that I realised quite possibly that the details on that rent card was yours as the surname matched my own.'

'I took the rent card when I left Matt, I didn't want him discovering that I had blown all the rent money on drugs and that it hadn't been paid. I must have dropped it when I was in labour.'

The two of them sat in silence for a few moments, lost in their own thoughts.

'Why come looking for me now?' asked Elle. She took a sideward glance towards Jenny.

'It was the right time. I'd gone to start the search so many times, but I was scared of rejection, I suppose. I talked it over many times with George and Wilson. If I'm honest with you, Wilson was apprehensive when George and I told him the truth.'

'Why?' I asked.

She took a breath. 'Because Wilson is adopted, and you're my biological child.'

'Wilson's adopted?'

Jenny nodded. 'George and I were unable to have children together. Wilson went through a difficult period as a child, and we didn't want him to feel anxious or rejected, so we only told him about you a few years ago, if that makes sense?'

Elle nodded. 'Has George always known about me?'

'Yes, from the outset. As soon as I knew we were serious about each other, I told him I had a daughter. He's been brilliant. He's the one who finally gave me the strength to start the search.'

'He sounds like a good man.'

'He is.'

'That day in the library…'

'Your birthday,' she said.

'You were using the computer.'

'That's when I started the search,' she confirmed.

'I sat at the very same machine when I started my own search. I always thought I'd know instantly if I ever stumbled across my mother, but there you were – so close by – and I didn't have a clue.'

'The night of the hen party…' Jenny paused.

'It brought it all back, didn't it?'

She nodded. 'I know I never miscarried, but when we discovered Eleni had lost her baby…' Jenny fought back the tears. 'I felt the way I felt when I left you that night.'

Elle touched her knee.

'I'd love it if you would be a part of my family and get to know us better.'

'I'd love that too,' Elle said, meaning every word.

Chapter Thirty-Six

Two hours later, Elle and Jenny were still sitting outside the café, talking about anything and everything. They had so much to catch up that they'd completely lost track of time.

Feeling a presence at the side of the table, Elle glanced up mid-conversation to see Irene and Wilson standing in front of them.

'Is everything okay?' asked Irene, with a look of confusion on her face.

Wilson looked equally confused, holding his rug and book. 'I've been waiting for you for ages.'

Elle and Jenny glanced at each other, then back at Irene. The look on her face had changed from puzzlement to astonishment. The penny had dropped and Elle discreetly nodded to confirm what she was thinking.

Irene touched Wilson's elbow gently. 'I think it might be better if you sit down,' she suggested.

'What's going on? Are you okay?' Wilson asked, looking towards his mum.

'I can leave you to talk privately,' Elle offered, glancing at Jenny.

She didn't know how Wilson was going to react to the news, or exactly what he knew about his mum's past.

'No, I want you to stay, Eleanor, and you too, Irene.' She smiled softly at Irene, who gave a slight nod.

'Eleanor?' Wilson queried. 'But your name is Elle.'

'Elle is short for Eleanor,' Irene said gently.

Jenny touched Wilson's arm. He looked at Elle. 'It's you, isn't it?'

Elle nodded. She didn't know how Wilson would be feeling. He'd become her friend over the last couple of months, and in an amazing twist of events, his adoptive mum was her biological mum.

'Yes, Wilson, Elle is my daughter.'

'But I thought Irene was your mum. Irene Cooper – Elle Cooper.'

'My real name is Eleanor Hansley. Irene is my foster mum, and I changed my name by deed poll a few years back so we'd have the same surname.'

'How about we walk back to my house to talk there?' Irene proposed. 'It's not too far and I'll put the kettle on. I think we could all do with a very strong cuppa.'

Ten minutes later, after taking the water taxi, they reached Irene's house. The second she opened the front door Buddy came bounding towards them, shaking his toy and wagging his tail.

'My gosh, he's grown,' Elle exclaimed, scooping him up off the floor and cuddling him.

'He's gorgeous!' Jenny exclaimed.

'Oh, he is – especially when he's asleep,' Irene said, chuckling.

They all settled in the living room whilst Irene made a pot of tea. 'Be a love, Elle, and grab that plate of biscuits from the kitchen for me.'

Buddy followed Elle into the kitchen. 'These aren't for you, little man. Here, have one of these instead,' she said, throwing him a chew from the barrel on the sideboard. He snatched it out of the air and scampered off towards his playpen.

After the tea had been poured, Elle looked at Wilson, who was clearly still taking it all in.

'How are you feeling?' she asked tentatively.

'I'm happy for Mum. She's waited for this moment for a long time.' He smiled at Jenny then hugged her. 'But I never expected to know you. It's quite unbelievable.'

Elle couldn't agree more. She'd never expected, when she woke up this morning, to discover that Jenny was her mother.

'But I think it's brilliant,' he added, a wide smile spreading across his face. 'I really do. I've seen what Mum goes through every birthday and Christmas. The heartache you must have both been carrying around, wondering who the other one is. This is a new start and I'm happy for you both.'

'Thanks, Wilson, that means a lot.' Elle stood up and extended her arms. Wilson mirrored her actions and they hugged tight.

Watching them embrace, Jenny brushed a tear from her cheek. Elle gestured for her to stand up. Irene followed and suddenly they were all hugging tightly, tears running down their cheeks. Buddy barked at their feet, not wanting to be left out, and Elle scooped him up in her arms. 'We're one big family now and we wouldn't leave you out,' she said, kissing the top of his head.

As soon as they sat back down, Jenny dabbed her eyes with a tissue. 'I still can't believe this day is here. For years, I've lived with the guilt of leaving you behind, Elle, of not knowing what happened to you. Every day the pain got worse and worse. Some days were better than others; some days I couldn't even bring myself to get out of bed. And some days I just existed. There was a part of me that was always lost,' she continued. 'However…' She turned towards Wilson and took both of his hands in hers. 'I can start healing now – I can build a relationship with Elle. *We* can build a relationship with Elle. Our family is complete.'

He smiled at his mum as she squeezed his hand. 'What a day.'

'Does anyone want some more tea?' Irene asked, pouring the last of it from the pot.

Jenny shook her head. 'No thanks, Irene. I've been nervously drinking it all morning.' She smiled.

Irene placed the empty mugs on the tray.

'Here, let me take those.' Wilson paused for a second and looked over towards Elle. 'Come on, sis, we can wash these up,' he said warmly.

'We can,' she said, genuinely touched by his words. 'I've always wanted a brother.'

Elle noticed a smile pass between Jenny and Irene as she and Wilson left the room together, heading into the kitchen. Wilson ran the hot water and put the cups in the bowl. He took a sideward glance at Elle. 'Jenny is the best mum anyone could have. Without her, goodness knows where I'd have ended up.'

Elle nodded.

'Jenny and George aren't my biological parents.' He began

washing the cups then one by one handed them to Elle to dry. 'I was taken into care when I was younger.'

Elle could relate, sharing such a similar past.

'My biological father is serving time in prison, and my mother took her own life.'

'Oh, Wilson, I'm so sorry.'

'They married young and my mother was fifteen when she had me... Being taken in by Jenny and George turned my life around. I couldn't love either of them any more than I already do. And now there's a new beginning for all of us. Wait until you meet George, you'll like him.'

Elle was in no doubt.

'I can't wait,' she said.

He grinned. 'Come on – let's get back in there. They'll be wondering where we've disappeared to.'

Just after they'd both sat down again in the living room, the front door bell rang, followed by Pippa's voice shouting down the hallway. 'It's only me.' Pippa popped her head around the living room door. 'I hope you don't mind. I dropped Buddy back a bit early...' She didn't finish her sentence, struck mute by the four pairs of eyes staring back at her.

'Is everything okay?' she asked, looking between them all. 'What's going on here? You texted me fifteen minutes ago asking me to come over... I thought you...' She looked towards Elle but stopped mid-sentence, not wanting to give away that Elle was meant to have met her biological mother today.

'Pippa knows where I was this morning,' explained Elle as Pippa perched on the arm of the chair.

Elle looked at Jenny who nodded, confirming it was okay to share the information.

'Pippa, meet my mother.'

With the look of puzzlement on her face, Pippa glanced around the room, not quite understanding.

'Jenny is my mother.'

Pippa's eyes widened as the realisation hit her.

'You?' she asked, amazed.

Jenny gave her a warm smile. 'Yes, me.'

'I wasn't expecting that.'

'We weren't either,' added Elle.

'But your name is Jenny?'

'I started using my middle name many years ago, and Hughes is my married name.'

Pippa shook her head in amazement. 'Wow! Just simply that – wow!' she exclaimed, standing up. 'Are you both okay? Happy? I'm so pleased for you both!' She hugged Elle first and then Jenny.

'Which makes you and Wilson brother and sister,' Pippa added, leaning across to shake his hand.

'It does indeed.' Elle gave Wilson a heart-warming smile.

'It seems to have been quite a day for everyone,' Pippa said, smiling as she checked her watch. 'And it's not over yet.' She tapped her watch then glanced at Elle. 'I've been over at the library and everything is in place for the book signing tonight. Aiden will open up and meet Noah as I knew you might have a few things on your mind, but we will need to get there as soon as possible. Is anyone else coming to the library tonight for Noah Jones's book signing event? It's going to be huge.'

'We wouldn't miss it for the world. It's not every day we get Noah Jones in town,' Jenny confirmed.

Elle's stomach was already doing somersaults at the sound of his name. She couldn't wait to see him.

Chapter Thirty-Seven

At four p.m., Elle and Pippa were sitting around the table eating an early dinner. They had another hour before they needed to head over to the library. Aiden had been dealing directly with Noah and his agent regarding the book signing and Elle was hoping that Noah would understand when she explained why she hadn't been in touch.

'How are you feeling about tonight?' asked Pippa.

'Nervous. I feel that I should have messaged him.'

'He'll understand. It's been quite a week for you. I'm sure your phone just beeped, by the way,' Pippa said as she placed her knife and fork across her empty plate.

'I'll grab it in a minute. Let's just sit and be comfortable for a minute before we wash up.'

'How are you feeling about today?' asked Pippa, taking her place on the settee next to Elle. 'It must have been a shock.'

'I can't even begin to tell you how I felt when I spotted Jenny sitting outside the café. I didn't want anyone being witness to what was about to happen.'

'I can imagine.'

'At first I just thought it was a coincidence, until she said she was waiting for someone.'

'How did the penny drop for you both?'

'I noticed she was a little on edge. Then I asked her if she was Cora Hansley. The shock on her face said it all.'

'Oh, Elle, I bet you were shocked too.'

'I was. It's all so surreal.'

'I know. It's a very emotional situation.'

'She's invited me round for tea next week to meet George, which I'm really looking forward to.'

'That'll be nice. And Wilson? He seemed okay with everything.'

'He was happy for us both. Changing the subject though, dare I ask – how's it going between you and Aiden?'

'It's going great,' she admitted. 'Except Louisa seems a little…'

'A little what?' Elle asked.

'I think she's a little what you'd call high-maintenance. We bumped into her when we were out earlier. She was with a man, which I think took Aiden by surprise. But when we took Theo home her mother let slip, he'd been on the scene for a while. It sounds like a case of what we said before – "I don't want you, but I don't want anyone else to have you either."'

'But on the whole is everything going okay?' Elle noticed a flush in her friend's cheeks. 'Actually, you don't need to answer, I know what that look means – it means it's going very well.'

'It is,' she replied with a beatific smile. 'Someone really wants you. That was your phone again.' Pippa nodded towards Elle's handbag.

'Oh! I forgot to look at the last message.' Elle reached towards her bag and grabbed her phone.

As she stared at the screen, her heart began to race. 'It's Noah.'

'What did he say?'

I hope you're well. I'm heading to the library after grabbing some food. I hope to see you later. X

Elle stared at the message and especially the kiss. Her pulse began to race.

'Let's go and make you look drop dead gorgeous ... not that I'm saying you aren't already drop dead gorgeous,' Pippa added quickly.

'The second text is from Irene.'

I'll meet you at the library tonight. Go ahead without me. I'm grabbing food with Arthur just before.

'Everyone's life seems to be going in the right direction.'

'And after tonight, let's hope we can get your love life on track. What are you going to wear?'

'Jeans and a nice top, and maybe those boots with the little heel?'

'Yep, come on then, let's get ready and you can go and bag your man.'

Elle laughed. 'Now wouldn't that just finish off my day perfectly.'

Pippa knocked on Elle's bedroom door. 'Are you ready?'

Elle had been staring at her reflection for the last few

minutes. It had been a day of nerves and excitement and tonight was no different.

'Ready as I'll ever be,' she said as she opened the bedroom door. 'Ta-dah! How do I look?'

'Absolutely gorgeous! You're going to knock him dead. It's just started to rain so I've ordered a taxi. It'll be here in a minute.'

'Great – I'll grab my coat and my bag.'

A couple of minutes later, the taxi beeped outside and they hurried towards it as the rain came down.

'Where to?' the driver asked as they climbed into the back of the cab.

'The Library on Love Heart Lane. It's in the grounds of The Heart of the Village on the Foxglove Farm estate.'

'Yes, I know it.' The driver put the car into gear and headed through the town of Glensheil.

Elle turned towards Pippa. 'I'm feeling really nervous, which I know is probably daft, and I'm hoping he's not too put out that he's being looked after by Aiden.'

'He'll understand when you tell him about today.'

Suddenly the car began to slow down.

They both looked out through the windscreen, where the wipers were swishing frantically in the rain.

'What's going on?' asked Pippa.

Up ahead blue lights were flashing. The cars on both sides of the road just in front of the bridge were at a standstill.

The taxi driver turned towards them. 'Looks like an accident. The road's been closed along with the bridge into Heartcross.' He picked up his radio and spoke into the receiver. The voice on the other end confirmed that one of the other drivers had just reported the accident.

'Are we going to sit tight, or make a run for it in the rain?' asked Elle, glancing at her watch.

'If they've closed off the bridge I'm not sure how we *can* make a run for it.'

Just at that second, a policewoman knocked on the driver's window. He wound it down.

'Excuse me, sir, but you might want to turn off your engine. The bridge has been closed due to an accident and we're asking everyone to stay in their cars. Unfortunately, there's no getting into the village of Heartcross until the accident has cleared.'

'How long will that take?' asked the driver.

'I'm sorry, sir, I can't say. But with the traffic backing up behind you, I think you're going to be stuck for a while.' The taxi driver nodded and immediately switched off the engine.

'I'll keep you updated,' she added before moving on to the next car.

Pippa attempted a feeble smile. 'Don't worry,' she said. 'I'm sure we won't be here too long.'

Elle pressed her face against the glass and saw a fire engine and an ambulance a little further up. She shuddered as her gaze took in something else. 'It looks like there's a motorbike on the ground.'

'Oh no. How awful,' replied Pippa. 'I bet the weather hasn't helped. This morning sunny and now the heavens have opened yet again.'

'We'd best text Aiden and tell him we're stuck on the other side of the bridge, otherwise he's going to be wondering where we are.'

Pippa rummaged in her bag and pulled out her phone. 'The damn thing is dead. I need to get a new one. It loses its charge way too quickly.'

'Don't worry, I'll text him.' She checked her bag then glanced towards Pippa. 'I've left my phone on the arm of the settee. Damn. Aiden will be wondering what has happened to us.'

Elle sighed. 'Never mind Aiden, Noah will be thinking you've stood him up!'

For over an hour and a half they sat in the back of the taxi. They were stranded. The bridge was closed and with the rain lashing down they just hoped they would be on the move soon.

Even though Elle knew it couldn't be helped and the situation was out of her control, she felt agitated. All she wanted to do was to get word to Aiden and Noah that they hadn't forgotten them and they were on their way even if they were moving nowhere fast.

They watched as the emergency services left the crash site and the wreckage was removed.

'The thing is, though, if people are going to the event from this side of town they'll have trouble getting there too. There will be no one there,' Pippa commented, glancing at Elle, who was checking the time for the umpteenth time.

'The event started ages ago. Aiden will be at his wits' end and think we've stood him up, and Noah will think his event is a flop.'

'The villagers will be there and the girls from book club. Surely word will have got round there's been an accident.'

'You'd hope so but we're so late.'

'The police are letting people through now,' the taxi driver piped up. 'Hopefully the traffic will begin moving again soon.'

The cars began slowly moving forward, making their way over the bridge. Finally, the library was in sight.

'Don't worry about payment, girls. I can't charge you for sitting there all that time in the traffic.' The taxi driver drove to the far end of the courtyard and navigated a three-point turn to face back the right way.

'Thank you, but please take your usual fare.' Elle opened her purse. 'At least we were out of the rain.'

Feeling Pippa nudge her she turned her gaze to the door of the library. Aiden and Noah were standing there in deep conversation. Aiden patted Noah on the back as a car pulled in front of them and then disappeared back inside the library.

With the engine still running, a girl stepped out of the car, and Elle watched as Noah put his arm around her shoulder and the girl leaned in and kissed him on his cheek. He climbed into the passenger seat and they drove off.

'He's left already.'

'Oh Elle, I'm sorry.'

Climbing out of the taxi, Elle felt deflated. They walked into the library. At the sound of the door opening Aiden spun around.

'Where have you been? Tonight was a complete disaster. We had a huge author in the building and barely anyone showed up, including you two. Noah has left. Everyone has left. It was embarrassing and look at the buffet that's gone to waste.'

'Oh, Aiden. We are so sorry. There was an accident and the bridge was closed.'

'You could have phoned, sent a message, anything.'

'I left my phone at home and Pippa's battery died. It's just been one of those nights.'

'Barely anyone turned up except a few from book club and

the locals. Noah kept asking where you were and I had no idea.'

'I'm so sorry, but the situation was out of our control. We saw Noah leave. Do you know who he was with?'

Aiden shook his head. 'He just said his lift was on his way.'

The door swung open again and Irene walked through it. 'Oh my gosh. I'm so sorry I'm late. It's manic out there. There was a huge crash and the bridge was closed. Arthur and I were sat in the queue for over ninety minutes. We couldn't go anywhere. I've been ringing you, Elle, but you didn't pick up.'

'I left my phone at home.'

'Where is everyone?' asked Irene, looking around the library.

'Obviously not here due to the traffic – or left because they'd been here for two hours and no one else turned up. I feel dreadful. How disappointing for Noah. Not the book signing he was expecting.'

Elle's mood had slumped to an all-time low. She was hoping that Noah wouldn't think she'd swerved the event on purpose, as that couldn't be further from the truth.

Chapter Thirty-Eight

T he next morning found Elle in low spirits. She'd barely slept a wink thinking about the previous night. Soon after they'd arrived at the library, Elle and Pippa caught another taxi home. The first thing they did was open a bottle of wine.

Elle couldn't get the image of Noah leaving the library out of her head.

She picked up her phone from the bedside cabinet and brought up his social media. On his Twitter feed there were a couple of retweets from the previous night but Elle could tell by the photo that the library wasn't crowded with people and she felt dreadful. The latest tweet was of Noah and the same girl he'd climbed into the car with. It was captioned: *About to paint the town red.*

They had huge smiles on their faces and Elle couldn't help but notice how gorgeous the woman was.

Snuggling down under her duvet she tried to block all thoughts of Noah from her mind.

Pippa tapped on her bedroom door. 'Hey, are you up?'

'Just about awake,' Elle replied.

'Here, I thought you might be needing these.' Pippa padded across the floor and placed a couple of headache tablets in Elle's hand along with a glass of water. 'We must have drunk a couple of bottles last night. I've also put some bacon under the grill. We need a little sustenance to soak up the alcohol.'

A loud beep was heard. 'The damn smoke alarm.'

Pippa hurried back downstairs to begin wafting at it frantically with a tea-towel until it stopped. Elle sat up in bed, swigged the water and swallowed the tablets. She willed her headache to go as later today she was meeting Irene, Arthur and Jessica at The Lakehouse restaurant, which was only accessible by boat. Hoping she'd feel a little more human in the next few hours, she pulled back her duvet and slipped on her dressing gown.

'Bacon butties are ready when you are,' Pippa shouted from the bottom of the stairs.

Elle had to admit it smelled good as she followed the aroma down the stairs into the kitchen.

Pippa was dancing around to a song on the radio when Elle walked in. 'Where have you got all your energy from?' she murmured, her head still pounding.

'I have no idea. Brown or red sauce?' she asked, sliding the plate of bacon butties towards her.

'Brown please.'

'It's this afternoon you're meeting Irene's new man, isn't it?' she said, tucking into her breakfast and catching the oozing sauce on the plate as she took a bite of the sandwich.

'Yes, Irene can't wait to introduce us.'

'Where are you going to?'

'The Lakehouse.'

'Very classy,' added Pippa, raising an eyebrow.

'I have no idea what to wear.'

'We can sort out your wardrobe after we've finished these.'

'Irene said that Arthur wants to treat us all. I'm just hoping I feel better after I've had a shower. At the moment, my head feels like it's not attached to the rest of my body and I'm feeling a little blurgh.'

'I can tell. You'll feel better after you've had something to eat. Did you contact Noah at all?'

Elle shook her head. 'I think the moment may have passed. Last night was a disaster and he left with a gorgeous girl.'

'It was definitely a catastrophic sequence of events,' Pippa agreed.

'Maybe it's the universe's way of telling me it's not meant to be. I'm just going to concentrate on today and meeting Irene's new man,' she said, knowing that she wouldn't be able to shake thoughts of Noah from her mind. 'What shall I go for? Jeans, dress or a skirt?'

Pippa glanced up towards the kitchen window. 'Blue sky and barely a cloud. What a difference from last night. It's still chilly out there though. How about that lovely floral dress you have with your navy cardigan and ballet slippers? That would be perfect.'

'Yes, I think you might be right,' replied Elle, picturing the outfit in her mind.

'I'll wash these up – you go and jump in the shower.'

'Thanks.' Elle handed Pippa her empty plate then climbed back up the stairs towards the bathroom.

———

Early in the afternoon Elle walked on to the wooden jetty outside The Little Blue Boathouse. The bright-yellow water taxi bobbed in the water with its engine humming. Stepping on board, she waved at Roman, the chief skipper of the boat. He flashed a warm smile then tipped his cap in acknowledgement. Once all the passengers were on board, Roman began to steer the boat slowly away from the jetty and as soon as they were in the open water, he began to pick up speed. Elle knew Irene was already waiting in the restaurant along with Arthur, and Jessica was due to arrive soon after.

She watched the view sail past, everything looking picture perfect: the sweeping bays and sand dunes, gulls hovering over the white cliffs, and Heartcross Mountain reaching for the sky. The boat eventually bumped gently against the wooden jetty where it bobbed in the water. The Lakehouse was absolutely breathtaking, the perfect place for lunch.

The inside of the restaurant was just as breathtaking as the outside, with its shimmering central dining bar and signature large windows overlooking the bay. There was striking art hanging on the wall and an ebony baby grand piano positioned in the far corner of the dining room.

Elle spotted Irene sitting with Arthur and gave her a wave as the waiter showed her to the table.

Immediately Arthur stood up and extended his hand. 'Pleased to meet you. I've heard so much about you.'

'Elle, Arthur, Arthur, Elle,' Irene introduced them.

'It's lovely to meet you too. This is the first time I've been here. It's just gorgeous, isn't it?' Elle sat down at the table.

'Jessica won't be long – she's just texted,' Irene said, picking up the bottle of wine. 'She's on the next river taxi. Would you like a glass?'

Elle placed her hand over her glass knowing she couldn't face another drop of alcohol. 'Just water for me, thank you.'

'Have a look over the menu. I'm having trouble choosing, there's so many options jumping out at me,' Irene said as she passed a menu to Elle.

'Thank you. Arthur, tell me about you. You met at the walking club, I understand? I want to hear all about it.'

Arthur shared the story of how he and Irene had bonded when they hiked over Heartcross Mountain.

'It so strange that I've lived surrounded by all this beautiful scenery and yet it was the first time I'd hiked to the top of the mountain,' Irene mused.

'It's on my to-do list,' shared Elle. 'I look at it every day from the library window and think the very same.'

'You must – and here's Jessica now.' Arthur waved towards the door of the restaurant and stood up with a wide smile on his face.

Elle swung a look towards the door of the restaurant and her eyes widened as she recognised Jessica. She was the girl who had picked up Noah outside the library last night!

Jessica was stunningly beautiful. She floated over to the table in the most elegant teal mini-dress, which gathered softly around her neck. She wore a tiny black cardigan and ballet slippers and her long brown curls bounced past her shoulders as she walked.

Visions of her and Noah seeped into Elle's mind again, and her mood slumped.

Jessica fell into her dad's arms and they hugged tight.

Irene smiled across at them and then looked over at Elle. 'Are you okay? You look like you've seen a ghost.'

'Of course! I'm all good,' Elle said quietly, telling a little white lie.

After Irene had brushed Jessica's cheeks with kisses, it was Elle's turn to be introduced. Jessica shook her hand with a smile then narrowed her eyes. 'You look a little familiar. Have we met before?'

'I don't think so,' Elle replied.

'It'll come to me,' she said. 'I never forget a face and you definitely look familiar.' Jessica studied her for a second longer before delving into her bag. 'Here, I've brought you a *Mamma Mia!* programme,' she said, sliding it across the table to Irene.

Irene beamed. 'I hope you've signed it for me.'

'Aww, I can do,' she said, whipping out a pen and scrawling her name across the photograph of herself before sitting at the table.

'I was telling Elle that you were in the production, and what a fabulous job you have,' Irene continued.

Elle stood up. 'Will you excuse me? I need the bathroom,' she said, wanting a moment to herself.

'Are you sure you're okay? You look so pale,' Irene asked, concerned.

'Maybe it was the boat ride. I've never been good on water. I'll just use the ladies' room. I'll be two minutes.' Trying to compose herself, Elle walked towards the bathroom. She couldn't believe Arthur's daughter was the girl who was with Noah last night. What were the chances of that? Elle leaned against the basin and stared at her reflection in the mirror. Taking deep breaths, she felt even more hungover than she had earlier.

She heard the door open behind her and Irene appeared at her side.

'I'm sorry to follow you but you suddenly looked awful. Are you sick? I know the water taxi can give anyone motion sickness.'

'It's not that. I'm ashamed to say I'm not feeling well …
probably because I had too much to drink last night,' Elle
admitted.

'I'm not surprised. You had an emotional day yesterday. It's
certainly not every day you meet your biological mother after
thirty years of separation.'

But that wasn't the reason she had been drinking last night.
She'd had way too much to drink because all she could think
about was Noah and the fact that she'd probably missed her
chance. Jessica was beautiful and they made a striking couple.

Once again the bathroom door swung open, Jessica
appearing in the doorway.

'The waiter's asking if we're ready to order, and Dad asked
me to come and check if everything's okay.'

'Yes, we're ready. We're just coming,' Irene said, giving Elle
a heart-warming smile before heading towards the door.

Jessica leaned against the wash basin while Elle washed her
hands.

'I've been racking my brain since I got here. I was sure I
knew you from somewhere, and it was only when Irene
mentioned you worked in the library that I realised who you
were.'

'Yes, I think we have a mutual acquaintance.'

'Elle. Yes – Elle. Noah's mentioned you a few times in the
last couple of weeks. It's such a small world – and such a
coincidence you're Irene's daughter.'

Elle's stomach twisted with embarrassment.

'It is,' she agreed, feeling foolish knowing that Noah and
Jessica had had conversations about her – and not only that,
but he'd had the cheek to sit in her living room, pretending he
was single and kissing her!

'Irene mentioned you travel all over the country

performing in theatre productions,' Elle said, trying to quickly divert the conversation.

'Yes, I love it! It can be a little difficult though when your loved one is on the other side of the country. It does get lonely but thank God for technology.'

'I bet,' Elle replied, brushing down her dress and managing to avoid eye contact. 'But you must be proud of his success too.'

'Believe me, his choice of career has nearly split us up on numerous occasions.'

Elle was quite taken aback by Jessica's response and was just about to ask why when Irene popped her head back round the door. 'Hurry up, you two. Jessica, your dad is getting a little impatient.'

'That's because he's hungry.' She smiled. 'He's always been the same. Grouchy!'

After the waiter had taken their food order, Elle sat quietly at the table listening to Arthur and Irene talk about their latest ramble. It was lovely to see the interaction between them. Irene's eyes were bright as they shared their stories and it was clear Arthur was a welcome addition to her life. But try as she might to concentrate, Elle's thoughts kept drifting to Noah. She was glad she hadn't messaged him now. What a fool she would have made of herself. The only future dilemma for her was Jessica being Arthur's daughter, which might mean she would bump into Noah at family gatherings. She knew she hadn't done anything to be ashamed of, but she also knew that she didn't want to see him loved up either.

It didn't take long for the food to arrive and Elle began to eat whilst she listened to Jessica talk excitedly about being cast in an upcoming production of *Les Misérables*. Arthur's face beamed with pride as she spoke.

'She was always one for dancing around as a child,' he said. 'She would sing at every opportunity. All my Saturdays were spent going from ballet to tap, drama to singing.' He looked at Jessica fondly.

'And it was all worthwhile,' Irene said.

'When do rehearsals start for your next production?' Elle asked.

'I have a couple of weeks off before the rehearsals start, then it'll be full on, all the way up till Christmas.'

'Christmas?' Irene exclaimed. 'That seems like a million years away.'

'It'll be here before we know it,' she replied.

'How does your partner cope with all your time away?' Irene asked, swallowing her last mouthful and putting down her knife and fork.

'He's learned to cope with it. He knows I love my job, and I love him. We just get on with it as best we can. We had a lovely night out last night after Noah's book signing. We met up with the cast of *Mamma Mia!* for a few farewell drinks. I thought I'd be a little tired today but I'm bearing up!'

'Elle, Jessica's boyfriend,' Arthur put in, 'is—'

'Noah Jones,' Elle interrupted, looking at Irene.

'Noah?' Irene repeated, puzzled.

Jessica burst out laughing. 'Dad *wishes* I was dating Noah.'

'At least Noah has a respectable job,' replied Arthur.

Elle and Irene looked at one another, confused.

'Pah!' Jessica rolled her eyes at her father. 'Dad thinks I'm about to marry the black sheep of the family.'

'I wouldn't go that far. I just wish he didn't feel the need to take his clothes off for a living.'

'Dan? You go out with Dan?' exclaimed Elle, thinking out loud. 'The guy from Eleni's hen do?'

'Yes, for my sins!' She smiled. 'He's my lovable rogue.'

'Definitely a rogue,' Arthur teased his daughter.

'As I said, Dad would have preferred me to date the sensible brother.'

'His job prospects are definitely more appealing.'

'Don't listen to him, Elle. Dan and my dad get on just fine – in fact, when they get together, they act like a couple of kids.'

'Indeed, we do,' Arthur confirmed. 'I just like to tease my daughter from time to time.'

'And what about Noah – does he have a girlfriend?' Elle asked casually.

'Noah? No. He's young, free and single,' Jessica answered.

Elle brightened up instantly, but felt a twinge of guilt for thinking he hadn't been genuine towards her.

Once their plates were empty Arthur asked for the bill.

'This is my treat,' he insisted.

'That's lovely of you, Arthur. Thank you,' Elle said gratefully.

'Arthur and I need to get back to Buddy. I can't leave that little rascal alone for too long. He's already chewed his way through my slippers and a new pair of trainers – not to mention the leg of the kitchen table.' Irene rolled her eyes as the waiter came back to the table with the card machine.

They all laughed.

Jessica glanced down at her watch. 'I've got another forty

minutes or so until Dan picks me up at The Little Blue Boathouse. Are you in a rush, Elle, or have you got time to stay for another drink?'

'I've nothing planned.'

'Fantastic, let's move over to that table by the window. Those chairs look a lot comfier.'

After saying goodbye to Irene and Arthur they ordered a couple of glasses of wine.

'I shouldn't really drink in the afternoon,' Jessica said with a twinkle in her eye. 'It usually sends me to sleep.'

'Me too,' Elle agreed.

They settled into the seats by the oversized windows, which looked out over the bay. Elle swallowed. 'I've got a confession to make.'

'Sounds ominous.'

'When you arrived, I was a little subdued because I recognised you from last night.'

'Last night?' Jessica asked, puzzled.

'Yes, my friend Pippa and I were on our way to the library when the bridge was closed off due to an accident. When the police finally let us through and we arrived, I saw Noah leaving with you.'

'Yes, Noah sent me a text. He said the night was disaster. Barely anyone turned up and, most of all, Noah had no word from you. He was gutted and kept checking his phone late into the night.'

'I'd left my phone at home by mistake.'

'He came out with Dan and me and got very drunk. All he did was talk about you. It's been great that I was touring Glensheil and it coincided with Noah's book signing – which he totally engineered, by the way.'

Elle raised an eyebrow. 'What do you mean?'

'He changed the tour plans because of you. He's been thinking about you since you last met and your name is always popping up in our conversation.'

'Noah talks about me?'

Jessica nodded. 'Absolutely! He definitely has a soft spot for you.'

A huge smile spread across Elle's face and a glow of happiness began to light up inside her. 'I have a soft spot for him, too.'

'Maybe that's something you need to tell him – because between you and me he's been waiting for a message from you.'

Just at that moment Jessica's phone beeped. 'That'll be Dan, he was going to text me after—' Jessica stopped mid-flow and looked up at Elle with wide eyes.

'After what?' she asked, staring back at her.

'After he dropped Noah at the train station.'

'Why is he dropping Noah at the train station?'

'He's going home – back to London. He said there was no point hanging around after you didn't show up or message.'

Elle's heart plummeted. 'But there were reasons. I need to try and catch him,' she said urgently.

Jessica picked up the phone. 'I'll ring Dan.'

Elle was relieved when he answered straightaway. 'Dan, how long until Noah's train leaves?'

Elle watched as Jessica balanced the phone between her ear and shoulder, then glanced at her watch. 'Thirty minutes.' She hung up the call. 'If you want to catch him you need to go now. The water taxi is just about to leave. I'll order you a cab from The Little Blue Boathouse and you might just make it. But you'll need to hurry.'

For a split second, Elle felt like time had stood still.

'Go!' Jessica ordered. 'Go and get your man!' She thrust Elle's bag towards her. 'I'll pay the bill.'

A mixture of panic and excitement surged through Elle as she hurried towards the exit of the restaurant.

'Let me know how you get on,' Jessica called after her.

'Will do,' she shouted back, but as soon as she was safely on the water taxi, Elle realised she didn't have her number.

Twenty-five minutes later the taxi pulled into the train station car park. Panicked, Elle paid the driver, hoping she was in time. Glancing up at the huge clock hanging from the red-brick wall she saw that there were five minutes until the train left. Elle quickly followed the signs to platform two, running as fast as her legs could carry her, weaving in and out of the other commuters, until she hit something solid and suddenly found herself stumbling to the ground, the contents of her bag spilling everywhere.

'I'm so sorry.' An apologetic man extended his hand and helped her up. 'That was my fault, I wasn't looking where I was going.'

'That's okay,' she said hurriedly, bending down to scoop up the contents of her handbag.

'Sorry again!' he called after her as she rushed onwards.

Out of breath but incredibly relieved, Elle spotted Noah at the other end of the platform.

She waved frantically and shouted his name but Noah didn't hear her as he stepped onto the waiting train.

'Noah!' Elle yelled again and began to sprint up the platform but it was too late.

The doors of the train shut and the whistle blew. The train began to move.

Quickly she rummaged inside her bag and grabbed her phone. She called Pippa, who, to her relief, picked up after a couple of rings. 'Pippa, are you at home?'

'Yes, why? Are you okay? You sound a little—'

'Never mind that,' Elle interrupted. 'I need you to go into the kitchen and text me Noah's number. His card is on the pinboard. Quickly.'

'Is everything okay?'

'Yes, but hurry.' She hung up and willed her phone to beep.

As soon as the number came through, Elle rang him immediately.

'You have reached the voicemail of Noah Jones.'

Damn.

She looked up but the train was out of sight. Noah was gone.

Chapter Thirty-Nine

A n hour later, Elle slumped down on the settee and kicked off her boots, sighing loudly.

Pippa appeared in the doorway. 'That's a loud sigh. What's up with you and what was all that about before?'

'It's Noah.'

'I kind of gathered it was something to do with him.'

'The girl last night – the one with her arms wrapped around him – she only turned out to be Jessica – Arthur's daughter.'

'No way. I bet that was a shock. What a coincidence,' Pippa exclaimed, sliding into the chair. 'And is she Noah's girlfriend?'

'I thought she was but it turns out she's with Dan.'

'Some girls have all the luck,' Pippa said with a grin. 'So why are you looking so glum?'

'Because Noah's gone back to London. He thought I wasn't interested because I didn't turn up at his signing and I didn't message. I think I've missed my chance. Jessica told me that last night was a disaster and he was constantly checking his phone for a message from me and now he's on a train back to London. I raced to the station to stop him but it was too late. I saw him step onto the train and before I could reach him, it left.'

'Oh, Elle.'

'That's when I rang you for his number, but it went straight to voicemail, and I … I couldn't just leave him a message. What would I have said?'

They were interrupted by a knock on the door.

'That'll be Aiden,' Pippa said. 'He was going to come round after he dropped Theo back with Louisa. I'll get the door.'

Elle nodded. Her head was spinning. Within the last twenty-four hours she'd met her biological mother, found out Wilson was her brother, got to know Arthur and Jessica – and Noah had disappeared back to London.

Hearing the front door shut, Elle looked towards the hallway and was just about to say hello to Aiden when her eyes locked on Noah, who was standing in the doorway wearing a lopsided grin. 'Cooper.'

Elle's heart began to race.

'Can I come in?'

'Of course. Where's Pippa?' Elle asked, looking over his shoulder.

Noah pointed to the front door. 'She's given us some space. Her words, not mine,' he said. 'She grabbed her trainers and jumped into a car that just pulled up outside.'

'That'll be Aiden.' Elle gestured to the chair.

Noah sat down opposite her. He stared at her in a way that caused her whole body to erupt in goosebumps. He was a vision of total gorgeousness.

'What are you doing here? I saw you at the station… I went… I'm not making much sense, am I?'

Breathe, Elle – in, out, in, out.

'I heard you shout at me as I got on the train, but by the time I realised it was you, the doors had closed. Then, as soon I got a signal, I received texts from both Jessica and Dan telling me not to get on the train because of you.'

'But you were on the train. How did you get here?'

'I jumped off at the next station and got a taxi straight here.'

'I'm so sorry about last night. There was an accident and—'

'I know you'd left your phone at home. Are we ever going to get this timing right?'

He looked at her with the most kissable smile she had ever laid eyes on.

'I hope so.'

Noah stood up slowly and then sat next to her on the settee. Her heart was pounding. He hadn't taken his eyes off her. 'Jessica explained what happened, but why didn't you message me? I've never checked my phone so often. It was more than I even check my book rankings!' He smiled.

'Please forgive me but I was all over the place yesterday. I've had a lot going on in my life… I met my biological mother.'

Noah looked amazed. 'I wasn't expecting you to say that. Wow. How did it go? How are you feeling? So many questions, I'm sorry.'

'It went well. Very well. It was even a bigger shock when I discovered we live near each other and not only does she come into the library but her son is my friend.'

'Double wow. I can't take this in. And yes, after that revelation, you're most definitely forgiven.'

'Neither could I at first, and thank you.'

Noah stretched out his arm. 'You have been going through it, haven't you?'

Elle leaned into his embrace and rested her head against his chest.

'I'm glad it's all coming together for you but you still could have sent me a message. I wanted to speak to you.'

'I checked my phone too,' she admitted, 'but there was no message from you either.'

'That's not true, I sent one yesterday saying I looked forward to seeing you.'

'Oh yes, you did. I'm sorry.'

Noah tilted her head towards his. 'You're beautiful, Elle Cooper,' he said and rested his head against hers. 'I remember the first time I ever set eyes on you – July fifteenth.'

'You remember the date.'

'Of course. I thought maybe you'd get in touch after you'd received your flowers.'

'Flowers?' she asked, confused.

'On Valentine's Day.'

'They were from you?'

'They were.' He gave her a sheepish grin. 'I suppose it was daft to think you'd guess they were from me after all that time. I should've been less mysterious.'

She smiled. 'I had no idea who they were from but they were beautiful – thank you.' Her heart was bursting. She furrowed her brow. 'You didn't by any chance send me a signed copy of Sam Stone's latest book as well, did you?'

'No. A signed copy of a Sam Stone book is very rare. Why?'

'It doesn't matter. What matters is that you're here now.'

'I was just thinking the same.' Slowly, Noah bent towards her and the electricity sparked between them as he kissed her softly.

'Elle…' He pulled away slowly but his gaze stayed locked

on her. 'You do know I fancied you the moment I set eyes on you, don't you?'

'Me too,' she murmured, willing him to kiss her again. 'But there's something I need to tell you.'

'Which is?' he asked, puzzled.

'I'm not after a quick fling. I'm not that kind of girl.'

'I'm glad to hear it. I'm not that type of boy either,' he reassured her.

'You live in London and I live—'

'One day at a time. We can work it out as we go along. I have a good feeling about you, Elle Cooper.'

'One day at a time,' she repeated.

'But I do have to go back to London tonight. I have a meeting with my agent tomorrow lunchtime.'

'How about you head back early tomorrow morning instead?' she suggested hopefully. She didn't want to let him out of her sight.

'Sounds like a good plan to me.'

———

Elle woke up at three a.m. entwined in Noah's arms, and was enveloped in an overwhelming feeling of happiness. For a moment she watched him sleep, before she kissed him gently and snuggled back into his chest.

'Mmm, what time is it?' he murmured.

'Three-ish,' she whispered. 'You've got another couple of hours before you need to leave. Try and get some more sleep.'

'Another couple of hours, you say? Who needs sleep?' he murmured, pulling her in closer. Elle was the happiest girl on the planet.

Chapter Forty

'OH MY GOSH! Look at that smile on your face!' Pippa exclaimed, pouring milk over her cornflakes.

'I have no idea what you mean,' Elle protested.

'Don't give me that! I heard all the whispering before someone sneaked out the door in the early hours. I take it it all went well?'

Elle nodded. 'Noah and I...'

'Yes?' she urged.

'Spent the night together and I'll be seeing him again very soon,' she confided, beaming and grabbing herself a bowl of cornflakes.

'That's brilliant! I'm made up for you, Elle! It's only taken how long?'

She laughed. 'Nine months!'

'Come on! Spill the beans – tell me what happened. I was surprised to see him standing on the doorstep,' Pippa said, shovelling cornflakes into her mouth.

'He'd heard me shout on the platform, but it was too late – the train doors had closed and it had started moving. Once his phone got a signal, he got messages from Jessica and Dan telling him not to get on the train. He jumped off at the next stop, grabbed a taxi and came straight here.'

'Aww, this is so romantic. It's like something that happens in the movies.' Pippa put her hands on her heart.

'I have to keep pinching myself. I can't believe this is happening to me.'

'What'll you do about the distance?'

'I was a little worried about that, but he said we should take it one day at a time, and he's right. What will be will be.'

Pippa squealed. 'Ooh, I think he's definitely a keeper. This is all *so* romantic.'

'Are you seeing Aiden tonight?' asked Elle.

'No, his dad is staying with him this week, and he doesn't get to see him that often. He said Theo is very excited.'

'You'll get to meet him though, won't you?'

'Yeah, hopefully. Aiden mentioned something about meeting up next weekend before his dad goes home. A meal out or something.'

Elle smiled. 'Long may all this happiness continue for both of us.' She hugged Pippa as her phone beeped.

'Aww,' she said, reading a text from Noah.

'Gosh, it must be love if he's already texting you. He only left a couple of hours ago!'

'I'm saying nothing!'

'Right, I'm in the bathroom first,' Pippa said, bounding towards the kitchen door. 'You can daydream out the kitchen window while you wash the dishes.'

'Cheeky!' Elle shouted after her.

A few hours later, Pippa was entertaining children in the reading corner while Aiden rearranged the crime fiction shelf and Elle trawled through her unread emails. Unless she wanted to speak to Russian women online or lift saggy skin without surgery, there really wasn't anything interesting in the inbox.

A shadow fell over her computer and Elle looked up to see Jenny.

Jenny smiled. 'Good morning.'

'Morning! What a lovely surprise! I wasn't expecting to see you.'

Jenny had a sense of calm about her and she looked rested. 'I was passing and just wanted to make sure you were okay after Saturday.'

'I am, and you?' Elle asked just as another email pinged into the inbox.

Elle took a quick glance at the screen and moved the mouse over the message as she briefly scanned the words.

'What night would you be free to come over and meet George? He's really looking forward to it.'

'Sorry, what did you say?' Elle's eyes were still locked on the screen.

'Elle, you're shaking. Are you okay?'

'Oh my gosh, oh my gosh, oh my gosh,' she repeated. 'I don't believe this.' A huge smile spread across her face. 'Jenny, I've won!'

'Won what?' she asked, confused.

Elle sat back in her chair and gasped. 'I don't believe this,' she muttered.

'Pippa! Aiden!' Jenny shouted over to them. Pippa was just wrapping up her reading session.

'Everything okay?' Aiden asked, hurrying over.

'I don't know,' Jenny replied. 'Elle's won.'

Aiden was joined by Pippa. 'Won what?' he asked.

Elle turned the computer screen towards them.

Pippa was first to finish reading the email. 'Holy blooming moly!' she screeched at the top of her voice.

'Shhh! You can't swear – it's a library!' Aiden hushed her but grinned.

Elle's stomach churned with excitement.

'You won, Elle! You won!' Pippa exclaimed.

'Is this real? I don't believe this is happening.'

There on the computer screen was an email from the organisers of the writing competition. Sam Stone had chosen her story as the winner out of thousands of entries, and this Saturday she was invited to attend a presentation and enjoy a three-course dinner at Starcross Manor. Her chest was heaving as she tried to catch her breath. 'I need to phone Irene!'

'That is amazing. Well done you!' exclaimed Jenny.

'I can't believe it! Not only have you won but you're going to meet Sam Stone! *The* Sam Stone – the *legend* that is Sam Stone!' Pippa almost shrieked.

Elle sat there, stunned.

'Your story's going to be published in a magazine too!' Pippa clapped her hands in excitement. 'I'm so chuffed for you, my clever friend.' She beamed, kissing both of Elle's cheeks.

'It's fabulous news, Elle,' Aiden said, also grinning. 'Congratulations. That must have been one hell of a story.'

'Aww, and look,' Pippa said, running her finger across the screen. 'You can take four guests with you.'

'I missed that part!' Elle exclaimed.

Pippa's eyes twinkled as she put her hands together and pretended to pray.

Elle's head was in a spin. Irene, of course, was her first choice, followed by Pippa, but then she had two invites left. Pippa would love to be able to take Aiden, and she wanted to take Noah, and there was Jenny too.

'I'm so proud of you, Elle. You deserve this,' Jenny enthused.

'Thank you.'

'Am I okay to share the news with Wilson?'

'Of course,' Elle replied. Jenny pulled out her phone and popped outside to call him.

'Would you like to come with me, Pippa?'

'Would I ever,' she squealed. 'Try and stop me!'

Then she paused.

Aiden placed his hand on the small of Elle's back. He must have read her mind because he gave her a heart-warming smile. 'Invite Jenny. Don't worry about me. I'll look forward to hearing all about it when you get home.'

'Are you sure?' Elle asked. 'I feel awful.'

'Yes, of course – but on one condition.'

'Which is?'

He grinned. 'Take lots of photos!'

'I will, I promise. Thanks, Aiden!' she said. 'Now pass me the phone. I need to tell Irene my news!'

Aiden slid the desk phone over towards her, and with a shaky hand Elle punched in Irene's number. She willed her to hurry up and answer it.

'Hi,' said Irene.

'I have news! Fantastic news!'

'Shush, Buddy, calm down,' Irene said. He was barking excitedly about something. 'News? Did you say news? What is it?'

'Are you ready for this?' Elle paused. 'I've only gone and won the Sam Stone writing competition!'

There was silence while Irene digested what she said, then a loud cheer followed, which made Buddy begin to bark again.

'Elle, I am absolutely delighted for you! You never cease to amaze me! I'm so proud of you!' Irene gushed.

'Thank you! I have to go now as I'm at work, but Irene…'

'Yes, Elle,' she said, catching her breath.

'I love you.'

'I love you too!'

Chapter Forty-One

Walking into Bonnie's to the sound of cheers and rapturous applause, Elle felt like a celebrity.

There were balloons in every corner of the room and congratulations banners pinned across the wall. News of her win had circulated quickly and tonight's book club was packed to the rafters.

Mim herself had become something of a local celebrity following Elle's win; the likes on her Facebook page had doubled and established authors were knocking down her door to come and do a talk at the book club. The local newspaper was also popping along tonight to photograph Mim and Elle with some of the other book club members. After all, if it hadn't been for Mim telling the club about the competition in the first place, Elle never would have entered.

Eleni was standing in front of the counter. As soon as she saw Elle she hurried over.

'Congratulations, Elle! Well done on your story, but how jealous am I that you get to meet the man himself on Saturday? You must be so excited!'

Elle was bursting with nervous excitement. Flynn Carter, a good friend of everyone in the community and owner of Starcross Manor, had given her a call on Monday evening to go over the details.

'Elle! Congratulations! What an achievement! It's always good to see one of our own shining through.'

That's what Elle loved most about the community of Heartcross – everyone championed each other and were always there cheering and flag-waving each other on.

Flynn told her that the presentation would begin at around seven p.m. Elle and the two runners-up would each be presented with a plaque, then Sam Stone would give a small speech about why her entry had stood out for him from the rest of the entries, before reading a small extract and presenting her with a copy of the magazine that had published the story. Once the presentation was over they would enjoy champagne and a three-course meal cooked by world-famous Michelin-star chef Andrew Glossop.

Elle had barely slept on Monday night after discovering she'd won the competition. Something had been playing on her mind and around three a.m. she'd texted Noah to see if he was awake. To her surprise he immediately phoned her and they'd spoken in hushed whispers for hours.

Noah had been absolutely over the moon that she'd won and even more excited when she'd asked him to attend the presentation with her.

'What's worrying you?' he'd asked. 'Why can't my budding superstar sleep?'

Elle had opened up her heart and explained the situation to him. He had understood exactly where she was coming from – she was worried about Jenny. She'd been delighted when Elle had invited her to the presentation, but now that Elle knew

Sam Stone would be reading an extract from her story, she was worried about its effect on Jenny. The story was about Elle's life – her unhappy childhood, and how she had felt abandoned – and it had been written with such raw emotion. Now understanding the full story, Elle didn't want to hurt Jenny – she'd suffered enough.

'You need to tell her and give her the choice to attend,' Noah suggested. 'You can't let her walk into the room and listen to the extract without being prepared. That would be unfair.'

Noah was right, of course.

Elle plucked up the courage to ring Jenny the following morning. It was the first time she'd actually dialled her number and she was feeling very apprehensive about how she would react. As Elle shared the details of her competition entry, Jenny listened in silence.

'Elle, I'm very proud of you and very grateful you've told me in advance, but I'm fine with it,' she'd said. 'What happened has made us the people we are today, and we can't change the past. I'd still like to come, if that's okay with you, but I don't want to make you feel uncomfortable.'

Elle reassured Jenny that she wanted her there by her side.

Now the nerves were kicking in. Elle couldn't believe she was going to meet Sam Stone. Noah had teased her when she told him how apprehensive she was about meeting him. She'd read every one of his books, but according to all the research she'd done, he was a recluse. There were no photos of him online and his private life was just that: private. He rarely made an appearance in public, and – Rona and Felicity had been right – he barely autographed anything, even his own books. Elle was truly honoured that he'd make the effort to present her with the award personally.

'He's just a normal bloke, you know,' Noah had said. 'He eats, drinks and goes to the bathroom just like the rest of us.'

Irene, Pippa and Elle were sitting in their usual seats in the teashop window and Rona dashed towards them clutching three plates of Victoria sponge.

'Just for you, my dear, and on Saturday, you let Mr Stone know if he wants to sample any of my finest cakes free of charge, he can just pop over here anytime.'

Elle laughed. 'I'll be sure to let him know.'

Mim had taken her place at the front of the teashop and in her usual style she clapped her hands and the room fell silent.

'Tonight, I would like to welcome our very own published writer, Elle Cooper,' she announced. Everyone turned towards Elle and clapped again.

Elle smiled gratefully around the room, then caught Irene's eye just as she was wiping away a proud tear.

'Thank you,' Elle replied once the applause had died down.

'Elle will be attending a very special ceremony on Saturday evening where her plaque and published story will be presented to her by the bestselling crime author ... Mr Sam Stone.' Everyone in the teashop let out a whoop. 'So tonight we have a little change to our proceedings. Firstly, I want to know – if you had one question to ask Sam Stone, what would it be? And secondly, Elle has agreed that she'll read us a short extract from her winning entry ahead of Saturday.'

Everyone turned towards Elle with admiring looks and clapped again. Now she was feeling really nervous; this would be the first time she'd let anyone know about her past except those closest to her.

'We're also expecting the local paper to turn up in the next hour to take some photos and interview Elle,' Mim added.

Elle grinned at Pippa. 'That's why you have a full face of make-up, isn't it? You're hoping to get in on the action.'

'You know me so well.'

'So,' Mim continued, 'if you could ask Sam Stone one question, what would it be?'

Immediately Isla waved her hand in the air. 'I'd ask: what inspired you to write your latest book?'

'What did you learn while writing your latest book?' added Felicity.

'What's your favourite underappreciated novel?' asked Eleni.

'Ooh, good question,' said Mim. 'Any others?'

Then Pippa piped up. 'I know one question you need to ask him.' She stared straight at Elle.

'Which is?'

The whole room fell silent.

'How did he know it was your birthday, and how did a signed copy of his book end up on your desk at work?'

'Yes!' Mim cried. 'Don't forget to ask him that!'

Elle's eyes widened. 'You're right, that's the question I'll be asking at the very first opportunity.'

'Elle, would you like to read us an extract now?' Mim asked as she shushed the room. All eyes turned towards Elle, who swallowed and took a deep breath. Irene gave her a reassuring look of encouragement. Elle prayed she could hold her emotions together as she looked down at the piece of paper in front of her.

Elle began to read.

'I remember my seventh birthday like it was yesterday. The winter brought another cold and dreary night and it was at times like that that I wished I could melt away like the snow outside and stop the ever-present pain. No one acknowledged my birthday. There was no cake, no cards, no presents and no friends for tea. I remember wanting the day to be over and after I put myself to bed I cried. No one came to see if I was okay... No one ever came. I knew I wasn't like any other seven-year-old, but I didn't know why. Why couldn't I have a loving family that rode bikes together, went for walks and enjoyed an ice-cream by the river?

'Lying in bed, the sense of abandonment felt raw – night-time was always the worst. Then, there it was again. The hushed whispers and the creaking of the stairs. The door opened slowly and light seeped into the room. I'd been here so many times already. I was bundled from my bed, wrapped in a coat that was way too big and told to wait by the front door. It felt like the middle of the night. The headlights of a moving car were fast approaching. The car stopped outside the gate. The only thing I was holding was my shawl. An owl hooted as a hand clutched mine and led me towards the car. I didn't look back.

'"*She didn't fit*" are the words that echoed all around me. Why did no one love me? Maybe I didn't deserve to be loved.

'Loneliness seemed to be my only dependable friend.'

Tears blurred Elle's eyes as she paused. The whole room was silent and as Elle looked up, she saw there wasn't a dry eye in the place.

'I don't think I can read any more.'

Someone started to clap and the rest of the audience followed their example. Then suddenly everyone in the teashop was up on their feet.

'I'm sure I speak for everyone at book club when I say

we're super proud of our very own Elle Cooper,' Mim called across the room, smiling at Elle through her tears.

'I'm sorry,' added Elle. 'My story didn't start off with the best beginning but it's certainly finished with the best ending.'

'You don't need to apologise to any of us.' Mim gave Elle a heart-warming smile. 'Teas and cake on the house for the next hour,' she announced.

Everyone clapped some more as Irene mouthed, 'Thank you' to Mim.

'I think I need something a little stronger than tea,' Elle whispered to Pippa.

'That is why I am *so* your friend,' she replied, whipping out a hipflask from her bag. She glanced at Elle's teacup, which was empty, and poured in the amber liquid.

'Drink up,' she encouraged. 'Do you want a drop, Irene?'

'Without a doubt,' she replied, sliding her cup towards Pippa.

'Here's to Elle,' Pippa toasted.

'Here's to Elle,' Irene agreed, giving her a heart-warming smile.

Chapter Forty-Two

As Elle waited on platform three, the station was alive with the hustle and bustle of Friday night commuters. Everyone jumping off the trains seemed to be in a hurry.

Elle checked the overhead display board. Noah's train had been delayed by around half an hour. Nervous butterflies swirled around her stomach. She couldn't wait to see him.

Perching on a nearby bench she thought about the presentation she would be attending tomorrow evening at Starcross Manor. She wanted to look her best, so last night when they'd arrived home from book club they'd talked outfits. Pippa had dragged every item of clothing she owned from her wardrobe and laid them out all over the living room. Pippa had claimed that she didn't have anything suitable to wear, and wondered aloud if maybe it wasn't too late to trawl the internet and purchase something with next-day delivery.

Elle was aghast. 'Pippa, you have everything from a little black dress – actually three little black dresses – to ball gowns, jumpsuits and skirts,' she pointed out.

'But this is a very special occasion! Not only do I want to do you proud, but there might be an opportunity to get a photo with Sam Stone!'

Elle laughed 'I knew there was an ulterior motive.'

'Penny for them?' Elle's thoughts were interrupted by a voice she knew only too well. She looked up to see Noah.

'Eek! That thirty minutes went quickly!' She scooted off the bench, jumping straight into his arms.

'I've missed you,' he said, kissing her.

'What a week it's been,' he said with a smile, swinging her hand as they walked along the platform. 'I leave you alone for five minutes and you end up winning competitions and getting your photo plastered all over the local press.'

Elle grinned up at him. 'It's so surreal! Last night I went to the book club and honestly, I felt like a celebrity.'

'Everyone is so proud of you – including me.'

'Thanks, Noah,' she said bashfully.

It was a fifteen-minute walk to Elle's house from the station and they chatted all the way. She'd told him briefly on the phone about her dinner date at Jenny's a few nights previously but now he wanted all the details.

Meeting George for the first time had been nerve-wracking, but he was absolutely lovely and had instantly put Elle at ease. Wilson had sat next to her at dinner and Elle felt a real sense of belonging. After the meal they'd sat around chatting, about everything and anything.

It was then that Jenny had asked Elle if she would help her choose her outfit for Saturday night.

'Come on, Wilson, let's leave the girls to it,' George suggested, as they headed out to the pub for a pint.

Elle had followed Jenny upstairs to a spacious bedroom

that had been decorated in a soothing colour scheme of white and duck-egg blue.

'Wow, look at those views,' she'd exclaimed, in awe of the acres of fields and the beautiful Heartcross church in the distance.

'Yes, it's fabulous, isn't it? How are you feeling about tomorrow?' Jenny quizzed, laying the outfits out on the bed.

'A little nervous. I'll be glad when the presentation is over and we can just enjoy our food.'

'What do you think of this?' Jenny asked, holding a dress against her body. 'I don't want to be overdressed or underdressed.'

'Mmm, I'm not sure about that one. I don't mean to offend.'

'What about this one?' Jenny held up a pair of black trousers with a spotted bow-tie blouse.

'Hmmm.' Elle hesitated. 'Maybe. I'm not sure though – it kind of looks like something you'd wear to an interview.'

'Yes, that's exactly what George said!'

They both laughed.

'This one?'

'That's the one,' Elle agreed, smiling. 'That looks lovely and the colour suits you.'

Jenny was holding up a navy chiffon dress that gathered softly around the neckline and fell to just below her knees.

'Perfect,' she'd said. 'I have a red cardigan that I can dress it up with and a matching handbag.'

'All sorted.'

'What are you wearing, Elle?' she'd asked then.

'I've borrowed a little black dress off Pippa. Honestly, she could open her own boutique with the amount of stuff she hoards.'

Jenny had laughed. 'I'm a bit like that with shoes,' she'd said. 'You can never have too many shoes.'

The rest of the evening had gone swimmingly and they'd arranged to meet outside the venue on Saturday night before they went in to the presentation.

'Here we are.' Elle bounded up the steps and unlocked the front door. Noah followed her into the hallway and tossed his holdall on the floor before giving her a sheepish look.

'I'd probably better hang up my shirt and trousers for tomorrow night. Otherwise, I'll end up having to iron them again.'

'There'll be a few spare coat hangers in my wardrobe – go up and help yourself.'

Noah kissed her on the cheek before disappearing up the stairs.

Pippa had left Elle a note on the table to say she'd gone round to Aiden's for tea and to meet his dad, but she invited them both to join them in the pub afterwards if they fancied it.

'What do you want to do?' Elle asked Noah, handing the note to him, when he came back downstairs.

'I'd rather curl up with you on the settee and maybe get a takeaway? Come here.'

He pulled her towards him and lowered his lips to hers. The kiss instantly sent her heart fluttering.

'How do you do that to me?' she murmured. 'You make me go weak at the knees.'

'Good,' he replied, his eyes locking playfully with hers. 'You have exactly the same effect on me.' He pretended his legs had given way and pulled Elle down on the settee next to him. With his strong arms wrapped around her he began nuzzling her neck.

'Let's order our food first, then you can take full advantage of me afterwards.'

'Spoilsport, but I am hungry,' he replied, sitting up. He spotted the signed Sam Stone novel on the table.

'Tell me the story behind this again,' he urged, opening the book.

'It was my birthday and it just appeared out of nowhere on the desk at work. It was bizarre! There was no one around and Pippa and Aiden hadn't seen anyone loitering.'

'You need to keep this in a safe place.'

'Have you ever met him?'

'No, he's a writer who seems to stay out of the public eye. I follow him on Twitter, but he barely posts.'

'Yes, I did tweet him after I received the book, but I never got a reply.'

'That doesn't surprise me.'

'But I'm going to ask him about it tomorrow. Let's get the food ordered. I'm starving!' Elle headed into the kitchen.

'Your phone just beeped.'

'It'll be Pippa. She'll be checking in to see if we're going to the pub. Just swipe the screen and look. I've not got a passcode.'

Returning with numerous menus, Elle placed them on to the coffee table. Noah stared down at the phone screen.

'Is it Pippa?' she asked, sitting next to him.

His eyes met hers and he passed the phone to her.

'Oh my!' There in her notifications list was a message from Sam Stone himself.

Looking forward to meeting the talented @ElleCooper tomorrow!

'Someone definitely has a fan!' Noah exclaimed. 'Like we said, he barely tweets.'

Elle didn't reply. She was still staring at the phone as her notifications began to ping off the scale from Sam Stone's followers.

Chapter Forty-Three

'How do I look?' Elle asked as she stood nervously in front of Pippa and Noah.

'You look amazing! Now come on – the car should be here any second,' Pippa exclaimed, grabbing her sparkly silver handbag from the table.

Noah looked gorgeous in a crisp pale blue shirt. He walked over to her. 'Absolutely beautiful. Enjoy today.' He softly kissed her on her cheek. 'And take a look outside.'

With a puzzled expression, Elle looked out of the window. 'Is the King visiting?'

Noah laughed. 'That is a Bentley and your carriage for today.'

'No way – that looks extremely posh.'

'Yes way, Flynn has sent it for you. He said you deserve to arrive in style.'

Elle put her hands to her heart. 'I don't know what to say. Everyone is being so kind.'

'Come on, we're going to pick Irene up en route.'

'Oh my gosh, have you seen the car outside?' cried Pippa.

'Heads are going to turn, travelling through Glensheil to Heartcross. I need to post a reel.'

Elle rolled her eyes in amusement as Pippa bounded out of the front door towards the car. Within seconds she had the driver striking different poses before she began filming inside.

'Only Pippa!' Elle laughed as they shut the front door behind them.

Fifteen minutes later the Bentley passed through the gatehouse and drove up the tree-lined drive of Starcross Manor.

'Wow, look at this place!' Noah exclaimed. 'I can't believe this is tucked away on the outskirts of Heartcross. It looks like something out of *Downton Abbey*.'

'It is such a fantastic venue,' Pippa agreed. 'And a great hotel.'

The car pulled up outside the entrance, and the driver opened the door for them. A red carpet trailed over the stone steps towards the Manor's impressive oak doors, where they were met by Flynn.

'Here she is, the woman of the moment. Congratulations, Elle!' A waiter stood beside him dressed in tails, white gloves and a top hat. He was holding a silver tray of flutes of champagne.

Flynn handed them each a glass. 'Welcome to Starcross Manor. I'm truly honoured that the presentation is being held here.'

'Thank you and thanks for the car, it was such a lovely surprise.'

'You're very welcome. Now, we have some members of the

press here who would like to take some pictures on you in front of the doors. Would that be okay?'

Elle was overwhelmed by the way she was being treated. 'Of course! I must say, a glass of champagne on arrival, all this attention… I could get used to this treatment. Is this what being famous feels like?' she whispered to Noah.

After the photographs were taken Flynn led them into the foyer, where Jenny was waiting for them. 'I saw you arrive. What a treat, a Bentley!'

'I know! Honestly, I'm feeling like an A-lister but I'm so nervous.'

'The presentation is being held in The Grand Hall,' Flynn told them. 'I'll let the main events organiser know you and your party are here. Is there anything else I can get you?' asked Flynn.

Elle shook her head. 'No, thank you, Flynn.'

He touched her arm. 'Enjoy your moment. Come on. I'll take you through to The Grand Hall.'

Elle's eyes swept over the room. Waiters were circulating with more champagne. Rows and rows of chairs were laid out in front of the stage, and in the centre of the stage was a microphone on a stand. When she spotted that, her nerves began to kick in and she took a huge gulp of fizz.

'Hey, steady,' Noah whispered. 'You don't want to be tipsy on stage. Wait until after the presentation.'

Elle knew he was right, but she needed a bit of courage.

Flynn checked his watch. 'Everything is running to time. Before the presentation starts you'll have the opportunity to meet Sam Stone.'

'What, now?' asked Elle.

'Yes, now,' replied Flynn, giving her a reassuring smile. 'Don't worry, he's human, just like the rest of us.'

Elle whispered to everyone. 'It feels like we're about to meet royalty.'

'I know,' replied Pippa. 'I'm very nervous too. This man is an icon.'

Elle linked her arm through Irene's as they followed Flynn towards an oak door marked 'Private' at the far end of the room. A doorman tipped his hat and opened the door wide.

Elle stepped into the room and did a double-take. She heard Pippa gasp. 'What are you doing here?' she asked Aiden.

He met Pippa's gaze and began to stutter. 'Oh— Oh God. You shouldn't have seen me just yet.'

They all stared at him.

'Don't be mad at me.' He too was dressed for the occasion in a suit and tie.

'Why would I be mad at you? Why are you here?'

'Aiden, is there anything else you need?' Flynn asked.

'No, I'll take it from here. Thank you.'

'Have fun, and I'll catch up with you all later.' Flynn wandered over to the side of the room leaving everyone looking at Aiden.

'What's going on?' Elle heard Jenny whisper to Irene, who shrugged.

'Aiden, spill the beans! Come on, what are you doing here? Please tell me you haven't gate-crashed the event.'

He smiled and motioned towards another door. 'I'd like you to come and meet Sam Stone – my godfather.'

'Your *godfather*?' Pippa raised an eyebrow in disbelief.

Elle stared at Aiden, open-mouthed.

'You're kidding us, right?' Noah probed.

'No. He's my father's best friend.'

'You kept that quiet,' Pippa trilled at the top of her voice. 'And your dad never said a word last night!'

'He was sworn to secrecy because I wanted to surprise you. Are you ready?' he asked Elle.

'I think so,' she replied, feeling her pulse race. 'I can't believe he's your godfather.'

Aiden was still smiling as he opened the door and swept his arm towards the man standing in the middle of the room.

'He's very handsome,' whispered Irene. Elle had to agree.

'Which one of you is the talented Elle Cooper?' Sam smiled as he walked over towards them with his hand stretched out.

'I'm Elle,' she replied shyly, shaking his hand.

'I'm very pleased to meet you. Your competition entry touched my heart in many ways and I'm not ashamed to say it actually brought tears to my eyes. It was an inspiring personal journey, full of raw emotion, and it deserves to be published. You're very talented. Have you ever thought about a career in writing?'

Elle felt herself blushing at all the compliments. 'Thank you,' she replied. 'And no, I haven't, but I work in a library and – can I just say – I love your books.'

'Thank you, that is very kind and who have you brought along with you today?'

Pippa stepped forward. Her smile couldn't have been any wider.

'This is Pippa. My best friend.'

Pippa didn't hold back. 'Fangirl moment!' She shook Sam's hand. 'I'm your biggest fan, I've read all your books, and I've loved every one of them,' she went on in a rush.

'And … breathe,' whispered Elle, making everyone laugh.

Pippa turned to Aiden. 'And I can't believe you never told me! What a cool godfather to have!'

Aiden smiled at her. 'I would have in time.'

'Does this explain where the signed book came from?' Elle looked from Aiden to Sam.

Aiden grinned.

'Guilty as charged,' Aiden said. 'I knew Sam was your favourite author and I wanted to spill the beans so many times, but I'd planned to bring him to the library this week when Dad was up visiting me – he lives relatively close, you see. But then you won the competition.'

Elle swiped Aiden's arm playfully.

'And this is Noah Jones, a fellow author,' said Aiden, continuing the introductions.

'Yes, I've heard of you,' Sam said, shaking Noah's hand.

'Thank you,' replied Noah.

'And this is Irene.'

'Hello,' Irene said, politely shaking his hand.

'And— Where's Jenny disappeared to?'

They all spun around but Jenny was suddenly nowhere to be seen.

'That's strange,' Noah said, looking towards the door. 'She was here a minute ago.'

'She can't have gone far,' Aiden replied. 'Anyway, it's time to take our seats. The presentation is about to start.' He glanced at his watch. 'Would it be okay if Sam and I came and joined you at your table for the meal afterwards?' Aiden asked, looking at Elle and putting his arm around Pippa's waist.

Elle smiled. 'Would it be okay? It would be more than okay.'

'I've got to go this way now,' Sam said, pointing to a different door. 'I'll look forward to chatting with you on stage and with the rest of you at the meal.'

Once they were through the door, Elle looked for Jenny but she was still nowhere to be seen.

'Where do you think Jenny's gone?' she murmured to Noah.

'I've no idea. Maybe the bathroom?'

'I don't want her to miss this presentation.'

'She won't, she'll catch us up,' Noah reassured her.

They all made their way towards the seats in front of the stage, and one of the organisers directed them to the front row.

'You need to save a seat for Jenny,' Elle whispered to Irene, who placed her bag down on the seat next to her.

Elle studied the hordes of people filtering into the chairs behind them, but there was still no sign of Jenny.

A few seconds later, Flynn stepped on to the stage and switched on the microphone. 'I'd like to welcome you all to Starcross Manor for this very special presentation.' The whole room hushed and all eyes focused on him. 'I've been a part of this community for quite a while now and it never ceases to amaze me, the talent that keeps popping up in this village.' He smiled at Elle.

'Jenny needs to hurry up! Otherwise she's going to miss it,' Irene whispered.

'I've just texted her but I've not had a reply.' Elle switched her phone to silent and put it back in her handbag.

'It's an honour for me not only to be holding such a presentation here today at Starcross Manor, but also to welcome to the stage the international bestselling author Sam Stone. His career has spanned over three decades, his books have sold over nine million copies and have been translated into fifteen different languages. Without further ado, please welcome to the stage – Mr Sam Stone.'

There was rapturous applause all around the room as Sam walked up to the microphone.

'Sam Stone is a very romantic name. He sounds like a movie star,' Pippa whispered to Aiden, all gooey-eyed.

Aiden placed his hand on her knee and squeezed it. 'It's not his real name, you know. It's a pseudonym.'

'No way. I never knew that.' Pippa swung a glance towards him. Just then Jenny appeared from nowhere and sat down next to Irene. She looked ghastly white.

'Are you okay?' asked Elle. 'We wondered where you had disappeared to. You look kind of pale.'

Jenny nodded. 'I'm okay.'

Pippa leaned forward to attract Elle's attention. 'Elle, did you know that Sam Stone is a pseudonym? He doesn't write under his real name.'

'Gosh! No! I didn't know that at all. What's his real name?' she asked, glancing over towards Pippa and Aiden.

'Matt Harrison,' Jenny replied, locking eyes with a very shocked Elle.

Chapter Forty-Four

The words 'Matt Harrison' hung in the air. Elle's heart began to pound.

Jenny nodded at her – it really was him. Elle's heart thumped even faster. All she could do was stare at the man on the stage in front of her – her father. Her past had hurtled into the present.

Irene nudged her. 'What are you doing? Get yourself up on stage, girl,' she whispered urgently, tapping Elle on her knee.

'Elle, go!' Noah nudged her arm.

Elle glanced up to find the whole room clapping and Sam looking in her direction. She hadn't heard him announce the winner of the competition. She was in a state of shock, oblivious to everything that was going on around her.

Aiden stood up and gestured for Elle to follow him to the side of the stage. 'You need to collect your prize.'

Finally, she stood up. Everyone was on their feet clapping. Irene dabbing at her eyes, proud tears running down her cheeks.

Elle took a sideward glance towards Jenny. She too was in a

trancelike state, staring at Sam.

Feeling like her legs were going to buckle underneath her at any given moment, Elle took deep breaths as she walked onto the stage. Sam shook her hand and presented her with the plaque before welcoming the editor of *Women's Writing*, who gave Elle a copy of the magazine in which Elle and her story were featured.

After a lot of handshaking, and once the room had stopped applauding, Sam cleared his throat. 'I'd now like to read you an extract from Elle's story.' He smiled at Elle. 'Is that okay with you?'

Elle managed a nod. Like a rabbit caught in headlights she was still staring at him.

He couldn't know who she was, but there was no doubt in her mind she was standing next to her father. She could see now how striking the resemblance was between the two of them, and wondered why she hadn't noticed it immediately. Elle had his eyes, his nose curved in the same way and his smile mirrored hers.

'It's okay,' he whispered, placing his hand over the microphone. 'Don't be nervous. I've got you.'

Elle glanced at Jenny as he started reading. She was on the brink of tears, and Elle felt herself shaking. Noah was glancing anxiously between them both, having realised something was going on. He mouthed, 'What's wrong?' at Elle, but of course she couldn't answer.

Everyone else in the room was listening intently to Sam, and, aside from the odd gasp, there was complete silence as the words of her story spilled from his lips. But then his words began to slow. He'd caught Jenny's gaze and kept looking in her direction. Elle knew he'd recognised her.

· · ·

As soon as the presentation was over, Elle saw Jenny leave her seat, followed quickly by Irene. The moment Sam walked Elle off the stage they were greeted by a sea of journalists, who wanted to photograph them for numerous papers and magazines. Elle could barely breathe, never mind smile, as the cameras flashed at them.

'Who's that woman you're with?' Sam asked as soon as the photographers had moved on to the other award winners.

'Jenny,' replied Elle.

'Jenny,' he repeated. 'Ah, my mistake.' His eyes darted towards the back of the room, but Jenny and Irene had disappeared altogether. 'I thought it was someone I used to know.'

Elle took a chance. 'Her full name is Cora Jennifer Hansley.'

Sam looked towards her in shocked silence.

'She's my mother.' Her voice faltered on the final word.

'Hey, congratulations, Elle!' Noah kissed her on the cheek. She couldn't acknowledge him; she was focused on Sam, reading the emotions crossing his face.

'I'm so proud of you,' Noah carried on, oblivious to the situation he'd just stepped into. 'For a minute on the stage I thought you were going to pass out. You looked like you'd seen a ghost!'

Elle tried to keep her emotions under control as the full meaning of the last twenty minutes hit her – she'd found *her father*!

Sam strained to see over the crowd, which included many fans clutching his latest book, hoping for a photo and an autograph. They were calling his name and squealing with delight as he looked in their direction, but it was clear he didn't even see them. It was Jenny he was searching for.

He turned back towards Elle and lowered his voice to a

whisper. 'We need to find her.'

Noah stared at Elle. 'What's going on?'

Her pulse quickened. 'I'll tell you later. I won't be long.' She followed Sam through the crowd, leaving Noah standing there, wondering what the hell was going on.

Ten minutes later, they'd searched everywhere. Jenny and Irene were nowhere to be found and their mobiles had been switched off.

Sam let out a defeated sigh and sat down on a settee in the foyer. 'I need to ask you something.'

Elle thought she knew what it was, and she was right.

'The story you've written – was it true?' Sam's eyes searched hers.

Elle nodded, swallowing the lump in her throat.

'But your writing suggests you're looking for your biological mum, so does that mean Cora – Jenny – is your adoptive mum?'

Elle shook her head.

'I don't understand, Elle.'

Elle took a deep breath. She sat down next to him.

'Irene is my foster mum. I've only just been reunited with Jenny. It's a long story.'

Sam dropped his head into his hands and was silent for a while.

'How old are you, Elle?' he asked finally, his eyes gleaming with unshed tears.

Her throat became tight, then her tears fell. 'I've just turned thirty.' As soon as the words left her mouth, she could see him doing the maths.

'You're Matt Harrison,' she said bravely. 'The man Cora

loved – the man she disappeared on.'

A tear ran down his face. 'She told you?'

Elle nodded.

'I loved that woman with all my heart. She just never came home. I thought she must be dead. I filed a missing-persons report, and I searched and searched, but there was no trace of her anywhere. My life turned upside down in an instant and I've never got over it. She was my first love. Not a day goes by when I don't think about her and wonder what the hell happened to her. And then after all these years, she appears out of the blue.'

Elle stood up and stared out of the window over the grounds of Starcross Manor. She spotted two familiar figures sitting on a bench. 'There they are,' she said.

Matt looked out of the window then hurried outside towards them, with Elle following close behind.

Jenny's face was stained with tears, and Irene's arm was draped around her shoulder.

'Cora,' Matt gasped, out of breath, as he stopped in front of her.

'Hi.' She managed a weak smile.

Irene squeezed her knee and stood up. 'Come on, Elle. We need to leave them to talk.'

Elle hesitated but then followed Irene's lead, looking over her shoulder as they slowly headed back inside.

'How are you?' Irene asked tentatively.

'I'm not sure. I really can't believe this is happening.' Elle halted and Irene took both her hands in hers. 'That's my father.'

Irene's eyes locked with hers. 'Yes, it is.' She hugged Elle as the tears fell.

'I've found my father,' Elle whispered in awe.

Chapter Forty-Five

One month later

'Are you ready?' Noah called up to Elle. 'The taxi's here.'

'I'm coming,' she shouted, hurrying down the stairs into the living room.

'Elle!' Theo came running towards her and she scooped him up in her arms and planted a huge kiss on his cheek. He giggled.

'Well, look at you, Theo! How handsome do you look in your suit and bow tie?' she exclaimed, putting his feet firmly back on the floor.

Theo grinned and held out his fist, which she bumped with hers.

'You look gorgeous,' Noah said, kissing her on the cheek with a smile.

'I'll second that,' Aiden said.

'Where's Pippa?'

'You'd think it was her getting married, the amount of time she's taken to get ready!'

'Oi, Aiden, I heard that!' Pippa said, laughing as she popped her head round the kitchen door. 'I'm ready!'

Theo ran over and squeezed his hand into Pippa's. She promptly ruffled his hair, and he beamed up at her.

The last month had been such a whirlwind. After the presentation, Jenny had finally confided in Matt what had happened all those years ago. Matt had been devastated that he'd been unaware of Jenny's addiction and how grief over her parents' death had consumed her.

Overnight, Elle had gained a father and the jigsaw puzzle was finally complete. Matt lived a half-hour away from Aiden's dad, on the coast. He'd invited Noah and Elle down for a weekend at the end of the month, which she looked forward to immensely. She couldn't wait to get to know him better.

'Where to?' the taxi driver asked as they all climbed in.

'Heartcross Church.'

The driver nodded and they were on their way.

'What a fantastic day for a wedding!' Pippa exclaimed, staring out of the window at the blue sky.

As they arrived, the church bells pealed and they could see Jack standing next to Wilson outside the entrance. They both looked exquisite in their three-buttoned waistcoats and kilts, each sporting a huge smile.

It was such a romantic setting, perfect for a wedding. Blooms danced along the edge of the large pond that lay in front of the church, and as they wandered over the bridge they could see a family of ducks swimming below.

'Such a stunning place,' Elle said as they reached Jack and Wilson.

'It's a perfect venue – very Scottish countryside,' Noah agreed, shaking Jack's hand. 'Congratulations, mate.'

Jack grinned from ear to ear. 'Thanks! I've got to get inside in a moment – apparently my wife-to-be is on her way!'

Guests began to file into the church, the men handsome in their kilts, the women wearing beautiful dresses.

Suddenly a proud Mim appeared from inside the church. The mother of the bride looked gorgeous in a duck-egg blue outfit with matching hat.

'Mim, you look stunning!' exclaimed Elle.

'Designed by Libby and I feel a million dollars.'

'I don't think you've met Libby yet.' Elle turned towards Noah. 'Libby is Flynn's sister and a fashion designer.'

'I've seen her work in magazines,' replied Noah. 'She's extremely talented and has evidently taken the New York fashion industry by storm.'

'In fact, here she is now.' Elle pointed towards the car that had just pulled up. Libby stepped out on the arm of her partner Guy Hart, Flynn and his wife Julia following behind.

'This is like a celebrity wedding. There's Andrew Glossop, the chef, and his wife Grace. And there's Drew, Fergus, Rona, Allie and Rory.' Elle pointed each person out to Noah as she reeled off the names.

'Irene and Arthur are already inside with Jenny and George,' added Mim. 'And you, Jack, you really need to disappear inside now.'

'I know, it's unlucky to see the bride! I wonder whose turn it will be next?' Jack said playfully as he glanced from Elle to Pippa.

'Time will tell,' Pippa replied.

As the horse and cart appeared at the end of the road Elle ordered Jack inside. 'Here's the bride! Quickly now!'

Eleni looked the picture of happiness in the horse-drawn carriage accompanied by Isla and Felicity, her bridesmaids.

'Who's giving the bride away?' asked Noah.

'Mim,' replied Elle.

Beaming proudly, Mim held out her hand as Eleni stepped from the carriage to a chorus of gasps. She was wearing an elegant cream A-line bridal gown, with a crystal-encrusted lace bodice and cap sleeves, and a chic tulle overskirt. Libby's design was simply stunning.

They all gave her a wide smile before walking under the floral arch that complemented the church's beautiful exterior. Inside, the church was decorated with bursts of ivory roses lining the pews, and white blossom artificial trees adorning the altar.

As the wedding music began to play, all eyes turned towards the back of the church and Eleni began to glide up the aisle, Mim beside her.

Jack beamed at Eleni as she made her way towards him. There wasn't a dry eye in the place.

'I do love a good wedding,' Pippa said, and promptly started to sob. Elle passed her a tissue then caught the eye of Jenny, who smiled across at her before turning towards Wilson, sitting in the front pew. Wilson had done his parents – and his sister – proud today, and Elle caught a special look between Jenny and George before George draped his arm around his wife's shoulder and kissed the top of her head.

Once Jack and Eleni were pronounced man and wife, Jack cupped his hands around her cheeks and kissed his bride. The whole church erupted in cheers and the bells rang out. After they'd signed the register and walked back down the aisle they stood for photographs in the entrance of the church, where they were showered with a rainbow of confetti.

'Ladies! This is your time,' Eleni announced, holding up the bouquet.

They didn't hesitate to gather in a semi-circle, Pippa pushing her way to the front. Eleni turned her back towards them and counted loudly to three before launching the bouquet.

All eyes followed the blast of colour as it flew up into the air and the waiting crowd of women surged forward with flailing arms – all except Elle.

And yet there was no stopping the bouquet as it travelled straight towards her and she caught it with both hands.

Everyone cheered.

'You know what that means, don't you, Elle?' Pippa winked at her.

She grinned. 'I sure do,' she replied, giving Noah a warm smile.

He wrapped his arms around her then bent his head and kissed her on her lips.

'I can't wait for the future,' Noah murmured.

Elle's heart soared. 'Me neither,' she replied, kissing him back.

'Eww, Elle that's naughty!' Theo cried, making slurpy kissing noises.

There was a ripple of laughter all around as Pippa scooped Theo up in her arms and smacked a noisy kiss on his cheek.

Theo's giggle was infectious.

'Time for a group photo,' the photographer announced. Everyone huddled together on the steps of the church. 'I love a good wedding,' Noah whispered in her ear.

'Me too.' Gripping the bouquet tightly, she held his gaze before turning to smile at the photographer. Her future was finally coming together.

Acknowledgements

I'm absolutely overjoyed to see my twentieth book published. I can't quite believe it! If this is the first book of mine you've read – hello! I hope you really enjoy it. If you've read my books before then welcome back, it's lovely to see you again.

This book was previously published as *Evie's Year of Taking Chances* and I've re-written it to fit in to the wonderful world of Love Heart Lane and adapted it accordingly. As ever this book is a team effort and the One More Chapter team are truly awesome. A huge hug to Charlotte Ledger, the captain of this magnificent ship, who turns my stories into books. Her love of romantic novels always shines through and it's wonderful to see this genre championed within the industry. She is without a doubt, one of the loveliest people in this industry. Thank you to editor extraordinaire Laura McCallen who works her magic and makes my books the best they can be. It's an absolute pleasure to work with you on each book and long may it continue. And last but not least huge thanks to Tony Russell, a copy editor who has frequent trips to Love Heart Lane.

Much love to my wonderful family, Emily, Jack, Ruby and Tilly. You are simply the best!

Woody and Nellie, my writing partners in crime. Woody has been by my side since book one and is often more of a hindrance than a help but I wouldn't have it any other way. Love you both.

Life hasn't always been straightforward, there have been a

few bumps in the road but I can honestly say life on my own is just wonderful. I have never travelled so much and I'm experiencing life like I would never have done before. There are two wonderful friends who I'd like to thank for accompanying me on my journey, Anita Redfern and Julie Wetherill. Things are never quite as scary with you two around. Our friendship is built on gin, laughs and of course cake … and just the fact you are both amazing humans. I am grateful and lucky to have you both.

A special mention to the Houston and Appleton families. It was such a pleasure to meet you the summer of 2023. We loved Tom's stories and you all made our holiday extra special – thank you so much.

Thank you to Estelle Maher and Sue Miller for my wonderful fiftieth birthday present – *The Little Library on Love Heart Lane* which has taken resident at my ramshackle cottage. As you can see, the illustrator put a special Little Library on the front cover of this novel, just for you!

Please support your local library they provide positive outcome for people and communities in many ways, beyond simply providing access to books.

Thank you, to you, my loyal readers. I know some of you have been with me from the beginning and some of you are just finding me now. Never underestimate how much your messages on social media are appreciated. They never fail to put a smile on my face. Thank you for choosing my books to read. It's the biggest privilege in the world to write stories.

Until the next book,

Lots of love,

Christie x

ONE MORE CHAPTER

YOUR NUMBER ONE STOP
FOR PAGETURNING BOOKS

The author and One More Chapter would like to thank everyone who contributed to the publication of this story...

Analytics
Abigail Fryer
Maria Osa

Audio
Fionnuala Barrett
Ciara Briggs

Contracts
Georgina Hoffman
Florence Shepherd

Design
Lucy Bennett
Fiona Greenway
Holly Macdonald
Liane Payne
Dean Russell

Digital Sales
Lydia Grainge
Emily Scorer
Georgina Ugen

Editorial
Arsalan Isa
Charlotte Ledger
Janet Marie-Adkins
Jennie Rothwell
Tony Russell
Kimberley Young

International Sales
Bethan Moore

Marketing & Publicity
Chloe Cummings
Emma Petfield

Operations
Melissa Okusanya
Hannah Stamp

Production
Emily Chan
Denis Manson
Francesca Tuzzeo

Rights
Lana Beckwith
Rachel McCarron
Agnes Rigou
Hany Sheikh
Mohamed
Zoe Shine
Aisling Smyth

The HarperCollins Distribution Team

The HarperCollins Finance & Royalties Team

The HarperCollins Legal Team

The HarperCollins Technology Team

Trade Marketing
Ben Hurd
Eleanor Slater

UK Sales
Laura Carpenter
Isabel Coburn
Jay Cochrane
Tom Dunstan
Sabina Lewis
Erin White
Harriet Williams
Leah Woods

And every other essential link in the chain from delivery drivers to booksellers to librarians and beyond!

Love Heart Lane Series

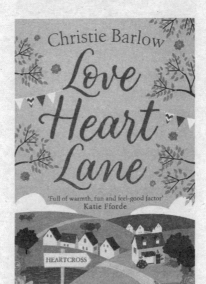

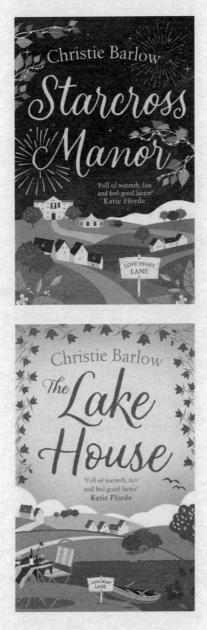

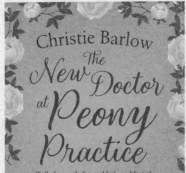

Christie Barlow

The New Doctor at Peony Practice

'Full of warmth, fun and feel-good factor'
Katie Fforde

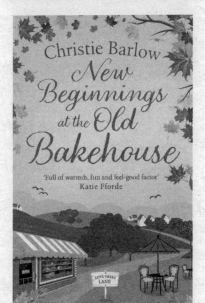

Christie Barlow

New Beginnings at the Old Bakehouse

'Full of warmth, fun and feel-good factor'
Katie Fforde

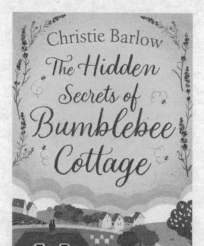

Christie Barlow

The Hidden
Secrets of
Bumblebee
Cottage

Christie Barlow

A Summer
Surprise
at the Little Blue
Boathouse

'Full of warmth, fun and feel-good factor'
Katie Fforde

Christie Barlow

A Winter Wedding at Starcross Manor

'Full of warmth, fun and feel-good factor'
Katie Fforde

LOVE HEART LANE